DRIVING ME BARKING

By JP Preston

2025

Butterworth Books is a different breed of publishing house. It's a home for Indies, for independent authors who take great pride in their work and produce top quality books for readers who deserve the best. Professional editing, professional cover design, professional proof reading, professional book production—you get the idea. As Individual as the Indie authors we're proud to work with, we're Butterworths and we're *different*.

Authors currently publishing with us:

E.V. Bancroft

Valden Bush

Addison M Conley

Jo Fletcher

Helena Harte

Lee Haven

Karen Klyne

Sydney Lear

AJ Mason

Ally McGuire

James Merrick

JP Preston

Robyn Nyx (RJ Nyx)

Simon Smalley

Brey Willows

For more information visit www.butterworthbooks.co.uk

This trade paperback is published by Butterworth Books, UK

CATALOGING INFORMATION
ISBN: 978-1-915009-85-2
CREDITS
Editors: Victoria Villaseñor & Nicci Robinson
Cover Design: Nicci Robinson
Illustrations: KC Lylark
Production Design: Global Wordsmiths

Acknowledgements

If it takes a village to raise a child, then it surely takes a vibrant hamlet to launch a book. My heartfelt thanks go out to Victoria and Nicci at Butterworth Books, to KC Lyark for the illustrations, and to everyone who has pitchfork prodded me toward the finish line.

Dedication

2024 was a year of mixed emotions for me:
the joy of finishing my first novel mingled with
the grief of losing first Pat, and then Annie.
Blood family and found family,
I'm grateful to have had you in my life.
RIP, guys.

Prologue
All Harps and Cherubs

YOU'D BE FORGIVEN FOR thinking that the clouds had parted and the sky had spontaneously filled with throngs of shining angels, all grinning their chops off and fiddling with harps and stuff the first time that I met Grier Campbell. Nope. No such celestial backdrop to our first encounter.

It was around lunchtime on an unremarkable Tuesday in November when her trademark Volkswagen campervan rolled up to our grim little camp at Greenham Common. Reb, Sally, Mrs Walker, Susan H, Sue G, and me were huddled under blankets around the campfire, feebly attempting to make light of the weather. I was, by now, something of a veteran Greenham Common protester, having spent the previous seven or eight months moving from gate to gate. I'd successfully managed to lose my failed student image. Nowadays, I was proudly strutting about the place in my newfound urban lesbo-warrior skin. After all, I'd left Muswell Hill as a gawky, reserved closet case. Now I was a real dyke; I could construct a sturdy bender tent that could house three or four women at a time, I could make a meal out of pulses and vegetables without so much as a sniff of animal flesh, and I was adept in the art of lighting fires in the perpetually drizzling rain—hell, I was even on to my second lover!

I'd run away to join the circus, and now I was the second assistant ringmaster. My input was regularly solicited by the action planners, and my aptitude for getting through the perimeter fence was much admired. Reb had done a good job on me, and in the spirit of true non-monogamous sisterhood, she was now making subtle moves to become mentor to a thirtysomething mother-of-three Marxist who had begun visiting us at weekends.

In truth, I was relieved. Reb and I had run our course; the relationship over in all but sexual terms. Politically and emotionally, we were drifting apart at a rate of knots but, on the nights when Rebecca came crawling into my tent, my heart and other organs raised the welcome flag and lowered the drawbridge. Rebecca was my sweet, sweet girl: an irresistible concoction of tactile tenderness and rampant hormones. The following morning, I'd sneak out to the fire before she awoke and return with a steaming mug of tea or hot chocolate for us to share. I cherished those brief intimate moments because I knew that the moment she dressed to leave, my lover Rebecca gave way to her alter ego, Reb the Dyke Warrior.

We never discussed this Jekyll and Hyde transformation, and no mention was made of her various lovers in the camp or back home in Brixton. I knew that I was just one of many, but I liked to imagine myself as the prime minister of Rebecca's harem, a sapphic first amongst equals. It was a kind of covert possessiveness on my part. I kept my insecurities to myself, and I never saw Rebecca exhibit any form of jealousy or otherwise un-sisterly behaviour.

On the second Tuesday of every month, we were visited by the good women of the Ladbroke Grove Women's Community Arts Workshop Collective. The "Posh Wagon," as Reb would remind us. It appeared that a group of feminist sisters had decided to show solidarity with us by taking up a collection. Not a cash collection, you understand. They had asked the women who used the workshop to contribute anything they could spare that might be of use to the courageous sisters who were braving the English weather to demonstrate their opposition to the stationing of cruise missiles at a military base in the God-forsaken Berkshire countryside. The response had been overwhelming and had just kept on coming. Soap and toothpaste were popular donations, as were tampons, sanitary towels, packets of Cup-a-Soup, and natural sponges.

Reb had sneered the first time the wagon had turned up. "Them posh cows reckon we stink!"

She was not alone in her criticism. Reb was the iconic leader of a sizeable band of working-class warrior dykes who denounced their middle-class sisters as being privileged part-timers who left all the real battles to their downtrodden working-class sisters.

"We don't need or want their conscience-massaging reparations," she'd declared.

For a working-class hero, Reb could be surprisingly articulate when she wanted. Some of the others had nodded their agreement, echoing Reb's vow to never accept a thing from the Posh Brigade. By the third month, much of the bluster of this political stand had waned. Word had trickled through to the boycotters; okay, the individually wrapped parcels contained useful stuff—soap, and toothpaste, and the like—but they also contained a few nice surprises such as candles, matches, teabags, little notes of encouragement, and sometimes, rolling tobacco.

All these enticements served to chip away at the resolve of the faithful who continued to say they didn't want anything that the Posh Wagon had to offer, but the killer blow came from an unexpected source. A rumour started to spread from gate to gate that Julie T from Birmingham had found chocolate in her package. A Crunchie and two Mars bars, I think. Political resolve was now stretched to breaking point, and many a fierce debate waged over the issue. I, of course, supported my lover's stance. I boycotted the Posh Wagon and never benefitted from the bounty or the Mars bar therein. I was a martyr to the cause, selflessly refusing to compromise my (Reb's) politics for a meagre square of the precious brown gold. I told no one that I actually disliked chocolate in all its forms. Except hot chocolate, that is...hot chocolate shared with a loved one.

So the Posh Wagon rolled in as usual, and the converted stepped up to receive their rations.

Reb sprang to her feet and slung her biker jacket over one

shoulder. "Coming?" She gestured towards her tent.

Sue, Susan, and one or two of the others followed and, for the life of me, I have no idea why I didn't. Reb was about to hold court, to preach to the converted. But I'd heard it all before and already been converted. I was feeling hormonally petulant and wanted Rebecca to notice my absence, to pop her head out of the tent door, wink at me, and call out, "Hey, babe," or some such endearment.

She didn't.

Before long, I could hear her muffled voice beginning the lecture for the day, the solemn evangelist reassuring her flock that they would indeed find salvation through their righteous abstinence. I didn't want to go without the tender intimacies that Rebecca considered politically oppressive to those non-coupled sisters amongst us. I wanted public cuddles and kisses, I wanted pet names and exclusivity, I wanted my Rebecca, and I wanted some minty toothpaste.

And so it came to pass.

I sprang to my feet and, with a cautious defiance, made my way towards the queue that was already starting to form in front of the Posh Wagon. Actually, I didn't exactly join the queue. I sort of shuffled in a half-embarrassed, half-defiant gait towards the line, then veered off at the last minute and repositioned myself against the base of a tree, about thirty feet away from the campervan. I watched the others come and go, like children visiting Santa's grotto. I saw Vicky Marsh (another of Rebecca's foot soldiers) glancing nervously around as she queued. She all but had a fit when she caught sight of me. I suppose I must've looked like Reb's general, leaning nonchalantly against the tree whilst drawing slowly on a meticulously crafted rollie. This is a look I have perfected over the years. On a good day, I can project a cool "I'm watching you, and I know what you're thinking" kind of vibe clear across a room. It usually provokes one of two reactions: either "Well, c'mon over then," or more commonly these days, "Urgh! Bloody filthy habit, smoking." On this occasion, the blood had visibly drained from Vicky's chubby cheeks and disappeared into her muddy Doc Martens.

I waited until the last of them had taken possession of their ill-gotten gains and trudged past me before I made my move. No sense in blowing my cover too early. I figured I'd just saunter along after the rush and casually enquire as to whether there were any tubes of toothpaste left. I could even make it sound like I was enquiring on someone else's behalf. Altruistic me, always putting my sisters' needs before my own. Yep, I could live with that. I put my best foot forward, unaware that Cupid, Aphrodite, and co. had been smoking some seriously wicked weed and were about to spring one of their best warped works on an unsuspecting dolt.

I wasn't expecting the song lyrics from "Just Another Girl" to slide over me the way they did. I'd only taken a step or two in the direction of the campervan when the sound of singing drifted my way. The woman was singing along to a track I knew by heart on her ghetto blaster. I rounded the back of the van armed with a swagger and a few well-rehearsed lines to utter, but when I saw her, I stopped dead. She had her back to me, and she was dancing. Dancing and singing along with one of my brother Frank's favourite songs.

I froze like a deer caught in the headlights. She didn't hear me approach and clearly thought that she was alone, because she continued with her swaying, hip-rolling step, enunciating the words with genuine feeling. I watched and waited, silently holding my breath, not wanting to intrude on what was obviously a private moment but unable to tear myself away. I ingested the scene before me. My mind took me back to the Goodge Street Incident, the time that I found myself sitting on the Tube opposite a dyke couple who were snogging the faces off one another. I knew that was a private moment too, but I had been unable to tear my eyes away from them. I had been mesmerised, my mouth gaping and my eyes magnetically locked on to their every move.

I was also powerless to stop the delicious tingling sensation that was coursing through my nether regions as I watched the dancer, and by the time I had regained a certain amount of respectable composure, she had turned around and was now facing me.

"Oh!"

Our eyes met, and her voice withered to a full stop.

"Oh," she said again, and then stood in front of me, head tilted down, hands buried deep in the pockets of her jeans.

Horrified at being caught in the act, I'm pretty sure that my face had flushed an embarrassing shade of beetroot. I looked at the ground and shuffled my feet a bit before I finally plucked up the courage to look again. Short woman. Smartly attired woman. Pint-sized, punky woman. Neither of us spoke for a couple of lifetimes, and then she strode to the side of the van, reached inside, and snapped the stereo off.

"Ah, erm...I don't think I have anything left to offer you."

Her voice came as a surprise to me. Not the tone or the words, but rather, the accent. I'd just spent the last six months or more conversing with women who had come from the length and breadth of this country and beyond. There were Scots, Brummies, Cockneys, and Germans, Welsh women, Scousers, and mad Mancs, but they all had one thing in common. To a woman, they were all working class. Well, I *assumed* working class as they all spoke with colloquial regional accents. I'd arrived with a standard London accent that allowed me to slip comfortably into the catch-all Cockney bracket, and I hadn't exactly gone out of my way to reveal my background to the others. That I came from a stable two-parent, family business background hadn't exactly found its way into conversations that were punctuated with references to childhood years spent in misery and hunger. It had seemed insensitive to mention my decent, loving parents and our comfortable home in leafy Muswell Hill when everyone else seemed to have survived their childhoods on erratic doley rations.

Everyone and her girlfriend could recount tales of alcoholic fathers or drug-addicted older siblings and years spent in ugly, draughty council estates that were crumbling with neglect. Up and down the country, vast swathes of my contemporaries were apparently struggling to tread water in the swell of Thatcher's yuppie revolution. And me? I would sit in silence, hugging my knees by the campfire during these conversations, occasionally nodding gravely to throw the others off my scent.

"That's Frank's favourite song... My brother, Frank... He's my twin." My cheeks had been ablaze, the firestorm rapidly spreading down my neck to join forces with the bubbling inferno that had had erupted in my core.

"Good choice." She gave me a flirty smile and stepped a little closer. "Seems like Frank has excellent taste in music...and siblings."

Rooted to the spot, I struggled to breathe, my heart pounded in my chest, and blood bubbled in my veins. I squeezed my eyes tightly shut and prayed that Saint Jude would shift me to the top of his priority list, and quick. The pint-sized vision of loveliness was approaching, and I was hyperventilating. Slate grey sky and pissing drizzle, the smell of grass and mud, wood smoke and petrol. Bang on cue, my stupid sensory overload problem decided to put in an appearance.

999? Fire service, please. Spontaneous combustion imminent.

"I'm Grier," she said and lightly grasped my elbow. "Hey, are you okay, love?"

"Fin," I gasped shakily, between heaving breaths. "Yes. No. Um...I think I haven't eaten enough today." Despite Grier's hand, which was now squeezing my shoulder—or maybe because of it—I was slowly regaining control of my lungs and forcing the oxygen to my dizzy brain. I bent over slightly and clutched my knees. I inhaled then exhaled slowly to a count of five, and all the while, Grier stayed with me, matching me breath for breath. Moments later, I straightened up, face to face with the loveliest juxtaposition I had seen in a very long time. Her pretty heart-shaped face was framed by a luxurious mop of dark brown curls, and her blue-grey eyes looked into my very soul. I stared and stared into her eyes, and she responded with a long, slow smile that sent a swarm of butterflies flapping their wings into my already rumbling stomach.

"Come on," she said, grasping my tightly curled fist in her soft fingers and pulling me towards her. "I've got a ham sandwich and a Wagon Wheel in the van that I'll split with you. You need to eat."

My swagger was returning with every step that I took with her. My fists uncurled, and I slid my hand into hers. "I am so ready to eat." I threw her a cheeky wink as I spoke. Had I been 100% recovered and confident, I might easily have added "you."

From Greenham Common to Hackney Marshes
One month later

I blame Carl for the fact that Tess and I ever got together. It's an odd relationship, him and me. I've known him for almost twenty years now, but I can't really say that I've ever liked him much. It would be overly dramatic for me to say that I took an instant dislike to him the day we first met, but I've gotta be honest; there was something a little unnerving about him. Still, in my wildest imagination, I could never have imagined the truth about him at the time. Saint John Nepomucene was well employed with that one. Old Johnny Nepomucene had always been one of my favourites. I'd always liked that the saint was a keeper of the queen's secrets, and I reckon he would have kept mine too. I fancied he'd had a hand in keeping some of my less than savoury confessions safe from the attentions of those around me, but he must've been putting in some serious overtime to deal with Carl's secrets too.

There had been frost on the ground that morning. I remember gazing dreamily at the naked, leafless trees through the window of Grier's bedroom and thinking how glad I was to be lounging in a cosy, warm bed in a squat in Hackney, as opposed to shivering on my lonesome in a crispy sleeping bag in a tent at Greenham.

Not that Grier's room had been anything to write home about, mind. The walls were covered in some tatty old peeling wallpaper from the 1970s and decorated with marker pen graffiti. I didn't have a clue what any of it said—I'm a one language gal—and this was all in French, or Spanish, or something I didn't understand anyway. The furniture consisted of a mysterious red metal trunk, a 1940s-looking dressing table, complete with flaking, distressed paintjob, and the biggest double bed I'd ever seen. Where they showed, the bare floorboards were grimy and sported large gaps from which cold, sharp draughts regularly emerged. I wasn't cold though. The huge double bed, which was fast becoming my idea of heaven, was perched on a brightly coloured woven rug and by my side, head resting on my chest and arms wrapped tightly around my waist, was the most perfect woman on God's green earth. Well, she was at that time.

For the first time in months, I was warm, comfortable, and well-shagged. I think I might have stayed like that forever if there hadn't been a sharp rap on the door.

"Hey, Gree! You up, girl?"

A deep male voice shattered my tranquil daydreams and, before I had chance to catch a breath, Carl Miller bounded in with a tray load of breakfast-type things in his arms. Madam Perfect, the newly crowned Queen of All That Is Lovely, chose that moment to peel away from the sensual nuzzling of my abdomen and leap out of bed. Cue one of my famous deer-caught-in-headlights moments. First priority was to drag the two duvets and the assorted pile of mis-matched woolly blankets up to my chin, partly to retain the warmth, but mostly to preserve my dwindling sense of modesty. Okay, I thought, this is weird. Some geezer's just barged into the bedroom, and my new sweetie is jumping up and rushing over to greet him with kisses.

I busied myself with the task of fixing my best lesbian separatist glare on him, hoping that the Goddess would smite him for his insolence. I wasn't sure which goddess, but any of them would have done at the time. Quite what Grier was doing, I didn't know. I watched and waited—well, neither floor nor Grier were about to swallow me up—so I had little choice really. She kissed him Frenchily on both cheeks, and then once again, rather noisily, on the mouth.

"Carl! Sweetheart! How long have you been back? You haven't met Fin, have you?"

To my toe-curling embarrassment, he slipped am arm around her naked waist, licked his lips, and grinned wickedly.

"Have now, mate!"

Um...yeah. I'd like to die now, please. Cue the conspiratorial giggling and hand-holding to which I would shortly become accustomed. After what seemed like an eternity, Grier released him and slipped back into the bed beside me. I considered indulging in a spot of haughty aloofness for a brief second or two, but hey, I was besotted and about to embark on a long series of forgiving the unforgivable as far as Grier Campbell was concerned. I welcomed her back into the sapphic realm with a nuzzle and a forced smile, before fixing this Carl character with a suspicious stare.

Carl positioned himself on the edge of the bed and began pouring the filth known as coffee into three mugs, flamboyantly waving away each and every groan and protest that I uttered with a camp swoop of his left hand. He began chatting excitedly to Grier, something about a beautiful boy in a nightclub in New York, and the pair of them hooted with laughter as they guzzled the foul brew. I should've learned the lesson that played out in front of my very eyes that morning, but I'm Thick-as-two-short-planks O'Sullivan so of course, I didn't.

I slipped into the Campbell/Miller household just before Christmas of 1988, and I suppose I became another fixture. At the time, the household consisted of Grier and Carl (or rather, *me* 'n Gree, and Carl); Alessandro the Italian communist guy; his girlfriend, Karen; and a bloke called Pete from Swansea, who may or may not have been sleeping with Carl. I could never tell. We stayed in that crumbling hovel for a week or two longer before being evicted by the good old socialist council of the London Borough of Hackney. Alessandro and Karen scraped the money together for the Channel ferry fare and set about thumbing their way to Tuscany, where they could wreak political havoc in sunnier climes. Pete announced that he was going to see his mum for Christmas, but he left with all his worldly possessions in a bin bag, and we never saw him again. That just left me 'n Gree and Carl. I know that it was the day before Christmas Eve because I recall battling the temptation to jump on a bus and slope off home to Mum and Dad's for the holiday. They say that love is all you need, but I seem to remember hankering after hot water and a spot of central heating when we first broke into number three Wallington Avenue and declared it a socialist-feminist squat. What a dump! Twenty odd years on, and it's one of the best-kept, most desirable properties in the area, and I own a third of it. Go figure.

I was well and truly done with the whole Greenham protest thing by that point. I will happily admit to anyone who cares to ask that I'd only gone for the wine, women, and song anyway. I know, I know. Not very PC, is it? I was a young, wannabe dyke, and it was the only way I could think of turning myself into an actual bona fide one. It worked, didn't it? I left Greenham, ostensibly to spend Christmas with my family. In reality, I was bored stupid with the routine hardship of protesting and just wanted to feel warm, and to feel Gree. I'd fallen absolutely hook, line, and sinker for the pint-sized Posh Wagon girl.

I consider myself to be a gangly, awkward-looking type, but Grier had clearly fancied the pants off me the first day that we met, and that wasn't something I was used to. After our first meeting that day in November, when we'd kissed briefly and clumsily and promised to stay in touch, I'd been surprised to wake up cold and alone in my tent the following morning with Grier on my mind. I briefly flirted with the idea of feeling guilty about it until I heard Rebecca's laughter in the distance, closely followed by a high-pitched giggle from whoever had been nominated her squeeze of that particular day.

Goodbye, guilt, and hello, righteous indignation. We'd only been an item for a matter of months, but I wanted more from Rebecca than she'd ever give me, and I knew it. I also knew that she would continue chipping away at, if not breaking, my heart with the rapidly expanding harem which she paraded before me on a daily basis. The morning after I met Grier, I swore an oath to myself. In my heart, I slammed the door shut on Rebecca forever, never to be revisited, no matter how hard she negotiated. That said, leaving Greenham was a must. I arose with a spring in my somewhat stiff step and set about the traditional leaving duty of redistributing my earthly possessions among the remaining women. Rebecca watched from the sidelines, but she didn't say anything to me. I said my goodbyes, hitched my rucksack onto my shoulder, and would have left things like that had she not shouted me over.

"Hey, Fin!"

I ambled towards her with a cocktail of melancholy and self-control bubbling up in my stomach. She was wearing that holey mohair jumper, but I don't remember if she looked upset or in any way concerned about my impending departure. I wasn't looking for that. I was too busy consigning her to the annals of women I have done, I suppose. I moved in close and embraced her in a back-slapping hug. "I'm going, Reb. Look me up when you get back to the Smoke, yeah?"

Far from being devastated, Rebecca had simply taken a step backwards, cocked her head to one side, and observed me with a squint. If I didn't know better, I would have said that she was surveying her creation with a critical eye.

Ah, yes, young O'Sullivan—go ye forth into the lesbian world with confidence, for I have taught thee well, my child.

Instead, she simply muttered something about keeping in touch before pecking me lightly on the lips and turning away. Not quite the sorrowful parting I had anticipated. I didn't know whether to be devastated or relieved. In the end, I opted for relief and put my best foot forward. Onwards and upwards. Away from sapphic sisterhood at Greenham and on to... I didn't exactly know what I was going to, but it sure as hell involved little Grier. Of that, I was sure.

Hearts and Cherubs too. My family made me.

If I'm completely honest, I never really felt completely at ease at Greenham. I spent my days huddled in blankets, listening to the life stories of the battle-hardened, working-class women of Greenham Common, and I had nothing I could tell them. No personal history that would make me a bona fide member of Thatcher's Nation of Outcasts and Malcontents.

Actually, my parents would've been my saving grace, credibility-speaking. The day that my dad overheard Father Jackson's thinly veiled racist put-down to my mum was the day that he decided to make a stand. He had left his own County Tyrone home just a month or two before and, like the good Catholic boy that he was, had been trying to settle into his new parish. He'd made a point of introducing himself to Father Jackson that first Sunday, just as Father Morrison had instructed before he left Omagh. Apparently, Father Jackson had been underwhelmed at the arrival of yet another poor relation from across the waters and had all but said so. But we are O' Sullivans, and we have more fibre than a barrel full of English monkeys could shake a stick at, or so Dad would confusingly tell us when we were young.

John Joseph O'Sullivan made sure that he arrived early for Mass the following Sunday, parked himself in the front pew—"best seat in the house, so it was"—and proceeded to make his great Irish presence felt. He sang the hymns with gusto and knelt to pray with an air of dignified piety that all the saints would envy. He repeated this brazen act the following Sunday and the Sunday after that. Having shoved his finger well and truly up the snotty nose of his new parish priest, he might well have let the issue lie on the fourth week…if it hadn't been for my mum, that is.

I never actually discovered what was said. Something uncharitable and casually racist, alluding to my mum's weight and the colourful dress she'd worn that day. Sunday best, probably. Dad had been standing at the church entrance, scowling at the dark grey sky and debating whether to put up his umbrella or chance it when he'd heard the remark. Apparently, he hadn't even noticed Mum, herself a London newbie—she'd been in chilly England for less than a week that Sunday—and was still shocked and wounded by the hostile, often downright aggressive reception her accent and skin colour seemed to provoke in her new countrymen. Aunt Pearl, who'd endured the London welcome for nigh on a decade already, was more than accustomed to hearing such comments. Apparently, she wasn't one of the docile, accepting Black folk who merely smiled in the face of the racists and laughed and joked along with them in order to gain acceptance. Nah. Aunt Pearl, tall and sinewy and as Black as a stick of liquorice, had a policy of full-on confrontation.

"Is what you say?" was her usual retort to whatever insults were being flung her way. Drawing herself up to her full five feet and eight inches, Ms Pearl Johnson would jut out her sharp chin and call out after whichever cowardly yob had had the poor judgement to take her on. "Hey, hey! Come y'here, bwoy! Come nuh? Is what, yuh 'fraid fi gal now? Come, mek I lik yuh down."

Then she would see them off with a slow, drawn-out sucking of her teeth. Usually. The olds would sometimes hint at the times that the tactic hadn't worked, lowered voices accompanying shakings of the head and sundry tuttings, but I never discovered what had actually transpired the few times that it hadn't worked. Aunt Pearl had a long, thin scar snaking down from the tip of her left eyebrow to just above her ear, and she didn't get that from grinning and apologising, I'll bet. I wish I'd had the guts to have asked her myself when she was still alive.

I am stung by a sharp pang of grief as I linger on the memory of my dearly departed favourite auntie. Aunt Pearl, alternately austere and benevolent in equal measures, the woman who taught me to plait hair and to tie my shoelaces. Somehow, she always had salt fish fritters in the fridge, and she always gave us 50p for sweets when we visited her. Right up until the arthritis got the better of her and she had to move to that nursing home in Finchley, Aunt Pearl always made us kids wait in the kitchen while she disappeared off into the bedroom to fetch "a lickle someting" to give us a treat.

There was this one time, about a year after she had died, I remember driving through Finchley on the way to a pickup and being floored by an overwhelming sadness. I'd pulled over to the side of the red route and found myself in an unexplainable flood of tears. I called Gree, stuttering over the radio to explain why I would be late in collecting the client that day. Gree, bless her, had simply jumped in a taxi herself and raced across London to get me.

Aunt Pearl was a fantastic individual: a Windrush pioneer who'd extended her home to her young niece, giving her more of a family life than she'd ever had back in Jamaica. Was she a closet dyke? Okay, counsel for the prosecution suggests that she never married (or showed the slightest interest in any blokes), was fiercely independent (resisted all offers and pleas from mum to come and live with us after Bernadette and Kath had moved out), and was quietly supportive of me and Gree (don't ask, don't tell) and our "lifestyle." She was also a member of the striking Ford assembly-line women who got the Equal Pay Act for all of us when me and Frank were too young to know what any of that was about. The unfriendly, often downright hostile locals made damn sure that Aunt Pearl knew she didn't own the place on a daily basis in those early days. I strut around like I *do* own the place, a brazen, mixed race, butch-ish dyke in the town that practically invented political correctness. I don't know I'm born, or so my dad would say. I don't know what I would have done in her shoes, but I do know that she was a better, braver, stronger woman than I could ever be. She was my hero.

Anyhoo, according to O' Sullivan legend, on this particular Sunday, my dad, on the verge of scurrying back to the near-derelict property on which he had just lavished his mother's fortune, had scowled and spun around on his heels in the doorway of the church, his blood rocketing to boiling point. He saw Mum, anxious and embarrassed, being ushered towards the front entrance by a tight-lipped Aunt Pearl. She was always devout, Aunt Pearl, and I suppose that the inside of a church was the one place on earth where she would allow such blatant racism to go unchallenged. For the life of me, I don't know why.

Aunt Pearl told me that he had looked her straight in the eye that day and read her thoughts, something along the lines *of I know, I know, but not in the church, okay?* He had opened and shut his mouth without speaking a couple of times (an O'Sullivan tradition) before turning to open the heavy wooden door behind him. Frosty January air had charged in to greet them, and Dad had winced on recognising Mum's apparent shock at the blast of freezing cold. Being a County Tyrone man, Dad was well used to the cold, persistent drizzle that erodes our sunny sides most of the year, making us Brits withdraw into ourselves and away from one another.

Holding the door open for them to step through, Dad had raised his umbrella against the driving winter rain and recalled his best and loudest Irish accent. "Here, ladies, please," he had boomed, motioning for Aunt Pearl to take the umbrella from him. "You may have brought us the warmth and the beautiful colours of your homeland, but I'm afraid all we can offer is this drizzling greyness by return. It hardly seems fair, but here's me best offering by way of compensation, if you'll accept it."

Aunt Pearl had been cautious, so I'm told, but she could not have failed to notice that the sound of his voice had wiped the smug smiles from the lips of the not-so-pious St Thomas's in-crowd, substituting expressions of curiosity, confusion, and downright agitation in their place.

"Tank yu, young mon."

She had accepted the umbrella with one hand, whilst motioning to Mum with the other. Dad had turned up the collar on his suit jacket against the cold and stolen a shy glance at my hesitant mother. Dad held the door as Mum stepped through, and their eyes met briefly before they both decided that the church steps were suddenly fascinating. The moment hadn't escaped Aunt Pearl's attention, and a well-timed clearing of her throat reminded them both that she was still there, and that they were still in the House of the Lord.

"'Twas the bloody English weather that brought us together," Dad would say with a wink. "Your mother tried to kill me with the pneumonia."

Then they would both laugh, their eyes seeking out one another across our crowded sitting room. I'd see that fleeting private look pass between them and wonder, with apprehension, whether anyone would ever look at me that way. Mum would then take up the story, embellishing the romantic here and omitting the racism there. I used to love listening to that story.

Dad comes from a long line of O'Sullivans, the bakers. He grew up in Omagh, watching his dad, grandad, brothers, and sundry uncles all run around serving the needs of the O'Sullivan and Sons' bakeries. Rory, the eldest brother was in line to inherit Grandpa Francis's business, and the twins, Brien and Gene, were destined to take over the huge Cookstown outlet. Calum, Uncle Martin's last remaining son had legged it to New York as soon as he had been able to raise the fare and looked unlikely to return. Dad's sisters, Siobhan, Ginny, Eileen, and Maggs had been expected to marry local gentry types and dutifully obliged.

Except for Ginny, that is. "Poor, sad Ginny," as my dad would refer to her, committed the most mortal of all mortal sins by taking her own life at the tender age of nineteen. That just left young John Joseph, wayward family misfit and apple of Grandma Fionnuala's eye. JJ had decided that he didn't want to accept his given station within the O'Sullivan hierarchy. Apparently, he had a bit of a fiery temper as a boy, though I've never seen any part of it in my whole life. As I understand it, Dad's refusal to roll up his sleeves and join the firm had been the thorn in Grandpa Francis's equally fiery side. Uncle Gene started to tell us about it once but, eyes blazing, Dad had raced from behind the counter to cut him off.

All I know is that there were fisticuffs between them and that the next day, Dad had stuck two fingers up to his own father and left for England. I don't know if Grandpa Francis ever knew, but I do know that Grandma Fionn had made him wait until she could fetch the money she had inherited from her mother from the local bank. John Joseph O'Sullivan the Wayward had landed in London on 5th August 1958 without a friend in the world, but with £5,000 in his back pocket.

Mum, on the other hand, was an only child for most of her life. Barely out of her teens at the time, Floreen Johnson had presented my Great-Grandma Sarah with a beautiful bouncing baby girl, my mum. According to Aunt Pearl, her father Albert's disapproval had been silent but deadly. Albert had belonged to Opus Dei and had no understanding of Floreen's lack of restraint. Why hadn't abstinence been enough for his own daughter, he had asked? He'd asked everyone, apparently. All and sundry, family, friends, and even visitors to the Johnson house had been submitted to his incessant questioning. By all accounts, he considered himself a reasonable chap. By all accounts, except for those of his children, I suspect.

Gerald, the eldest boy, had fled to the States and entered into the fellowship of the Jehovah's Witnesses. Strikeout one. To his father's abject misery, his brother Donald had accepted Haile Selassie I as his saviour, swapping his neatly clipped, post-war flat top for wild and unruly dreadlocks, and this at a time before Bob Marley had globalised the concept. Strikeout again. Great-Grandpa Albert had frowned and sighed and frowned again, before declaring that his last child, Pearl, would have no opportunity to veer off the rails.

He would ensure that she would make something of her life. Pearl, he declared, would be leaving the fold for the golden opportunities offered by the magnificent mother country. Standing shoulder to shoulder with those who had braved the Blitz and come out smiling, Pearl would represent the Johnsons of Kingston, Jamaica, their loyal cousins from across the waters. Pearl would valiantly put her back into the post-war rebuilding of the greatest country in the world and when she had settled in, she could relieve him of the pre-teen, whose tiresome mother, my grandmother, had burdened him with.

Floreen Johnson had fled her home accompanied by one Neville Anderson, whose speciality, it transpired, had been making babies. There were rumours. Neville was the father of Jeanette Thompson's boy. Neville had been caught in an un-Christian clinch with Father O'Halloran's young sister, and she barely fifteen years old. Though she had married Neville before they even got on the boat to Miami, Floreen had entrusted their first-born daughter to the care of her parents, with the intention of sending for her when they had settled in New York and earned enough money for the fare. Initially full of hope and anticipation, the letters to her young sister, Pearl, began to reveal that Floreen's marriage wasn't going quite as planned. After a time, the letters had simply stopped coming altogether.

Ten years passed. Baby Marcia had become a shy ten-year-old and Auntie Pearl an upstanding seventeen-year-old member of the parish. When Albert answered the London Transport's recruitment advert on Pearl's behalf, even more tears had been shed in the Johnson household, not least of all by Sarah, who would now lose her last child to a world outside of the island. Ten-year-old Marcia had begun to count the weeks, months, and years before she could join her beloved auntie in the country revered by her grandad and tepidly described in the letters that came from Aunt Pearl.

Mum said she hardly remembered her own mother. Like Pearl,

she had grown up calling Great-Grandma Sarah Mummee, and Great-Grandad Albert had been Daddee. She used to say that she remembered being heartbroken when her mum had tearfully kissed her goodbye for the last time, but that the biggest wrench she had felt had come when Pearl had taken her leave.

"I send fi yu, no worry 'bout dat. I send fi yu, hear?"

I never asked Aunt Pearl how she had felt about being deported by her dad to this chilly island. I didn't reckon she'd have slagged him off anyways; to do so would have been considered disrespectful of her elders, and she was always so proper about such things. I couldn't think that I'd ever slagged my olds off either. It wasn't that I shared Pearl's morality about such things, just that...I thought they were okay. *More* than okay.

The sharp stab of desolation which accompanied this thought took me by surprise. I pictured them sitting on the porch of their retirement home out in Jamaica. He'd be reading the copy of the *Mirror* that he'd spent half the morning finding, and she'd be pottering around the garden, examining the mangoes, ackee, and bananas for ripeness as they hung on the trees. Maybe one of the neighbours had joined them and was shielding his eyes from the hot sun with one hand, taking a long, slow sip of cool coconut water.

I sighed. If they'd been here, five minutes around the corner in the flat above the shop, or even ten minutes in the opposite direction in the house I grew up in, I would have hightailed my sorry arse over there sharpish. I'd park my moody backside on a kitchen chair, eyes fixed on the table's swirling wood grain. I would grunt my yes/no replies to Mum's gently probing questions, and she would have set a mug of tea and a thick slice of hard dough toast dripping in butter in front of me. And then, moving behind my chair, she would have slipped her arm across my chest, seat-belting me to the chair and to her body behind it. She'd have pressed small sharp kisses to the top of my head, and we'd have been still. Dad would have ambled into the room, then stopped dead in his tracks, his eyes searching for mine, then Mum's, and then mine again.

"Women!" he'd have declared in his mischievous, mocking tone. He would make as if to steal the toast from my plate, and Mum would have laughed and swatted his hand away, all the while keeping me pinioned.

"Dad!" I'd have said in an exaggerated tone, rolling my eyes at him. Releasing her grip, Mum would have gently squeezed my shoulder before crossing the room to pop more bread in the toaster.

"What?" Hands outstretched, he'd feign surprise.

And then the smiling would begin. Dad's wide eyes twinkling. Mum's smile small and shy, beaming love across the room as she tried in vain to reprimand him with her eyes. And then there was me, reluctantly admitting to myself that, despite the heaviness in my heart, the world was not going to fall in on me. Not today anyway.

My Dental Fetish

Present Day

Say love me or leave me and let me be lonely
You won't believe me but I love you only
I'd rather be lonely than happy with somebody else.

You might find the night time the right time for kissing
Night time is my time for just reminiscing
Regretting instead of forgetting with somebody else
There'll be no one unless that someone is you
I intended to be independently blue
I want your love, don't wanna borrow
Have it today to give back tomorrow
Your love is my love
There's no love for nobody else

"Love Me or Leave Me" by Nina Simone with lyrics by Gus Kahn.

"Can't we have some proper music on now?"

There's nothing in this world quite as effective as a smart arsed five-year-old to drag you back to the M1 of reality. The wheels of my fantasy love machine (a shiny black BMW 3 series) veer swiftly back onto tarmac, and I return to earth with a reluctant start.

Instinctively, I grip the steering wheel a little tighter and flick a glance in the rearview mirror. The road behind me is as clear as it was the last time I checked, all of ninety seconds ago. Today, the road ahead is populated with a sparse sprinkling of vehicles. Fewer cars than I normally see at this time of day and, unusually, a fair number of motorbikes. Half term daddies out playing with their toys, I decide, a smile playing on my lips. The separated and the divorced skiving off on their boy-toys, employing me and people like me to manage the kids that they should be spending quality time with, giving their baby mummies a break from parental duties. *Yes, and half term daddies pay the rent.* No. I purse my lips and raise my eyebrows. Paid the rent, *paid* the rent. Paid as in the past participle of the verb *to pay.* Or something like that. I dunno, I'm thinking more and more about school and university and all that stuff these days. Turning forty'll do that to you, I guess. I'm on a countdown now, and part time daddies will continue to pay the rent for seven more days. And then? More lip-pursing and a little lip-biting. I just wish I had half a clue as to what's waiting for me after. Twenty-some years after my time at Greenham Common, and I'm only now about to make a conscious decision about my life. To proactively decide my future rather than just let it happen to me, to proudly and confidently stand on my own.

Maybe.

I cut Nina Simone off dead in the middle of yet another exquisite note. With a little help from some nameless pirate station belting out some tuneless house or garage track, I placate the youngster in my back seat. I steal a quick glimpse in the rearview mirror at my godson, Ade Junior, who is swaying from side to side in his booster seat and mouthing God knows what, as this particular "tune" has no lyrics. Another sigh, and in doing so, I notice one or two fine lines emanating from the corners of my eyes. I scowl a good-un and return my gaze to the road ahead, remembering just how I'd gotten myself roped into this in the first place.

Ade Oworu Senior has excused himself from his usual half-term childcare responsibilities in order to participate in some obscure golfing tournament in Guernsey. The case for the defence goes something like this; every year, McClelland, Mansfield, Palmer and Clarke Solicitors are represented by Geoff Palmer and Simon

Clarke, leaving David Mansfield Jnr and co. to hold the fort. Old Mr McClelland is, of course, always available as backup, but no one ever calls him in to help, even with a tricky case. Ade himself has only ever met William McClelland once (during his job interview) but he has, on occasion, overheard other colleagues muttering in nervous whispers about late night phone calls and outrageous demands from the "Old Man."

This year, Geoff Palmer was having to be talked out of leaving his Coronary Care Unit bed at the Sunnydale Clinic. Note to self: there are no dales in London and, even if there were, they'd be grey, overcast, and piddling with rain. Word has it that Old McClelland himself has expressly forbidden his attendance. Says he's found a great golfing stand-in, and that there's absolutely nothing for Geoff to concern himself with, apart from making a swift and full recovery. They say that Palmer's blood pressure increased to 158 over 106 when McClelland phoned to give him the news. Golf is Geoff Palmer's life 365 days of the year, and the bi-annual Legal Eagles Charity Cup is his Christmas and Easter devotion. So, according to Golfer Geoff, whoever Old McClelland has in mind as a stand-in had better bring the cup home this year. Word has it that Palmer has promised to handwrite and personally deliver the bastard's P45 if he doesn't. Whoever *he* is.

"And so you see, m'lud, in mitigation, I respectfully submit that there is a three-line whip on my attendance. I have to go." My old mate, Ade Senior, had been in the kitchen leaning against the brushed aluminium fridge, watching his wife plough through a pile of ironing when he began his summing up. "If I want to keep my job, my head, and my reputation, that is. If I am ever to become Mr Adebola Oworu of McClelland, Mansfield, Palmer, Clarke *and* Oworu, that is."

The Honourable Yemi Oworu QC had simply rolled her eyes skyward and shaken her head. "We'll survive," she had muttered, almost absently, clearly trying to find a solution to the half-term childcare crisis. "Have fun with your playmates," she had told him, without any obvious malice. She had continued slipping the mound of freshly ironed shirts and blouses onto the waiting wooden hangers, fastening only the top button of each before moving on to the next. Then she had paused for an ominous second or two, cocked her head to one side, and observed her somewhat nervous husband through narrowed eyes. Ade's eyes had hit the deck, as he clearly anticipated her words.

In a tender movement, Yemi had smiled, reached out to him, and drawn a finger over his shiny bald head, before letting him have it. "Just don't get drunk, babes."

I shake my head at the memory of the way he winced. I slip a gear down to third, give the Beamer some welly, and glide past the cruising Tesco's van before sliding back into the comfort of the slow lane. Everyone knows about Ade's whiskey standoff. Ade loves an Irish whiskey, his favourite being a Connemara twelve-year-old peated single malt. This, given the opportunity, he would consume till the cows come home, and when they lived with us, he and Frank used to do just that on a regular basis. Without the cows though. Trouble is, though Ade adores the whiskey, the feeling's far from mutual. He drinks, he gets pissed, and, truth be told, he's an amiable drunk. It's not the whiskey-drinking; it's the throwing-up and the hangovers that are the problem, and Ade knows it.

Cut to the quick, Ade had blurted out the first vaguely rational thought that had entered his head. "Can't we get Fin to take him to your mother's each day? Or to football camp, or to...I don't know, the dentist or something?"

The broad smile on his wife's face had flickered briefly before the furrowed brow had settled in. She reminded him that I was finally throwing the towel in on my private hire driving career, or taking an extended leave of absence, at the very least. With an exaggerated tut, Yemi said he should have remembered such an important detail about one of their oldest mutual friends. That it would be insensitive of them to ask me to postpone my long overdue holiday in the sun.

With his back against the wall (fridge), Ade had then thrown in what he had perceived to be his trump card. "She'll do anything for you though. She's always fancied you, you know."

My stomach had plummeted to my boots, and I had been mightily relieved to be standing just out of sight in their hallway when he'd dropped that one. Rubbing away at the pain of that gut punch, I'd stomped noisily back into the kitchen in time to catch Ade grinning and Yemi rolling her eyes.

"You know I'm only kidding, right?" He'd raised his eyebrows at me.

I'd known well enough that Ade had been only half kidding, so I half forgave the grinning idiot when he slipped his arm around my waist and pulled me in for a hug. Of course, he'd been unable to resist saying, "Remember, I put a ring on it," before he let me go.

Yemi's lips had curled upwards for a second before she composed herself. "Out!"

We stood together, hand in hand, watching the bozo sashay away, belting out Beyoncé's "Single Ladies" at the top of his voice.

"Men!" she said, releasing my fingers and returning to the task at hand. "Make me a lesbian, Fin, so I don't have to deal with this shit."

I'd laughed long and hard at that one. I fetched a glass from the cupboard, slid into a chair at the kitchen table, and helped myself to the peanut punch that she had made earlier. "No can do, mate," I said, still chuckling. "I'm fresh out of rainbow dust this week, and besides," my heart did a minor flip when Yemi looked up from the ironing board to meet my gaze, "I love you just the way you are."

We smiled at one another, enjoying the marshmallow sweetness that hovered in the air between us. When Yemi opened her mouth to speak, I already knew what she was going to say, so I pre-empted the question by adding, "Of course I will, hon," and we remained in comfortable silence until it was time for me to leave.

Contrary to popular belief, one I haven't disabused them of, I really don't have a holiday in the sun lined up. Truth be known, I've been dreading the time when I'll become a gentlewoman of leisure. I briefly flirted with the idea of taking (really) early retirement, but I know that won't do. Everyone's expecting me to announce that I'm going back to finish my degree or something equally studious but...I just don't want to. I'm happy to take a break for a bit, but I honestly can't think of anything I'd rather do than zip around the streets of London in the Beamer all day long. Ade's right and wrong though. I *do* have a real soft spot for Yemi, but it's because she's a fucking amazing individual, and because she was so sweet to me when Grier left, and not because I want into her knickers. In your sad and lonely straight boy dream, Mr Oworu.

Speaking of knickers, mine are feeling decidedly tight as I walk young Ade into the dentist's waiting room. For most folk, the smell of mouthwash and the posters of other people's decaying molars combine to create a most distinct turn-off. Most folk associate these things with pain and suffering. Pervert that I am, however, the smell of a dentist's waiting room causes an altogether different reaction in me. I usher Ade to an empty seat and pull the Spiderman beanie off his shaven head. He begins his usual squirm of protest, but I'm not listening.

I'm squirming myself, adjusting my Levi's and trying to fan cool air to the blush that I feel rising above my collar. I shove one hand into the pocket of my jeans and lean casually against the wall behind me. I'm trying to look cool. Well, not *cool* cool, just not, well, the way that *she* makes me feel. Ade has noticed my nervous posture and starts pulling faces at me. Some of them are really quite inventive, and it helps keep my mind off the woman on the other side of the door who we're about to see. I cross my eyes, pull out my ears, and poke my tongue out at him. Of course, she chooses to make her entrance as I do so.

"Ade Oworu?"

She looks around the waiting room from left to right. Ade is climbing down from his seat and reaching for her hand, and I'm still squirming. I'm impaled on the infrared rays that are beaming from her stunning Kohl-lined eyes. I try to smile and say something, anything. I can't.

"Hello, Fin."

Her voice is rich and luxurious, like gooey, melted chocolate. She's smiling at me over her shoulder as Ade leads her to the treatment room. He stoops under her arm and into the room.

Alyssa lowers her head for a moment and then, shooting a mischievous glance in my direction, says, "Are you coming, Fin?"

I'm struggling for words. I'm wrestling with a pair of rogue knickers. I'm allowing Alyssa Gianaris to lead *me* into the treatment room. Her fingertips make the merest of contact with my shoulders as I squeeze through the open doorway, but I nonetheless feel a bead of sweat roll down my back. *Do not go there.* I'm a week away from the start of my life of leisure, and I do not need the complication that another liaison with Alyssa would bring. I don't want to go there again, especially with my current emotional condition and the twisted soap opera that my life has become. She will suggest, and I will resist, resist, resist.

We met early last year when I first brought Ade in for a check-up. Apparently, I sent her gaydar through the roof, and she flirted mercilessly with me throughout the consultation. She's absolutely stunning, and she makes love like a Eurostar express going downhill on an icy day. She asked me out for a drink, which became a bite to eat, which in turn became a late drink in some trendy Islington bar. Of course, I had to scuttle off home in the not so wee hours (Kingsbury to Heathrow scheduled for five a.m. the following morning) but I spent the next couple of weeks making unscheduled visits to her flat or to the dental surgery on a near daily basis. Her eyes are the colour of Caramac, and she has this incredible mane of luxurious black curls that I'm hard pushed to resist sinking my fingertips into. Her teeth are straight and white (what else would you expect of a dentist?) and she smiles widely and often. She's gorgeous—what can I say? But... There's always a but with these things, isn't there? She drinks too much, and I can't stand her druggie mates. *Yeah.* I grit my own imperfect teeth and repeat my Alyssa mantra. *Resist, resist, resist.*

After an uncomfortable ten minutes, young Ade is all done. No cavities detected, and no fillings required. Alyssa embraces him, clasping his reluctant head against her luxurious bosom before she leads him back to the waiting room. My thoughts begin to drift in the direction of said bosom, and I have to physically shake my head to dispel the memory of her smooth, expansive breasts in my hands, and the feel of my tongue across her dark brown nipple.

Inhale and sigh; it's all I can do to stop myself from rushing across the room and planting my trembling lips firmly against her white-coated chest. My sizzling cheeks betray my salacious thoughts for all to see and, of course, Alyssa catches and interprets my juvenile stare. Flashing me a dazzling white glance of her perfect pegs, she smiles and beckons me on. She actually draws a finger down the side of my blazing cheek as she leads us toward the door and, in a voice dripping with honey and promise, she tells me that I must come back and see her soon.

And that's the crux of my whole being, folks. I'm a forty-year-old mass of fucking rampant dyke hormones, destined for a lifetime of wild impulse-led decisions and the heartache that inevitably follows in their wake, and it cannot go on. Something has to give. I thank God for the cool, passion-killing drizzle that pervades my senses as we cross the car park to my wheels, and I resolve to do better in my future dealings with women. Yeah, right.

Languishing in Hot Water

IT'S FRIDAY. RECLINING IN my fragrant tub, I resist the urge to cry out, "Thank fuck" or some such utterance, but Friday it is, and I have made it through half-term week without incident—without major incident, that is. I have driven young Ade to tennis lessons, drama classes, Granny's house, and cousin Jide's house. I've even taken him swimming—mental note to purchase a new cossie—and allowed myself to be splashed, harassed, and cannon-balled. He's a good kid, a real little sweetie, and I've enjoyed spending the time with him. My penultimate week's work has been something of a pleasure, a sort of pre-sabbatical. Now comes the hard part; I've got seven days to come up with some exciting holiday option. Seven days before I say farewell to the Driving Ambition Collective (what's left of it) and head off for the glamorous, exciting second phase of my life, which is currently emblazoned with a big fat TBC. Just one week before Grier and Madam arrive too. Time to sink deep into the bathtub and practice opening my eyes underwater, I think.

It's not working for me today. Usually, my bathtub antics absolve me of all worries and/or adult responsibilities but right now, I am fully aware that when the sun rises tomorrow, I will be just six days away from Grier being here in my/our house once again. She'll be here, wishing me well in my adventures to come. She'll be moving confidently among my workmates, housemates, and family members. Laughing and joking, she'll be the life and soul of the party. *My* bloody party. Ten days ago, I turned forty. Now my sister, Bernadette, is about to turn fifty, and we're going to jointly party like it's 1999. I gulp a breath. My brother Frank's not here to celebrate our birthday, and my...Grier will be. Well, she's not *my* anything, really. Another gulp. Bernie will welcome Grier back like...like a sister, I suppose. She's always liked her, and her fiftieth birthday party wouldn't be complete without Grier's presence. I couldn't object to her inviting Grier any more than I could explain why I'm dreading her arrival. She'll breeze back into my life with a wink and a smile, and only the two of us will know what transpired last New Year.

Cue a little rippling of the water. I'd add more hot, but I haven't been soaking long enough to need it. Only the two of us. Who the fuck am I kidding? Ripple, ripple, minor splash. I'm struggling to figure out how I feel about it all. I've nothing to be ashamed of; I'm a consenting adult. Grier and I have known each other for the best part of my adult life. It was the most natural thing in the world for her to slip into my bed that night. We didn't have to. I didn't need to. We just...did. In a way, it was good. A sort of closure, you could say. After all, we still care about each other, don't we? Well, I care about her. This is where I exhale deeply, trying to convince myself that this is indeed the state of play. My Catholic conscience is not entirely convinced, and the name *Tessa* jabs me sharply between the eyes.

I rub the palm of my hand against my forehead in small, tight circles. What's wrong with this water anyway? I thought that water was supposed to have soothing properties. Healing, even. All I'm getting from this tub is bloody wrinkles. I rise abruptly, catch sight of myself in the triptych art deco mirror across the room, and emit an overly dramatic sigh. Three forty-year-old women stare back at me with a glum expression. Their kinky brown hair has become flecked with grey here and there. Exactly when did that happen? I raise my head in defiance and poke my tongue out in their direction. The ensuing grin barely registers on my lips before my whole being freezes. I hear a noise, a tiny sound, rising from the ground floor. It is neither ear-piercing nor blood-curdling, but I hurriedly draw the towel around my shoulders, protection against the chill that has descended upon me on hearing it. I squeeze my eyes tightly closed, and I dig my teeth into my lower lip.

Tuh-tuh-tuh-tuh-tuh-tuh-tuh-tuh.

The sound of a bicycle wheel gently spinning as it is carried into the hallway stops. I can hear muffled voices engaged in amicable conversation. I screw my eyes tighter. My heart is beating so loudly that I imagine it leaping out of my chest and thump-thumping its way across the cold floor. I watch in fascination as it hops across the chequered tiles, leaving a smeared trail of my lifeblood in its wake. Only when I visualise the valves pumping and the severed arteries trailing behind it do I force myself back to reality. This is ridiculous. I try to compose myself, to force that errant organ to chill out. It's no use. My heart's trying to work its way up my windpipe and out of my mouth. We both know that Tessa's back, and we have to perform our normal functions in her presence, come what may.

I shiver and resolve to change the topic of thought which has so rudely interrupted my daydreaming. What is it about us human beings that compels us to stick our big toes up the spout of the cold tap when taking a bath? I had been merrily contemplating my navel, my never-expanding waistline, my tiny breasts, and that recently arrived grey pube that's been sent to try me, but now? I throw off the inadequate protection of the towel and plop back into the tub.

I stretch out my entire body in the water before employing *my* big toe to add hot water. I force myself to inhale slowly, deeply, and repeat the calming process. With a little effort, I persuade my sorry self to begin squeezing all panicky thoughts from my mind, employing the warm scent of Issey Miyake to deodorise my inner-city lungs. Mm. I take fleeting comfort from the familiarity of that smell. I'm here in my own perfumed bath, in my own snazzy house, in a rather nice residential street in north London. I'm an Executive Director of the company I co-founded a lifetime ago, and I'm just about to take a well-earned sabbatical to do something exciting and worthwhile. Or do nothing at all, which is looking increasingly likely as D-Day edges menacingly closer, and I have exactly zero plans. Six days. I'm also forty years old and girlfriend-less, and I can't decide if that's okay or a modern-day Greek tragedy.

Alyssa Gianaris. I groan and plunge my head under the water. *Stop thinking about that bloody woman.* Adopting my best Mother Superior expression of displeasure, I wag a disapproving finger at my wayward self. Regrettably, this is not enough to prevent me from entertaining a fleeting image of Ally's naked, voluptuous body lying in the middle of my king-size bed, a come-hither smile, inviting me...um...thither. I'm having a momentary lapse, one of my familiar loss of self-control moments, and I'm lurching from one scary reality to the next. *Get it together, Fin. Six days.* Things will be different then...won't they?

I'd sworn off women for the past several months, but I guess I'm having a vulnerable moment. I've been avoiding the good doctor all this time, and we both know it. I ran away from Alyssa the other day when all she wanted was a swift fuck-buddy session. And then there's Grier. Well, Gree'll be on her way here very soon. She'll be my guest for the weekend. She'll be sleeping in the spare room, just a matter of feet across the landing from me. Her and her bloody poncey girlfriend, that is. I roll my eyes and poke my tongue out in the general direction of Barcelona, I fancy, then cast my eyes around the bathroom for reassurance. My bathroom, my safe bathroom in my safe house, I think to myself. I have a lot to be grateful for.

Truth be told, it had been Carl's house before it was mine and Gree's and Carl's, but that's beside the point. He'd been the one to come up with a mortgage when the benevolent Housing Association had offered to flog us the crumbling wreck of a squat, as it then was, for a meagre sixty grand. Carl had been gainfully employed by Channel Four at the time, so it'd been easy for him. Me and Gree had been struggling to keep the Driving Ambition Collective afloat but within a year of him buying the place, we had also signed away our freedom to a three-way mortgage, becoming capitalist wage slaves and bourgeoisie homeowners in one fell swoop.

Not long after we had liberated number three Wallington Avenue, the lesbian jungle telegraph directed Reb to our crumbling doorstep. She quickly moved into the top room—*Tessa's room*—and Grier persuaded her to join us as a DAC driver. Living and working with my girlfriend and ex-girlfriend was surprisingly uncomplicated, though I must admit that Reb's nonchalant attitude to my lovey-dovey relationship with Grier did cause me to pout. A big bit of me had wanted her to be driven to jealous distraction in the face of my affaire du coeur, but she never was. That's Rebecca for you: brazenly non-monogamous and accepting of pretty much anything. Except the patriarchy and capitalism, that is.

Our enthusiastic foray into the realms of the rat race had proved too much for Reb's pristine politics. Reb's upper lip had curled in disdain at the suggestion that she join us, and she upped and went south (a betrayal I still haven't come to terms with). We were *North Londoners*, a proud tribe who only ever ventured south under duress, and in packs. Reb nailed her colours to the South London mast and, though she continued working with us and we continued to socialise and bump into one another at demos and the like, relations were never quite the same after that. Her place in the house had been filled by Alison and Claire the builders, who'd started fixing and rebuilding stuff and by the time they moved on, we were basking in two-bathroomed luxury. The entire house was cleared of woodworm, splinter-shedding floorboards were sanded and varnished, mouldy wallpaper was stripped, walls replastered and rag-rolled, and hey presto! Carl the Director and Grier the Photographer had a suitably plush north London residence. Oh, and then there was me, of course.

"Oh, get a grip." I splash water at my face.

And now I'm bloody talking to myself. Squeezing my eyes tightly shut again, I rub my index fingers across my eyebrows and bite my lower lip some more. Multi-tasking, I call it. It's comforting, sort of. When I finally open my eyes, I'm still sitting in the claw-footed tub of my smart black and white bathroom, but I am no longer alone. Tessa's relieving herself on my bog, glaring at me with a pronounced frown. She does that when the top bathroom's out of bog roll. Uses my bathroom, I mean, not frown. Actually, she usually frowns as well. Frowning's all she's done in my direction of late. In fact, this is probably the longest period of time we've spent in such close proximity over the last few months. Since the New Year Fiasco, that is. Since I decided to be brainless, gutless, and batshit crazy all rolled into one.

Seconds pass before it finally dawns on what's left of my frazzled mind that she's waiting for me to deliver the answer to some question or other that I haven't actually heard. Cool as you like, I open and shut my mouth, then I glance sideways. "Eh?"

What? It's a perfectly valid utterance for someone of limited communication skills like myself. The bathroom invader's scowl deepens. She puffs out a snarled exhalation as she rips a length of toilet paper from the roll on the wall. She has my number of course, and I hate that in a woman. She wipes herself with the bog roll and stands before dropping it in the loo, watching as it swirls away down the pan. She makes me wait deliberately, methinks. She also makes me think like her, and I hate that in a woman too. Especially in the same woman. I've long since stopped being weirded out by the fact that she can have a wee in front of me with such blasé abandon. Maybe it's a northern thing—everyone and her whippet piling into the bathroom at the same time—I dunno. I'm actually holding my breath when she finally she speaks again.

"When's t'Royal Visit kicking off?"

She hoicks up her jeans and turns her back on me as she washes her hands in the basin. I watch her drizzle the liquid soap into her left palm and then rub her hands together with a swift circular motion. She slops the suds right up to each wrist in turn, before plunging them under the running cold tap. I've seen her do this a million times and each time, I've felt a tiny shiver in the base of my spine. My overactive imagination tells me that Dr Tessa

Beckinsale—Becks to her mates—is actually a retired surgeon-cum-serial killer who is living in my house with the express purpose of doing me in on a dark lonely night when she's got me alone. Only she's already had me alone on several nights and each time, she's taken me to her cluttered hovel of a bedroom with a very different intent than murder. Tessa glances over her right shoulder at me, eyebrow cocked in question, awaiting my answer. My heart betrays me by conceding a minor flutter.

"Grier's on her way, via Amsterdam," I say, rippling the water for no good reason. I clear my throat. "She'll be here next Friday night— They'll be here, I mean."

Dr T waves her hand theatrically as she crosses the room to get a towel from my airing cupboard. As she passes the head of the bath, she pauses and, for a split second, I think she's going to kiss me. I close my eyes, raising my head in anticipation, but the desired contact doesn't occur. Instead, she lets out a sort of low snort and places her hands firmly on her hips. Now she looks like my mum when she's on the verge of telling me off.

Jabbing her index finger into the centre of my forehead, she spews forth her words of endearment. "Oh, fuck off, Fin."

Yeah. Not exactly the reaction I'd been looking for. She's one cool fucker, the good doctor; gotta love that coolness. Except when it's fixing its icy fingers around your throat, of course. Tessa crosses the room and before she reaches the door, she turns and gives me her trademark crooked grin, causing a minor flutter to jolt my stomach. She's about to say something, I know it. I pray for a tidal wave to kindly put me out of my current misery but nothing happens, and I lie, naked and vulnerable, motionless under her callous gaze. Simultaneously, I love her and hate her.

"So, Her Majesty'll be here Friday? Poor you!"

As she takes her leave, I catch sight of the granite expression fixed on her face, and a pang of guilt, or sadness, or something rumbles deep in my belly. Tessa's not a mean-spirited soul, or rather, she wasn't before me. I've made her into a malicious harpy, presumably fashioned in my own image. Or Grier's. I snarl and splash a little in my bathwater, and I know she's right. Gree's coming and once again, I'm all of a lather, so to speak.

This therapeutic bathing's a heap of crap, and I've decided that it's time I got up and got on with life and all that. Allowing myself one final exaggerated sigh of despair, I rise theatrically from the perfumed waters, reach for my bathrobe, and cross the floor to the basin in three swift stomps. I grip the porcelain rim as if my life depends on it and force myself to look in the mirror. Staring back at me are a bunch of haggard O'Sullivans, all in need of a good haircut. We know that we can't get to Harry the Barber's to restore my usual, razored sharpness this side of the party, so I grab a tub of gel and take charge, smoothing down the sides and twisting the curls into a carpet of inch-long, bumpy baby dreads. When I twist my neck left and right to check my handywork, I'm pleasantly surprised by the results. I'm actually able to enjoy the moment for a second or two before the familiar crushing weight of expectation bears down on my chest, and the scowl returns to my face. I stare long and hard at the mirrored cabinet doors before I force myself to prise them open. Another sigh.

Inside lurks the magic bullet that will change my life, or so they say. Before I can change my mind, I pop a tiny tablet from the blister pack, sling it into my mouth, and swallow without water. I don't want to do it, but Cal's made me. My old mate made me promise to attend the appointment she made for me with my GP last week, made me swear that I would follow her instructions, even if I didn't want to.

I don't want to. I barely taste the coating when the anti-depressant shoots down my throat, but I grimace anyway. I'm on day three of these so-called helpers, and I don't feel any different. Tell me again why I'm doing this, Cal? Will it keep Grier in Barcelona and out of my house and my head? Nope. Will it waggle a magic wand over Tessa and miraculously turn her into somebody who wants to talk to me? Nope again. I sigh and force my tightly clenched jaw to soften a little. It's going to be a long week of anticipation. If I had more than half a brain, I'd allow myself a minute to acknowledge the tiny stabbings of misery that have accompanied Tessa's departure. I miss her, and I'm very much aware that I do indeed have but half a brain when it comes to women.

I Need a Paddle

I'M LYING ON MY stomach, flopped diagonally across my bed and barely breathing. That close encounter of the bathroom kind with Tessa has really knocked me for six. It's been nearly four months since the New Year Fiasco, and I'm no further forward. No further up shit creek, and my paddle's still AWOL. My propensity for masochism elbows its way into my thoughts, stealing me away to watch a miserable rerun of New Year's Day in glorious technicolour. Like nudging a damaged tooth with my tongue, I have to give it a prod just to see if it still hurts. I fall into the void of that awful memory.

I couldn't look at Tessa at breakfast that morning. Our eyes briefly connected across a kitchen filled with the human remnants of the previous night's party. Carl hugged his coffee mug, eyelids heavy with a lack of sleep and an excess of illegal substances. Darren danced about the place, frying Cumberland sausages and looking as fresh as a daisy, as usual. Some boring geezer from the Beeb who, I seem to recall, spent most of the night droning on about Dr Who to anyone who'd listen. He looked like he'd wandered into the wrong house but hadn't had the good grace to make his apologies and leave. Then there was me, looking shifty of course, and Grier. Gree was darting to and fro, digging up jars of jam from the cupboards liked she'd never been away. When Tessa buzzed into the room with a smile on her face, I dropped my head and pretended to be flicking something off my T-shirt. I supposed it took her all of thirty seconds to ingest the scene before her, to put two and two together. Time had stood still, with the clock on the mantelpiece upping its vocals to a deafening level. *Tick, tick,*

tick had never sounded so ominous. By the time that Carl spoke, I had died and gone to hell in a sidecar.

"Well, here's the African queen herself! When'd you get back, and how'd you like the Cape, my dear?"

He paused his familiar ninety to the dozen chattering to accept a bite of the sausage sandwich proffered by Darren, his long term on-and-off and then on-again partner. Tessa had returned late the previous night following a visit to her mum and little sister, who had relocated from West Yorkshire to Cape Town with her stepdad. That morning, across the kitchen divide, I studied Tessa from beneath my lowered lids. She moved to the fridge, pulled open the heavy doors, and selected a carton of juice. Then I watched her drain the last of the carton into a clean mug before leaning back against the fridge door and taking a large slug. Not once did she look at me. She knew.

"Yeah. Yeah, it was brill. Stunning place. Simply beautiful."

I could all but feel the strain in her taut voice, but still I did nothing, said nothing. A muscle in my right thigh betrayed me when Grier plonked herself down at the table beside me. I suppose I must have jumped, or flinched, or something. I prayed heartily to St Fiacre, patron saint of taxi drivers and sundry other folk, that the earth might open up and swallow me whole, pausing briefly for a polite burp of acknowledgement, but no such luck. I sat motionless, rooted to the spot, feeling the eyes of two expectant women burning into my cowardly lowered head. Had they heard my heart thumping double time against my ribcage? Had they known that a prolonged agonised scream was readying itself in anticipation of my lips parting to facilitate its exit? *I'm sorry. Don't ask me to explain; I can't.* I didn't know what was going on. I couldn't think. My head was throbbing, and I couldn't catch my breath. I could smell the singed edges of the toast on my plate, feel the warm glow coming from the overhead light, but I couldn't speak.

"I must dash, sweethearts," Grier said, patting my thigh as she rose from the table. "I really want to catch up with Izzy at the Tate before I head back."

Sliding slowly away from my side, Grier smiled broadly at Tessa as she made a point of squeezing past her to the door. Neither one of them spoke, but I saw a muscle in Tessa's jaw clench, felt the heat of Grier's smugness. All the while I was deafened by the rush of my blood ringing in my ears. I was a spineless little shit then, and I'm sure as hell no better now.

Tessa had flown halfway around the world to get back for the party, to get home to me, and my heart had danced a pretty good Samba when she walked into the room that night. I'd been standing talking to Grier on my right whilst propping Alyssa up with my left arm. For no good reason, I glanced across to the living room door and there she was, looking healthy and bronzed, and sporting a very sharp and very dykey new haircut. I remember smiling, and then grinning even wider when she caught sight of me looking at her. She must have dropped her bags off in her room before coming in, because she picked her way through the mass of assembled bodies on the makeshift dance floor with her empty arms outstretched, inviting me in. I just couldn't stop grinning. I think about it now, and I feel a hard knot of anxiety rise up my chest, forcing its way to the back of my throat where it emerges victorious as a tiny, mournful sigh. If I was a philosophical type, I'd weigh up the relationship between anticipation and dread but for now, O'Sullivan the Uneducated simply recalls the delicious wave of pleasure experienced at the sight of the returning Dr Beckinsale.

Did we kiss? I seem to recall planting one on her newly bronzed neck and murmuring some minor endearment as I drank in the familiar scent of pear and freesias, but I don't remember a snog or anything. Thinking about it now, through Carl's filmmaker kind of lens, I wonder how we must have looked to others, standing in the middle of the party embracing one another. How we must have looked to Grier, left holding the sozzled Alyssa after I had abruptly broken off from our conversation to greet my lover. Why am I such a bozo? It might all have been so different if only I'd said goodnight to the ex and the old ex there and then and galloped up the stairs with the good doctor. But I'm an arse, aren't I? I let her go, allowed her to slip through my fingers and slope off to bed while I did the responsible hostess bit and drove the inebriated Alyssa home. Why couldn't I have gotten pissed myself that night? Why, in the name of all that is holy, did I have to tuck Alyssa up in her bed (having comfortably resisted her less than subtle invitation to revisit our past "arrangement") and then fall for Gree's masterplan? *Don't try to kid a kidder, Fin. You can fool some people sometime, but you can't fool all the people all of the time—you know why.* I squeeze my eyes tightly shut and grimace, as I expel Bob Marley's words and the uninvited self-admonishment from my mind.

I left Alyssa's with a spring in my step and a tightening in my Levi's. I was going home, through the empty streets of freezing north London, to the woman I loved. *Maybe loved.* I tanked it home, carefully observing the speed limits of course, and then I made the worst decision of my entire life. Standing in the doorway of her room, I watched Tessa sleeping the sleep of the jet-lagged for a few moments before I silently crept away. I had been intent only on going to brush my teeth before slipping back to Tessa's room and into bed next to my sleeping beauty. But...Grier. Well, Grier in my room—formerly our room—waiting for me with champagne, two glasses, and a massive spliff. I can smoke as much as the next dopehead, but the alcohol'll get me every time. Grier knew that, but I can't make any excuses. I'm a fucking arse, as Dad would say, and I know it. I think Grier has always known it too. I groan aloud as the memory fades to black, and I bump back into the present.

And now Tessa's back, and I'm back. By some flukey coincidence, we're both in the house at the same time for a change, and soon Grier'll be here too. Tessa's been down to the kitchen I suppose, but I hear her sprinting up the stairs two at a time, heading past my door on her way to her own room, and I'm lying on my bed listening to her footsteps. She's gone to change her clothes. I visualise her plonking her bum on her bed, shucking off her shoes, and shedding her work clothes with careless abandon. Sports bra, Sloggis, and then just smooth freckled skin. My lips are slightly parted, the breath catching in my throat. I squeeze the bridge of my nose with my thumb and forefinger. "Don't. Just don't."

Since the Griergate thing, I've shown my true moral fibre by studiously avoiding Tessa. It's easy. She gets up at around 6:45 a.m., by which time, I'm usually en route to my first pickup. Call me an antisocial weirdo, but I quite enjoy those long, dull airport runs. Everyone else hates them, because they take up half the day and don't pay that well. Unless you get a good tip, that is. Well, I don't really need the money (on account of the payout that me, Gree, and Rebecca got when the DAC was taken over by Servall), and I love driving through the empty streets of London at that time of day. Most of my early morning customers are long-standing arrangements who ask for me when they book. I just turn up at the control station on a Monday, sign the previous week's job sheets, and pick up my bookings for the coming week. One airport run a day for five days makes me enough dosh to live on for the week. Thereafter, everything I earn is spendies and, if I continue doing the Friday and Saturday night West End jobbies, I'll remain a financially comfortable girlie. If I continue being a boring, stay-at-home cheapskate with nobody to spend my money on, that is.

Mornings are a doddle—I'm up and away before Tessa and Carl have yawned, blinked, and sworn at their alarms—and with a bit of cunning planning, it's pretty easy to avoid Tessa in the evenings too. On Mondays, I've been hanging out in Caroline's kitchen 'til late. Kevin, the husband, usually pokes his head in around seven thirty-ish enquiring about the possibility of dinner or something, but I think he's getting the message. We sit in Cal's kitchen all night, nibbling olives and downing chardonnay (well, *she* does; I keep an oversized tea mug in her cupboard for such occasions). We drink and chat and argue and guzzle 'til she's sozzled and I'm waterlogged. Then we play the "why are you really here?" game for a minute or two, at which point, I make my excuses and leave.

I nearly told her last week, I swear. My lip started quivering when she asked after Tessa, but I just about managed to say I hadn't seen much of her lately (true), and that I must be off as I had five a.m. pick-up (lie). Cal had stared at me with drunken eyes and said nothing. The silence had screamed and nagged at my ears until I finally blurted out something about telling her all about it sometime.

"You will when you can."

Bloody Caroline with her professional hat on. It drives me barking, that. Still, at least she allows me to sit and chill without judgement, and it gets me out of the house. A bit of me thinks if she just came out and asked, I'd probably spill my guts to her. That's not her way though. On Tuesday evenings, I'm cool 'cause Tessa has football practice and doesn't get back 'til gone ten. I can stride through the front door with confidence and hang out in the living room without fear. The house is so much quieter these days, but Carl's home more than he used to be I guess, and for some odd reason, my sister, Deborah, has been popping in regularly since the band got back from that Germany tour. Deborah and the Uberdyke drummer, that is. Sometimes Tessa has a match on a Wednesday, so I play that one by ear, but Thursday is the day that she holds her tutorial at the house. Half a dozen dozy, badly dressed students sitting in my living room discussing the cultural significance of the Wetwang skeleton or whether Aethelflaed is a better shout than Boudica for the true English heroine of all time. I haven't a clue what they're on about, and I don't want to know. Anyway, that Kylie, or Kellie, or whatever her name is always hanging around, and she makes me uncomfortable. There's something a little off about a twenty-year-old Aussie undergraduate blatantly pursuing her tutor. Okay, Tessa says she's not technically Kellie's tutor and that Kellie's a "bloody smart young lass" who's going to go far in the world of academia, but all I see is a rampant baby dyke throwing herself at my housemate.

Housemate.

I ponder that one for a second or two before the niggling in my stomach forces me to abandon the thought. Somewhere in my consciousness a low, dark voice attracts my attention.

If she's just your housemate, why do you care who's chasing her?

I don't know, now go away.

Last night, Deborah came for tea (not dinner, you understand. Dinner's what she was having with the weirdo drummer later that evening), and she was quizzing me, Christ knows why, about Tessa. I had one eye on the clock, knowing that She Who Must Be Avoided would be putting in an appearance at seven, and I needed to be outta there. I blame her for all this. Well, not *all* of it. The screwing-yer-ex-in-the-face-of-your-current bit is all my own work. But as well as Carl, Deborah is partly responsible for me and Tessa becoming a bona fide *item* before the Cape Town trip. Was that a conspiracy? Now that I think about it, wasn't it Deb who encouraged me to go to that sodding football match in the first place? I try to piece together the sequence of events that led me back to Tessa's bed that night. We'd gotten together at that loony Goddess weekend, merrily tripped our way through a sizzling honeymoon period, and then I'd gone and banjaxed the thing. We'd been getting on so well. I'd been relaxed, happy, and comfortable spending time with her, so why had I felt that pressing need to backtrack and withdraw from her? Would I have gotten through it? Or had I needed my baby sister's intervention to guide me back to Tessa? Well, back to before everything went tits up in such a blazing ball of fire anyway.

Tessa mentioned that her mate couldn't make it to the Leeds Utd/Spurs game on Friday morning, and I got a call from Deborah that afternoon telling me I should go with her. Get myself out of the house, go see what Frank used to rave about all those years ago. Oh, and bring Tessa over for dinner at their place after. What was that look on her face when I told Tessa I'd be interested in going with her if the ticket was still free? Chuffed certainly, but not altogether surprised, I think. Did Deborah set that up? Was it coincidence that she called me on my mobile at the very time that I was driving a comically glum Tessa home from White Hart Lane? My own car had been in the garage for the weekend, and I didn't have a hands-free kit in the replacement, so when Deborah called, it had been Tessa who answered. Naturally. Had the two of them conspired to get me to agree to dinner with her and the Uberdyke? *God Fin, you really are thick sometimes.* I scowl at the ceiling above, eyes unblinking.

Flipping myself over on the bed, I rest my head on my arms, pulling myself back to the present. Last night I pulled a moody on Deborah. Said I really didn't have anything to say about Tessa and, by the way, was late for a previous engagement. Big fat lie. I'm getting good at that. Mental note: must have a word with St Fiacre, my patron saint, about my recent crimes and misdemeanours. Or get myself into a confessional box. Probably both. I'm aware of Tessa's footsteps pounding ever closer as she now descends, heading for the front door. She's on my landing now, and I'm staring at the bedroom doorknob, holding my breath. This can't be healthy. I sigh and, gripping the bed sheets with tightly balled fists, I sigh again when she moves on.

Sister-Whacked

I'M RUNNING DOWN A long, dark corridor which has Gothic, flaming torches mounted on the walls either side. I don't know why I'm running, but I know that I need to. Finally, I arrive at the end of the corridor, and in front of me is a narrow door. A strange, small wooden door. Tessa would know if it was Elizabethan or what, but I just know that it's a door. Locked? I turn the black wrought iron handle, which is shaped like a steering wheel, and it slowly swings open in front of me. I step over the threshold and find myself on a football pitch in a huge stadium. The crowd is cheering wildly as I start my run, and then suddenly, I'm joined by people in football stripes. I recognise Kathleen from down the road, who gives me the thumbs up. She is surprisingly light on her feet for a woman of seventy-seven. I feel encouraged. Then she runs past me, and everyone else becomes freeze-framed. The crowd is silent, frozen mid-motion. I see their faces, all contorted in a motionless group stare. They are no longer cheering for me. They're trapped, fixed at this point in time, unable to alter their behaviour in any way, and it's my fault. This, I know; I just don't know why.

"Come on, come on! Over here. I'm open!"

I have no idea what she's talking about 'til I see the ball at my feet. Tessa is jogging to my left. She is looking at me, pointing downwards to her right-hand side, urging me to pass the ball. I can't. I try to move, but I appear to be wearing flippers, and the ball just rolls harmlessly away from me to the feet of a motionless player. As it rolls over her toe, the player comes to life, and I recognise my sister's girlfriend, the Uberdyke. She's laughing. Laughing at me. And then all the other players come to life. They're laughing and passing the ball amongst themselves. The crowd is once again animated. I try to join in, but I'm wearing flippers. I'm wearing frigging flippers.

Tessa is by my side, jogging backwards with apparent ease. That's a pretty good party trick. I've seen her do it before, the one and only time I went to watch her play. She looks great! I want to kiss her, and I flip flop a step closer before someone darts between the two of us. Kellie the Irritating Aussie has shrunk to about three feet tall and is jogging alongside Tess. They both circle me, gawking like they've noticed a huge zit on the end of my nose or something. Cocking her head to one side as she looks up at me, Kellie whispers something to Tessa, who bends down so that she can hear. She cups the Aussie's tiny head in one hand and plants a sweet kiss on her minuscule lips.

"She doesn't know how to play."

They look at me and laugh loudly, holding onto one another for support. That sodding baby dyke is laughing at me. A whistle blows somewhere in the distance, and I catch sight of a man in black with the whistle still between his lips. It's my brother, Frank. I try to call out to him, but the words tumble broken and unintelligible from my lips. He fixes me with a confused expression for a second, then turns his attention back to the others. He slips an arm around Tessa's waist and affectionately punches the Uberdyke on the arm. They leave the pitch together, laughing and joking. I feel tears welling up in the corners of my eyes, but before they have half a chance of rolling down my cheeks, they are upstaged by a trickle of freezing cold water streaming from the top of my head. I spin around (within the limits of my footwear) to find that my dad's sponging down an imaginary cut on the side of my forehead with some foul-smelling watery concoction. He's dressed in a track suit and carrying a bucket of water. I know he's talking to me because his lips are moving, but I can't hear what he's saying. I strain to hear him, but all I can make out is something about being a "star player," a "big disappointment," and "getting stuck in in the second half."

"Dad, I miss you. I miss you both so much."

He can't hear me. He is suddenly on the other side of the pitch, and he looks like an old man. This time, the tears do come. I sit down in the centre circle, flippers flopped in front of me, and allow myself to cry. I don't know exactly what's wrong, but I do know that it hurts. I hurt, and I know that the Magic Sponge can't fix it.

My eyes snap open, and I squint against the sunlight streaming in through the open blinds and steady my breath. *Sodding dreams.* I'm awake, safe and sound in my room, but the hollow feeling in my chest remains. Jesus, Mary, and Joseph, what was all that about anyway? I wriggle onto my back and drape my arm across my eyes, thinking of my dad and how much I miss him and the silly banter we shared. Dad sent me a brill birthday card that I keep on the bedside table. A hand-painted picture of a lanky dancer with a big smile that made me laugh out loud when I opened it. Then I'd had to swallow back a half sob when I read what he'd written inside:

Save a dance for your old man, my precious girl. You're always in my heart, Fionnuala.

Nothing arrived from Frank though. The autographed picture of the current Spurs squad, my gift to him, remains unopened in the back of my wardrobe. Will I ever get the chance to give it to him? I force my lips into a tight line, scowling to stop the tremble that this question brings.

I hear voices coming from the ground floor. Downstairs, probably in the kitchen, Carl is talking to a woman. A second or two passes before I recognise the voice, and when I do, I immediately pull the duvet up over my head. Bugger! It's Saturday, and my sister Deborah's come to discuss next week's musical selections for the party with me. I'd been putting her off for such a long time that I finally gave in under her torturous interrogation the other night. I try to project myself to another time and dimension, but of course, I fail. Sister Mary Agnes always said I lacked concentration and willpower, but I bet she's never even tried astral projection.

I hear her footsteps as she reaches the first landing. Deborah, that is, not the good sister.

"Come round on Saturday," I'd said, giving her my best scowl. "Bring breakfast."

"Will that be breakfast for two or for three?" A devilish grin lit up her angelic face.

Smart-arsed little brat. She knows full well that I'm not currently engaged in any bedroom liaison activities. I pause for a second to wonder whether or not she's aware of the reason for my chaste status. She probably just thinks I'm an old git who's lost her touch. Old git, I can live with, whereas the alternative reality starts my head reeling again. The footsteps draw nearer. She pauses outside the door before flinging it open with gusto.

"Knock! The door's there for a reason, y'know."

Okay, I'm not exactly Mother Theresa of a morning. I like peace and quiet, and I crave solitude. I love that first hour's driving in the morning, especially in the springtime. Roads clear, pale hazy sunshine just peeping over the horizon. No music, no radio, no conversation. Nobody grilling me about my future plans or my current romantic situation. Just me and the tarmac. Now my Saturday morning solitude has been shattered by the arrival of my baby sister, and she's early. She strides through the door, kicking it closed behind her before she sets a tray down on my bedside table. I grimace when the pungent whiff of coffee invades my nostrils.

"Coffee's for me." She plonks herself down on a corner of my king-size without invitation. "Your tea's in the pot."

Well, that's something I suppose. I throw a look of gratitude in her direction and turn my attention to the tray.

"You brought Beigel's? You're a star, Debs!"

Smoked salmon and cream cheese—my favourite. She's come with a peace offering. Only we're not at war, are we? She pours the steaming black stuff into my enormous mug and adds milk before handing it over. Her expression is shifty, a little anxious maybe, and

I'm feeling all sorts of guilty. Again.

It's an odd relationship we have, me and Deborah. Not so much a case of love/hate as one of endure/urge to slap silly. My earliest memory of her is the day that we had our photos taken. The day that is never to be repeated in the history of the Family O'Sullivan. It was Easter Sunday when a photographer came to the flat to take a bunch of family portrait pictures. I was five years old, and he was a strange looking man: all red hair and freckles, and with the biggest nose I'd ever seen. But when he spoke, he sounded like my dad, so I figured he was probably okay, and I proceeded to stand exactly as he asked. Head tilted to the left, now to the right. Holding hands with Frank, etc etc. Then came the cruncher—the O'Sullivan ladies all together.

Three chairs were brought out, and it was a modern-day miracle that anyone could find three that vaguely matched in our place. Mum sat in the middle, with Bernie and Kath, the teenagers, on either side of her. The baby was passed to Mum, who placed her proudly on her lap, right in the centre of the picture. Naturally, I had tried to oust her, tried to worm my way onto Mum's lap, but to no avail. The brat was given centre stage, and the ensuing picture features Mum beaming down at her, with me standing behind, grinning, arms held aloft, as I challenged the camera to not find me the most interesting person in shot. When I look at that photo, I always think that Kath looked somewhat detached. She is looking directly into the camera with an expression of defiance and boredom. Even then. It always scares me how little we knew about her, how we all failed to see her struggles.

"Bernie's given me her list," Deborah says, between nibbling morsels of Danish pastry. "I just need to get yours down, and we're good to go."

I stop chewing, then I blink and swallow. My chest tightens, constricted by the guilty knowledge that I haven't been in contact with our older sister since way before Christmas. Since the day that we sat silently holding hands in that hospital waiting room.

Bernadette had let slip that she had an appointment to discuss her radiotherapy progress one day and, in spite of my usual bumbling awkwardness around all things emotional, I knew that I couldn't let her go alone. Her husband Paul, she had argued, was so emotional that he wouldn't have been much use to her if the news had been bad, so she hadn't told him. We'd argued about that for a while before she relented and agreed to let me drive her to hospital.

Of course, once we arrived, there was no way that I was going to let her hear the news alone so, as much by chance as anything, I ended up being the one to hear the good news first. I'm not worthy. It should've been Mum, or Paul, or one of the kids who was there to absorb the relief and joy, but I was there, for what it was worth. I'd been there to squeeze Bernadette's hand when the radiologist began his update, my eyes glued to the laces of my trainers as I silently pleaded with God. My mum's in Jamaica, so far away, and I don't know what I'd do if I lost Bernadette too.

"H-how's she doing?" I ask. My voice has dwindled to a stuttering whisper as I thump my chest, pretending to choke on my bagel. Deborah thumps my back with a little more force than the situation warrants, and I hold up a hand, motioning her to stop. By the grace of God, I somehow manage to resist the urge to throw her down on the bed and choke her senseless. Why is it that she brings out the killer instinct in me? I know that the stupid emotions rattling around inside me with no place to go aren't her fault, but bloody hell! I take one look at Deborah's face and fratricide pops into my head, front and centre, simply because she has the misfortune of being in my miserable company right now. That and the fact that she's...Deborah.

"Oh, she's fine," Deborah says, pausing to examine her perfectly painted fingernails for no good reason.

I just about manage to suppress a jealous snarl as I curl my hand into a ball to hide my own ragged, nibbled ones.

"Says she's missed you lately, Noo."

I need to grip the duvet to steady myself at her use of the old family nickname. Deborah's words, casually dropped into the conversation, douse my inner guilt fire in accelerant, igniting the dormant smoulder into a furious blaze. *I know, I know that. I'm a crap sister—to you, to Bernie, to Frank…to MIA Katherine.*

I can tell you absolutely nothing about my sister Katherine. Except that she's a junkie, I think. I haven't seen her since she stormed off to Newcastle with that miserable, wife-beating, smack-headed moron of a husband, and that was over twenty years ago. I'd like to express some regret about that situation, but I feel nothing. I just don't know her. We grew up in the same house, but I can honestly say that I don't know the first thing about her. Except that her junkie husband broke Frank's nose.

Kath had turned up battered and bleeding one day, and I remember Frank grabbing his jacket and storming out of the flat in a fury, while Mum had fussed over and comforted Kath. I just sat there at the kitchen table, staring at my hands and feeling awkward and useless until Dad came in, and all hell had broken loose. I'd never seen my mild-mannered father so enraged. I don't think Mum had either. I think someone had secretly superglued me to the kitchen chair, because I was unable to move. I'd been totally rooted to the spot as Dad had raged and gritted his teeth, and Mum had cooed and gently fussed over Kath. I saw the looks that passed between them, the urgency emanating from Mum's eyes to his, and the volume of unvoiced pleas for calm. After what seemed like a lifetime, Dad walked across the room and knelt beside Kath's chair. He gathered her into his arms and whispered things to her that I couldn't hear. I remember her calmly nodding as he spoke, then she sank into his embrace, finally releasing the great sobs which she had been working so hard to contain. I just continued sitting there in silence, doing nothing, offering nothing, because I knew that I had nothing inside me for my sister.

Then Frank had suddenly appeared in the doorway, sweating and breathing heavily, with an expression on his bloodied face that I still can't put a name to. He looked at my dad, ignoring my shocked mum's attentions, and gave him an odd sort of bloke-to-bloke nod, which Dad returned. I remember thinking, *What the fuck?* when he plonked himself down in the armchair, but he had been oblivious to my presence. He looked across the room at Kath and winked. That's all. He just winked at her. Later that night, Frank told me that he'd gone around to Kath and Ben's to confront him but had ended up laying into him without uttering a single word. Apparently, Ben had told Frank to mind his own business but that had just further riled him.

"My sisters are my business," he told me later that evening, his voice splintering with emotion. "Always will be."

I wouldn't say he was a hard man, but he's always had a bit of a habit of smacking people who mess with us girls. I don't care if it's macho or aggressive; it's something I've always been able to rely on, and I appreciate it. He was serious that night, I know, but where is he now? *God, I need you now, Frank.*

I reluctantly haul myself out of my reminiscences, trying to focus my dizzy mind on the matter in hand. I've always got on great with Bernie, but me and Deborah have an altogether more complicated relationship. I grimace as I watch her through my narrowed eyes. Deborah is gazing into her compact mirror, pouting as she applies another layer of lipstick to her already perfectly painted mouth. Her larger-than-life persona is sucking all of the oxygen from the room—my room—and I'm irked that she's oblivious to this dynamic. Sister Clare pops into my mind, tutting and giving me the eyebrows of admonishment at my lack of Christian charity. I wrinkle my nose and mentally dispatch the sanctimonious old penguin with a flick. The image of the elderly nun, habit billowing as she flies through the air screaming, "Jesus, Mary and Joseph and all the saints" momentarily comforts me.

"God, you're in a world of your own today. Where the fuck are you?"

Snapping out of my melancholy, I refocus on my bedroom guest. She's lounging cross-legged on a corner of the bed, her back against the foot post. I smile and shake my head. Since we were kids, I've thought of her as being the Golden Child. You know, every family's got one. The sacred, most blessed. The everything-I-touch-turns-to-gold one. Deborah's beautiful. That screaming bundle with a head full of yellow curls that Mum brought home from hospital grew into a pretty little girl, and the pretty little girl developed into this beautiful and talented woman. Deborah's always been just perfect in just about everything she does. Bernie looks like Mum, Frank too, and I look just like my dad but with tits. Barely with tits, but I'm just a female John O' Sullivan and still as skinny as a teenager. My corkscrew curls are a sandy-tipped brown colour and grow backwards from my forehead in a wild fury. The odd rogue grey has crept in over the past few years, and now they're beginning to announce their presence and lobby for acceptance. Like Dad's, my eyes are blue and whilst freckles might be cute on a six-year-old, I think they're less so on a fully grown woman. Much less so. Deborah's smattering of perfect freckles looks like God Himself pencilled them in across the bridge of her also perfect nose. My own imperfect nostrils flare and relax.

"Aw, fuck, you know." That's me, always erudite. I bite my lip at the unexpected depth of misery in my tone. Deborah inhabits a world chock full of rainbows and unicorns, whereas my world consists of a grim landscape of oily black quicksand. She wouldn't understand even if I had the inclination to tell her. We don't have that sort of relationship, which is maybe surprising, considering we shared a bedroom for the most of our childhood, until she upstaged me by leaving home for university. Me and Frank had stayed at home and enrolled in the same law degree course at the same uni that Tessa now lectures at. But Golden Girl Deborah buggered right off to Edinburgh for three years before sauntering home with an honours degree in her back pocket. And it was a first-class one, of course.

By that time, I had become a shifty, doley drop out and a lezzie to boot. Deb was cool with all that, and I suppose she did try to get me involved in her predictably captivating life, gigging across London with a jazz band at the time, but I was arse over tit in love with Grier then and made my excuses at every opportunity. Like I've done for the past few months, sulkily avoiding spending time with Deborah and her girlfriend, Juno, when all she does is be nice to me. The thought sends another guilty shiver through my body, and I turn towards her.

"I'm fine." I wave dismissively. My voice cracks, reminding me that I am anything but fine, and I need to swallow hard and blink back the tears that I know are readying themselves at the corners of my eyes. God, I'm tired. Deborah's brow wrinkles when she fixes me with a soft gaze. I can do nothing to prevent the startled sharp sniff that belies my words.

"No, you're not, Noo," she whispers, leaning closer to me. "You're..." She shakes her head as she searches for the words.

My eyes focus on the grain of my wooden bedpost as I wrestle to forestall the flow of hot tears that are itching for release. I can't remember exactly how and when she came out but last summer, my baby sister was canoodling in corners with a beautiful, tattooed Brazilian woman. Nowadays, the sight of two women snogging doesn't turn so many heads, but these two certainly do. It's as if God had put his hand in the dyke jar, pulled out one dark one and one fair one, and then dipped the both of them in the beautiful-and-talented jar. Me? I think I'm the Frankenstein's monster version, the one cobbled together out of spare bits of misery and angst and shoved into the last lanky body on the shelf.

Deborah's become the O'Sullivan family lesbian, and I'm...I'm an "also ran," once again relegated to miserably skulking in my little sister's shadow. It's only been a year or so since Deborah dumped Robert (drummer number five) after getting drunk and shagging my ex. That's Rebecca and not Grier, though I wouldn't put it past her either. I was gobsmacked when Deborah slept with Rebecca, gobsmacked and livid at the pair of them, but I put that one down to Deborah's irresistibility factor and Rebecca's shag-'em-all philosophy. Next thing I knew she'd binned off Robert and left the band. When she introduced Bernie and me to Juno, her new band's drummer, we both visibly winced in anticipation of what would surely follow.

I poke a finger into the cream cheese that's threatening to escape from my bagel. Deborah smiles a knowing smile at me. She's seen me do this a million times, the bagel thing and the dismissal thing. It's what I do when I don't want to talk about something. Something important, usually. Something that I really should discuss with another human being for the sake of balance. Something that I won't discuss with another human being without the influence of a dozen or so wild horses. She backs off, as she has done so many times over the years. I'm grateful, so I decide to throw a few pleasantries into the pot.

"How's it going with the Girl from Ipanema then?" I ask. Okay, I admit it. I cannot have a simple conversation with Deborah without taking the piss. Big style. One of us in this room appears to be getting a shit load of good lovin' from a hot and talented dyke, and it ain't me. This is not the natural order of things. I'm the dyke in this family. I'm the one who's supposed to be merrily cruising on the lez boat, but I'm a big fat failure in that department right now. "Sorry. I'm sorry, Deb. How are you and Juno getting on?"

She squirms a little, then she carefully places her coffee cup on the floor, brushes invisible crumbs from her chest, and looks me in the eye. She claps a hand across her mouth, as if to stem the stream of truth which she is struggling to contain. When she lowers her hand, there's a shy smile on her lips.

"Um..."

Breathe in, breathe out, repeat. Deborah's unexpected bashfulness has given me a much-needed reprieve from sinking into my own misery and memories, and I grasp the opportunity with both hands. I sit back and wait for her to continue.

She lowers her head again and chews on her perfectly lip-sticked lower lip for a second. "I asked Juno to marry me."

I must be having a caffeine rush by proxy, 'cause I've suddenly gone all wobbly. I stretch my palms out over the cool white sheets. Yes, I am still in my own bed, in my own house. It's just that somebody's shot me into another dimension. I shake my head in an attempt to rid myself of the fiery mixture of disbelief and outright jealousy which, having started in the pit of my stomach, has worked its way to my throat and is threatening to burst messily out of my ears if I'm not careful. I try to speak, but I actually have no idea of what I want to say. Eventually, I exhale a noisy breath, inhale deeply, then sink back against the pillows, arms folded in anticipation. We regard one another with apprehension. Okay, so we're still both silent, but at least I've moved the silence up a notch or two with my articulate *on the brink of saying something important* shuffle.

"Say something, Noo."

Or not. Back to me then, I guess. It's only then that I realise that Deborah is waiting for something from me. The Golden One actually needs my input, and that makes me nervous. I open and shut my mouth twice before I squeeze out a feeble, "Wow!"

I manage to brush aside the tiny demon (dressed rather fetchingly in red leather and armed with a pointy toasting fork with which she is assaulting my conscience) before opening my mouth to speak again. "Deb, you've known this woman less than a year and—"

"Nine months." She shakes her head soberly. Her left hand is again clasped over her mouth, but I still clock the broad grin that she is trying to conceal. "Nine months." She giggles. "And I want to spend the rest of my life with her. Christ, Noo, you have no idea how hard it was for me to tell you that."

Baby Sis has now visibly relaxed somewhat and is lying on her back. She tucks her hands behind her head and is absently raising and lowering her legs, emitting tiny grunts and groans with each exertion. The Golden One is baring her soul to me whilst absently exercising her bloody abs. Only she could do that. For her, life is effortless; things and people come and go. Exercise is as effortless as breathing. Golden hair, blue eyes, tan skin, firm body. She can play guitar, bass, and keyboard. I resist the urge to puke my jealousy onto my rather lovely Ikea duvet cover and turn my attention back to the matter at hand.

They certainly look like they were made for each other, and I've never seen Deborah happier than she's been of late. I run a finger along the edge of the mattress and tell her so. A slimy tendril of misery quickly wraps itself around my throat, and I have little will to resist. It tugs me slowly toward the familiar black quicksand, whispering nauseating snatches of half-truths.

"You have no one who loves you like that... You weren't smart enough to see out your degree course... Everyone you love leaves you."

"Pah!" I am unable to contain the dejected exclamation that forces its way from my pounding chest. I skew my head downward in an attempt to free myself from the tendril's grasp, intent on refocusing my jittery self on Deborah's voice. Too late. Deborah's been talking, baring her soul to me, and guess what? I've been wandering off into my head again, thinking about myself. Now she's looking to me for some response. To what, I haven't a clue. Seconds pass before she turns her head, smiling her irritatingly sweet smile at me.

"...so since she won't tell me, I guess I'm biting the bullet and asking you."

She gives her uniquely ebullient chuckle which reminds me, of course, of *her*. It was one of the first things I noticed about Tessa, that wholehearted laugh that seems to come from a bottomless pit of mirth deep inside of her. How can anyone so intellectual, so brainy and serious have such a lyrical laugh? Tessa laughs and giggles all the time, and it's infectious to those of us around her. Before I have time to drift away on that sweet thought, my S&M-attired devil returns and invades the proceedings by inserting a sharpened knitting needle into my heart.

I'm absently rubbing my left breast with a small circular motion.

On realizing this, I drop my hand and return my frowning gaze to Deborah. Her raised eyebrows are fixed in an expression of confusion. I have no idea what she's just said to me, but I know that it has something to do with Tessa. I'm unable to meet her gaze. Ever the driver, my eyes do a quick left mirror, right mirror, rearview mirror manoeuvre before sinking to the floor. Or in this case, my geometrically patterned duvet cover.

Deborah patiently awaits my response. Eventually, I conjure up half a brain and a set of vocal cords. "Sorry, Deb. Miles away. What did you say?"

Even before she repeats herself, I know what she is going to say. My devil girl is now using a small metal hammer to whack the hell out of the strategically inserted knitting needle. The ensuing vibrations are causing ripples of pain throughout my sweating body. I absently return to rubbing my chest in anticipation of what she is about to say. The dreaded, unspoken question which has been silently playing on the lips of all of my friends for the past few months. The question that I have been walking over hot coals to avoid answering. I've always known that it would raise its beastly dragon's head at some stage, but I'd just assumed that when it happened, St George or someone would weigh in and slay it for me. Glancing around my room, I notice a distinct lack of Catholic icons lining up to rescue me, so I clear my throat and await my cue.

"You and Becks," she says, winding her words cautiously on an invisible retractable thread. "What happened with you guys? I thought you were all love's slightly more mature dream?"

My chest undergoes an involuntary huff-huff. Usually, I'm able to laugh, cough, or throw out some off the cuff, self-disparaging remark, which serves to throw people off the scent. Smell of fear, more like, Cal would say. And now my sodding little sister, Queen of the Beautiful People, knows that my cage has been well and truly rattled. If I could manage to lock up the cage doors (with myself inside) and then swallow the key, would they all bugger off and leave me alone? Deborah has left her designated corner of my duvet and is making her way over to my side. It's all I can do to stop myself from screwing my eyes tightly together and whispering my usual mantra: I'm not here, I'm not here, I'm not here... I do manage to knock out a quick plea to St Fiacre though, enquiring if he responds to teleportation requests.

"Hey?"

The compassion in Deborah's voice catches me off-guard. St Fiacre doesn't come through for me, but my baby sis is certainly trying. She eases herself down on the bed, uncomfortably close for comfort, catches my eye and refuses to drop the connection. Her face is soft and open, and I know that the listening ear she's offering is genuine. I'm suddenly and unexpectedly touched by her concern, and I feel my resolve crumbling. I know I won't escape this encounter—she has me pinned up against the headboard of my own bed—without some sort of offering. She will prod and poke and harass and poke some more until I crack and confess. I can visualise the rubber hoses and thumb screws she has in store for me.

"Fin, what's happened between the two of you? You two are made for each other, so what on God's green earth has fucked it all up?"

God, I know I'm in trouble now she's used my dyke name. She's stopped being my baby sis and is talking to me dyke to dyke. That means that I can't avoid the question, and I can't lie either. I think I'm trying to speak, but my gasping throat is giving out nothing at all. My stupid girlie tear ducts are threatening to embarrass me but, with the help of my auto swallow reflex, I'm winning that battle.

I'm so weary. I'm tired of keeping up appearances. I'm tired of putting my best foot forward, and I've had enough of the pretence. I go about my daily business as normal and the days and weeks go by, but I'm so exhausted by keeping it all in. I screwed up. I screwed up when I screwed Tess over, and I've got no excuses. I wish I could think of a good reason for my pathetic behaviour, but I can't. It's all my fault, and there's nothing I can do to fix it now. I'm so miserable.

"Debs…" It's a start, I suppose. A tiny, girlie squeak has forced its way out of my lips, and Deborah is patiently waiting for the rest to follow. Except that I can't find the words. I don't know how to tell her how incredibly stupid her sister is. That her big sister, the cool, successful business dyke is a pathetic loser when it comes to women. I want to tell her, but I'm just not able. I want to throw off the mangy old German army greatcoat that is my protective armour against all things emotional and walk blinking and naked into the warm sunshine of vulnerability.

Finally, I give up the struggle and sink my head into my hands. When Deborah places a gentle hand against my cheek, I don't flinch. I raise my bowed head. "What did she say?" I ask her.

Yeah, yeah. I do want to tell her but, if my dad's a man of few words, then I guess I must be the dyke of a thousand procrastinations. Deborah moves back a touch, and I find myself missing the proximity. My eyes must visibly widen as she begins to recount details of her social contacts with Tessa over the past few months. Apparently, Tessa has been dining at Deborah and Juno's place on a regular basis. Every Sunday afternoon to be precise. Deborah cooks the lunch, Juno and Tessa watch the football and consume the beers. I can image every detail.

I see her sitting cross-legged on the carpet. In my mind, it's a trendy, large Aztec design rug despite the fact that Juno's actually from Brazil via Belgium. Uberdyke's parents are diplomats who spent many years in Europe before retiring back to their home country. Her first language is French, I think; she has that sexy, accented English speaker thing down to a fine art. I imagine the two of them laughing and joking around, clinking their beer bottles noisily together as they toast some football detail or other. I see Deborah enter the room and run her elegant fingers through her lover's crinkly cropped hair as she passes and, on seeing this scene before me, the lump of jealousy in my throat grows ferociously.

What's wrong with this picture? It should be me, that's what. It should be me in love and in domesticity, entertaining a mate at home. Instead, it's the newbie O'Sullivan dyke, unquestionably cool lover in tow, entertaining the very smart and very sexy Tessa Beckinsale.

Okay, Deborah's scowling. She's clocked my emotional sleight of hand and is wondering whether or not to allow me to get away with it. Her expression is one that I can't interpret—confusion, annoyance, something—before her lips curl downwards with resignation.

"Oh, you two! All I can wring out of her is—" She casts a harsh look in my direction.

Like a small green houseplant carelessly left outside in the midday sun, I start to wither and squirm under her beaming rays. I pray that St Fiacre has green fingers and will swoop down and carry me into the cooling shade. Apparently, he doesn't.

Deborah sucks in her breath. "She says that you don't want to be happy. She always drags the subject away from the two of you before muttering cryptic stuff about having been there and done that. Nothing that makes any sense though, Fin. That's why I'm asking you."

I pick at the seam of the duvet cover with my fingernail struggling through the swirling fog that has descended on my mind. Tessa's saying nothing, it seems. Oh, shit, I almost wish that she would. Ever gracious, the good doctor declines to slag me off.

In a flash, my head is filled again with memories of Tessa. I see her smiling face, her chipped front tooth, her greeny-brown eyes twinkling as she throws me a wink. I see the two of us in this bed on the morning that she left for Cape Town. I'm lying on my stomach, head resting on my folded arms. Lying on her side, she is gently tracing a line down my back with her warm fingertips, and as I turn my head to face her, she places a soft kiss on my shoulder and says, "You can be happy, y'know. It is allowed, sweet thing."

Darling Tessa fades into the ether, and I'm left with a lean slice of longing and the interrogations of my little sister. I clasp my hand across my face and I chew my lower lip in earnest. Tears, *real* tears, have tricked their way from my Judas ducts. I surrender. I can't fight the swirling surge of emotion that's overtaking me. I give in, sink into Deborah's arms, and allow the grief to seep from my injured soul. And then I start to tell her my sad and sorry tale. From the beginning.

In the Confessional

DEBORAH'S LOOKING AT ME with an air of mild boredom, barely concealed beneath a veneer of put up or shut up impatience.

I jettison the repellent images of Grier and her latest lover having sex from my consciousness after having allowed my toes just the merest of dips into that familiar murky pool of my pain and torture. I've been there so many times that I've been given a season ticket.

"So." Deborah tilts her head thoughtfully after listening to my rambling. "Reb didn't steam up to London on her white charger to haul your arse back to romantic land, but you didn't care 'cause the whole Grier Campbell lurve thing had gotten you square on the jaw, right? Oh, and this has exactly what to do with you and Becks?"

I consider getting annoyed for a second, but I let it pass. Bloody hell. I can't take all this touchy-feely bonding stuff; it's unnatural. This is my cue to throw off the duvet and leap out of bed. I turn my back on her at the sink and fiddle about with my toothbrush, willing her to change the subject. When she doesn't, I utter silent curses, fiddle some more, and long for a return to awkward silence. Well, I can be sulky and silent at the same time, can't I?

Not for long, apparently. Deborah cuts clean through the wishy-washy reminiscences and asks me straight out what happened at the New Year party. I moodily begin the arduous task of filling her in.

"Are you fucking barking?"

Deborah leaps to her feet and is looming ominously over me. I am the ill-fated deer, about to fulfil its roadkill destiny. And there was me thinking that this baring of souls stuff was supposed to be therapeutic. You know, I tell you something dark and ugly, and you pat me on the head and murmur platitudes about everything being all right. My baby sister's sitting—no, pacing—in judgement of my foul and wicked deeds.

I close my eyes and picture myself as some obscure Christian martyr. I am St Fionnuala of Haringey, about to be brutally executed by the secret lesbian protocol police for my inexcusable foray into the realms of bad judgement and sheer bloody stupidity. I'm looking thin (what else?) and drawn (in a cool, Gothic sort of way) as I plead my sorry case before the Council of Lesbian Elders. I'm wearing a stripey prison uniform and my trembling hands, clasped tight in cold, steel handcuffs, are joined together in a solemn gesture of prayer. I appeal to God, the Goddesses, and all the saints. The Elders are undecided. They murmur to one another and nod their heads emphatically before fixing their combined gazes on me. I'm sure that the one on the far left fancies me.

"Jesus H on a pushbike! Are you even listening to me, Fin?"

Yeah. Actually, no. "What?" Reality check, and for my sins, I'm still sitting bolt upright in my own bed, in my own house. My rottweiler sister has plonked herself on one corner of my sanctuary and thankfully has her back to me. She shakes her head, and I brace myself for the diatribe that will surely follow.

"Grier Campbell's the most self-centred, manipulative cow I've ever had the misfortune to meet."

"Don't hold back, Debs, say what you really think," I say. I did a stupid thing. Okay, that bit, I'll accept. But, hey, nobody died by my hand, did they? The memory of Gree's petit mort by my hand fleetingly ignites a set of emotions that I'd rather not experience right now. I have to physically shake the wayward thoughts from my dizzy head before I'm able to return to the rack of guilt that my sister has been busy erecting for me.

"...waltzes in and fucks up your life...AGAIN. Christ, Noo, what were you thinking?"

I hear the ping of a microwave when Angel girl pops into my head. *The truth, the whole truth, and nothing but the truth, she tells me. This is your chance to unburden yourself. Are you ready, Fin?* I look at Deborah, radiating judgement in front of me, and shake my head. "I wasn't thinking. That's the bloody point, isn't it?"

Angel girl gives me a hard stare. I silently plead with her for understanding. Sometimes, the whole truth is too much truth to deal with all in one go. All of a sudden, I've had enough. I've been banging my head against a brick wall on this one for the past four months, and nothing's changing. I'm not changing. Gree's not coming back. I know that she'll never come back to me, to our home. I'm not sure how I feel about that, but I do know that Gree's not the sole cause of my grief, not even the primary one. I take a deep breath and grip the bedpost before turning my attention back to my sister. "Deb, I don't care about Gree, not anymore. Okay, I slept with her when I should have been with Tess, but that's not it either."

I squirm in discomfort. When Gree first leaned in to kiss me that night, I could've pulled away. I could've gone after Tessa that morning. I could have approached her at any time in the past months and pleaded my sorry case, made my peace. If I'd wanted to, that is. And I do want to, don't I? I'm staring at my perfect little sister, aware that she has something that I don't. She's serious about Juno, and she'll fight tooth and nail to make a life with her. She'll risk my derision, my downright mean and nasty streak, because she has what I lack. My sister Deborah is held aloft by one fine and healthy backbone. Before her writhes her spineless sister, forty years a belly-crawling coward. I gnaw my lower lip ragged as she voices her thoughts.

"It's not unforgiveable, Noo," she says, drumming her fingers on her lips. "The situation is recoverable. I'd forgive Juno, I guess."

When she turns to face me, I see nothing but concern in her eyes, but I'm still feeling shifty, unable to hold her gaze. There are too many secrets and lies chasing each other around in my head.

"Are you sure, Deb?" I absently grab a pillow and clutch it tightly to my chest for support.

Deborah cocks her head to one side. "Oh, yeah," she says after a time. "Of course, I'd have to kill the other tart, slowly and painfully, but...I figure it's best to get the relationship howlers out of the way right at the beginning, right? It's gotta be worth giving it a second shot, Noo."

"Second shot? If it was you, Deb, would you give a *third* shot to some fuckwit who'd already proved themselves to be—" Oh shit, where did that come from? *Stop talking, Fionnuala. Put your lips together and just can it.*

Deborah stops talking mid-sentence and regards me with narrowed eyes. It's too late for me to say that I don't want to talk about it. I hear the distant ka-ching of that particular penny falling onto a polished wooden floor somewhere, and I watch as the twitchings at the corners of her mouth develop into a full-blown smile. She bounds across the bed with puppy-like enthusiasm, sidles in uncomfortably close to me, and nudges my shoulder with her own. She raises her hand to her mouth again to cover her rising grin.

"Well, fuck me! That wasn't your first get together? After we all had dinner that night and played that butch game thingy—that was hilarious, by the way—it wasn't your first get together, was it?"

I need only shrug. Deborah knows that she's caught a big un, and she's enjoying herself as she reels it in. I'm transported back to the shared bedroom of our childhood and the annoying brat who always wanted to know the details of what I was doing or what me and Frank had been doing. Only this time, the room's become a dark little confessional, and the brat is wearing a dog collar and chewing on the ornate golden crucifix that has hung around her neck since her First Holy Communion. Smug, she throws the song list in her hands over her shoulder with a dramatic flourish.

She leans in closer, still smirking. "Go on then!" she says, all but salivating in anticipation. "Let's have it."

I inhale a deep breath, then puff out my cheeks, and exhale wearily. Another sigh. "Okay, fine, fine. But if you really want to understand, I'll have to –"

Take you back to the start of my catalogue of dodgy decisions? Walk you across the hot coal of memories that are intruding on my days and haunting my nights? 'Fess up to my unenviable history of relationship bloopers?

"I can't just jump into the here and now, Deb," I say. "We've never done this stuff before, you and me, so I guess I'll have to... put it into some kind of context." I roll my eyes at her obvious glee. If all roads lead to Rome, then I'm pretty sure that all of my past indiscretions have led me here, to the point at which I'm cajoled into revealing the details of my relationship with Tessa. I take a deep breath. "If you really want to understand, then I need to start with when Tessa and I first got together. Really together, in the biblical sense, I mean."

Deborah looks at me like I've suddenly grown an extra head. *Yeah, you think you know, clever clogs, but you don't know the half of it.* I raise my eyebrows and plough on nonetheless. "So, remember when I disappeared off to Somerset for the weekend with Tessa's lot?"

Hiding Stuff from Your Mates

"HOW COME WE ONLY ever see you once in a blue moon these days? Godparents are more than just people who turn up with cool birthday presents, you know?"

Sitting cross-legged on the floor of Yemi's living room, sipping a cool glass of fresh carrot juice, I'm slowly beginning to unwind from the stress of my ridiculous Saturday morning. I fight the urge to retreat into my familiar cocoon and instead allow my gaze to wander around the room. I recognise the multi-coloured rug that I'm parked on as being the same one they used to have in their bedroom when they lived with us. *Us.*

My head skews to an angle as I contemplate that word. Do I mean us as in we, the old gang from way back in the day, from before Yemi got pregnant with young Ade? Or is that us as in, that scruffy band of merry urban revolutionaries dedicated to fighting the oppression of the masses through cunning application of the law by providing cheap taxi rates for working-class women? Not sure where Carl fits into all this, mind. There was me and Gree running the Driving Ambition Collective, providing transport for all of London's women and children at very reasonable rates, whilst charging the arses off the leftie London councils who employed us as part of their community transport initiatives. There was Ade and Yemi, the solicitors, working all the hours God sent on immigration issues and bail cases, paying us rent and cheerfully ignoring the arctic draughts and temperamental hot water boiler which regularly withheld its bounty out of sheer spite. There was Jo and Buzz, the brickies, and their mate Claire, providing quality building work across the capital without so much as a *What cowboys worked on this before? It's gonna cost you for us to put it right.*

My gaze comes to rest on a soppy anniversary card which has been jauntily parked on the mantelpiece above the ornamental-but-functional "real" gas fire. God! When did we all get so old? I remember the first time I met Yemi as if it was just last week. I run my hand through the mop of twisted curls adorning my head, mindful of the somewhat brutal homemade hack-job I had been sporting on that first day. Now I'm thinking of Grier again and how she always liked me to look a little butcher than I was comfortable with. Ha! That's a laugh. Gree as the little femme, I mean. Something about her genteel west London accent marked her out as a pint-sized femme in baby Docs. If bedroom walls could talk...

"What is it with you tonight, Finbo?"

Yemi has caught my vacant, probably gormless expression and she, more than anyone else who knows me, knows what that means. I am disturbed, distracted, mentally dishevelled, and I can't hide it from my old mate. Delaying the inevitable, I spring to my feet and head for the kitchen, busying myself with the worthy task of replenishing the tea and bickies. Of course, Yemi follows me, looming in the doorway like an ominous but elegant member of the Spanish Inquisition. I suppose I should expect that, with her being a QC and all. This is the woman who insisted on barging into my room to bring me tea and sympathy after Grier buggered off. This is the friend who endured my deranged ranting, the sobbing and the wailing, and still returned for more after my needy emotions had left her exhausted. Carl kept a low profile when I was in danger of being sucked under by my grief, as I remember. Well, he's Gree's mate, isn't he? *Yeah, and the rest.* Right now, Yemi knows there's something amiss, and she's intent on coaxing a light thread of truth from my reluctant lips.

"What are *you* doing here anyway?" I ask, struggling to make my wavering voice sound a little less shaky. That's good. Change the subject and turn your back on her as you do the brew.

Yemi is having none of it. She pursues me into a corner of her rather lovely family kitchen with a professional ruthlessness that I find both frightening and reassuring. I spend my life dodging the awkward. In situations with strangers and conversations with friends, my tried and tested strategy for survival is to simply extricate myself at the earliest opportunity, but I know that this won't work with Yemi. Exactly one week after Grier left, Yemi was the one who braved my wounded animal, self-pitying ire to bring me support and comfort. And tea, by the bucket load. Yemi was the one who phoned in sick for me, just at the point when Reb and the others were considering dumping me for someone more reliable. She also did a lot of the bringing my mates up to speed stuff. Left to my own devices, I wonder if I'd ever have told them that I'd been humiliated and dumped by the love of my life for some nutty professional lesbian with bags of dosh and a Barcelona penthouse.

Yemi's stout frame is comfortably rocking a soft sweatsuit combo this evening, her plaited hair swept from her face by a wide kente print hairband. A sharp contrast to her usual wig and gown professional self, tonight, Yemi is my comfort blanket mate. She places her hand on my shoulder, her touch causing an involuntary shudder to rack through my scrawny frame. I choose to ignore that warning shiver, deftly swinging the fridge door open and busying myself with the hunt for milk amongst the bottles of posh spring water and the admittedly attractive jugs of fresh fruit and vegetable juices.

"Come on, Houdini, what's up with you now? You know you're going to tell me, so just open those tight lips of yours and start spilling."

With one nimble sidestep, she has positioned herself between me and the contents of her fridge and is running her soft gaze over my face in search of clues. Maybe Ade was right about me after all...but I'm a seasoned professional in the art of avoidance, so I jettison that thought and swiftly grasp at the lifeline which appears before my own baby blues. "What, no vino?" I gesture to the fridge shelves, which she is still guarding with her body. Yemi's face flashes a strange conspiratorial expression which I am unable to interpret, but she steps aside and allows me to finish my avoidance tea-making task. Before I have chance to figuratively high five myself however, she is impatiently jabbing me in the ribs.

"Spill, O'Sullivan," she says before stomping off to the living room armed with a six-pack of Little Ade's Penguins. "I might not be well enough to attend that goddamn boring dinner with Mr and Mrs Mansfield, Clarke, and Palmer, but I'm not sitting and looking at your ugly mug of mystery all night without something to keep me going."

She continues to mutter under her breath as she attacks the chocolate bars in the living room, while I delay the inevitable by shuffling and stirring my tea in the kitchen. Not quite what I had in mind for my weekend's entertainment when I woke up this morning, all this emotional, grilling stuff. First the Golden One and now Yemi. I'll have to give her something, so I swallow a sip of reassurance tea and head for my inquisitor's lair. Returning to my cross-legged stance on their familiar old rug, I tentatively sip at my tea, burning my lip and vaguely enjoying the sensation as I do so.

"Deborah came round and gave me a thorough third degree this morning, that's all," I say, after a time. "Says she wants to go over the set they're playing at the party next week and then proceeds to spit roast me on the subject of..." My voice begins to splinter with emotion and I can't continue.

Yemi does not prompt. She has curled her elegant body into a comfortable recline on the old green sofa and is stirring her tea with a brisk circular motion. I have no reason to back out, to clam up, to flee the emotional intrusion, and her natural tranquillity coaxes the words from my lips with ease.

"Tessa." My eyes are now firmly locked onto my steaming beige liquid. Her name seems to have become entangled in the rising steam and is now twirling its way toward the ceiling, haunting me like some mischievous swirling ghost.

"Tessa?" Yemi looks confused for a moment, then smiles a little. "That's Becks, isn't it? I forget she has a real name! Beaming Becks is called Tessa, ha! Go on then, what about her?"

I realise, with a somewhat miserable jolt, that I have unwittingly opened the conversational door. I have admitted that I call her Tessa, and as everyone else refers to her as Becks, it follows, ergo, that I must use her first name in private, not public. In intimate, cloak-and-dagger private, and as a form of endearment. For the second time today, a bubbling wave of emotion courses through my veins, and I am unprepared for its ferocity. Month after month of carefully stashing my feelings in my emotional vault are rolled away in an instant and, in Yemi's company, I want to stop fighting. I carefully place my mug on her driftwood coffee table and draw my knees to my chest, resting my head on my folded arms.

"Yem?" *Please don't hate me for being such a hideous human being but...* "I don't mean to hide stuff from you, but I'm a bit scared to tell you. My whole life is a fucking disaster zone. Not just one aspect, the whole nine yards. I can't sleep, I can't think... Most of the time, I have trouble even breathing. I just can't stop thinking about the past, and I think I'm about to explode. I've done some terrible things, been such an arse."

This might just be the longest sentence I've ever uttered, and I don't quite know how my brain had co-operated with my mouth to make it happen, or why. But I started so I'll finish, I guess, and I plough on. "I really like Tessa."

Yemi smiles, but the mirth drops from her face when she looks at me. "Okay," she says slowly. "You're both adults. Why's that a problem?"

"It isn't... It shouldn't be..." I shrug. "We got together in the autumn, and it all just clicked into place." I try to dislodge the delicious snapshots of Tessa that invade my mind. Tessa smiling at me, Tessa gripping my hand as we kick up dry leaves in the park, Tessa's uncontrollable fit of giggles when I discover that ticklish spot on her hip with my tongue...

Yemi shuffles on the sofa, lets out an inelegant burp, and mutters an apology. "Why do I get the feeling that there's a big ol' *but* about to waddle in here?" She smothers another burp with her hand.

I wince and distract myself with a mouthful of tepid tea when I feel my heartbeat crank up a notch. "Oh, you know me, Yem." I throw my arms out wide. "I was falling hard and fast for her, so the only thing to do was back the hell out and quick. I went AWOL on her."

"Fin!"

The exasperation in her voice jolts me sideways as if I've been struck, but when I work up the courage to steal a glance at her face, her eyes project their familiar warmth at me. I hold up my hand. "She didn't let me get away with it though. She came after me, and we reconnected. Tessa's kind and gentle...and so patient with my shit." I'm about to drift away on a sweet Tessa memory when my jaw suddenly tightens. My whole body jolts, and I inhale sharply as tears begin to well in the corners of my eyes. *And then I went and...* Yemi motions me closer, and when I shuffle near, she begins retwisting my budding dreadlocks, a small act of intimacy that gives me the confidence to continue talking.

"Remember the New Year's Eve party?" When she murmurs acknowledgement, I squeeze my eyes so tightly together that it hurts. Then I drop the bomb. "I slept with Grier," I whisper.

"Eh-eh!"

Her scandalised exclamation has me twisting around, trying to look at her. She pauses for a beat, before firmly tugging my head back into position. I yelp in pain and indignation. "Ow! Goddammit, Yemi!"

She widens her eyes at me before cupping my chin with one hand. Then she lightly smooths her fingertips across my scalp with the other, and I relax into her touch. She re-applies her attentions to my scruffy head.

"Tell me," she says, gently nudging my back with her knee.

My learned friend's tone is even-tempered and coaxing, so I

swallow down the lump in my throat and continue to spill the beans.

When it's over, I remain huddled on the floor at Yemi's feet, wiping the tears and the drizzle of clear snot from my face with the Wet One that she has handed to me. I had come here to babysit, yet, while Little Ade was comfortably tucked up with sweet dreams rattling around his young head, here I was demanding the kind of nurturing care that his mum was supposed to be having a night away from. I prepare to admonish myself, but instead my eyes follow Yemi, who is moving uncomfortably across the room.

"Terrible indigestion," she says, rubbing her stomach with her hand. She makes no comment on what I have just told her but instead, squats before the TV cabinet and searches through the rows of DVDs. By the time she turns to face me, I have done a passable job of regaining a semblance of decorum and have even managed to scrub most of the tell-tale signs of emotion from what is probably my blotchy face. After silently fiddling with the player for a minute or two, she lumbers across the floor, hauls me to my feet, and guides me gently to the sofa. I don't protest when she carefully lowers herself down beside me, not even when she lifts my hand and places a gentle kiss on the inside of my wrist. With all the tenderness I would wish from a lover, she strokes a baby dread from my forehead before pointing the zapper at the TV, shattering the silence that had descended upon us.

"Don't drive back. Stay over tonight, Fin," she says, still clasping my hand between her cool fingers.

Her endlessly deep brown eyes cause my own to prick with tears as I'm warmed by the intensity of her gaze, her non-judgemental compassion and, if I'm honest, her striking beauty. I love this woman. Quite simply, I harbour a depth of platonic feeling for her that I can't explain to my dyke mates. I prepare to drift off on another sorrowful mental tangent, but I'm interrupted by the sound of the film beginning. With a grin, I acknowledge the ritual we're performing, and I allow myself to draw closer to the darling beside me, momentarily allowing my head to loll on her shoulder.

"Yeah, I think I will," I say, gratefully accepting the warmth she is offering. "But only if I can be Thelma this time." We both laugh, and for a few brief hours, I really feel that there may be some hope for me if this wonderful woman doesn't recoil in horror from my sad and sorry tale. Oh, she'll give me her learned opinion all right, but the morning seems a long way off and for now, I'm content to cuddle up on Yemi's sofa and allow her to retwist my budding dreadlocks.

A Month of Sundays

NORMALLY, I'D BE A bit of a stickler for bathing only in my own home and in my own bath. Today though, I've thrown caution to the wind and allowed Yemi to usher me into her cosy little guest bathroom with promises of sandalwood and peace and quiet. Little Ade's been up for a couple of hours now, and I chose to ignore the less than subtle hints that I should join him by pretending to be asleep when he came calling at half six this morning. But I have responded positively to Yemi's coaxing. A well-presented mug of tea of a morning will always do it for me and, having perked up my puffy red eyes a little, I know that I must prepare myself for another emotionally charged day.

Hot and bubbly sandalwood-scented therapy rises from the bathwater. She knows me so well. The scene is set as I gently lower my bones into the lovingly prepared tub but once again, I find myself unable to shake off the miserable spectre of self-loathing which has been needling my weary soul for the past few months. It finds me, seeks me out in my rare moments of calm, to scratch at my shoulder with its cold, skeletal finger. The acrid whisps of mist that swirl around the hem of its cloak rise menacingly to engulf me, to drown me in a fog of bitterly growled taunts.

You did this to Tessa. You can't take it back now. You're a coward. What will you do when Grier arrives, eh?

Lying on my stomach, I plunge my face into the steamy depths and hold my breath, counting, hoping, waiting for something to happen. *I'm a witless coward. Get me out of here.* In pressing me to unburden the story of how I met Tessa, Deborah has no idea what she has unleashed. I long for, *ache* for, the warmth, laughter, and inner peace that eludes me. I hate this version of myself. Those freakish panic attack episodes used to only happen every now and then, whenever I was particularly stressed out, but this past week they've been blindsiding me on a daily basis. The frosty tide of guilt and panic which rises and retreats inside my inwardly bruised body leads me to momentarily contemplate confession and the morning service at St Martha and St Mary's. I could be there in fifteen minutes if I got a spurt on. That particular comfort blanket is swiftly tugged away by the forces of reality. I'd be done with Mass and all by eleven, say eleven fifteen, and then what? Back home to the house I love with the company I can't be with. The thought of being in the same room as Tessa causes my heart to step up a beat, and I find myself absently rubbing warm sandalwood water across my eyes and temples.

> *Trouble in mind, I'm blue*
> *But I won't be blue always*
> *'Cause the sun's gonna shine*
> *Through my back door someday*

Nina Simone always nails it for me. "Trouble in Mind" just about sums me up, Nina. Yeah, yeah. Someday soon, please. I quietly whisper the song to myself but stop short of the bit about laying my head on a lonesome railroad line and letting the 2:19 train ease my troubled mind. I'll pass on that one, thank you, ma'am. Deborah asked me, or rather demanded that I go through the details of how me and Tessa became an item, and I had simply reeled it all off. Words unspoken for the longest time, a secret made public becoming a reality. No place left to hide now that it's been spoken. Now it's real. Gingerly, I hold my face in the palms of my hands and groan. Give or take a month or so, it's been the best part of a year since the whole Beckinsale saga began and, to my mounting dismay, I realise that I'm no better at managing it now than I was then.

I stand on the bathroom's well-worn duckboard, enjoying the cool solidity of the thing after my hot and hurried bath. I'm wearing the sweet-scented bathrobe that Yemi has laid out for me, rubbing my thick hair dry with an equally fragrant bath towel. I've always seen myself as the poor relation of Ade and Yemi, I suppose. Looking back, I've always held the professions of my family and friends as being worthy and arty, with myself a mere driver, the menial interloper in their midst. Executive Director is a fancy way of saying that I attend a dozen or so board meetings of what's left of the Driving Ambition Collective but in reality, I'm just a driver. No lofty title, no letters after my name. I'm just your average, common-or-garden variety taxi driver. It doesn't matter that I started and ran a successful business. I'm still nowhere near their league.

Shivering in Yemi's bathroom, I suck my teeth and shake my head, hoping to dislodge the bittersweet memories of the old gang that have flooded my mind with anguish. I miss Aunt Pearl. I miss my mum and dad, and I miss my absent brother. The intensity of those losses comes in the form of a heavy, jagged rock, which has lodged itself between my heart and ribcage, maliciously shredding chunks from my tender insides with every breath that I take. Somewhat surprisingly, I have no idea what I feel about Grier.

So why the fuck did I do it then? I know the answer to that question, but I can't acknowledge it. I make a decision. Yemi's bathroom mirror is the place where I will take a long, hard look at my life and formulate the genius strategy which will pluck me out of my current quicksand predicament. Tessa and Grier, both expecting something from me. Me, squirming with indecision in the mire, accelerating my descent with every movement. Hm. Maybe not. Maybe I'll also ignore the fact that I'm supposed to announce to the world what amazing sabbatical plans I have lined up in four days' time. I move about the room, fiddling with toothpaste here and bath toys there, and I leap about a foot in the air when I step on one of Ade's brightly coloured squeaky bath toys.

I'm fully clothed now and, though I'm initially attracted to the comfortable sounds of a family breakfast that are rising from the floor below, I hold off a little longer. I'm desperate to organise the roller coaster events of the past year of my life into some sort of order, into something I can live with without the crushing guilt and remorse that has been suffocating me of late. They say that misery loves company, but I don't want to inflict my ugly wretchedness on this lovely family.

Grier's coming. I've spent eight years of my life ducking and diving to avoid having a meaningful conversation with her and look what happened last time we met. And Tessa? When the pain of my racing heart snagging on the jagged rock joins forces with my shallow gulping breaths, I slide into a heap on the bathroom floor, unable to stop the gasping sobs from escaping the confines of my tightly pursed lips. I bury my face in a towel to muffle the sound. Am I destined to die alone, in pain and, somewhat inconveniently, on Yemi's rather lovely bathroom floor?

Ten minutes later, I'm finally sitting in the kitchen and Ade Jnr is perched precariously on my knee, cheerfully munching his way through his peanut butter on toast. Most of it is managing to find its way to his stomach, although it should be noted that a sizeable quantity appears to be hell bent on attaching itself to my jeans. I clock this but right now, I really couldn't care less. Yemi's kitchen is a safe and warm place for me to be on a Sunday morning, and I'm making the most of it. Clearly, Yemi has been up for hours, and I enjoy watching her glide around her domain, organising stuff as she goes. The load in the washing machine finds its way to the tumble dryer, my cornflakes are introduced to their milky other half, the Sunday paper magically appears on the table's edge. Absorbing the scene before me, I have a heartfelt longing for all that I survey. How sweet would it be to belong to this family? Sweet kid, gorgeous and talented woman, and... In walks Ade Snr, blowing away my cobweb dream.

"Folks!" He ambles into the kitchen in search of the coffee and porridge lovingly prepared for him by his wife.

Casting a smile in her direction, he rubs his hand over Jnr's crinkly, shaven head before plonking himself down with a slight groan in the captain's chair. The impending junior partner of McClelland, Mansfield, Palmer, Clarke, *and Oworu*, impeccably dressed in boxers, vest, and flip flops beams another tender smile at his wife, raising his eyebrows slightly. Yemi returns the smile, holding his gaze for a second or two before nodding at him, lightly brushing her palm across her stomach.

"Still got that indigestion, Yem?"

I have inadvertently popped the invisible balloon on which their gentle moment had been delicately balanced, so I guiltily lower my eyes to stare at the solid oak dining table.

Yemi clearly suppresses a smile as she turns to retrieve a jar of honey from the larder. This she places beside her husband's porridge bowl, stooping to plant a light peck on his shiny, bald head. Ade Snr slips his arm around her waist, and once again, I feel like an intruder, a trespasser in their blissful coupledom. In all the time that I have known these two, I have never seen them anything other than besotted with one another, and it has always felt good (if not a little voyeuristic) to be around. When they lived at the house, there would be weeks when we would barely catch a glimpse of them as they zipped from library to college to work, but then they would always appear on the Sunday morning, rustling up breakfast in our damp and draughty kitchen, as it was then. Two couples and a spare part. It had always felt that way but just lately, I've begun to question whether I was that spare part and not Carl, as I had previously believed.

"Don't think you can get out of finishing the Scrabble, Fin." Ade's mischievous face bears a somewhat disturbing resemblance to the boy on my lap. "I may have been alcohol-impaired last night, but I'm as fresh as a damn daisy now, and I'm armed with legal words that you can't even begin to imagine."

I am caught off guard by the chuckle which escapes unchecked from my miserable being. Last night, feeling emboldened by the power of *Thelma and Louise*, I had indeed challenged Mr Competitive to his favourite pastime and, according to the board, finished up languishing twenty odd points behind the master at close of play. I'm starting to get that warm and fuzzy feeling. Right now, there is nothing that I would enjoy more than to escape from my misery by winding Ade up. That he imagines there's even an outside chance that I can catch up, maybe even beat him, is a start, and I'm certainly game.

For the first time this week, if not longer, my smile is one of genuine pleasure, as I rise to my full five feet seven and a half inches, relocating Ade Jnr to a nearby chair as I do so. "Bend over, son," I say, pointing a finger at big Ade. "You're about to get caned."

Hands on hips, I taunt him with my best cheeky smile, along with a solemn promise to abuse his sorry behind all over the board. Yemi groans and rubs her back before announcing that she's heading back to bed. And so begins Super Challenge Sunday, which kicks off with the unfinished Scrabble and ends with Othello (best of three) by way of Yahtzee. By the time I find myself kissing them goodbye on the doorstep, I am intellectually bloodied and bruised, and Ade Snr is performing a scaled-down conga with his son in the hallway.

When I finally make my exit, I note that the sun is shining, and I actually feel good.

That sort of shit never lasts long, does it? I literally sprint down St George's Avenue to the car, such is my levity, only to find that some bastard has smacked a lump out of the driver's side door. I drop to my knees, stroking my fingers over the ugly white scar with a degree of tenderness that should really be reserved for lovers and loved ones, though I do indeed love my car. It's my work, and I do most of my best thinking whilst driving it. There's a fine line between intelligent thought and self-absorbed wallowing though. I squeeze the rubbery key fob and wait for the hazards to flash on and off before climbing in.

Inside, the air is still and calm, warmed by the hazy spring sunshine, and it smells like sweeties. Not from young Oworu this time, but some strange spray stuff that I got from Joshie the valet guy who does the DAC cars each week. Plunging my key into the ignition, as I do a zillion times every day of my life, a nagging realisation presents itself; I'll miss my job after next week. Okay, maybe I'm not the suave and sophisticated professional person that I should be at my age, but maybe I could tell everyone that I actually enjoy my work, that I have no desire or ambition to do anything grander. Maybe. I'm forty years old and pretty much unemployable, and on that chilling thought, I glance at the space where my missing side mirror should sit before positioning the car to join the traffic and head for home.

They say that home is where the heart is, but as I wait to join the A406 super highway to home, I'm really kind of hoping that it isn't where the sister is. It's barely twenty-four hours since I was subjected to Deborah's roller coaster ride through my emotions, and though I had pushed the memory from my mind and soaked up Yemi's hospitality, the minute I start to think about home, it's all there again. Deborah and Juno's sapphic bliss; my inability to put a name to the feelings I have for Grier or move past them; the size eight boot with which I have stomped over my relationship with Tessa; the chill that accompanies the realisation that I will have to play nice with Grier and her poncy girlfriend in the very near future. And the icing on the cake—me, hopelessly flailing all over the shop. *Fucking great.*

Return of the Native

THE ANGRY BLARE OF a car's horn toots me back to reality and, realising that the traffic is once again moving, I quickly shift into first gear and away. My fuddled, troubled mind has apparently decided to take a break from driving, leaving my world-weary bod to carry the can and get me home from Yemi's.

The Sunday quiet streets of north London are as familiar to me as the back of my hand, and I race my way through them, speed limit permitting, towards nowhere in particular. I don't want to go home. I don't want to lie in brooding silence across my under-utilised king-size, holding my breath, ears straining for sounds of life from above. Tessa will be in right now. Sunday morning's her marking time, and I know that she'll be up there, body stretched leisurely across her own bed, surrounded by a number of disorderly heaped towers of books and papers. Her half-moon glasses will be perched in a curiously attractive manner on the edge of her straight nose, her left eye half squinting in concentration as she silently mouths the words on the page. She will lie like this for an hour or two before uttering some string of expletives and leaping to her feet.

"Ar, shit...is that the time? Bugger, bugger. Gonna be bastard late again," and she'll leap to her feet. Then, I'll catch the faint sound of cupboard doors slamming, various thuds and scrapings, and then finally, her customary humming as she slams her bedroom door and comes tripping down the stairs, past my door, and away. She'll sling that bike of hers onto her shoulder, maybe pausing to yell a parting acknowledgment to Carl, before slamming the front door with a crash. Every fibre in my body will plead with me to stay put, but I'll race to the window and watch her mount and ride away.

Then I'll throw myself back onto the bed, lie on my back, and stare unblinking at the ceiling until my eyes hurt. Pathetic, much?

It's too late to take evasive action though. I'm already turning into the avenue on autopilot, my eyes darting from left to right seeking a suitable space in the white CPZ marked bays. Being Sunday morning, I'm forced to drive past the house and park at the far end of the street, close to the junction with the main road. Another sigh as I lock up. I don't want to go home just yet. I can't. I take a left onto the main road and continue walking on to the Broadway. Strolling, hands plunged deep into the pockets of my jeans, I have no particular place to go. I just wander. Eventually I commit to a Sunday paper and allow the penetrating drizzle to force me homeward. The sun had been out when I left Ade and Yemi's but after the twenty-minute drive across North London, the sky is leaking again. Glancing skyward, I pull a face and manage to summon my trademark scowl-cum-smile. *Go home, you silly cow!* I put my best foot forward, take the doorsteps two at a time, and punch my key into the lock.

I step across the threshold and, to my dismay, hear a most unwelcome sound: Tessa's laugh. Vibrant, clear, and inimitable, it reverberates around the dark hallway. *Oh, shit, oh, shit, oh, she-it!* I'm being drawn into the vortex of her presence by some invisible string. Her laughter, the levity in her voice...these things echo through my frazzled mind. I want to be in her presence. I want to be close to her, but I know that that's just not possible.

Carl's in there too. Haven't seen him for a couple of days, and I really should go in and catch up, but I know that, with Tessa present, I'm an interloper who would burst the balloon and ruin the scene. Could I just get away with sneaking past the living room and tiptoe-bolting up the stairs before anyone notices my arrival? I'm just putting this plan into operation when I hear her voice again, loud and clear, bouncing from beyond the closed living room door.

"Fin!"

An icy chill slowly sinks into my bones. It's too late to sprint away unnoticed, and I know that I'll have to face her. Months of tactical avoidance, executed on my part with a soldierly precision that...erm, that Grier's military Grandpa Walt would have been proud of.

Dr Tessa Beckinsale, object of all of my current hopes, dreams, and fears, steps backwards through the door, which she has wrenched ajar. I remain motionless, pinned against the wall by the power of her eyes. Her lovely, soft greeny-brown eyes are twinkling in that customary way of hers, and I'm harpooned on the end of her gaze. It's been such a long time since I last saw that mischievous twinkle, and I swear that I need the dado rail's solid support to prevent me from slithering down the wall in a mushy heap.

Her sandy hair, fully recovered from its Cape Town hairdressing ordeal, is threatening to conceal her left eye. She's gorgeous, and I'm gawking, entranced as she scoops a few strands between her fingers and banishes them behind her ear. *Oh fuck, fuck, and thrice fuck!* She's beckoning me over, and I know that I've got to pull my skinny arse together and start behaving like a real grown-up. I take a step towards her, steeling myself for the altercation, but fully ignorant of today's particular rules of engagement.

We are standing maybe a couple of feet apart now, as she again beckons me towards the living room door. My mouth's gone all Sahara on me, but even if it hadn't, my brain's rice pudding. And God, I want to kiss her! What the fuck am I thinking? How totally psychotic is that? I need to speak, to say something about this ridiculous chasm I've carved between us, to beg her for the loan of a healing shovel, which I would willingly wield, night and day in an effort to get the two of us back on level ground. I need to do something, say something, *be* something other than the pathetic creature standing in front of her, whose heart is pounding out pain and pleasure in equal measures.

I open my mouth to speak but of course, no words. No sounds emerge. She has this effect on me. I know that she always will and all I can do is allow my gaze to sink into the carpet pile. Who am I kidding? I'm always like this, ever the long-limbed, tongue-tied introvert.

It seems like an eternity has passed since she first called my name and yet here I remain, stagnant and rooted to the spot. When she finally puts me out of my waking nightmare, her voice is warm and dripping levity, just as I remember it having been, all those months before. I have no idea what I've done to deserve this civility.

"We've got company, Fin. C'mon!"

There's something a little conspiratorial in her tone that I can't put my finger on, but I allow her to nudge me through the doorway into what was once my favourite room in the entire house. I see Carl standing in front of the bay window and, for a second or two, I fail to notice the man sitting in the tatty old Chesterfield armchair by the window, the one that used to be Frank's favourite piece of furniture. The two of them break off from their conversation mid-sentence, and the visitor rises to greet me. In front of me stands a handsome, well-built bloke dressed casually in joggers and a polo shirt, sporting short, well-kept dreads. A warm smile unfolds broadly across his face, revealing a flash of gold tooth. Upper left incisor to be precise, the mirror image of my own dental jewellery. He strides across the carpet and stands in front of me, still grinning, eyebrows raised, arms outstretched, and still silent.

I'm unable to speak, absorbing instead every detail of his still youthful face, his short, manicured fingers, the very slight tinge of grey at the roots of his spikey dreads. Finally, he stretches out an arm and touches me lightly on the head. He needs to stretch of course; I'm still half an inch taller than him. I'm unable to process the scene before me. I think someone's shoved a golf ball down my throat because I can't speak, but worse than that, I feel my body betraying me once again. I bite my lower lip and swallow down the big girlie sob which is threatening to humiliate me in mixed company. No chance of controlling the single hot tear which is solemnly rolling south, heading for my chin and beyond. My eyes have decided that his trainers are of far greater importance than his face, but I nevertheless move forward and tightly grasp the tip of a dreadlock. The silence is finally broken when we speak in unison.

"Peanut."

"Noo."

I'd like to say that what follows involves a load of grinning, arm-punching, and back slapping, but the reality is so much more unattractively girlie. He wraps his broad arms around my shoulders and, may the patron saint of butch dykes everywhere forgive me, I sink into them, blubbering unintelligible reproaches at my long-lost brother.

Peanut Allegory

Francis Xavier Eugene O'Sullivan has always had a funny-shaped head. At the age of forty however, he appears to have grown into his nickname with a vengeance. Surveying the familiar contours of his long-lost face, my mind wanders back to that breezy Sunday morning in March when my brother first became Peanut O' Sullivan. I remember it clearly because it was the one and only time I ever saw my dad cry. We'd all just got back from Mass. Kath, Bernadette, Mum, and us two, all elbows and giggles as we battled to be the first through the shop door. Still living above the bakery then, y'see. Two and a half bedrooms, a half decent living room, and a kitchen with barely enough room to swing a dead cat without dislodging the wall mounted pots and pans. Words like cosy and snug spring to memory but the truth is, we lived on top of one another, and Frank and I were getting to the age where we needed separate bedrooms. So, that Sunday morning I had bustled my way through the door ahead of my brother, the wiry beating the pudgy hands down once again. I soon stopped dead in my tracks though.

There were two big men in the shop, two men I didn't recognise, wearing rough jeans and stern expressions. Suddenly I was afraid. The men were behind the counter, and Dad never allowed anyone behind the counter except for Mrs Gannon, who served the customers, and us lot. Hard and fast rule, it was. My eyes scoured the contours of the shop for clues as to what might be going on, and then I spotted Dad. He had been standing with his back to me, shoulders hunched and with his face cradled in his hands. It had taken me all of a nanosecond to realise that he was crying.

Crying! Like what we did when we'd had a fight or broken a toy. I launched myself with fury and all the strength my seven-year-old frame could muster, laying into the nearest big, strange man. Frank ambled into a similarly aggressive stance.

"You leave my daddy alone!"

Apparently, I had been a furious mass of bony kicks and punches. The poor bloke had taken one look at me and swept me off my feet with one hand, deftly tucking me under his arm.

"Woah, now, little peanut head." The other man had placed one hand on Frank's head to halt his progress before the two had looked at another with bewilderment. They had then turned and stared expectantly at my dad.

"Johnnie?"

A woman of very few words, my mum. By this time, she had crossed the shop floor and was holding Dad's lowered head in her hands. Their foreheads were touching and though I could hear the whispered exchanges that passed between them, I couldn't make out the words. He had slumped into Mum's embrace for a brief moment or two, nodded twice in response to her whispered remarks and then, at last, he had drawn in a rasping breath and turned to face the stunned gathering.

"Well, John Joe?" The older one, the one with the rough, unshaven cheeks, had leaned back against the counter, head cocked to one side, demanding an answer from Dad.

Dad wiped his eyes with the back of his hand, pinched the bridge of his nose for a moment or two, and then slipped his arm around Mum's expansive waist. Something anxious hovered in the still air around us, and for all my earlier aggression, I suddenly felt scared.

Dad drew his scrawny frame up to its full six-feet-two. "Gene, Brien, this here's my family. Here's my wife, Marcia," he said. Softly.

Nobody spoke, and nobody moved. Only the clock on the wall rose to the occasion, marking the eternity of silence that was threatening to swallow us all up with a formidable tick, tick, tick.

"Your wife, John Joe?"

Another million or so years later, the older one pulled off his cap and took a step forward, hand outstretched to Mum. His hair underneath was a mass of flattened red curls. Corkscrew curls like Dad's, only ginger.

"Eugene O'Sullivan, Mrs," he boomed in a rich lyrical tone, a baritone version of Dad voice. "And here's me brother, Brien."

Brien had apparently needed a second invitation. Eugene O'Sullivan used his redundant cap to batter his brother's arm, and Brien shuffled forward and shook Mum's hand firmly. Stepping backward, he had then repositioned his own cap and concentrated on surveying the chequered lino floor.

I still couldn't fathom what was happening in front of me, but Bernie apparently did. Joining my parents behind the counter, I watched her slip her hand into Dad's before asking something about Grandma. Grandma? As far as I was aware, my family consisted of Mum and Dad, my two sisters, Aunt Pearl, my twin, Frank, and, of course, the Golden One. No uncles, cousins, grandparents. Just us. Except for the faded photo in the silver frame, that is. Treacley thoughts began sliding slowly into my consciousness. I remembered talk of a grandma. The striking woman with the cheekbones who surveyed us with sombre gaze from the silver frame in the centre of our mantelpiece. Wasn't she a grandma or something? God, was *she* my grandma? Did I really have a granny after all? On the Easter Sunday of my seventh year, I realised that my dad had a mum, and I had a grandma. Oh, and that I was Black, Irish, and middle class to boot.

All of this races through my head as I stand there in my brother's arms. After a time, I'm able to stop snivelling on my brother's Northern Ireland polo shirt. I wipe snot away with the back of my hand, disentangle myself from his embrace, and attempt to digest the scene before me. Carl the filmmaker, grinning from ear to ear, clasps his hand together with a camp flourish, before making a show of wiping an imaginary tear from the corner of eye. Tessa, *my*

Tessa, is pretending to arrange a pile of papers on the sideboard. For someone who professes not to give a shit, I'm doing an utterly crap job of controlling myself when she's around. Cue a little more foot-shuffling and plunging of hands into jeans' pockets. Frank's the only one who appears to be unfazed. He hasn't changed much either. Maybe a little older around the eyes but he still has the same stocky build, the same clipped, spikey dreads, and the same Cockney wideboy tone.

"God, sis! Anyone'd think you'd seen a ghost, ya big jess!"

A stifled giggle reminds me that my ex-whatever-she-was is witnessing my foray into the realms of the uncool. I want to say something cool and decisive, but she's wielding that emotional magic wand of hers, and I've gone all tongue-tied and gawky again. Fortunately, Frank slaps me on the back of the head and rescues me from further embarrassment.

"Ow! Where've you been, you bastard?" Although I sound seriously annoyed, I know that he has clocked the smirk tweaking the corners of my mouth upwards. "And where's the sodding milk, mate?"

The last time that I saw him, Frank'd been in an unusually morose mood. I remember him sitting at the kitchen table, head in hands, grunting half answers to my brusque questions, as I hopped back and forth preparing for my morning pickup. A to Z, bottled water, sunglasses. "What's with you this morning, anyway?"

He raised his head briefly to look at me and for a split second, I thought he was going to say something important. Then a warm arm had snaked around my waist from behind, and I had lost a minute or two in a romantic clinch with my darling Gree. When I finally and reluctantly disentangled myself, physically and emotionally, he was standing by the sink, scowling and shoving his arms into his battered old jean jacket.

"Where are you going?" I hadn't really meant to sound so...so accusatory, but I suppose I might've come off that way. Frank really had nowhere to go. No job, and no reason to be up at six thirty on a weekday or any other day for that matter. His days were one long round of watching TV, smoking spliffs, and lamenting the fact that the love of his life (a hard-faced airhead with zero redeeming features by the name of Shar) had run off with another bloke. Well, not exactly "run" and not exactly "off." It had been three weeks since dodgy Shar had informed my hapless brother of her clandestine shagging of Mark the Roofer, but she still lived just across the Broadway from us, and he still saw them both down the local each Friday night.

With hindsight, I regret not having been there for him at that miserable point in time, but I knew that she was a cow and always would be, so I'd concentrated on trying to raise some oomph in him. That and being famously in love with the irresistible Grier Campbell, of course.

"Milk. We're out of milk," Frank had practically spat out his words as he'd bolted through the door.

There had been a bit of tension between us in the preceding week, but I'd rationalised that life was a bit like that when you were thirty years old and still living with your sibling. I was rapidly becoming a snotty, Thatcher-leaning capitalist scumbag, while he was skating perilously close to the unfulfilled-potential/dole-scrounging dopehead bracket. Frank had slipped out for a pint of milk, and I'd charged headfirst into another day's worth of delivering folk to their chosen destinations across London. I hadn't given him a second thought that day, not when Gree had messaged me to arrange a lunchtime quickie, nor when Cal had dragged us off to the pictures that night.

No, I'd simply run my eyes over the note he'd left pinned to the dartboard on the kitchen wall the following morning and assumed that he'd be back after the weekend. Which bit of "Need to be away from here right now" didn't ring the alarm bells which were to clang their way through my consciousness in the subsequent weeks?

My leather-clad demon is once again ramming her pitchfork

into my solar plexus, her face glowering with ugly distortion. Somehow I'm responsible. I let my brother go, like I let go of everything and everyone of any importance in that period of my life. A single thought had occupied my stupid, romantic head back then, and it came in a five-foot-nothing package. Before I can allow myself a quick meander down Soppy Street, my demon jabs me again, and I force my thoughts to return to the here and now. To Frank, and to the shuffling, grinning Tessa. She's enjoying this. I can feel her eyes boring a hole in the back of my jean jacket. I have to get a grip, take control, regain some dignity in front of my...my whatever she is to me.

"Ar, shit! Football practice. Time I wasn't here."

Tessa's voice is light and friendly and causes my stomach to flutter. The way that she speaks, the words she chooses, her accent, her tone. I'm in such a bad way. I shuffle around to face her, but she's already halfway through the doorway. For a brief moment our eyes meet, but then she drops her gaze and looks away. Demon-girl cackles as she rams me with her pitchfork once again.

"Good to meet you, Frank."

"You in later, mate? Catch a beer or something, yeah?"

Whaaaat? My brother's just gone and done the thing I've been incapable of these last months. Frank and Tessa are trading skin like they've known one another all their lives and all I'm left with is a faint whiff of No. 19. Who the fuck wears perfume to play football anyway? I follow her movement down the hall, not visually, simply anticipating each footstep on the polished floorboards as she approaches the front door.

Now she's slung her bike onto one shoulder and is gripping her keys between clenched teeth as she struggles to negotiate that rather handsome stained glass and wooden door. I yank my thoughts back to the here and now again: the present, this room, and the two blokes who are grinning all over their smug little chops at this dizzy dyke's obvious anguish.

"Jesus, Noo! What d'you do to that one? I mean, I like her, and

there's obviously some sort of thing going on with you two, but..."
Frank widens his eyes and waggles his fingertips at me. "Tell me everything. Now."

My brother has been back in my life for exactly ten minutes, and he's already grilling me on the intricacies of my soap opera life. He settles himself down in the centre of the battered sofa, gesturing to me to plant myself beside him. I remember that sofa when it was brand new, and the trouble Frank, Gree, me, and Carl had getting it through the narrow front door—well, Carl supervising, that is. I'm wondering how to break the news now. How to tell him that I lost my darling Grier so many years ago now, that I'm a big old girlie mess these days, that I hurt all over and burst into tears at the drop of a hat and, and, and. How to explain exactly what I did to the lovely woman that he's just met. Stalling for time and the space to conjure up a credible spiel, I suggest Sunday lunch at the pub. Carl immediately declines. He's waiting for Darren to arrive, so it's just me and the peanut against the world. Just like old times.

Facing the Reggae Music

I'M GEARING UP TO tell him. Within a couple of hours of the Prodigal Brother's return, he has me shuffling my baseball boots and swirling my pint of weak shandy in his favourite corner of the Green Man: to the left of the big window, behind the pool table. Seems that not a lot changes around here. By sheer coincidence, Mark the roofer was in too when we first arrived. Apparently, Shar had buggered off about a month after Frank had left, which, as it turns out, was the best thing that could have happened to Mark because it had led to him jacking the roofing in and getting that job with the council. And meeting Mrs Mark the roofer. And having the twins. And buying the flat. And living happily ever after. And blah-de-blah-de just talk amongst yourselves and leave me out, boys. 'Cept of course they don't, and he won't. Of course.

"So where d'ya meet that one, and how come she's living in the house?"

Lager boy Frank has an annoying habit of going off the conversation at a tangent and then veering back sharpish and without warning or the use of indicators for that matter. I'm just starting to wonder what has changed about big bruvva in the past decade when he kicks me under the table. Not that annoying habit, apparently.

"Ow! What? What are you on about now?"

The house? Strange, I've always considered the house to be Frank's home as much as mine. After he graduated, Frank spent so much time sleeping on the living room sofa that we finally relented and let him move in. Okay, so he didn't throw hard cash into the pot when we first blagged our way to becoming mortgage slaves—he was doing his doley drop out thing when the rest of us were selling our principles out for a tenants-in-common mortgage—but after he left, I simply boxed up his meagre possessions and shoved them in the back of the cupboard in my room, assuming he'd be back and wanting his room again. His room's been empty since Biker Boy Bill left, thankfully taking his entourage of dolly biker's molls with him. I shudder at the memory of Carl's poor judgement when it came to choosing rent-paying housemates. Biker Boy Bill and Straight Charlie being just two of the lust objects he subjected us to over the years. Actually, I liked Bill. Bill could cook and loved to flaunt himself in front of a drooling Carl. Carl's the one who has irritated me most over the years. I'm not fooled by his camping it up. Underneath that frivolous and flamboyant exterior lurks the cold-blooded heart of a reptile, this I know for sure. The only human being on the face of the planet that he wouldn't sell down the swanny is, of course, Grier. I know it, Darren knows it, but what they don't know is that I know why.

The party line about those two is that they met in college, shared digs, and ended up in a squat in Brixton together afterwards. What they don't know is that I once drove a certain Arts Council exec by the name of Elizabeth Taylor from Elstree to Blackheath. Elizabeth had been pretty loose-lipped during that journey, particularly after I had confirmed that yes, DAC member Grier Campbell had indeed attended the same art school as her.

"I wondered," she said thoughtfully as she absently plucked invisible lint from her Chanel blazer. "I saw the name—Grier's such an uncommon name, isn't it?—and decided to book your company for old time's sake." She laughed, entirely without mirth, and looked away.

Yes, I confirmed, she was the pint-sized, curly-haired, gay political activist that Elizabeth remembered. I would have told her that she was my pint-sized love goddess if she revealed her former association with my then-current girlfriend. I nearly hit a parked car. The Beamer threatened to blow a gasket. Took me a minute or two, and several glances in the rearview mirror, to compose myself enough to casually enquire as to what she'd been like then.

It's probably best not to ask a someone who has been cruelly dumped by the one they love to offer an unbiased opinion on the said individual's character. I did know that, having been treated to a right royal character assassination by Cassie (Gree's girlfriend-before-me), but I can honestly say I really didn't see the ton of bricks that Elizabeth was about to drop on my head coming. Cassie, I rationalised, was bitter and twisted, having been cruelly abandoned by the love-struck Campbell days after we had first met. Couldn't expect her to remain president of the Campbell fan club after that, I supposed. 'Twas a dirty job, but I was certainly prepared to roll up my sleeves, shuck off my jeans, and engage wholeheartedly in the task.

"Mindfucker is the best way I can describe her," Elizabeth said, her lips pursed like she'd just sucked on a lemon.

O-kay. By this stage, I had pretty well gotten used to the negative press generated by Grier. I got it. Everyone hated her. She stood accused of everything from arrogance to zealotism by just about everyone I came into contact with, but I reassured myself that that was the old Grier. My Gree, the new, adoring sex goddess bore no relation to the fiend described by a surprising number of her "friends" and acquaintances. A nervous laugh forced its way out of my lips as I tried to concentrate my whirring mind on the woman with the buggy who was approaching the zebra crossing in front of me, toddler in tow. "God! Really?"

I laughed uneasily, mentally willing my passenger to issue a full retraction. Go on! Tell me you're only pulling my leg, tell me Gree treated you like a queen, didn't she, eh? Tell me she was the best thing that ever happened to you, that the sex was amazing, and that you were a fool to ever let her go. Please? I've never been big on mind control. Elizabeth had simply laughed, more of a snort than a laugh really, before folding her arms across her cashmere-covered chest. For a minute I thought that was going to be it, her pearl of wisdom cryptically bequeathed to a mystified devotee of the League of Campbell worshippers but unfortunately, Elizabeth was just getting warmed up, and there was something about her tone that sent a shiver down my spine.

"Of course, she may have changed... I mean, we're talking twenty years ago... God! When did I get so old?"

I was going to respond with some murmured platitude out of Catholic politeness, you understand, but the usual diatribe came spilling from Elizabeth's mouth before I could. A sorry tale of betrayal, duplicity, and downright meanness of spirit, and I drifted away from the blistering attack after a minute or two, but Elizabeth didn't appear to notice. She seemed to be enjoying herself, so I returned my attention to the boy racer to my right, the narrowing of the road ahead, and the ensuing bottleneck, of which I was about to become a member.

"So, as you can imagine, her running back to the hubby was the last straw."

Some evil demon thing had filled my mouth with hot new potatoes, 'cause I was unable to utter anything resembling an intelligible word. I hunched my shoulders and clutched the steering wheel tighter, aware that I had just spun around in my seat to face Madam Deep Gob whilst doing forty on an A road. "Sorry...what?"

I tried desperately to make eye contact via the rearview mirror. Elizabeth was applying yet another layer of lipstick as she spoke, so I couldn't catch her eye. Oh, come on, come on! With exasperated impatience, I waited for her to catch up. Well, I began drumming my fingers on the dashboard and sighing. Finally, she took the hint.

"The infidelity, I could have coped with. Okay, nobody enjoys being deceived, but that's life, I suppose."

I was losing the will to live, or perhaps it was the will to allow Elizabeth to live. I wanted to pull over on the dual carriageway with no hard shoulder, grab her by the ears, and tug until she confessed that she'd made it all up. Somehow, I didn't think that would work though. The word infidelity had burned into my solar plexus like a cattle prod, kick-starting that familiar shallow-breathing nonsense which normally served to underline the rising panic in my nervous self.

"I mean we all make mistakes, of course we do. And we learn from them. We come out and tell the world that we are women loving women. Some of us choose to sleep with every woman we lay eyes on before scurrying back to our husbands, presumably to deny that any of it ever happened." Elizabeth sighed.

Whaaaa? Just run that one by me once again, will you? There's no husband. There's no geezer lurking in the shadows, or I'd know about it, wouldn't I? I've seen her mail; it's all addressed to Ms Campbell. That's Ms as in not married to a geezer, isn't it? My inner demons immediately set to do battle. Normally, my money would have gone on Ms Reason and Logic, but something about Elizabeth's embittered Southern Counties' annunciation had declared Ms Self-pitying Paranoia the clear winner. I'd heard enough. At that point, I wanted to pull over and eject the malicious cow, seeing her off with a defiant mouthful of witty and clever retorts. This would have been after I'd managed to quell the golf ball of sickening panic that had been working its way north from my stomach since I'd heard the word husband.

Saved by the right-hand turn! By the time I'd negotiated the Beamer into a generous parking space in posh Leaside Terrace, Elizabeth the Mouth was pulling down her mini skirt in anticipation of her exit from the vehicle. One of those knees-together-slide-out-at an-angle jobs, I think. Making a hasty decision to play the butch card, I had raced out to open her door, tactically avoiding the pile of fresh dog shit that was steaming on the pavement squarely in front of her door. I remember her smiling as she accepted my hand. Then she'd told me that she rather liked me and asked me my name. Okay, yes, I was flattered, and I flirted back a little, leaning back against the motor as she fished in her handbag for the fare.

Elizabeth had tottered her way halfway up the stairs toward the front door before my ego had subsided, and my paranoia returned. "Um. Do you remember the name of that guy?" I tried to make my voice sound light as I squeaked out my burning question for all the world to hear.

I have a picture in my head of that moment in time; willowy, power-suited posh gal perched on the top step of a smart London terrace, pausing in front of the shiny, black front door. Keys in hand, she paused and turned to me with a slight frown, as if ninety minutes wittering on about the bad old days had somehow exhausted her. At this point, I would've claimed that these posh girls had no stamina, except for the fact that I knew one who had a shitload, and I was the one with the waning energy.

"Hmm. Can't quite remember. Extraordinary that. Harrison? No. Something...erm...oh, gosh, I can picture him now. Very pretty boy! Was into films."

Oh, dear God! Flaky Elizabeth made me want to throw myself to the ground in a kicking, screaming tantrum. I accepted the proffered notes, allowing her to fingers to linger a shade longer than necessary against my own. What? I'm a private hire driver. I take customer service seriously.

"Thank you, Elizabeth. I'll make sure I let her know that I ran into you today." I'm nothing if not a charming flirt, y'know, and my fragile ego adores being lightly caressed by an attractive, slightly older woman. I was almost over myself by the time I yanked my door back open, preparing to scoot back up the South Circular and to my non-transgressing girlfriend in lightning quick fashion.

I tried to calm my relationship anxiety by insisting that I'd misheard Elizabeth's parting call. I'd climbed back into the car, and a large lorry had thundered past on the opposite side of the road, when she'd called out over her shoulder. She said it all right, I know she did. Carlton. Carlton the film studies guy. I slowly and reluctantly digested the fact that my girlfriend had been/was married to her gay mate, and that, despite the fact that we had all shared a roof for several years, no one had thought to tell me. I cringed and fumed, turning the knowledge over in my head, but I didn't confront Grier. She could have told me if she'd wanted to, but in all the years we were together, she never did. It's the only thing I have ever really held against her.

"You picked her up in our Student Union bar? Christ, Noo! What the fuck were you doing there anyway?" Frank sups his pint and wipes his lip with the back of his hand. "I could never drag your miserable arse in even when we were studying there."

Studying? Seems like an entire lifetime ago, and someone else's lifetime at that. I was crap anyway; left halfway through the second year while my smart brother went on to pick up his law degree with honours. Said long-lost brother rapidly metamorphosised into my mildly irritating, soon-to-become downright irksome, brother. Sitting opposite me in the familiar corner of what was once our local is the Dorian Gray of the O'Sullivan family. His unlined face remains supple, his clipped beard ungreyed by the ravages of time. His eyes still twinkle with mischief, the corners barely hinting at the crow's feet which should, by all accounts, mark his descent into the abyss of fortydom and middle age. Still a little soft around the middle, I note, as I shuffle in my seat and tug at my own waistband.

Without the security of my trusty canvas belt, I'd be wandering around like some surly gangsta with my jeans hanging off my hips. Still, no sign of that so-called middle-aged spread that I've been looking forward to. Nah, guess I'm just destined to be a shapeless beanpole all my adult life. I'm changing the subject, of course.

Frank pushes his chair back and scrutinises my face with earnest. What does he see in me after all these years? I focus my attention on choosing a bag of crisps from the pile that he dumped on the table on returning from the bar. Clearing my throat with a nervous cough, I cross and uncross my legs, and then tug absently at a single, grey-rooted curl just above my left temple. "I didn't exactly pick her up."

I pause to take a deep slug of my lager shandy. I don't want to be here. I don't want to be trapped in this trendy dump feeling the alcohol starting to spread through my veins. I don't want to talk about Tessa or even think about her, for that matter. Frank's just spent the last thirty minutes telling me how well rid of Gree I am, and now he's moving on to Tessa.

He flaps his hand dismissively. "Whatever," he says, "I've just met her and already I know that she's a quality upgrade on Grier fucking Campbell. Christ, that woman..." He squeezes his eyes tightly shut, pinches the bridge of his nose, and shakes his head.

Accustomed as I am to hearing negative comments about Gree, coming from my brother, the words are painful to my ears. "Grier's not as bad as everyone makes out," I say, perhaps a little too quickly. The sharpness of my tone catches me a little off guard. Why do I feel a need to charge to her defence after all that has happened between us? Frank is staring at me, unblinking, his lips slightly parted as if he wants to say something. I don't want to hear it. I take a deep breath and look away. There's a flying ant walking across the edge of the table, and my gaze is firmly glued to it. Right now, I'd swap places with that bloody bug in an instant. I bet she doesn't have to explain to her thirty thousand siblings exactly how and why she's let the colony down. Or perhaps she does. Perhaps she's flying off to join a new colony where nobody knows her and her extended family. Perhaps...

"I'm getting old here."

I watch the ant fall drunkenly off the table's edge before returning my attention to his face. He's grinning that wide-mouthed, gold-toothed grin at me again. Plank! I rub the palms of my hands down the outside seams of my jeans, nervous habit number 112, if I'm not mistaken. "I'd promised Carl I'd get a girl in for the spare room, on account of the Straight Charlie business and all, and I'd done nothing about it. And he was coming back from San Francisco at the weekend—Carl, not Charlie—and I remembered that it was almost term-time, so I went looking for a student. I met Tessa in the Student Union. That's all." I slump back into the spongy soft leather sofa and cuddle my glass. There, I said it. It occurs to me that this is the first time that I have talked about the Straight Charlie business with anyone other than Carl; it's still so painful. Somehow, I want to tell Frank though.

Frank sips his pint, before folding his arms across his chest and waggling his eyebrows at me. "Who dat?" he says, smiling that dopey smile of his.

My nostrils flare, and the smile on Frank's face falters. "Charles Anderson the Second," I say. "Some shit-for-brains-but-loaded public school boy who Carl met at work a year or so ago." I'm vaguely aware that my lips have twisted into a snarl to accompany the ugly memory. "Charlie became a fixture in our spare room for the remainder of that week, and when Carl suggested that Charlie stayed in the house while he was finishing up in San Francisco, I had no reason to object and didn't." I should've. *I was spineless then, and I'm still spineless now.*

"Noo? What's all this about, mate?"

When Frank's voice hauls me back to reality, I have to swallow hard to regain my composure. He needs to know who I am, what I've become since we last met. "Charlie moved his bimbo girlfriend in, and then his mate and *his* girlfriend," I say, trying to sound casual. "So, it was me and a houseful of weed-fuelled strangers."

Frank throws his head back and roars with laughter. "Typical Carl," he says. "He's away with the fairies when it comes to people. He'd invite a serial killer back for breakfast if he liked the look of his shoes." When he catches the look on my face, he turns a little pale. "Shit, Noo. I'm sorry. What did you do? What did you say to them?"

I swallow and reach out to touch the edge of the table to steady myself. It hadn't exactly been my finest hour and despite the fact that I've opened the door to it, I'm reluctant to revisit this particular memory. "Oh, you know me, Frank. I bottled it." I'd love to tell him that I went all *Xena, Warrior Princess*, shrieking a blood-curdling ululation that drove him and the other from the house, screaming in terror. I can't do that, so I shrug my shoulders, feigning indifference. "I just hid in my room, hoping they'd leave me alone...and they did, most of the time. Except for that day when he barged into my bedroom."

I'd been almost paralysed with fear when I saw Straight Charlie leaning against the door frame, half in and half out of the room, the oversized joint between his lips shedding its powdery ash down his T-shirt and onto my floor. My hand trembles when I reach out to pluck my glass off the table. I pause to take a reassuring glug of my shandy, under Frank's watchful gaze. "I said, 'I want you out of my house, Charlie. You and the rest of your freeloading entourage need to find another home to wreck. Tonight.'"

"Good for you, mate," Frank says.

No, not really, I think to myself. Before I can decide on how to edit the memory for my brother's consumption, my internal DVD player shoots me back into the action, and I relive the memory of that awful moment when I found myself standing nose to nose (well, nose to chest) with the wanker.

Okay, yes, I did resort to violence. I had never hit anyone in my life, except for Paula Dunning when we were eleven, but she was a racist cow and had it coming. Charlie Anderson was just a ridiculous, overgrown public schoolboy living in a self-destructive drug haze. Unfortunately for me, he was living it in my house at the time, and my patience with the chemically afflicted wasn't exactly abundant. Screaming like a banshee, I swung my fist in the general direction of his face, only to land a distinctly girlie punch somewhere in the region of his shoulder blade. That was it, all I had at the time. Game, set, and match to the interloper.

"Shit, Noo, shit." Frank thumps his fist on the table, rattling the glasses. He raises an apologetic hand to reassure the startled drinkers around us before slumping back into his chair. "Tell me," he says, his voice laced with concern. "What did you do?"

What did I do? My thoughts return to that miserable day, remembering how I'd stood for a brief moment clutching the banister for the support that my trembling legs demanded, before bolting down the stairs and out of the front door. No tears, no rage, just an overwhelming, all-consuming vulnerability. Charlie and crew had effectively kicked me out of my home, and I wouldn't be able to return until they had gone. What was worse, I just bolted out of the house leaving my house and car keys in the middle of my bed, neatly at the disposal of the spliffing, snorting masses.

I found myself pounding the pavement without the slightest clue as to where I was going or what I was going to do when I arrived there. On that sobering thought, my trembling legs came to an abrupt halt, preferring to take root in the middle of the pavement. I allowed my eyelids to slowly slide closed, noting with a little surprise the absence of the annoying, hot tears which generally accompanied my bouts of high emotion. I might have remained rooted to the spot for the remainder of the day, had it not been for Candy. My glassy eyes focus on my brother's diamond ear stud.

"Remember Candy?" I ask him. Candy's a big ol' shaggy mongrel, lumbering and affectionate, who belongs to Kathleen and Dennis, the retired couple from across the road. She'd been a puppy last time Frank was here. Frank looks at me with a "what the fuck" look as he unhooks the top button of his Fred Perry, settling himself in for the long haul.

"The neighbour's dog, right?" he says, scrunching his eyebrows.

The expression on his face indicates that he has no idea where my story's heading, that this is a right royal tangent, even for random-brained me. I scramble my way through filling him in on the relevance of my meanderings.

I'd been accustomed to seeing Candy taking Kathleen for a walk twice a day back then, but I'd never seen her out in the street by herself as she had been that day. I'd like to say that on that occasion Candy had raced over to me, barking frantically, raising a paw, beseeching me to follow her, in true Lassie fashion. The reality's a little less dramatic, but come over to me, she did. It was only after I had raised myself sufficiently from my pit of despair to think about stooping to scratch the shaggy one's bearded chin that I had heard the cry. So faint that I first thought that I imagined it, but then it came again, accompanied by an unmistakable sigh of despair.

"Candy! Come back, girl!"

Would it be ungracious of me to admit that, as I sprinted across the street in the direction of the cries, I had been spurred on by the thought of the set of keys which, I remembered, Gree had given to Kathleen for emergencies years before? Hey, I would've gone anyway. I'm that sort of a neighbour. But even so, I'd still been shocked to come across poor Kathleen sitting on the bottom basement step clutching her left ankle. Her face was as white as a sheet and though she tried to sound cheerful as she retold the story of her fall, I had instinctively known that she was scared shitless, and that I would need to take charge.

"Don't move, Kathleen, that looks bad," I said, placing my hand on her shoulder. "Give me your keys, and I'll go in and call an ambulance."

Waving off her protestations of "Oh, I don't want to make a fuss, dear," I made short work of relaying the details to the ambulance service dispatcher, phonetically relaying the address and postcode.

"Whisky Alpha Lima Lima India November Golf Tango Oscar November... Yes... I'll check... I'll be right back." My heart punched out a presto beat as I scurried around Kathleen's house, locating her handbag and other necessities. "Here you go, Kathleen," I said, easing a pillow behind her back as I draped a duvet over her shivering body. "They're asking if you take any medications. What should I say?"

Her ashen face contradicted her cheery tone. It seemed that Kathleen was getting greyer by the minute, and I worried that she might lose consciousness. When she flapped her hand in the direction of her handbag, I grabbed it from her, located the packets of tablets, then raced back to the phone to relay the details to the waiting controller.

Frank takes another slug of beer and draws his tongue over the froth on his moustache. "Good job you were there, Noo," he says, almost absently.

"What, me?" I huff out a self-deprecating laugh. "I'm crap at all that caring-sharing stuff. I barely know which way is up." I shrug and fan my hands out. "I called an ambulance, and I called Dennis. No knowledge of rocket science required, mate."

Frank gives me an exasperated look and makes a sound gurgling in the back of his throat when he thumps the table. "See, that's it, right there, Noo," he says, the razor edge in his tone catching me off balance. "You're always putting yourself down. What would I have done in that situation? I dunno, but you..." He pauses to trace a line down the condensation on the outside of his glass, before tilting his head and smiling. "You just jump in and take charge when you need to, mate. You might not be all that when it comes to looking after yourself, but when other people need you..." He stares into his beer. "You da man, Noo." His face softens a little, and he grins. "Always have been. You'd be my go-to in any crisis."

I feel the blood rising to my cheeks under the scrutiny of his warm gaze. My eyes are shiftily avoiding making contact, but he pursues me until I relent and look at him. Deep brown eyes project warmth at me, coaxing a smile from my lips. I shrug and look down at my hands, silently willing him to change the subject.

"Ah, well..." I say, nervously smoothing the palms of my hands over my thighs.

"Ah, well nothing, Noo." Frank grins and raises a finger in the air. "Looks like you've forgotten that you're the O'Sullivan Superhero, and it's my job to drag you, kicking and screaming, back into your cape."

He gives me a wink, and I smile back at him as my shoulders begin to relax. There's a crumb of truth in what he says; I used to have an uncanny knack of being able to hurtle into action when I needed to. I'd sprinted home to call 999 when dozy, teenaged Aaron Jacobs had ignited his dad's garden shed, and I was the one who dragged that inebriated girl away from the carload of leering men that she was about to join that night when we were at college.

I'd endured her endless tirade of expletives, driven her home, and safely delivered her into the grateful hands of her concerned flatmates because it was the right thing to do. When did I stop doing that? When did I become a worrier, paralysed by fear and insecurity instead of being a do-er?

Frank leans across the table to poke at my arm. "So what happened then?" he asks, waving his fingers at me to continue.

I watch the bubbles in my shandy chase one another for a second or two and allow myself to feel the warmth of the cape he has draped around my shoulders.

"That's it, really," I say with a shrug. "I waited with her for Dennis to arrive, got us a black cab home when she was all patched up—God, those things are so slow—rustled up beans on toast for three... Then I told them my sorry tale and graciously accepted their offer of the use of their sofa for a few days." I wish I could've told him that I'd been so strengthened by their support that I charged back to the house and evicted the squatters single-handedly but in reality, the minute that Dennis reported that the sponge collective had left the house, I simply let myself back in, collected my toothbrush, keys, phone, and some clothes, and left the house as I found it. Dirty, dishevelled, and with the TV left blaring. I did stop to leave a note for Carl. Sellotaped it to the castor oil plant in his bedroom and hightailed it out of there before the sponge collective returned. Never thought that I'd be as pleased to see bleedin' Carl Miller as I was the day that he finally arrived home from San Francisco. Could've kissed the bastard when he came over, armed with flowers and an apology to accompany me back home. Well, nearly.

Frank's eyebrows do that funny twitching thing that he does, and his jaw clenches.

"I'm sorry, Noo," he says softly. "Sorry that I wasn't there when all that was going down."

He looks genuinely perturbed. My stomach gives a little flutter, and I smile a little. "Nah, it's no biggie," say. "Gotta learn to stand on my own two feet sometime."

"I know," he mumbles. "Me too. I needed to learn how to be a real person without you by my side. That's why I stayed away up in Newcastle after Ayia Napa. Of course, I had to let Mum know that I was back, but I made her promise not to tell you. I know that was a crappy thing to do, but..." He sits back in his chair and raises his hand. "I swear by St Damian and...um...his brother that I'll never just up sticks and leave you again, Noo."

We both chuckle. I was always hot on my knowledge of obscure saints. I used to practice reciting their names and causes while he practiced reciting the names of Tottenham Hotspur players, past and present. He'd offer a Jimmy Greaves, I'd counter with a Saint James, son of Zebedee. Phil Gray became Saint Philip the Apostle, and Ossie Ardilles earned him a Saint Oswald of Northumbria. Once, he thought that he had me with Gary Lineker but with no Saint Gary, I had insisted that St Garai was the same thing. Dad raised an eyebrow, Mum beamed and nodded, and so that had been that. Pious girl 1, Footie boy 0.

"Good." I nod my head. "Good, 'cause God knows, I'm crap without you, bruv."

He nods his head vigorously, takes a long swig of his pint and emits a satisfied murmur. "Yeah, you are, sis," he says. "I mean...just what *is* going on with you and Becks? Tell me everything!"

Demon girl jabs me with her fork, and I wince. *I will tell him. I know that I have to, and soon, but—* Frank drains the dregs of his glass while I re-acquaint myself with the bubbles in my own. He holds out a hand to me, and we link fingers.

"You're a fucking hero, mate," he says quietly.

I'm warmed by the pride that radiates from his words. Changing the subject, he fills me in on his reunion with Kath, his job at the Law Centre and his girlfriends (past and current). I relent and bring him up to speed on the Great Flood, the Goddess Conference, and the shameful New Year debacle. Well, the airbrushed, sanitised version I gave to Deborah and Yemi anyway. By the time I finish speaking, I'm a bit of a mess. My voice has become a hoarse whisper, my cheeks let me know in no uncertain terms that they are burning crimson, and my eyes are brimming with tears.

Frank leans forward and squeezes my shoulder. "You'll sort it out, Noo," he says. "We can sort this."

He gets it. He gets me. He meets my watery stare with his own steady gaze. I feel a familiar twinge in my chest, a long-forgotten sensation of panic and calmness battling one another with the calm steadily gaining the upper hand. Frank has neatly landed a rabbit punch squarely on Demon girl's nose. I hear her indignant protests as she shoots backwards through the air.

I'm so glad Frank's back.

Frank's Back

THE OFFICIAL FAMILY RUMOUR regarding the Disappeared One was that he had gone to Spain. Laughing boy's eyes twinkle when he sets me straight on that one.

"I went out to get milk, and bumped into Aero at the bus stop," he says, smiling broadly and exposing his sparkling incisor.

His eyes get that soft glazed look, like he's slipped out of the pub and into some sweet memory of the past. I frown, waiting for him to come back to the here and now. Frank's always been the realist, the level-headed counterpart to my absent-minded, daydreaming self but right now, he looks like he's away with the fairies. A raucous cheer erupts from the pool table area, and he snaps back to our conversation.

"Aero." He looks at me expectantly. "You remember Aaron Jacobs, right?"

Aaron Jacobs, the school pied piper, the nutter who persuaded Frank to be strapped into a computer chair and allow the others to launch him down the slope in the park and straight into the concrete duck pond. The unrepentant maniac who scribbled "Top Geezer" on Frank's resulting wrist cast—yeah, I remembered Aero all right.

"I bumped into Aero at the bus stop. He was on his way to spend the summer working in his brother's bar in Ayia Napa. Told me I should come too. Sun, sea, sand, and booze—I mean, everyone loves a barman, right? Sounded good to me." He shrugs, as if stating the obvious, and I bristle in my seat. "So I went."

He presumably clocks the scowl on my face because he holds up a finger at me while he while he swigs on his pint. I wait, silently cursing the idiot's boy swagger.

"Mate, it was mental. Well wicked! You had to be there."

Aero had scribbled the address on the corner of Frank's *Daily Mirror* and all but begged him to join him. There would be girls galore and a bar job to boot, he'd promised, and it had been all the persuasion Frank had needed. He'd sauntered off home with a smile on his face and, finding the house miserably empty, he had simply packed a pair of jeans, a spare T-shirt, and a toothbrush.

"Have passport and nothing else to do. Will travel." He spreads his arms out in a ta-da gesture.

I resist the urge to slap him around his peanut head. "What, and you didn't think to leave a note or something?" My rasping voice is probably a little more emotional than I intended. Frank says nothing. My usually articulate brother opens and closes his mouth, and then slumps back into his chair, biting his lower lip. It's a family habit; we O'Sullivan's have this avoidance thingy down to a fine art. We also have ragged lower lips.

"I was going to tell you," he says, swirling the beer in his glass. "I was... You were..."

Something about him isn't right, even I can see that, and it sets my Spidey senses tingling. We're sitting in the boozer on the corner, wading through a whole heap of catch-up small talk, and now he's going all weird on me. I try to press him on it, and he gets all evasive, but there's definitely something on his mind that he isn't telling me. Not like Frank at all. Or maybe I just don't know him at all after all this time. He takes another large swig from the glass, and then gives me a smirk. Somehow, I get the feeling that he isn't exactly smiling behind it.

"Water under the bridge, mate," he says at last. "We both had stuff going on back then, and some things are best forgotten, know what I mean?"

Um...yeah, no, sort of. My brow furrows. Frank takes up the story again, and I lend him half an ear. It's only when he starts talking about the things I don't know about that I start paying attention.

"So," I say, slowly drawing the word out. "There was a brother," I shudder at the thought of another Jacobs dipstick in the world, "a bar, a job, and more women than you could shake a stick at." Try as I might, I fail to conceal the resentment that saturates my tone. "But you didn't come back at the end of the summer, did you? You didn't even let me...us know that you were alive." That my brother would just up and leave me behind without a second's thought exasperates me, and the thought that he'd obviously enjoyed himself during our separation rankles. I look around for the support of my flying ant, but she's long gone. No, I'm on my own with this one. Feeling all kinds of fragile, I nervously sip at my drink and try to ignore the glee in Frank's eyes. Cosmas and Damian be buggered, if he can have such fun absconding once, he can do it again. The thought drains the saliva from my mouth, leaving me fighting to swallow. Something resembling guilt briefly washes over Frank's face, and he looks away for a moment before reeling back.

"I did get in touch," he says. "I sent Mum and Dad a postcard."

"A postcard? That grubby, dog-eared scrap of cardboard was supposed to let us know that you were okay? That you hadn't been abducted by aliens and were lying somewhere on a spaceship with a probe up your jacksy or something?" I proper scowl at my memory of the postcard. The photo of a nameless sunny beach, Frank's scrawling handwriting, the fact that Mum'd had to pay the excess postage because the plank hadn't used the right stamps.

> *Hi Mum, I'm gonna be working in Cyprus for a bit. I've got a cool job and a nice place to stay. Don't know when I'll be back. Say hi to everyone, Love Frank.*

It had grated on me. Astonished and bewildered by the fact that my brother had made such a monumental leap away from me had both stung and saddened me at the time. Swallowing back her concerns, Mum had muttered that she was "glad to hear that he was okay." Dad had proudly declared him to be "away to sow his O'Sullivan wild oats, so he is." And me? I'd fretted and whinged on to Grier about being abandoned by him. Grier, I recall, had pointedly asked me if I was going to spend the whole evening worrying about my brother or kissing her. I'd chosen the latter.

I clear my throat and straighten a beer mat in an effort to dislodge the embers of desire deep in my belly that the memory stokes. We're not here to talk about her, after all.

Frank's grin is suitably sheepish. "Yeah, well," he says, "I wasn't really thinking straight at the time. Too busy living the life."

He flashes me his best charming smile, warm and broad, and I silently curse myself, knowing that I will be letting him off the hook. I've missed him more than I care to think about. "Frank, that was worst postcard in the history of crappy communications. Ever. D'you know that?" My reticent smile prompts him to grin even harder at me, and a chuckle escapes his lips.

"Yeah, I guess," he says quietly. Then he perks up in his chair. "Noo, it wouldn't've been your cup of tea but...it was mental, mate!"

He's right, of course. I don't do "mental" arms-in-the-air, mega dance activities. My pastime of choice will always be an introverted, leave-me-alone-in-my-bedroom-with-a-book kind of thing. Of late, I'm more likely to be found splayed out across my bed, brooding, worrying, and maybe crying to myself, but I don't tell him that. Instead, I lock those images away in my deal with later vault. By the look in his eyes, I can tell that he's just itching to tell me all about it, so I roll my own eyes and huff out a breath. "Go on then. You may as well tell me about it."

"Oh man!" he says. "You should've seen the place. Strobe lights, glitter balls, shish kebabs—the works. Me and Aero thought we'd died and been fast-tracked to heaven in a limousine." He drains the remainder of his beer and swipes his cuff across his lips to remove the foam beard which has settled on his actual beard.

"We did six nights a week, grabbing some shut-eye on the beach during the day, then we'd go back to the bar to do it all over again. 100% mental mate, mental."

"Um…yeah, you said that, Frank." I bury my fidgeting hands in my jacket pockets and resist the urge to mutter, *Give me strength.* "So, you made a shit load of dosh then?" I say. "I mean, what with the unlimited supply of booze and the free accommodation, it doesn't sound like there was a lot to spend it on. You must have been minted when you came back."

Lager boy shifts in his chair and squints. "Um…"

I throw my hands up at him. "What are you not telling me, Frank?"

He grimaces and scratches his fingers through his beardy cheek. He has guilt written all over his chops, and I'm all confused. I mean, hadn't he gone off to seek his fortune and return as the financially conquering hero?

Leaning forward, he beckons me with a finger. "Okay," he whispers. "But don't tell Mum, yeah?"

Later, standing in the fake marble toilets of the Green Man, scorching my fingers under the hand drier, I shake my head again. Only Frank the Plank could get himself into such a spectacular mess. Ably aided and abetted by the clueless Aaron bloody Jacobs, of course. Dumb and bloody dumber. Frank's just filled me in on the sordid details of his sobering stint as a suspected international drug dealer in the not so lovely Ayia Napa Police Detention Centre, and I need a moment to process it all. Apparently, the clueless duo had found an abandoned rucksack in the bar's toilets which, to their childish delight, had contained a pair of genuine Prada sunglasses, some geezer's passport, Axe deodorant, and a shedload of banknotes.

Frank laid claim to the sunglasses, slung the backpack onto his shoulder, and they merrily skipped off to stash the loot in their digs. Except they hadn't gotten that far. The moment they'd stepped out into the sunshine, they found themselves handcuffed and whisked off into the custody of the local police.

I withdraw my hands from the dryer, groaning at my reflection. I look about as worn out as I feel. It's been hard to reconcile the fact that Frank had been languishing in a prison cell while I was luxuriating in the arms of my beloved Grier. I take a moment to wrestle control over the feelings of remorse that erupt in my chest.

Where were you when he needed you? the spectre hisses into my ear.

My hand absently swipes at my ear, cutting short my more than likely descent into the gloom. Yes, I'm a hopeless mess of a human being, but I silently pledge to be a better sister before I scurry back to join him.

Frank's not at our table when I return, but I soon spy him over by the pool table, chalking up his cue and chatting amiably with some random stranger. That's Frank for you; he can befriend anyone. Anytime, anywhere. Me, I'm more of a pull out a book and radiate "Don't speak to me" vibe kind of person. When he catches sight of me, he beckons me over.

"Hey, Noo." He nods at the man standing next to him. "We're going to play doubles with Calum and his mate, yeah? Best of three."

Disappointed that I'll have to wait for him to finish his story, I ignore the heat rising in my cheeks and force a polite smile. I spend the next fifteen minutes playing a reasonably competent game, simultaneously squeezing down the growling anxiety bubbles in my gut. My eyes reassure me that my brother is here, safe and sound but... I perform my sibling pub duty adequately but bow out and escape to the relative safety of our table at the earliest opportunity. Frank saunters off to the bar to order something hot and deep-fried for us and another pint for himself, and I wish I had half the effortless swag that he radiates.

"What?"

The aroma rising from the bowl of chips Frank's wafting under my nose informs me that I've been zoning out in my daydream again. I blink a couple of times to reboot my brain, swirling a chip in the garlic mayonnaise dip for want of something better to do with my hands. "Er...international drug dealer?" I pop the chip into my mouth, taking pleasure in the incredulous look that he gives me.

"How can you?" He gesticulates at the steaming chips which by all accounts, should be too hot for anyone to handle. "I mean, surely your mouth must be—"

"Made of asbestos?" I like my tea and my food eye-wateringly hot, and Frank's not the first to have noticed my quirk. "Multi-talented, bruv," I say and wink. My shoulders begin their descent from their high alert position as I relax back into conversation. Somehow the dozy git always manages to make me feel better, and I can't resist adding "and don't call me Shirley." Silence. I look at him, he looks at me. I pop another scalding chip into my mouth and waggle my eyebrows, and we both burst out laughing. I remember the first time we watched *Airplane* together at the fleapit cinema in Finchley, and how we clung to one another, tears rolling down our cheeks. My cozy stroll down memory lane takes a hair-pin bend when the image of a laughing Tessa floats into my mind. Tessa. Earnest Tessa, my laid-back brainiac, whose sophomoric humour teases out the playfulness in me that I thought long lost. I tilt my head askew, frowning as I acknowledge the fact; *Tessa reminds me of Frank*. I swear I hear a ping notification that my warm and fuzzy jar has reached its functioning level. I pray that it's enough to keep me afloat when my stomach lurches, my brain reminding me that she is no longer *my* Tessa.

Frank wipes a tear from the corner of his eye with his sleeve. "Right," he says. "Um...international drug dealer, I'm not. White, six-foot-four, Cameron James Watkins, I'm not." He pauses to swipe a chip from the bowl but winces when it burns his fingertips. Dropping it back into the bowl, he wrinkles his nose at me. "Your mouth's fucking unnatural, you know that?"

"So I've been told, mate." I blow on my fingernails and mock polish them on my T-shirt, while Frank mimes sticking a finger down his throat and retching. I chuckle, motioning with my hand for him to continue the story.

"Yeah, well," he says, warily eyeing the chip bowl. "It only took them three weeks to figure it out. The real Cameron Watkins trying to cross into Greece with a rucksack full of Es and no passport was a bit of a giveaway too. Aero was bloody useless!"

Aaron, it transpired, had run around like a headless chicken, splashing Frank's hard-earned cash on a series of ambulance-chasing lawyers who had been happy to relieve the gullible numpty of the cash before vanishing into the ether.

Frank sighs. "It wasn't all that bad, though," he says. "I got a lot of sleep...and the food was better than we'd been getting, so..."

The image in my head of a grim-faced, unshaven Frank rattling his tin cup along the bars of some seedy, Victorian cell is swiftly updated. I can just imagine the plank cheerily accepting his tray of freshly cooked food from the guard, and asking for salt and "Coke, not that diet stuff, mate." I mentally roll my eyes. Only Frank could land on his feet in a situation like that.

"They let me go...eventually, and I went back to the bar." He chomps on a chip. "But I was skint by then, and I just wanted to go home."

I steel myself for the next harrowing instalment.

"I managed to wrangle a ticket home off Aero's brother's mate. I wanted to go, he wanted to stay." He waves his hand in the air. "All it took was a couple of beers and twenty-five quid to get him to part with his ticket. A couple of calls to the airline, a touch of good old Irish blarney, and I was touching down in Blighty," he says, smiling at the memory. Then he frowns. "Unfortunately for me, I was touching down in bloody Newcastle airport," he says.

We stare at one another before blurting out in unison, "It's home, Jim, but not as we know it."

Our easy laughter and the familiar warmth that being in his company brings is a stark and welcome contrast to the abject misery to which I have become accustomed of late, and I welcome it with open arms. I sink back into my seat, savouring the sound of my brother's voice as he talks me through the details of his reunification with our sister Kathleen, the only person anyone in this family has even known to reside in that area. Kath, our long-lost sister, voluntarily exiled to the frozen north with her miserable, waste of space husband, never to be seen by the O'Sullivan clan again. Except by Frank, that is. Chancing his luck, he'd presented himself on the junkie's doorstep with a grin and a cheery, "Hi, sis!"

Kath had been well into her recovery when he arrived there. She had dumped the moron, lost some time in and out of rehab and, by the time Frank arrived, had been clean and sober for a couple of years. At the time, big sis had moved into the realms of the gainfully employed and was studying part time for her degree.

"She hated us all," he said. "Felt like we let her down when she needed us most. Everyone but me." He lets out a sudden laugh. "Well, me, she loved, of course...because I'm handsome, and adorable, and her favourite brother."

Mum and Dad had worried over and whispered about Kath after she had run off with the scumbag, but I had merely rolled my eyes, silently mouthing *good riddance* to myself. Now, to hear she hated us and had felt abandoned... Bile bites at the back of my throat. My leather-clad demon tries to interject, toasting fork held aloft but I'm able to swat the bitch aside. That's the power of two, you see. I'm a better person, a *stronger* person when Frank's around. He was at Kath's graduation. The only O'Sullivan to witness Mrs Katherine Dionne Walsh, junkie waste of space, emerge from her northern cocoon as Ms Katherine O'Sullivan, BSc (Hons) Psychology.

I'm feeling fifty shades of guilty that we hadn't all made the trek up there to see it, to shower her with the support and admiration that her monumental turn around deserved. Of course, it wasn't like the rest of us knew she was graduating, but still... Add the fact that Peanut Boy has been gainfully employed as a solicitor these past years, and suddenly I'm feeling like the black sheep of the family again. Why am I the only one who doesn't have a degree? More to the point, why does it matter so much to me now?

Frank springs to his feet, holding out a hand. "C'mon, curly girlie," he says, cheekily ruffling my hair. "I need fresh air, and you need vitamin D, ya pasty thing. Let's go to Epping for some real food."

Suppressing a sigh, I rise to my feet and follow him, scowling at his impertinence before succumbing to a genuine smile. Maybe I am all kinds of screwed up but with my brother by my side, I'm better.

"So, you got dumped by the Cow, what, eight years ago now? And you've been fucking and dumping Becks for the past six months?" Frank chews rapidly and rhythmically on his mouthful of roast beef.

I drop my gaze to my plate, willing its contents to impart the wisdom I will need to survive my brother's grilling. The pinky beef slices are giving nothing away, so I slather one in horseradish and force it between my lips. Breakfast at Yemi's seems a lifetime ago, and I know that I should eat, but I'm still not hungry. Walking in the crisp clean air of Epping Forest with Frank had temporarily recharged my emotional energy, but now? My mind transports me from this cosy, country pub dining room on the edge of Epping Forest to the raucous sports bar where I know Tessa will be right now, and I drink up the vision.

She'll be wearing a training top over her football shirt, her body still sweaty from her exertions on the field. She'll have removed her shin pads, and her rolled down socks will reveal muddy skid marks on her shins. If I nuzzled in to place my mouth on that sweet spot where her neck joins her shoulder blade, I'll discover a magical, salty region that pulses aromas of grass and mud and sweat and Tessa, which commands me to lick and suck and— I inhale so sharply that I begin to choke on the partially chewed contents of my mouth, and the horseradish assaults my sinuses, making my eyes water.

Frank looks at me like he's just noticed an enormous zit pulsing on the end of my nose or something, but he says nothing. He pours a glass of water and slides it across the table to me, and I gratefully gulp it down, washing away all traces of horseradish and visions of Tessa in one fell swoop. I contemplate the fire, the gentle orange glow and the smell of wood smoke that are emanating from the grate. I'm a mess. How long I can keep this up? I give Frank a look, one that I hope transmits "Back off. It's not that simple."

He spears a carrot with his fork. "You fucked the Evil One on New Year's Eve under the nose of your then-girlfriend, so to speak. She ain't talking to you, you're playing hide and seek at home, and now you're gearing up for Campbell's return this weekend. What'd I miss?"

I force myself to swallow. He cuts through the crap and hit the target so squarely; how does he do that? He nudges a broccoli floret aside with his knife, relegating it to the outer rim of his plate before stapling me to my seat with his penetrating gaze.

"But you ain't happy, Noo, and you look like you've been that way for some time. Really, mate. When was the last time you were really happy?"

My stomach lurches and the blood freezes in my veins. I'm William Tell's kid, back against the tree waiting for the impact. Oh sure, there's an apple perched on my head for him to aim at, but when I squint through my tightly closed eyes, I see the rubber-suckered arrow heading for my forehead. I see it but am unable to duck out of its path. Schooom!

Crooked Grins and Alcoholic Sins

I DO KNOW THE last time I felt truly and blissfully 100% happy but I side-stepped Frank's bear trap, batted the question away with a raised hand and a look that I fancied strongly conveyed a "Don't go there" message. I threw him a bone by reminding him that he'd asked me how Tessa had come to be living in the house and filled him in on that saga instead. So how did I end up with Dr Tessa Beckinsale instead of the student I'd gone looking for? As I lay in bed that night, I let myself drift into the memory of that fateful day.

Attacking the campus stairs two at a time on that summer's afternoon, I grinned a right smug smile to myself, basking in the sheer genius of my yet-to-be-executed master plan. Students! They were a dozy, last-minute set of individuals, and my old college was a bottomless pit of available dozies. The bored receptionist in the Students' Union block had lowered her magazine just about long enough to grunt an acknowledgement to my request. After an ever so brief head to toe assessment of my gangly self, she waved me in the direction of the Welfare Office notice board with a flail of her pointy, painted fingernail. Cruella bloody de Vil or what?

Feeling ludicrously cocky, I winked back at her before hoicking my jeans from hip to waist (fruitless task though it was) and racing off, partially written notice board ad in hand. Genius! It read: *Lovely room in lovely Rainbow Muswell Hill household available to lovely woman. Immediately.* I was happy with that. Rent would be negotiable, and applicants could call me on my mobile. Carl would be home sometime on Sunday, and that would give me all of Saturday to scrutinise the possibles and show them the house. Easy peasy, lemon squeezy! My feet barely touched the ground as, card and pin in hand, I advanced on the unsuspecting notice board. My confidence took a swan dive however, when I spied the small crowd hovering around the accommodation board.

A potential merchant banker, a couple of skinny Goths (male and female, matching set), Barbie and her sisters, and a badass bruva complete with back-to-front baseball cap and jeans hanging even lower than my own. My fingers inadvertently tightened on the card, and I had to work some to resist the rising urge to flee while the going was good. I veered abruptly away from the noticeboard crowd, positioning myself casually (and coolly, I hoped) against the opposite wall while I regrouped. Goth and Gothena were arguing in fierce whispers over potential locations and for a mad moment, I vaguely considered wading in and giving them an early Christmas present. Until she raised her voice...

"It says 'mature students,' Jack." Gothena's voice was a thin and cracked whine, the pitch of which was liable to set the wine glasses ringing. "I'd rather live at home with your mum than a bunch of old strangers. Why can't we just stay at yours?"

Young Jack, clearly unimpressed with his girlfriend's lack of ambition, grunted his derision before slumping to the corridor floor in a clanking heap of black leather and Celtic silver. I lowered my eyebrows before turning on my heels to leave. Bad idea, students. Bad idea! I would've been down the corridor and out of the door if my path hadn't been obstructed by a certain someone. Standing in front of me in the middle of the corridor was a scruffy, fresh-faced young woman scowling slightly in the direction of the notice board. Short of squeezing up against her on the left or right, there was no obvious way of getting past. Cue the O'Sullivan awkwardness: a kind of all over tingling of the body, accompanied by that familiar low whisper.

You're a long, flat, weird-looking geek. People will always stop and stare.

Worse still, I quickly realised that the woman had spoken to me and, having momentarily popped my head into the O'Sullivan bucket of self-consciousness, I failed to hear a word she had said. Right on cue, the blood raced to my cheeks. I prayed fervently to St Fiacre: I'm a taxi driver, get me out of here. Unfortunately for me, this mantra didn't yield the desired result. I'm beginning to believe that St Fiacre thinks I'm a crap driver or something. Fortunately for both of us, the woman lowered her gaze from the intense heat radiating from my face.

She smiled. "Still nowt there? If I don't get sorted by t'weekend, I am Donald Ducked!"

And then she laughed, and I laughed too. There I was, a thirty-eight-year-old dropout, standing amongst a group of bleating, sixth form rejects, laughing at nothing at all with this complete stranger who, apparently, had stolen the Laughing Policeman's laugh. It was funny, she was funny, and when I looked again, I saw an attractive, young woman displaying a broken incisor.

"You and me both," I said, still enjoying the levity of the moment. I really can't explain what it was about her, but somehow, when she fixed her smiling eyes on my own shifties in that corridor that day, I felt a sense of calm and familiarity. Gaydar, some would say, but for no apparent reason, I found myself thrusting the partially written card into her hand. Smiley girl ran her eyes over it in an instant.

"Aha! Tis I, tis I, methinks, tis I!"

She handed the card back to me and stood smiling, chipped tooth and all. I couldn't help but wonder if I'd made a serious error of judgement. I mean, what the fuck was she saying? But before I could stutter through a retraction, she threw her head back and released that captivating laugh once again.

"Sorry, sorry," she said, though it sounded like she was directing it at herself rather than me. "I'm Tessa—everyone calls me Becks— and I'd love to see the room, if you think you could live with a history nerd like me."

A calculated risk; I did the maths. Laughing Tessa was certainly the best of a pretty poor bunch, and the silver labrys around her neck weighed heavily in her favour. Ever the introvert, I stole a sideways glance at her to properly register what she looked like. Greeny-brown eyes and sandy, light brown hair, and startlingly deep dimples in her pale, freckled cheeks. I liked the way that she kept sweeping her grown-out fringe behind her ears for safekeeping as she spoke, only to have it escape within seconds each time. Yeah, I clocked that she was as tall as me, but more solid. A gym babe, perhaps? Certainly not a fashion victim, I noted with approval.

She was wearing a tatty old pair of Levi's, roughly chopped off just below the knee, and a bright red vest which forced my eyes to linger on her not unsubstantial breasts. It was the vest, honest. We introduced ourselves, shook hands formally, and when I gave her the address to meet there in an hour's time, I did so with a surprising lack of apprehension. What wasn't surprising was her reaction to the house. It's lovely, even if I do say so myself. The top room's huge and the kitchen's cosy, and I told her that holding weekly tutorials in the living room wouldn't be a problem. We sat in the kitchen and drank tea.

"So what are you going to tell me about yourself, Ms Beckinsale?" I asked, hoping that she didn't notice my blushing cheeks and the forced confidence in my voice. I cleared my throat and grounded myself by locking my eyes onto the blood red, poppy-printed teapot between us. *Get a grip, Fin*, my inner life coach growled, *your wallflower's showing*. A peal of her infectious laughter warmed the room, momentarily letting me off the hook.

"Oh, I'm as boring as they come really," she said, leaning back into her chair. "I'm from West Yorkshire—God's own country."

She thumped her chest as if the statement and the gesture would somehow give me all the information I needed. I rolled my eyes and curled my lip in mock disdain. I resisted the urge to ask how she'd come to chip her tooth, and why she hadn't been to the dentist about it. "Oh, God, not another northern monkey? Coming down here with your 'thees' and 'thas' and stealing our women."

She giggled and gave me a lop-sided grin. An actual,

child-like giggle that somehow managed to unlock the social tension squeezing my shoulders into a knot at the prospect of having to have a real conversation with her.

Her eyes twinkled as she took a glug of her tea. "From what I hear, it don't take a lot to get yer knickers round your ankles, you lot... Southern floozies, the lotta ya."

"Fuck off, Tyke!"

Another laugh and another slug of her tea before she turned serious. "Okay, alrighty. Tessa Beckinsale—I told you that, right? Thirty years old, lecturer in History and Women's Studies at the uni, lover of meat pies, Leeds United, and all things Elizabethan. What about yerself?"

My heart stepped up a beat. This was the point at which I would have to reveal my lowly taxi driver status, the point at which her eyes would glaze over as she absorbed the fact that I existed outside of her intellectual sphere. Relocating my gaze to a swirl in the table's woodgrain, I mumbled, "Fin O'Sullivan. Lover of...um... lesfic and bacon butties. Taxi driver, for my sins."

Tessa growled, actually growled, and I flinched in embarrassment. When I dared to glance at her, I was relieved to see the corners of her mouth twitching upwards in a smirk.

"You lot're fucking lethal," she said. "Always cutting me up on t'left hand turn when I'm on me bike."

"Arrogant, kamikaze bastards, you cyclists. You think you own the roads, and the Highway Code applies to everyone but you. And don't get me started on Lycra."

Tessa opened her mouth to speak, then she abruptly snapped it shut, her brow creasing. There was a brief silence, followed by a chuckle, then a full-blown smile. Then we both laughed. An hour or so passed in easy conversation. She seemed to take pleasure in winding me up and making me blush, and I surprised myself by how quickly I relaxed into bantering with her. When she left that evening, having somehow managed to drink more cups of tea than me—no mean feat I can tell you—I patted myself on the back and basked in the smug warmth of my dexterous handling of the room-renting situation. Carl was on his way home, and the room had a dyke occupant.

Life looked good to me back then.

Hormones Rising

MOST PEOPLE HAVE A bit of a negative thing about mornings but for me, particularly of late, weekday mornings have become a welcome change. How long have I been spending my weekends shiftily shuffling about the house in my tatty bathrobe, doing little other than avoiding Tessa? She didn't come home last night, and I have to admit that I was more than a little surprised at my own jealousy. Jealousy of whoever she spent the night with, I mean, not of the fact that she spent the night with someone, if that's what she did, of course.

Slipping sharply from third to second, I take a left corner too quickly and find myself mounting the kerb slightly. A short, round woman in a duffle coat scowls her disgust at me, and I shoot her an apologetic grimace in return. I glue my eyes to the road ahead, the bin bag in the centre, that annoying traffic-calming island, and the bicycled Dread cutting me up from the left. It's nearly seven, and I've got my skates on, merrily speeding to Queen's Park and beyond. The logical conclusion for Tessa not coming home last night is that she spent the night at Deb and Juno's place, and I'm going with that explanation right now. I'm also well aware that the indignant tiger moths in my stomach are duelling with good reason though. I mean, what if?

Yeah. My life seems to be an open-ended soap opera these days, and the script writers are none too kind. A cursory glance at the clock on the dash confirms that I'm ludicrously early for this morning's pick-up, so I head for Operation Big Breakfast. With a head full of Tessa, secrets and lies, and the Brother Man's return, I ran out of the house without so much as a cup of tea in my stomach.

Mum'd kill me; she always made us kids down at least one bowl of Cream of Wheat before she'd let us leave the house of a morning. Cue miserable guilt seeping into my consciousness from far-left field. I haven't called my parents for months and months now, and I dunno if they're alive and, well, living the life of several Reillys way out there in the Kingston. What I do know is that Frank's back.

I swing the car into a space on the Broadway just in front of Maisie's Cafe. Dunno who Maisie is or was, but these days Mad Gil the Gooner serves a mean toasted bacon sandwich and gives free refills of tea to boot. The café windows are already reassuringly steamed up; seems like I'm not the only nutter out and about at this ungodly hour, when most of London's still tucked up warm and cosy in their beds. I pick my way through tables occupied by manual workers tucking into Full Englishes, nod at Gil, and grunt my order.

"Take a seat, love. I'll bring it over."

Don't mind if I do, son. Gil's a hefty-looking geezer with bushy eyebrows and fat, pink sausages for fingers. He is dressed, as ever, in jogging pants and a vast Arsenal shirt, which is struggling to cover his protruding belly. I come here a couple of times a week and have been doing so for more years than I care to remember, so Gil is quite used to me, and I'm quite comfortable with him. I'm more than aware of the furtive glances and whispers I trigger amongst the men though. Yeah, yeah. I'm a long, lean, Black dyke dressed in black. Get used to it, boys. I sigh, my first of the day, wishing I really was that confident around other human beings. I'm about to go off all maudlin when Gil delivers my egg and crispy bacon, side order of bread and butter, and a suitably oversized mug of tea.

"D'you see the lads last night, eh, eh?"

Gil's eyes are gleaming as he dispenses his culinary bounty. The man's a complete nutter when it comes to football, and though I've known him for some time, he hasn't abandoned the idea of converting me to the fold. The sporting fold, that is. Gil's cool with me being a dyke on account of him having a gay nephew (his sister's boy, who Gil's been a second father to). Gil went round his sister's house and "gave her what for" when she and her husband were less than positive about the gay teenager in their midst. This I know because he retells the story every other time I come in. He makes me smile, Gooner Gil.

"Mate, I keep telling ya, I bleedin' 'ate football, and even if I didn't, I'd be Lillywhite. My brother'd kill me if I so much as looked at another team."

Sad, but true. Frank's been back for less than twenty-four hours, and he's already been enquiring about tickets for Saturday's home game. My response has tickled Gil, and he walks away laughing, deftly swinging his vast frame down the aisle between the tables as he returns to his serving counter.

"You wanna do yourself a favour and come down the Emirates sometime, Fin. You and that other sad bastard over there."

Gil gestures towards a lanky young man in painters' whites who is sitting with his mates in the front window. This is the cue for the rest of the group to indulge in what I imagine passes for lighthearted (expletive-loaded), building site banter, with the unfortunate tosher being the object of their ridicule. Said geezer finally rises to his feet, pulls his T-shirt up and over his head, raises his arms, palms outstretched, and reveals the cockerel tattoo on the left side of his chest. Despite my football aversion, I smile and raise my mug in salute as, ignoring the volley of verbal abuse, he launches into a shaky rendition of "Tottenham till I die." I'm briefly tempted to join in their carousing but, right on cue, my leather-clad, conscience-stabbing demon appears. In the blink of an eye, I'm catapulted back to the pressing worries of my current life.

Ach! I'd barely finished filling Frank in on the sorry tale of the good doctor and I yesterday, before he drop-kicked me with that statement about not being happy. What was I supposed to do with that?

I'm distracted from that thought by the sound of wooden

chairs being scraped over ceramic floor tiles. The builder boys are leaving. Even the sight of a bunch of daft lads arguing over whose turn it is to get the bill fails to produce a smile from my tightly pursed lips. Tessa, Queen of Yorkshire, is well and truly in my head this morning, and I have a feeling that tutting, sighing, and shaking my head ain't gonna do the business for me today. There's no denying that deep down I *am* unhappy, and the Tessa stuff's only a small part of it. I can remember, down to the second, the last time that I was truly happy. The acid in my stomach gurgles. I've lost my appetite, and I don't want to go any further down this road. I don't even want to finish my tea. I rise from my seat, cross the café, and plonk a handful of coins on Gil's counter.

"Gotta go, mate. Didn't realise the time."

Waving away his kind, half-hearted protestations, I all but bolt out of the door and onto the empty Broadway. God will, I know, forgive my tiny white lie. He will understand the electric chair jolt that surged through my body when I allowed myself to own up to the truth about my unhappiness. The awful, shameful truth. How long have I spent pretending that everything is hunky dory, pushing the reality out of my mind? Frank makes me confront myself, damn him. Deborah annoys me, pokes, and prods me into tossing unwelcome thoughts around in my head before I manage to bury them under a pile of other to-dos, but Frank? Frank slips an arm around my shoulders, quietly whispers, "What is it, Noo? How can I help?" in my ear, and I've reached the end of my ability to procrastinate.

Mentally pencilling in a long overdue confessional session for this Saturday, I scurry back to the familiarity of my car, where I'm briefly comforted by performing my usual start-up routine. Briefly. I head off towards my pickup, acutely aware that the bubbling nausea in my stomach will nuzzle, nudge, and eventually force me to take the time to revisit the scene of my last happy moment.

Unfortunately, this morning's client always likes to work on her laptop in silence when we go to the airport. Works for me usually but today, I find myself longing for conversation and inane chit chat, anything at all to stop my brain from dragging me back through time and memories. Naturally, it ain't happening. I turn left, I turn right, I negotiate roundabouts, dual carriageways, and a fair chunk of the M25, and my passenger sits with her head in a laptop, oblivious to my mental anguish. I smile at a little girl on the zebra crossing in front of me. Her two front top teeth are missing, and she has bobbles in her hair. Her mum is clasping her hand tightly, gritting her teeth as she negotiates the hordes of travellers and their hordes of designer luggage milling in front of the airport. Those two aren't travelling today. I think they're probably here to meet someone. Mum's anxious, the girl's excited, and I wish I was her instead of my miserable self.

Cue a half prayer to Saint Christina the Astonishing in the hope that she'll make it happen. She doesn't, of course, and I'm left opening the car door for the client, nodding and smiling professionally, thanking her profusely for the meagre tip. And then I'm alone again. I'm driving back to London with the windows open. The cold, damp air is whipping my cheeks, burning my earlobes, and causing a thin drop of transparent snot to seep from my icy nose. I'm on auto pilot, driving with a fury, trying to put distance between myself and the memory.

I can't.

I'm not going home, not now. I can't face them, the people who know me so well. It's four days till Grier arrives and when she does, I won't be able to face her either. Not while that memory is still gnawing away in my gut anyway. When the Epping Forest turn off comes into focus, I change lanes and take the slip road. I pull into the car park, jump out, and find myself a suitably gloomy place to mope.

PM Tea

I'M LYING ON THE still damp grass, staring at the sky. It's blue, unusual for this time of year, methinks. And there I go again, thinking like her. I'm AWOL. Okay, maybe that's a bit dramatic. I could claim to be taking my lunch break, I suppose, but I did the Gatwick drop and now I don't want to go back. It's Monday, and the office will be full of people, and noise, and other stuff that annoys me. Finance Girl (whose name I can never remember) is in on Mondays, along with Jeanie the Motormouth Controller, and the valet guys, all gossiping nineteen to the dozen. Why are blokes such gossip hounds? My miserable mood demands answers, and that blue sky's not offering any. I'm sure that the cloud on the right, the puffy, angry-looking one, is pointing a finger at me. Can clouds actually have fingers? This one's got three, and I swear one of them's just identified me from a line-up of useless specimen earthlings.

My inner angels and demons are offering no assistance either. Red Leather Girl is prodding me with a toasting fork and Wedding Dress Girl is looking sorrowful, but they're both asking *me* what's up. Like I'd know. I'm glad that Frank's back. All my life, he's driven me barking bonkers, but it's a kind of irritation that I can live with. Usually. I'm the eldest, nine and a half minutes to be precise and though I've always been the one to take the lead in whatever we've done, I've always cast one eye behind myself, just to keep a lookout on what he's thinking and doing. I reckon God created me first but got a bit distracted when it came to allocating personalities. Frank's way more together than I am and should definitely have been the older, wiser twin.

I wipe the salty trail from my cheek with the back of my hand and shield my eyes from the weak spring sun to scowl at the pointing cloud and beyond. Day after day, and week, month and year after year, I've been dragging my sorry carcass out of bed. As the sun has risen, so have I. I've performed my rituals, interacted with the world at large. I've passed the time of day with my mates, cried at the usual sad films and love songs.

It's not enough.

I'm treading water and have been doing so for much longer than I care to remember. And that's just it really; I don't care to remember. I haven't been happy for such a long time, and it's not about Gree, Tessa, or even Sue before her.

"Pah!"

Sue was sweet, a thoroughly decent, caring woman, and I stole two years of her life. For two long years, I let her believe that I'd have a real, grown-up relationship with her one day. Shifts permitting, Sue made dinner for me a couple of times a week, extended her Florence Nightingale work to her relationship with me. She never made any real demands or asked any difficult questions of me. Like a little prince, I was free to come and go as I pleased. Sex, even romance, were both optional in that relationship. Sue would patiently wait for me to "open up" and in the meantime, whatever I wanted was just fine.

When she finally 'fessed up that she was planning to move West (country or London, I wasn't altogether sure) with that really nice junior doctor woman, the one who was on the permanent night shifts, I felt nothing at all. They had started seeing each other romantically about a month before she made her tearful confession. Among the snatched canteen coffee moments and the corridor nods and winks, it just sort of happened. She hadn't been looking for it, she said as she pleaded for my forgiveness. She really hadn't meant to hurt me...

She didn't, and I wasn't. I felt sorry for her, really. I had slouched low into the soft Starbucks sofa, rubbing my eyes with my fingertips and feeling all kinds of miserable. I was sorry that I'd given her so little, and sorry that I'd made her feel bad about wanting more of me. That she felt guilty and felt the need to explain herself to me for wanting more than I'd given her had brought it all crashing home. Whatever had gone on in her mind, I'd been idly treading water with her. It hadn't been a relationship so much as a parking bay. I had parallel-parked in the safe warmth of being Susan Barrett's girlfriend, and I broke her heart along the way.

I'm not going back. My eyes are narrowed in desperate concentration as I search the scurrying clouds for inspiration. The spring dampness of the earth beneath me is seeping through my clothes and into my bones, as if the earth is trying to reclaim me, sorry body and soul. If I lie here, all still and silent, maybe the ground will gradually suck the life from my bony bod, finally opening up to swallow the lifeless bag of bones that was once Fionnuala O'Sullivan II. Named after my grandma, y'see. The image of that formidable matriarch glaring her disapproval from the mantelpiece photo jerks me out of my self-indulgence and into an upright position, hugging my knees for support.

I *do* remember when I was last happy, the moment when I last felt a pure and harmonious mellowness, coupled with a wave of general well-being, and the memory causes my lips to purse, and my eyes to screw themselves tightly shut. I pinch the bridge of my nose and puff my cheeks out, but neither action helps. I pray to an assortment of Catholic saints and icons, but that doesn't help either. A little more eye rubbing ensues before I spring to my feet and stride purposefully towards the coin-gobbling meter which is renting me London street space by the six-minute slot. Red-eyed and with a face like a well-smacked arse, I slide behind the wheel of my trusty cocoon, turn the key in the ignition, and flick a CD into life. Of all the songs on all the compilations in all the lonely cars of this world, it had to be Nina. Madame Simone bursts forth from my speakers, imploring me to break down and let it all out. I don't. I exhale a long, slow breath. An eerie calm has settled on me. I lean forward, slowly, purposefully, and position my head on the leather-clad steering wheel. What the hell is it about Nina Simone that reminds me of Grier, reminds me of the last time I was truly happy? The demon girl prods her pitchfork into my stomach, cackling wildly as she forces me to watch the replay of that night in full HD. Fine. So be it. I close my eyes, lol my head back on the headrest, and let the bittersweet memories come...

I'm moody and restless, shuffling my Docs and squirming in my seat. Grier pauses for a brief moment, pulls back from her tripod-mounted camera, and throws me a pleading look. In return, I bare my teeth in a not altogether mock glare. I have absolutely no desire to be trapped in a musty old music hall on a Saturday night, surrounded by the Political Lesbian Great and Good, watching the Artistic Lesbian Crap and Crapper strut their gut-churning stuff. Gree's still pleading though. Answering her gesture with a smile, I too plead silently and for all I'm worth. Lover girl shakes her beautiful head and returns her attention to the camera. She is sporting a luxurious head of curls, like a dark dyke Annie amongst the variously shaved masses. At her insistence, Harry the Barber has obliterated all traces of the famous O'Sullivan corkscrew curls, leaving me with a sharply razored flat top. I feel like a sheep in August, but hey, she likes it, and God, I like her! I'm trying to be magnanimous about this; my darling Gree's an artist, and this is work. Later, I too will work, safely and soberly driving several of these artistes—and I use the word loosely—to their chosen destinations, and it will be her turn to wait for me. Finally, at night's end we will be reunited and crawl under the duvet together to continue our all-consuming passion for one another, the thought of which creates a smouldering warmth within my jeans. Sucking in a breath of air, I return my gaze to the stage, vowing to be more supportive and less horny.

The act is just about rounding off. The two women on the stage are shrieking in unison, arms flailing wildly, as they beseech the audience to "stand firm." I slump a little further into my seat in solidarity. The audience erupts in a cacophony of shrieking applause—God, these feminist types don't do anything quietly—and I politely slap my palms together a couple of times. And then, from speakers positioned I don't know where, the soothing sound of Nina Simone wafts my way. Now that's more like it. I close my eyes to savour the delicious moment and feel a sweet, warm breath against my ear.

"Mm, darling one! Wish I could skive this one and whisk you off home right now."

Darling Gree, you and me both. When I open my eyes, my Grier is smiling down at me as she positions herself on my knees, straddling my thighs. Her eyelids are heavy with unspoken desire, her lips parting slightly as she moves in to kiss me. She is so very beautiful, and I am hard-pressed not to throw her to the ground and have my wicked way with her there and then in the Upper Circle of the Hackney Empire. Instead, I slide my hands inside her T-shirt, wrap my arms around her waist, pull her in close, and attempt to sail down her throat with my tongue. She breaks away from my tonsil Olympics for a brief moment, just long enough to mesmerise me with her beautiful eyes.

"You'll never know how much I love you, my sweet. It's quite impossible to put a value to it." Her low, husky whisper speaks of passion and lust.

Then she presses her body firmly against my own, nibbling at my ear lobe as she murmurs promises of the explicit kind. I see her face, I see us, as if from above, two bodies wound tightly together, heat emanating in smoky shafts from the union. Never, never in a million years could I have imagined that it would be possible for me, wimpy uncool O'Sullivan, to be so utterly, deliriously happy. My eyes are filled with a glorious vision of my own sweet Grier, leaning in to express her love for me in kisses. I am full, I am complete. I am happy.

Frowning, I jerk my head back front and centre, and the car park materialises in sharp focus. In my head, I hear the sound of a stylus being abruptly dragged off a vinyl record. "Fuck." I blink away tears and mentally slam my finger on the pause button before the memory can re-run the moment I became truly unhappy. I need to move, literally and figuratively, away from my past.

I turn the key and head home. It has finally dawned on me that I'm days away from my next period, hence the bullets for nipples, the niggling tenderness in my lower back, and worst of all, this stupid snivelling at the drop of a hat. That said, I forgive myself for snarling at the evil pedestrians who deliberately step out in front of me when I'm doing twenty-five to thirty, and for cutting up the flash Audi TT bloke, just because. In my infinite wisdom, I decide that I have spent far too much time in my own head of late, and as I inch the car into a tiny slip of a parking space with the dexterity of a pro, I promise myself that I will be more sociable. It's time to lose myself in some silly time with the prodigal brother and catch up with the soap opera that is Rebecca's current love life. I cut the engine with a flourish and celebrate my newfound resolve by popping a couple of Feminax. Then I remember that I still have the Tessa situation to negotiate.

Being Monday, I don't expect her to be home, but I let myself in with ninja stealth anyway. All appears quiet on the north-eastern front as I step into the hallway, so I head for the kitchen in search of milk to wash the pills down. This house is never completely empty, even when we're all out at work. By the third or fourth step, I can smell garlic wafting from beyond the closed door, accompanied by a reassuring sizzling. My stomach reminds me that I haven't eaten since this morning's half a butty at Gil's, and knowing that it couldn't possibly be the kitchen-phobic Tessa inside, I enter with confidence.

The man standing at my kitchen sink with his back to me is peeling potatoes. Barefooted, he is dressed, as usual, in shorts and vest. Doesn't he own anything else? I'm surprisingly happy to see him, and I cross the room with a leap and a bound to greet him. Well, okay, not quite a leap and bound, more of a swaggering shuffle really, but it's a positive shuffle.

"Hey, Fin!" He turns and, holding his wet arms in the air, he proffers a cheek in my direction.

My lips smack soundly against a stubbly cheek as he puckers up to kiss fresh air. He looks genuinely pleased to see me, and I'm enjoying that response right now, given how rarely it comes my way. "How's it going, Dazza?" I retrieve a carton of milk from the fridge, which I sniff with suspicion before gulping a large mouthful.

His face contorts into an expression of utter revulsion. "Oi! Use a glass, can't you?" He points to the stack of freshly washed crockery on the draining board. "Remind me not to let you anywhere near my kitchen."

I blow him a kiss and plonk myself down at the table. I toy with the idea of continuing the wind him up by sticking my feet on the table but reject that one on the grounds of it being a bridge too far for the unfortunate chef. Darren returns to the task in hand, and we remain comfortably silent for a minute or two before engaging in our usual manner.

"What's for—"

"Chicken casserole with dumplings."

The said chicken, I note, has already been browned and is snuggling at the bottom of the dish under a mound of freshly diced carrot and swede. Darren returns his attention to the spuds in the butler sink, a slight frown playing on his eyebrows as he mutters to nobody in particular.

"And I suppose you want me to—" I rise to my feet.

"Yeah, great. You can blanche the beans for me." He pauses and stirs the simmering pan of stock before taking a minute sip. "A little olive oil, a sprinkling of flaked almonds, and we're good to go."

Domestic Goddess, I ain't, but I can hold my own in a kitchen, Mum made sure of that. I haven't the foggiest idea why Darren Tolley is in our kitchen on a Monday afternoon, but I'm certainly not one to turn my nose up at home-cooked food, and these days we have a pretty easy-going relationship. Wasn't always like that, mind you. The first time that Carl brought him home, I was tempted to run around the house nailing down the valuables and adding locks to all the doors. Okay, so none of us actually had any possessions of value at the time, but you get the drift. My impression was of a young, junkie rent boy. He's actually only five years younger than me (and fifteen younger than Carl), but he's always had an elfin, artful dodger look about him. He's not coy about his early sex worker years, in fact he reeled off his entire life story to me one afternoon, over a half bottle of whisky and an ocean of tea. He hadn't been looking for sympathy—he's probably the most resilient person I've ever met—but I'd immediately warmed to the guy, awarding him honorary little brother status in my heart that day.

What are the chances of a shifty, junkie rent boy running in to, literally running into, the arms of someone who was prepared to give a shit at the worst moment of his life? You know me, I'm not exactly Carl Miller's fan club secretary, but I have to give him credit where it's due. When Darren all but knocked him off his feet that day, Carl's response had been to buy the guy a sandwich and a cup of coffee. Carl says he'd noticed Darren around before that meeting, had given him spare change, and passed the time of day with him on several occasions. Carl says that Darren had pursued him like a banshee, enticing him away from Johnny, his boyfriend at the time, by supernatural means. Dazza claims that Carl was ludicrously cheap, willingly becoming his sex slave for the knockdown cost of a short Interflora campaign. The truth, I suspect, lies somewhere between the two (with sordid details that I really don't care to know), but Carl and Dazza swiftly became an item, and Johnny became toast. I don't suppose I can denounce him as a home wrecker too vigorously, on account of me being the fly in the ointment between Gree and that Mad Cassie woman. Not one to stand on ceremony, Gree had waited a full twenty-four hours after our Greenham Common meeting before leaving a message on Cassie's answerphone. Gay men are far more civilised about these things. Apparently, Johnny had simply shrugged and kept Carl's on-loan leather bike jacket. That and his Carl Zeiss zoom lens *and* his bicycle. I would've taken a bullet between the eyeballs in defence of my relationship with the lovely Grier in those days, that's how smitten I was back then. And then she left me, wounded and pining, eight years ago. Hah! This reflection brings me spinning back to Dazza and the casserole, the here and now, and the impending arrival of Grier and her girlfriend, Novia bastard Delgado, now a mere four days off.

Dazza's whistling as he slices up the spuds, and I'm pulling the string off the runner beans with all the dexterity of a sous chef. Having completed his catering college stint, he's gone all celebrity chef on us, but I'm certainly not complaining. We used to have a rotation system for our Friday night house dinners; Carl would cook a roast dinner one week; I'd do macaroni cheese and fried chicken the next. Of course, when Gree was here, she used to surprise us with something seafoody—prawns, or scallops, or something—loads of garlic and chopped coriander. We excused Frank from kitchen duty on the grounds that we wanted to spend our weekends out clubbing and the like, as opposed to being in a close clinch with the toilet bowl. Later, on the Fridays that Tessa wasn't rushing off to Leeds for the weekend, she would order pizza for us.

Tessa. I pause, bean in hand, thinking about the time we spent together when things were, you know, normal. I didn't really notice her around the house in the beginning. I was just smugly satisfied with the fact that I'd managed to pull off the find-a-housemate thingy. Carl liked her from the off though. I'd come home some evenings, and they'd be sprawled across the sofas in the living room, gabbing on about Puritans, the Industrial Revolution, or the representation of women in the post-modern era. She always tried to drag me in, protesting as I tried to escape, attacking the stairs two at a time. I really can't hack it with those intellectual types, so I don't even try. I always left that stuff to Gree and her crowd.

The final de-stringed bean hits the bowl with a satisfying ping. A cursory check of the pan of water simmering on the cooker reveals that we are good to go, and I prepare to dump my beans in their blanching bath. The near-naked chef releases a near-girlie scream of horror, and I stop dead in my tracks, beans held aloft.

"For fuck's sake, Fin!" Darren charges across the room and snatches the bowl from my hands. He has the manic look of a man possessed. "Slice them first, you savage dyke!"

"I'll slice you in a minute, son."

Darren throws his head back and laughs with real amusement. "You're soft as shit, my friend. I know it, you know it, and those frigging beans know it. Give."

He plucks the knife from my hand and frowns into the bowl, checking for evidence of my culinary incompetence. I acknowledge his grudging nod with a lavish bow, drawing circles in the air with my right hand.

"I am Don Alejandro of Castile, and I have come to torture your heretic beans," I say, surprising myself with a quick giggle. Darren chuckles and throws his arm around my shoulder. I lean into him and place a loud sloppy kiss on his forehead. "You have a knack of making me smile, Daz," I say, the gloom of the day finally lifting from my weary being.

Darren squirms. "Um...yeah, but...and don't torture me, I forgot to tell you."

I scowl when he drops his arm and moves quickly away from me. He chef-chops the beans before dumping them in the pan with a swoosh. Then he turns back to face me and delivers the G-Bomb.

Not Friday. Wednesday.

Grier will be arriving two days early, the knowledge of which cluster bombs my brain with panic, interspersed with bittersweet memories of long ago. And just like that, the swirling grey gloom returns, inching its venomous claws up my body, threatening to swallow me whole. And, just to compound my misery, the tell-tale sound of Tessa's bike wheels echoes up the stairwell. Perfect timing.

I'm praying that she'll plonk down the bike, and simply turn and sprint upstairs to her room. *Oh, please. Oh, please!* Frank told me that I could sort this out, but he's not here now, and I'm a jellyfish, minus the sting. I thank God that the price of alternative London accommodation and the proximity of Tessa's workplace have combined to keep her ensconced in the room above me. It's torture to have her so near and yet so far from me, but I really don't know what I would've done if she'd upped and left after my New Year shenanigans. I inhale a sharp, shallow breath, and my hand moves instinctively to soothe the ache in my wounded chest. I'm living on borrowed time, very much aware that this uncomfortable living arrangement can't continue indefinitely. I request the assistance of various saints and icons; *please let her just go straight to her room so I don't have to face her now.*

No such luck. She attacks the polished brass door handle like a woman possessed—maybe by a genuine need for food, it being teatime and all—and then, before our recent past has chance to flash before me, she flings open the door and marches on in. She's hot and sweaty from the cycling, and a long strand of sandy hair has glued itself to the side of her face. Her cheeks are glowing pink and shiny. Now where have I seen that particular look before? Our eyes briefly meet across the garlicky kitchen, then mine automatically hit the deck, but not before clocking her half snarl of indignation on seeing me. Those mock-slate floor tiles hold a certain fascination for me right now. It's funny, but I'd really never noticed that the grout in between the tiles is also grey.

I clear my throat and scrape my chair back a touch, shuffling as if about to rise and do something important, and thankfully, Tessa chooses to ignore me. Darren, who has been perched on the washing machine, watching us like we're contestants in a reality TV show, wriggles himself to a standing position and flashes Tessa a grin. She squeezes her body behind my chair to cross the room to kiss him. Her hand brushes across my shoulder as she does so, the very faintest of touches, and for a split second, I find myself unable to breathe. Those tiles are fascinating, I swear to God.

I'm sick and tired of this situation, literally. This malignant silence between us causes the acid to rise in my stomach, and my limbs to ache. I'm a forty-year-old woman, sitting at my kitchen table, stealing sly glances at my thirty-two-year-old housemate who is, of course, so much more to me. I've been pretending that I can go about my business avoiding her, pretending that it's possible to ignore the thunderous silence which pollutes the air whenever we're together. I can't. I don't want to. I want to resolve this nightmare once and for all. I just don't know how. "I'm sorry" doesn't seem like enough when I've lobbed a hand grenade and blown our lives apart in one stupid move.

"How can you possibly resist? My dumplings are legendary!"

Darren is poking her in the back now, as she pours herself a large mug of orange juice. She turns, grinning her chipped-toothy grin at him, and raises an eyebrow. I watch them from the safety of my bowed head.

"Sorry, I have plans tonight, O, my Master Chef!" she says, giggling.

As she sweeps a clump of sandy hair behind her left ear, my heart performs an Olympic medal-winning somersault in response. She has plans, she has a date, she is seeing someone romantically, and it ain't me. I don't know why I'm surprised at this revelation, but I am knocked for six. In all my arrogant pondering, in all of my extensive navel contemplations, did I really imagine that she would spend the rest of her life in weeds, lamenting the demise of her momentous romance with the irreplaceable Fionnuala O'Sullivan?

Dazza is teasing her and, somewhat unusually, she is allowing it. The acorn of anxiety that planted itself in my stomach when she sauntered through the kitchen door is spreading its tendrils of misery through my body, inching up my windpipe. I swallow hard. Twice. Somewhere in my head, a gospel choir harmonises to a cruel crescendo the name of my chief suspect, the irritating student woman I do not wish to acknowledge.

"You've got a hot date, you dark horse, you!" Dazza's beautiful eyes are glinting with the gossipy delight of it.

Still smiling, index finger pressed to her tightly closed lips, Tessa shakes her head. She strides to the fridge to replace the juice carton. A "Don't go there" sign looms darkly above the three of us.

"Ooh-err, Becks!" Darren emits an irritating squeal of delight before cupping both hands over his mouth. "Don't tell me it's that Aussie kid?" He stoops to check the casserole, which is fragrantly bubbling in the oven.

I pray to a cocktail of specially blended Catholic saints for an earthquake, tidal wave, or anything that will bring an end to the torture of hearing about it. Accidently, and faster than a speeding bullet, my eyes have shot from the floor to Tessa's. My emotions are written all over my miserable face, and I'm humiliated that she has seen it. I'm a suckling pig, basted with this titbit of unwanted information, apple in mouth, impaled on a bloody hot spit. Dazza continues to crank the spit handle. Bastard.

A sharp intake of breath, a screech of chair legs, and I rise from the table. I'm flustered, awkward and ungainly, but my need to get out far outweighs my usual desire to be cool. I need to lie down, to rest my burning cheeks on the cool cotton of my duvet cover. I need to derail the train of images of Tessa and the Aussie which is pulling in to my jealousy station. My hand reaches out in an involuntary spasm of a movement to straighten the salt and pepper mills on the table, buying a few precious seconds in which to regain a modicum of composure. I know that she's watching me, but I can't bring myself to return her gaze.

"Right." At last, a sound escapes my lips and thankfully, my voice is relatively even in pitch. "Um...I've gotta go. I'll see you later, Daz." And then, incredibly, I turn to face Tessa. Her head is slightly bowed, but her eyes are turned up, eyebrows poised in question. "See you tomorrow then, I guess." Where that came from, I have no idea. Why I choose to make my conversational debut at this particular moment in time, after all my months of sulky silence and avoidance, I really can't say. Maybe the conversation with Frank and all the ruminating are having an effect. Tessa locks her eyes onto my own for a second, no longer, and then looks away.

"Yes, I'll be here, Fin," she says cooly. "Just as I have been every single day. I live here."

A rogue muscle in my cheek jumps into a visible wince. I cannot get out of there and into the sanctuary of my bedroom fast enough.

What the hell was all that about? I'm trying to make sense of my hell's-in-my-kitchen moment earlier and not getting very far. I'm sitting at one end of the table, pushing my fork around a plate of half-eaten casserole, trying desperately to avoid a particularly moody-looking dumpling. Frank has been filling the boys in on the whole *Peanut O'Sullivan: The Missing Years* saga, and I've drifted off into my own little hellish world again.

The boys are gabbing on about God knows what, hooting and squealing like a bunch of pre-pubescent girls. What I'd give to be able to legitimately bow out, to escape back to the safety of my bedroom, and pop a couple more Feminax right now. It's too late to make my exit; their voices rise with excitement as they cheerfully debate some trivia or other. Unfortunately for me, I hear my name and, before I know what's what, I find three sets of eager eyes turned my way.

"Eh? What?" Forcing a chunk of chicken breast into my mouth, I look at them all. Directly opposite, Frank is nodding expectantly as he scratches his beardy chin. To his left, Carl is cleaning his glasses with the sleeve of his cashmere jumper. His head is bowed, but his grin is nonetheless evident. Leaning behind Carl, arms draped around his neck, Darren is giving me the mischievous, as opposed to downright evil, eye.

"Lindsey."

He says the name like a fait accompli, as if its very mention will propel me into a state of great enlightenment, which I will share with them all. I am none the wiser. They've obviously been discussing some celebrity, though I can't for the life of me figure out why they think I might have input. Two gay boys and a metrosexual must surely have a wider knowledge of matters current than the antisocial, geeky dyke in their midst. I grimace and shake my head, returning my attention to the dumpling in hand.

"Dyke or Hasbian?"

Dazza's starting to worry me now. He's staring at me in earnest, his long-lashed almond eyes demanding a reply. Frank tries to suppress a giggle, which emerges as a snort, his shoulders heaving in silent mirth. Carl finally gives up on his stab at self-control, allowing his tightly pursed lips to slacken and the broad grin to light up his face. Darren has, by this stage, completely lost it; he's gripping the back of Carl's chair for support as he giggles like a child. I'm aware that I'm missing something here, but I'm really not in the mood for it tonight. I push my plate aside and rise from the table, preparing to take my leave. "Aw, fuck this," I mutter at no one in particular. "I'm off to bed."

That proclamation kills the giggling...for a second or two, and then all three start up again. Somewhere in the annuls of my miserable mind, a penny clanks noisily on a stone floor and a 100-watt bulb illuminates my consciousness. I stop in my tracks, midway between the table and the door, spin around to face the three witches, and point an accusatory finger at Daz.

"Fucking hash fudge, you bastards!" I say, slowly drawing each word out.

The guilty boys collapse in a tittering heap, and I struggle to suppress a chuckle myself. Odd are, Dazza's to blame for this, so I advance on him with all the menace of a woman scorned. "Give."

Darren knows that he's been busted. I won't stop until vengeance is mine, and he knows it. He empties the contents of his shorts' pockets onto the table and steps back, leaving me to examine the evidence before me. A packet of red Rizla with one corner missing, a pair of nail clippers, a couple of fivers, a handful of silver coins, a jewellery bag stuffed with grass, and finally, a small lump of dark brown stuff wrapped in cling film. Never one to stand on ceremony, I pounce on the thing, unwrap it, and pop it into my mouth. A familiar tang hits my taste buds, the essence of good times in bygone days. As I chew, I take time to savour the aroma before swallowing it down. I don't much feel like staying up and giggling with the lads tonight, what with the hormonal mood I'm in, but this serendipitous offering will certainly help the Feminax go down in the most delightful way.

As I pass Frank's chair, he grabs my thigh and gives it a squeeze. "Good to be home, sis," he says, his red-rimmed eyes twinkling.

I am struck by the realisation that we are all still behaving like the daft kids we were when we first met. We've refused to grow up, but time's moved on anyway, and it ain't about to wait for us to catch up. Shifty dole boy is a practising solicitor, disco bunny art boy is a successful film maker, and rent-a-twink is a jobbing chef. That just leaves me then, and Gree. What will this socially inept dyke become when she grows up? And the $64,000 question? What has become of Grier these last eight years? I'll leave that one alone for tonight, preferring to mock-slap my brother about the head as I take my leave instead.

"Good to have you back, Peanut," I say. "Really good, bruv." On the other side of the kitchen door, I hesitate and hover at the foot of the stairs. I don't know if I'm overly hormonal or just getting old, but I feel a stab of sadness on leaving the giggling trio. They all seem to have managed to slip into their middle ages seamlessly, retaining the essence of their youth in the process. I, on the other hand, seem to be stuck treading water in a stagnant pond, but I know that it can't last forever. I'm all too aware that unless I do something, *change* something about this miserable existence of mine, the thick, slimy reeds will envelop me and drag me down to where Ophelia awaits with open arms.

You're So Young, and I'm So Old...

MY BEDROOM HAS ALWAYS been a safe haven, a sanctuary from all of the world's ills. After Gree left, I holed up in here, unwilling and unable to face the world at large, in my gloom. A slight shuffle and a minor rearranging of the pillows accompanies that particular thought. I'm warm, comfortable, and suitably stoned, cocooned in my luxuriously thick duvet as I draw deeply on a well-crafted rollie. Inevitably, I fall into the thinking about the past again.

In all the time we had together, I can't remember me and Gree ever arguing. We just didn't. We got along well together, never really disagreeing on anything of substance. Day-to-day disagreements would lead to a sulky strop of varying intensity on my part, always accompanied by a delicious period of make-up intimacy, crafted and orchestrated by Gree. A half smile ventures onto my frowning face at that particular memory, and I exhale a sharp, smoky lungful. Fat rings of grey smoke chase one another towards the ceiling. I'm thinking of Gree, her impish eyes drawing me in as, one hand on my belt loop, she would plead her case and ultimately get her way. I would have given her anything, done anything she had cared to ask for. I loved her so completely back then.

Straining to reach the ashtray on my bedside table, I crush the life out of my rollie with venom. Yeah, I had loved her unconditionally, and yeah, we had never seriously fallen out about anything that couldn't be resolved with more of our fast and furious lovemaking. But ultimately, and despite all of the above, I still wound up sobbing and clutching my duvet as my beloved raced away from our relationship and our home, Barcelona-bound. A long, slow inhalation of breath, and I reach for the comfort of my baccy pouch again. It's a slender, dark brown leather thing, and it has my initials on it. It was a present from Gree a million years ago. I'm aware that I will, I *must*, play out the final days of my relationship with Gree in my head. I've done it before, a million times or more, believe me, and I still have no answers. I just don't know why she left, why I let her, and why we haven't gotten back together after all the time that has since passed.

And then there's Tessa. Funny, sweet Tessa, who terrifies and delights me in equal measure. I think about that day we spent on the beach at Southend and remember the tenderness with which she wrapped the blanket around my shoulders when I'd shivered against the bracing wind. I remember her voice, her soft murmurings about nothing in particular, as I had bitten my lips to prevent myself from uttering words that I knew that I would surely regret. *Remember what happened the last time you said that to a woman?* Demon girl had appeared that day in the nick of time. Probably.

My eyes are drawn toward a lumpy shadow in the middle of the ceiling, a remnant from the Great Flood, and I'm again reminded of my own peculiar obsession with the two women who bob in and out and in and out of my life. Grier. Tessa. Five-lettered, black widow tormentors who, despite my best efforts, continue to draw me in with their invisible threads even as they pay attention to others caught in their web, leaving me swinging. I shift and squirm under the duvet as I suck on that thought. I've been staring so hard at the water stain on the ceiling that my eyes are filling with water, and I have to blink hard to force it back. Well, that's my story, and I'm sticking to it. I've FUBARed our relationship as far as Tessa's concerned, but try as I might, I still can't explain what happened with me and Gree. One moment we're canoodling in the Hackney Empire and next thing I know, she's running after that sodding playgirl (whose name I can barely speak without spitting, cursing, and crossing myself twice) out of my life and into a new one with *her*.

There was something funny going on with Gree and the Playgirl that night. I haven't a clue what, but I do remember clocking a series of minor incongruities which, by themselves amounted to not a lot but, when woven together, might suggest to the neutral observer that all was not well.

A woman takes to the stage. A tall, startling individual with handsome dark features and a Sinead O'Connor haircut, whom I clock with a casually disinterested glance before receding into my usual daydreamy position. She is half lit by the spotlight, and she stands unmoving as an eerie mist swirls across the stage. There's a bongo player somewhere in the wings, and she's pounding herself into a frenzy. I shoot a pleading look at Gree. *Take me home now, or at least shoot me.* But she just squeezes my hand and fixes her eyes on the stage. I sigh, maybe a touch too heavily, and slump back in my seat. Bongo Lady reaches her orgasm, and the stage is once again plunged into darkness. I long for a pair of joke glasses, the ones with the pictures of eyeballs on the front so that you can fool everyone into thinking that you're awake, when really, you're anti-socially asleep. When the light returns to the woman on the stage, I'm a little unnerved. She's still standing motionless, but her head is jerking around in a creepy spasm, her wild black eyes hunting something in the audience. I pray to God that it isn't me she's after and attempt to concentrate, at least a little.

After an eternity of torture—shouting, wailing, banshee-impersonating—she stops squawking, and the spotlight fades, plunging the stage into darkness. As one, the audience begins to whoop and cheer, and Gree slowly lifts her head from the camera. If I had been a little more observant, a little less self-absorbed maybe, I might have noticed the haunted expression on her ashen face, the curious way that she clapped her hands together, slowly at first, and then with urgency, but all the while, entirely without pleasure. But I didn't. I just nuzzled into her fragrant neck and whined like a spoilt toddler.

"Can we go now?" Again, cocooned in my own little needy

blanket, I half clocked but failed to respond to the writing on the wall. To what was written all over her face. To all but innocent ol' me, a shadow had crept over me and Gree, brooding and malevolent, choking the oxygen out of our carefree, blissful relationship. I all but whooped when she told me that I should go and meet her back at home while she finished off her work. And when she finally crawled into our bed, hours later, I shrugged off the fact that her body stiffened when I slipped my arm around her waist. I nuzzled in closer, burying my face in her sweet-scented hair, oblivious to the fact that she was staring wide-eyed into the darkness, her jaw clenched tight.

There's a knock at my door and a grunt requesting entry. Peanut's head emerges, and I wave him in. Peanut Head traded me his ear buds for the loan of my laptop and superfast internet access a few days ago, a temporary measure which means that he's now seated a few feet from the end of my bed, chubby fingers pounding his thoughts into my keyboard. I never really use the thing so am happy to do the trade. Frank says he needs to keep in touch with "his people" on Facebook and answer some of the mountain of emails that are clogging his inbox. He has a laptop of his own, only he's left it at Kath's, and he's not going back there 'til after the weekend. Am I bothered? Nah, I've got the better deal. I'm tucked up safe and sound, hot water bottle strategically placed across my belly, smiling dreamily to myself as Frank's selection of reggae, old and new, washes over me.

I've decided that tomorrow is soon enough for me to start worrying about the whole Tessa and the Irritating Aussie thing. The remainder of the evening has been given over to smiley, floaty calmness for a change. My be-harped angel-girl has done her best to tut tut me into a guilty corner, but I'm not having it. I've banished her, along with the leather-clad demon girl who had been doing her utmost to cattle prod me into her swirling, whirlpool of jealous paranoia. For one night, maybe one night only, folks, I have resolved to take a rain check on the soap opera that is my real life, awarding myself an evening of indulgent dropping out with my own company.

I can't remember the last time that I allowed myself some guilt-free daydreaming. Normally, I'm more of the it's-all-my-fault kind of individual, absorbing all the world's ills like some big ol' Catholic sponge. Lurking somewhere in the back of my mind is an unassailable truth. Pathetic though it may be, I've found a crack in the gloomy mantle of my life, a tiny chink in the oppressive black sky above, through which I have glimpsed weak fingers of pale sunlight.

I spoke, Tessa spoke, and the world didn't end. The world didn't end, and she didn't batter me to death with a verbal or literal baseball bat. Actually, we've never argued about anything, the good doctor and I, but maybe that's the problem with us. We fit together and get along with one another, but we don't talk. I've spent months studiously avoiding situations where the two of us might find ourselves having to have a conversation—*the* conversation—and not only has it *not* lessened the oppressive tension between us, it has also actually escalated this powder keg situation. Somewhere outside of my cloud nine existence, I'm aware that Frank is standing at the end of the king-size, regarding me with raised eyebrows. I raise a protective hand to the earphones that I have come to know and love and have decided to keep. Wriggling myself to a sitting position, I free up my left ear and grant my brother the audience that he is requesting. "'sup?"

"Pub?"

He gives me a look the look that says, "You really are a pathetic creature, sis," before striding purposefully toward the door. He shakes his head in disbelief as he does so, and I'm far too mellow to worry that it's anything to do with me. Frank exits with a brief nod, and then, I am alone once again, just me and my soft and creamy contemplations.

We don't talk, the good doctor and me. There's no need, we've already said it all. You know that lesbian thing about sex on the first date and moving in and exchanging cats on the second? 'Cept we didn't swap cats or have sex on the first date. We haven't dated at all. I cast my gaze up to the top left-hand corner of my ceiling. I've spent such a long time trying to force Dr T out of my head, yet, here I am, floating along with nothing but warm and fuzzy thoughts about her, about us.

How did we come to sleep together that first time anyway? No, not the pre-Cape Town Caper. That wasn't the first time, as Deborah's thumb-screwing had me admit the other day. God, not even the Home Alone weekend, when we found ourselves alone together, rattling around this big ol' house. Sex in the kitchen had felt like such a good idea at the time. Hell, it had seemed churlish not to. Funny things happen in the heat of an Indian summer. I'm dredging the annals of my hazy mind now, trying to work out exactly how I first came to slide into.... cordial relations with her.

Top left-hand corner of the ceiling in my room is getting more than its fair share of my attention again. My right hand is, somewhat tellingly, clasped across my mouth. Somehow breathing through my fingers is conducive to intelligent thought for me. An ancient goddess, a conference weekend somewhere in the depths of the West Country, a gaggle of the good doctor's female students, and their designated PCV driver succumbing to a flu virus two days before. These things conspired to get me to agree to ferry the nutty shower to their assignation, unwittingly agreeing to spend a night sharing a lumpy bed and room (both were lumpy, I kid you not) with the aforementioned leader of harpies.

Why the fuck did I agree to risk life, love, and limb, negotiating a rusty old minibus (with dodgy power steering and non-electric side mirrors) through the rain-battered countryside on my weekend off last autumn? Because she asked me to. That and the fact that I knew that Gree was planning a surprise royal visit that very weekend. Rebecca had let it slip that Grier had invited her over for dinner at the house—my house— on the Saturday night. That's the other thing about being a lesbian. You both keep all the friends, meaning you end up in the same space sometimes. In this case, she ends up in my space. If there's really only six degrees of separation between all people, the lesbian community has artfully managed to hone it down to two, three tops. Dinner with two of my exes? No, thank you.

Before then, I'd pretty much managed to avoid having to see Grier and Madam. Eight years is a lot of ducking and diving, especially when the object of your duck-diving still owns a third of your house and commands the adoration of its other resident. I'd made an art form of my ability to suddenly and coincidentally be called away on family business or the like, right on the morning that they had been due to arrive. Over the years, I managed to limit our meetings to a mere handful. The first time I cried a lot, begging her to come back to me. The second time, I tried to kiss her on the stairs, fumbling through my desperate emotions, with her poncy girlfriend not six feet away in the spare room. Strikeout, and strikeout again. By her third visit, I'd regained my trademark moody cool, managing both civility and detachment for three days and two nights under the same roof.

Rebecca had made me sad and Grier had cleaved me in two, so when Tessa pleaded the case for me venturing down the M4 corridor with her on that wintry Friday in October, I grasped the challenge with both hands. We had already crossed the "bedfellow" divide, so sharing a room with her had held none of the usual fear of intimate proximity. Just a few weeks before the Great Goddess thing (okay then, our first fuck weekend), Tessa and I had somewhat reluctantly become what she laughingly referred to as *bedfellows*. Circumstances had conspired to place the two of us in my bed every night for nearly two weeks. A combination of the Great Flood (of Wallington Avenue, not the Old Testament) and the Great Deadline (or Carl's dizzy lack of planning, as I saw it).

One fine Sunday evening, a little over a year ago, I returned home from a delicious weekend in the arms of one Alyssa Gianaris, but I don't wish to dwell on that...on her...right now, to find Claire the plumber and Carl the dipshit engaged in solemn conversation. My first thoughts ran along the lines of "Nice to see you, Claire. Now I'll just slope off to my room," as did my second thoughts really. No such luck. I was informed by the gruesome twosome that there was a problem. We'd had a bit of a leak but no need to panic, Claire had come round the minute Carl had phoned. Lucky she was in. Yeah, yeah, I get it. The water had been shut off at the mains, and we were no longer in danger of being washed away. Okey dokey, I was cool with all of that.

Problem was, that wasn't the problem. The problem was that the tank in the loft had rusted away in one corner and developed a leak. Carl had been gone, flitting in and out because of deadlines, and hadn't noticed.

I'd been holed up at Casa Gianaris since the Friday night so had no knowledge whatsoever of the impending catastrophe of biblical proportions. Tessa, whose bedroom is between mine and the loft, had been away on her customary football weekend. From the day that she moved in, Tessa had quietly come and gone without really making an impact on the household routines. She had slung her bike over her shoulder of a morning before pedalling off to uni. Every evening, she would return, sweating and usually grinning, pass a few pleasantries with myself and Carl, and then retire to her room. Apparently, she wasn't much of a telly person; she always resisted our best efforts to indoctrinate her into the *Coronation Street* Sad Addicts Society. In fact, apart from her attendance of the Friday night "family dinner" club, I hadn't spent any time with her at all.

Funny that. Looking back, I seem to recall her sitting and chatting (or debating, should I say?) with Carl when I was out of the house. Yeah, I would come home late at night to hear his low growl and her infectious laugh emanating from the living room. Despite my love-hate relationship with him (mostly I can't stand the bastard, resenting every bone in his lying Campbell husband body), I have to admit that I'm really quite used to sharing my space with him. I suppose it was my fault that we never really became a household threesome, me, Carl, and the doctor. I knew that the two of them were getting along pretty well, and I liked her well enough, but I kept finding my gaze wandering up and down her body whenever she spoke to me. How embarrassing is that? I kept making excuses not to join the two of them in conversation, finding reasons why I needed to scoot off whenever she came and plonked herself down on the sofa next to me. All those months! All that time, I guess I was secretly attracted to her (so secretly that I failed to let myself in on it), and I did whatever I needed to in order to keep my pathetic, teenaged lusting a deep, dark secret. Sad case, O'Sullivan! She made me laugh though. She's genuinely funny, her quick-fire witty remarks always had me grinning in spite of my miserable self.

Every other Saturday, at the crack of dawn, she would sling a rucksack over her shoulder and scoot off to King's Cross, heading for the pitch at Elland Road and the arms of her long-distance girlfriend. Of course, the water tank had chosen one of Tessa's football weekends to share its contents with the rest of the house. Drip, drip, drip. The water had seeped into the loft floor, hour after hour unchecked. Finally, the sodden ceiling in Tessa's room could endure no more. Collapsing under the strain, it had given the errant stream of water a means of escape, and the stream had gratefully accepted. Free! Free, at last. The stream had continued its drip, drip, dripping and, now joined by lumps of plaster and splinters of long-rotted floorboard, created an ugly grey torrent of stinking slush, which had spread out and made itself at home all over Tessa's bedroom.

That weekend, and the week preceding it, Carl had been working overtime like a thing possessed. Massively behind on the production of some feature film or other that he had been working on, he had finally, in my humble opinion, cracked up. It was Sunday, and the deadline was Friday. Carl needed to work with Frankfurt Lukas for at least another three days, and the exhausted Lukas had been tearily threatening to jump ship and return home. For the previous month, Lukas had been working from morning to night on a task which should have been completed in less than a fortnight. He was skint, exhausted, and one step away from jacking it all in. In his infinite wisdom, Carl had persuaded him that what he needed was a good hot bath, a home cooked meal (cue the frantic messages left on Darren's answerphone), and a few nights' sleep in a cosy Muswell Hill (spare room) bed. He knew of just such a place...

Lukas had been swayed, particularly after Carl had offered a cosy Muswell Hill sofa to Laura, his assistant editor, in a last ditch bid to stop her from abandoning the project altogether in favour of attempting to get her foot back in the door of the flat from which her ex-girlfriend had just evicted her. Lukas had had his own reasons for wanting to be close to the lovely Laura at this difficult time (bizarre reasons, as she was clearly never going to be interested in him), but hey! He moves in mysterious ways, and Carl Miller moves in Cor Blimey permutations of His ways. Carl had needed the pair to remain committed to finishing the project to deadline and by a stroke of supreme (and, truth be told, admirable) manipulation, he'd managed to convince both to set up camp in our house for a mere five days longer, after which they would be free to disappear into the ether with their well-earned pay cheques and his blessing.

No such luck for me though. I had to stand (slouch) in the hallway, pining for my crisp cotton sheets (weekend with Alyssa equals not much sleep), listening to Carl ranting on about the disastrous timing of the...um...disaster in hand. Brilliant timing, Carl. That left us with no room at the inn for bedroom-less Tessa to bunk down in. I would have drifted off completely if I hadn't caught my name being mentioned and clocked the expectant joint gawp from those two.

"What?" Eyes left, and Carl is beseeching me to do something. Eyes right, and I see that Claire, head tilted slightly back, has folded her arms across her chest and is waiting for me to say something.

Oh, shite, not again. I didn't have a clue what they'd been talking about, and I was just seconds away from being caught out. Lucky for me that Claire had always been a right gobby madam with a flair for the dramatic then.

"Well," Claire said, idly running a finger through the dado rail dust, (I hate that in a woman... Someone who does dust inspections and the like), "you've still got that massive bed, haven't you, Fin?" She paused, probably for dramatic effect, and lightly grasped the arm of Carl's Superman T-shirt to draw him in.

Deciding that speechlessness was not an option in the current circumstances, given that they were clearly intent on me offering to share my room with Tessa, I started up with my usual inarticulate stuttering. No, no, and thrice no...and mainly just because. In the depths of my stomach, a rather agitated butterfly began a solo tango. Demon girl provocatively licked her lips and threw me a wink, before jab-jab-jabbing her pitchfork after the butterfly. Angel girl, preoccupied with attempting to save the butterfly's life, still found time to rebuke me with a pointed *be nice* glare before scuttling off.

I decided that I needed to see the destruction for myself in order to come up with a creative excuse, so I feigned interest and asked Claire to show me the damage. Gotta admit, I was more than a little shocked when she pushed open the door to Tessa's bedroom to reveal the stinking, sludgy wasteland beyond. It was serious. Yep, the room was uninhabitable... Poor Becks would have to move out for a bit... My brain slumped into a manic meltdown as I tried to be sympathetic to the circumstances and adamant that my king-size was not the answer at the same time. And then, right on cue, *she* arrived home.

The Great Flood

SHE CRIED. NO, NOT big ol' girlie sobbing and snotting all over the shop crying, but that day, when faced with the rancid wasteland that had once been her bedroom, Dr T's lower lip definitely quivered. She tiptoed across the room, cautiously picking her way through the manky piles of books, papers, and magazines to which I would later become accustomed. Tessa's idea of housework is to sort her manic clutter in loosely relevant piles. I watched with a somewhat peevish fascination as she moved about the room, lifting and examining papers here and kicking away sodden articles of clothing there. Occasionally, on encountering some sopping article or other, she groaned or emitted a low curse.

And while Claire had taken the tour with her, and Carl fussed and sympathised, I remained motionless on the second-floor landing, leaning on the door jamb for support. When the tour came to an end, when Tessa was finally satisfied that she had indeed lost all of her second-years' essay papers, countless paperbacks, and that disturbingly life-size poster of Kylie Minogue, now forlornly clinging to the wall, sadly water-stained and a shadow of its former sunny self, I clocked a series of nods, winks, and raised eyebrows between Carl and Claire, punctuated by the odd glare in my direction. They clearly wanted me to ride to the rescue, the mighty heroine offering the use of her boudoir and saving the day—ta-da! I was seething with the manipulative injustice of their conniving, but I was also genuinely sorry for Laughing Tessa, whose gloomily clenched jaw was contradicting her monicker. Carl gave a little cough. For the life of me, I have no idea what came over me, but I mounted my white charger and came over all John Wayne. "Ma'am,

I'd sure be mighty pleased if y'all would accept ma hospitality..."

Nah, I didn't say that. Avoiding eye contact, I focused on soggy Kylie and spluttered an invitation to share my room, my king-size et al, while the repairs were made. I was torn between turning Carl to stone with my evil eye and offering reassurance to the no-longer-laughing Tessa. To my surprise, I heard a voice, *my* voice, cutting clear through the soggy, sombre silence. "We've been through worse in this house Becks, Carl'll tell you. It'll be okay." Tessa stared at me in disbelief and cast her eyes around the sludgy room before returning her gaze to me.

"I...I'm happy for you to share my room while we get it sorted." I was desperate to banish the look of abject misery from her face. Somehow, that misery was seeping into me and dragging me down, and I think I would've done anything, offered anything to bring a smile to her face. When I realised that I was staring at her, I cleared my throat and dropped my eyes to the slushy floor. "You can set your desk up by the window to work, and my bed's plenty big enough for two. Don't worry, we've got you covered," I muttered and gently nudged a pile of grey slush aside with my toe. All eyes were on me. Carl silently mouthed the words, "Thank you."

Had I really just said all that? I winced slightly and dug my hands deep into my pockets as I leaned on the door frame, knowing that it was too late to rescind. What the fuck, Fin? Grown women don't just invite total strangers into their beds. At least, they don't without having salacious ulterior motives. *Whoa, wait! Are we really doing this right now?*

"Ar, mate, I don't want to put you out, but..."

They were halfway down the stairs and heading for my bedroom door before I'd even managed a customary splutter. Claire, followed by Carl, followed by Tessa. She stopped and glanced over her shoulder at me, her warm eyes seeking mine in the half light of the stairwell. She smiled, I smiled, and then nodded in the direction of my room. She waited for me to catch up and then stood back as I opened the door for her.

"It really is no problem," said the Fin who had taken over my body as the Tessa who was about to take over my room stepped cautiously over the threshold. Unlike hers, my room was a showroom of neat and tidy; St Zita would have been proud. She allowed her army kit bag to slide from her shoulder to the floor, her eyes fixed on the elephant in the room or, more specifically, my king-size bed.

"I'm...um lefthanded, so I always sleep on the left."

I didn't dare to look at her. Had I been bold enough to shift my eyes from that fascinating line where the rug ends and the floorboards begin, I might have clocked the slight smile that was playing at the corners of her lips. As it was, it took the warm depth of that familiar Beckinsale laugh for me to drag a shy glance at the attractive woman who was perched on the right side of my bed, her hand smoothing out my already smooth duvet.

"I'm really grateful." She ran her fingers through her tousled hair before another peal of her infectious laugh warmed the room. "And I don't snore!"

I plonked myself down on the bed beside her. "Says who?" Well, she'd thrown it out there and despite all my sulky miserableness, I am nothing if not a serial flirt. The words flew out of my mouth before I could reel myself in. Laughing Tessa with the soft green-brown eyes and the sport-toned bod was sitting on my bed looking...actually, looking pretty hot. And there I was... Actually, what the fuck was I doing? My leather-clad demon girl, busy stoking the furnace in my jeans, threw me a knowing wink, and I knew that I had to get a grip and take control, or risk losing all control. Inarticulate, hormone-fuelled Fin had been poised in the wings, gearing up to return, a situation I was desperate to avoid.

"Says me girlfriend, Em," Tessa said with lightning speed. Then the grin fell from her face. She pursed her lips and frowned. She sucked in a deep lungful of air, then exhaled, slowly. "Ex. Emma, me ex-girlfriend," she said, slowly punching out the words.

Her hand moved from my duvet to her forehead and began

massaging, her fingers and thumb moving in small tight circles across the skin. I wanted to speak, to murmur some banal platitude to fill the silence but as usual, my mouth opened and closed without uttering a word. I'm good at that. Once again, my polished floorboards started to look fascinating. I allowed the silence between us to drift on.

"What a weekend!" I was relieved to note that Tessa's voice had almost returned to the jovial tone to which I'd become accustomed. "Dumped. Okay, that had been coming for a while now. I'm sad, yes, but can't say that I'm heartbroken or owt. Flooded, though. That were unexpected." She shook her head and laughed, actually laughed, as she spoke. "Folk say disasters come in threes. I'm just waiting for a fucking anvil to fall from t'sky on me head."

"Locusts," I mumbled.

That beautiful laugh of hers has always had the ability to whack my funny bone and, not for the first time, I found myself unable to stop myself from grinning and joining in.

"Locusts?"

"Locusts." I jumped to my feet and stood in front of her, reading from the imaginary clipboard in my hands.

"Says here, Locusts...ten million. Special delivery for a...Mrs Beckinsale from a Mr ...um Od. G. Od. Angry and bitey, blah, blah, blah... Where d'ya want 'em, sweetheart?"

She threw her head back and roared with laughter, pounding her palm on the bed in applause as she did so. The woman had merry in her veins, and I was on a roll. I swivelled in a small circle before becoming Tessa herself.

"Now then, steady lad." I stretched my lips into a dour, frowning, downturned line as I stomped around the room, twanging my imaginary braces.

"Oh, I do *not* sound like that!" She laughed, pointing a warning finger in my direction. "You watch yourself, O'Sullivan."

Wriggling herself back against the headboard of my bed, she narrowed her eyes and shot me a fake angry look, before folding her arms across her chest and crossing her legs neatly at the ankles.

A tiny breath puffed from my lips. It had been an age since I had last had a woman stretched across my bed, and I kind of enjoyed the snapshot image before me. And she was oh, so easy to wind up! I made a comic descending whistle noise culminating in a sharp dunk and then allowed myself to fall dramatically onto the bed, clutching my head. "Ar, hey! That's t'second fucking anvil today!"

How long had it been since I'd laughed like that? My shoulders were heaving as I defended myself from the pillow assault that Tessa subjected me to. We descended into uncontrollable giggles, and I actually rolled off the bed and onto the floor in the midst of the attack.

"I *do not* sound like that, and I don't swear that much."

When I was finally able to tilt my head in her direction, Tessa was shaking her head and wiping tears from her eyes, her broad grin revealing the chipped tooth that I'd clocked the first time we met. Still there. An ocean of calm unexpectedly washed over me, and I started to feel my shoulders drop and my spirits lift. This room-sharing was only going to be for the next two weeks; I could manage that many days with Laughing Tessa. Hell, I might even enjoy it.

"Yes, you fucking do," I said.

Silence. Then more laughter. More than my bedroom had heard in a very long time.

Misery Acquaints a Woman with Strange Bedfellows

AND SO, IN THE autumn of last year, Tessa and I became official bedfellows, a practice that she assured me had at one time been common in this country. Somewhat astonishingly, far from resenting the personal space invasion, I actually quite liked having her there. The only downside being that my bedroom moved from ship-shape to bomb site in one fell swoop. Carl dredged up a small clothes rail, a prop from a set at work, and Tessa set about piling her "work drag" onto it.

At home, she always wears a vest or T-shirt with a pair of long shorts or jeans and depending on the weather, flip flops or scruffy trainers. For work, it's a different matter. She irons a shirt (I mean, who does that these days?) and a pair of chinos or cigarette trousers, slips on her loafers or brogues, and dons a blazer. When I see her in this attire, I know that she means business; she is every inch the professional woman and I have to confess, I think she looks pretty damn hot. I love her shirts. Classic stripes, ginghams, and paisleys with button-down collars and always ironed within an inch of their lives. If my lecturers had been half as attractive as she is, I might have gotten through my arid degree, and my life today would be very different. I am somewhat in awe of this woman who effortlessly commands respect at her prestigious workplace and grips me tight and holds my gaze in the heat of her shuddering orgasm.

I crash back to the here and now with a thump as my stomach turns and my bladder informs me that I need a wee. So much for playing in the past. My sneering devil girl prods my belly with a sharpened pitchfork, forcing me to read the *Out of your league* placard she is waving in my face. Angel girl is trying to nudge her aside. They are full on wrestling but of course, demon girl is so much stronger. She has better weapons. Poor angel girl is soon defeated, but not before she flashes me her own placard, emblazoned with three simple words: *She likes YOU*. Devil girl is stomping her victory dance all over my body. I sigh and grimace, reluctantly shaking myself out of my daydream as I slope off to the bathroom, because we both know that the devil's right. Academic Tessa was always out of my league, and yeah, she had liked me. Until I'd shoved my low-brained stupidity right up her nose, that is.

The bathroom floor tiles are cool under my bare feet as I prod the toilet flush and watch my own blood swirl away down the pan. I have slipped into my cosy red PJ bottoms and a tatty old *Nobody Knows I'm a Lesbian* T-shirt, and I'm happy to report that my medications of choice appear to be doing the trick. A little smirk twitches the corner of my lips. I am safe in the knowledge that tomorrow's first run is Barking to Luton airport, and I don't have to pick up until 8:45 a.m. I'll still wake up at the crack of dawn, but the thought of tea and toast in bed before work will be a welcome change to my routine. I pad softly back to my room and slide under the duvet with a small sigh of contentment. Of course, devil girl is not yet done with me. She laughs maniacally as she hijacks my phone's soothing playlist, leaving the reggae version of "The Bed's Too Big Without You" pounding in my ear buds. I roll onto my stomach, stretch my arm out into the expanse of unoccupied mattress, and gouge the crisp unruffled bedsheet with my fingernails. "Tess." The tiny, all but inaudible, whisper escapes my lips, and a fat tear sears its way down my cheek. Staring miserably into the darkness of my room, I do not stop it.

Me and Tess had bumped along very well as bedfellows before *the thing* had happened. That night, somewhere in deepest Somerset, I laid in the bumpy bed in the lumpy room desperately trying to make sense of what had happened, of what had been real and what had been a dream. Had Tessa really scuttled over to my side of the bed and snaked her arm around my waist that night? On the night of *the thing*, I had been half or mostly asleep when she tiptoed into my room, silently shucking off her clothes in the darkness. Had she embraced me, spooning her body into mine as I had laid on my side facing the window? Had she felt my heart hammering inside my ribcage as I pretended to be asleep, or had I really been asleep? The following day, with the paint fumes subsiding to a tolerable level and Claire declaring Tessa's room once again habitable, that had been that. Tess moved back to her own room. No time to discuss the previous night's encounter—*the thing* that may or may not have actually happened—but I doubt I'd have broached the subject anyway. After that night, I became awkward in her company (even more awkward, if that was possible), my heartbeat fluctuated and sweat pooled in the small of my back whenever I was in her company. Now, sharing a room with her at the inn, I was faced with the prospect of once again sharing a bed with her, and I still didn't have a clue how to act around her.

As the sound of the downstairs door slamming and a cacophony of rowdy goodnights drifting up to the lumpy room, my body jerked into a paralysing combination of fight and flight. Tessa's voice, Tessa's laugh, and her urgent whisperings were heading my way. I knew that the Irritating Aussie was lodged on the top floor, and the image in my head of the two of them giggling and whispering together ignited my jealousy touchpaper. When the slow footsteps came to a halt on the landing outside the bedroom, I was suddenly seized with a rush of jealousy and exasperation. After throwing off the duvet, I sprang to my feet, raced to the door, and flung it open, armed with my fiercest righteous indignation face, ready to confront the brazen hussies beyond.

Next thing I knew, I was sprawling on the floor under a tangled mass of arms and legs. Muffled groans were followed by peals of laughter. Laughter? This wasn't going quite as I had imagined. Scrambling from beneath the pile, I tried, uselessly, to muster a death ray glare at the giggling women on the floor. Not easy when you're wearing bunny jim-jams, I can tell you. Tessa was lying on her back underneath a clearly inebriated Kellie. Another woman, who I recognised from the bus journey, was opening the door opposite, quietly chuckling to herself. She crossed the small landing and helped Tessa raise Kellie to a slumped, half standing position, using the wall to support her.

"Thanks," the woman whispered to Tessa as she had led/dragged Kellie to their bedroom. "I've got it from here."

"Good night, Sam," Tessa slurred cheerily. "And may the Goddess go with you!" She stepped back into our bedroom and closed the door with her bum. Leaning against the door frame, she had fixed me with a huge grin, her glassy eyes seeking mine.

"You're drunk." I fully intended to give her a severe scolding but the corners of my lips twitched with amusement, and my voice had decided that a bubbly squeak was the appropriate tone.

"Y-es. Maybe…a bit. But I'm still in control of all me faculties, and I am still standing. See?"

She held her arms out to the sides and stood on one leg to prove her point. Satisfied with her efforts, she flashed me her widest, most endearing smile and laughed that laugh of hers. Annoying as she was, she made a lovely drunk. A lovely, beautiful, and quite enticing drunk. A groan of irritation escaped my lips. I wanted to be annoyed but found myself filled with an unexpected glow of warmth and, as I watched her struggling to relieve herself of her clothing, something else too. I physically shook and turned my back on her half naked body in order to suppress the tingling sensation rising from my core. When I was able to claw my way back to land of the living, I realised that, in her bra top and knickers, Tessa had already slipped between the covers and was lying sprawled out, flat on her back, droning on at no one in particular.

"Of course I couldn't let that slip of a lass out-drink me. Yorkshire pride and all that. Yes, I did get a bit tipsy, but I were t'last man standing. Woman standing. Oh, my Goddess!"

A small laugh, and then a full-blown guffaw. That gorgeous sound that had me fighting to control my own giggle reflex. "Oh, give it a rest, you piss artist." I plonked myself down on her side of the bed and fixed her with what I hoped was a harsh scowl, even though I was struggling to keep a straight face.

"But you should have seen their faces when I downed the first one. And then...then I launched into an amazing rendition of "The Hymn of Aphrodite." God, I were reet on fire!"

She gave herself an almighty air high five, almost knocking me off my perch as she did so. "Oh, put a sock in it, Tessa! I'm warning you. Just bloody shut up, woman."

Tessa cocked her head to one side, momentarily considering this disruption of her self-congratulatory monologue with a raised eyebrow. How she does that I'll never understand. She slowly looked me up and down, raising her glinting eyes to meet mine and fixing them there. Finally, she tucked her hands neatly behind her head, pouted her lips and raised both eyebrows in defiant challenge.

"Make me."

She was taunting, teasing, and downright hot as hell. What the fuck? I mean, what the actual? Drunken Dr Beckinsale was laying down a challenge, possibly flirting with me, and I was rooted to the spot. Tick tock, tick tock, tick tock. I was wasting time thinking instead of acting.

I scrambled wildly over the bumpy bed and launched myself on top of her, pinning her body to the mattress with my own and smothering her yapping mouth with my lips in a long, firm kiss. Okay, this wasn't exactly what I'd had in mind for the evening. My sole intention had been to one-up Tessa, to outdo her brazen flirting by shocking her into silence with an out of left field kiss, but now? Now I had an electrical bolt of arousal surging through my entire body, the same body that began to mould itself against hers, without my permission, I might add. Entirely of their own accord, my lips softened, withdrew slightly, and began softly grazing over and around Tessa's mouth. When her lips slightly parted in response, my eyes snapped open (when had they closed?), and I forced myself to pull away, to release Tessa's wrist that I'd pinned to the pillow above her head, and to urgently seek out her eyes. This couldn't be happening, right?

"Not drunk, Fionnuala," she whispered breathlessly, raising her hips from the bed to reunite with mine. She slipped her hand inside my top, grazing the small of my back with her fingertips, and in a small voice sodden with desire, breathily asked, "What kept you?"

Nobody, but nobody, ever calls me by my actual name. Coming from her lips right then, the sound reverberated in the air, spreading over my goose-bumped skin like a warm honey kiss. Before I had had time to bask in it, Tessa squirmed from under me, propped herself up on one elbow, and placed her palm flat against my now heaving chest.

"Bunny jammies have got to go," she said, a slight smile playing on her gorgeous mouth.

"Oh, shit!" What on earth had possessed me to pack these? My hands felt like I was wearing cricket gloves as I struggled to free myself from my pyjamas. Tessa got to her knees and began helping me with the shirt buttons. I was torn between ripping the shirt off, buttons and all, and liberating her voluptuous breasts from their sporty incarceration. In the end, she took care of the irksome buttons, deliberately taking her time in doing so, as I ached for more skin contact. She planted a series of small kisses against my ribcage, trailing her tongue and lips upwards to my own breasts, causing my breath to come in short, jagged pants. When her tongue touched my hard nipple, my head unexpectedly jerked back as my body experienced a dizzying electrical storm of arousal. I was in serious danger of being swept away on the crest of a tidal wave of orgasm at any moment, and she knew it. When she brought her head back to my level and returned her attention to my mouth, my knees buckled.

"No stamina, O'Sullivan?" she murmured into my mouth,

before plunging her hot tongue deep.

I could only moan in response and fill my lungs with the woody fragrance of her hair. When she backed up a notch and whipped her bra top off in a single fluid movement, I emitted a small involuntary cry. I was definitely out of control. I half considered slapping her down with a slick and witty retort to stall for time, but... Well, I had my hands full with exploring those sumptuous full breasts of hers, the ones that I'd fantasised about on more than one or two occasions. They were beautiful. *She* was beautiful. Why hadn't I made this happen sooner?

Tessa pressed her body tightly against mine, sucking gently on my collarbone as she did so. I gently gripped her buttocks with impatient hands and dived right in.

"You're beautiful," she gasped between pants, her eyelids heavy with desire.

My heartbeat quickened to a frenzy. Beautiful? Nobody ever told me that I was beautiful. Hot. Sexy, maybe, but beautiful was a new one on me.

"Beautiful," she said, lazily trailing her trembling hands over my blazing skin, "and I'm going to make you come so hard, you'll know it for true."

I was on the brink before, but the passion in her whispered words ignited a cauldron of craving inside me that had thundered me into evasive action so that I didn't peak too soon. How had this woman propelled me into such a frenzied state so quickly? More's the point, how could I deal with the annoying sensory overload that was threatening to ruin the moment? The roaring pulse of blood in my ears, the weird orangey glow of the bedside table lamp and the shadows it cast in my peripheral vision, the smell of old wooden furniture and clean cotton bedding, my mind and body about to explode and shatter like a stone fragment hitting a car windscreen. I squirmed and wiggled myself out of her delicious grasp to slow her down and refocus my mind. My body wanted to sprint to the finish line, to launch itself against the tape in a panting, heaving fury but by the narrowest of margins, my logical mind wrestled control over it. *This is Tessa*, it reminded me, *not some random fast fuck.* A curious image of my fifteen-year-old self decked out in my fencing sabre and lamé shot into my mind. *Balestra*, it whispered.

Deep breaths, long, slow kisses, and delicate teasing touches drew gasps and moans, all the while hinting at what was to come. Engage, disengage, parry, and riposte. For me, sex had always been fast and furious, but not with Tessa. Before that night I hadn't had sex with another human being for such a long time that a part of me had been reluctant to acknowledge the significance of the situation I found myself in. I hadn't wanted to fumble my way to a quick release that night. I had wanted, *needed*, to savour every delectable inch of her.

Thankfully, Tess promptly got onto the same page. She cupped my head in her hands and grinned. "Mm, alrighty," she murmured, drawing me back into another agonisingly teasing kiss.

Though the setting could have been more romantic—both of us were acutely aware that we were a mere ten feet away from two of her students—I can honestly say that it was the best sex I'd ever had. She promised much and delivered in spades.

By the time I croaked, "Shit. Fuck" at my beeping alarm and reluctantly stole myself away from our delicious tangle of limbs, long before the sun had had time to put in an appearance, the following truths had become self-evident:

Tessa's smile shoots me up with warm and fuzzy.

Tessa's skin is as smooth as a carefully polished stone, apart from her knees and shins, which look like a battlefield.

Tessa has an appendix scar, and a Leeds Utd tattoo on her left shoulder.

Tessa tastes tangy and salty, and tasting her drives me crazy with want.

I want more Tessa. Much more.

When Tessa stirred a little and cocked a half opened bleary eye in my direction, I leaned in and kissed her softly on the ear.

"Last woman standing," I said in a cocky whisper, reminding her that she had been the one to bring our previous night's liaison to a conclusion. "In an old woman, old skool stylee."

"No. Oh no, no, no! Oh dear God, we haveta stop!" She had groaned in the wee small hours of the night before, capturing my hand from between her thighs and relocating it to the relative safety of her belly. "I need sleep. *You* need sleep if you're going to get us safely home in one piece, and what the fuck have you done with all t'bones in me body, Fin? I'm a fucking jellyfish!"

The inelegantly sprawled heap of Dr Beckinsale raised her rubbery arm in my general direction and beckoned me with her fingers. "Get theeself back in my bed, wench," she said, with her face still plastered to the bed sheet. "But please could you get me a glass of water first?"

"Nah," I said, with what I hoped was an irritating nonchalance. "I'm off to find a cuppa."

Tessa groaned and cursed me in no uncertain terms and with a raft of creative expletives, but when I returned ten minutes later, armed with a mug of tea, a black coffee, and a steaming bacon butty, she was up and dressed on the edge of the bed, freshly showered and towelling her curly hair.

"Mm," she murmured, softly lacing her fingers into mine. She carefully stowed the coffee mug on the lopsided bedside table and wrapped her lips around the breakfast offering. "Oh, so good. Did I say thank you, thank you, thank you?"

She attacked the butty like a woman possessed, pausing only briefly to chug a large swig of coffee before returning to the butty-ravishing.

"I dunno about thank you, Tess. All I seem to remember is, "Oh, God. Oh, my God. Fuck! Oh, God, Fin. YES!" The smile on my face was broad and smug as I blew on my fingernails and mock-polished them on my shirt. I was pleased to see the sudden pink flush that hit her cheeks before continuing in a fury up to her scalp. She grimaced as she stopped chewing, her eyebrows shooting to the top of her head in a panic.

"Oh, holy fuck," she gasped. I swear I saw a lightbulb ping on and hover above her head. "Did I... Was I...loud?" she asked.

"No point in whispering now, Tess." I gave her a wicked grin. "I mean, last night you were oblivious to the banging on the wall and the ceiling, and to your tortured students yelling, "Shut the fuck up" at you...and when those wolves started howling in the distance—"

And there it was, that slow heart-melting smile once again lighting up her face. A split second's pause, and then she lunged, propelling herself rugby tackle-style at my knees.

"Too slow, my dear," I said, wagging my finger at her. "Oh, ow. Fuck!" In my attempt to avoid the incoming tackle, I'd veered sharply to my right and ended up cracking my head on a menacingly evil wooden beam that was randomly jutting out of the wall. I reeled backwards with the impact and landed flat on my arse in the middle of the floor. Tessa's laughter filled the air as I sat on the lumpy carpet rubbing my temple. I swear I saw stars.

"Anvil from heaven," Tessa said, giggling at my scowl. She scrambled across the floor and knelt beside me to examine the rapidly developing bruise on my temple before softly whispering her verdict in my ear, "I think you'll live."

She brushed the spot gently with her soft, coffee-scented lips and tilted her head to look at me. My swagger chose that moment to desert me, and I was saturated with a syrupy shyness. I wanted to lean in and kiss her, but a rigid ball of anxiety had taken root in my chest. "What happens now, Tess? When we get back, I mean?" My small voice, loaded with pitiful neediness, escaped my lips before I could reel myself in. The kiss she pressed to them barely registered in my consciousness before she drew back sharply.

"Oh, shit. I'm going to be fucking late."

She flew around the room shoving papers, pens, and sundry items into her rucksack, pausing only briefly to rub a thick blob of gel into her unruly damp hair before swiping her fingers through it. It was as if I wasn't there.

She flung the door wide, poised to exit, and looked back at me. "Fucking hell! Sorry, sorry. I've got to go."

But she didn't go. She slammed the door and rushed back to me, holding out a hand to help me off the floor. Then she kissed me so deeply, so passionately that I gasped, and my wobbly knees struggled to keep me upright.

"I'm so bastard busy at work this week that I don't think I'll be home much before t'weekend," she said. "Will you have dinner with me on Saturday night?"

I know I'm not exactly known for my articulacy but even I was surprised by my inability to string a sentence together. I simply nodded my head, vigorously, and basked in the warmth radiating from her whole-hearted smile.

"All you can eat buffet?" I asked and gave her a sassy smirk when my bravado reappeared with a thump.

Tessa gently cupped my cheek with one hand, opened the door with the other and said, "Fionnuala, there's no place on earth that could satisfy your appetite."

When she closed the door behind her, I flopped back to the floor with a big stupid grin on my face and made carpet angels with my arms and legs for much longer than any grown woman should.

Tuesday's Child is Full of Grace (Sometimes)

"It's only a couple of days, Noo, and this time, I'm definitely coming back."

As ever, Frank saw through my fake cheeriness and sensed my need for his reassurance when I dropped him at the airport. Frank had called me at lunchtime, throwing me completely off kilter by asking for a lift to Luton Airport. Something had come up, and he needed to get back to work for a couple of days, he told me. He needed to sign off on a few things, to pick up his car and a few bits and pieces before the weekend. Not least of all, he needed to check in with Asha, his girlfriend.

It made sense, and I agreed to take him, inwardly struggling as I'd been to contain the icy fingers of panic tightening around my chest, threatening to squeeze the life out of me. I zipped him up the M1 in a pouty silence, broodily nibbling the skin off my lower lip before pulling up a little too sharply in the drop-off zone. To reconnect with my brother after all the years apart, only to have him ripped away from me within a meagre forty-eight hours felt like a cosmic low blow.

"So, I'll see you on Friday then?" I hadn't meant it as a question but my weakly squeaked tone betrayed my inner misery. I slumped back in my seat, fighting the urge to cling to his shirt sleeve as he exited my car. Instead, I faked nonchalance. I was a grown woman; surely I could take care of myself in the coming days, couldn't I?

Frank rapped noisily on the window, motioning impatiently with his hands for me to open it. "Noo." Leaning on the open window, he focused intently on me. "Like I said, St Damien and his brother, um...whatsisface? Y'know...Patron Saint of twins geezer?"

A chuckle burst from my lips, and I rolled my eyes skyward before smiling and slowly shaking my head. Footie Boy 0, Pious Girl 2. "Cosmas, Frank. It's *still* St Cosmas."

Frank grinned, and my angel girl stuck a pin in my misery balloon.

"Yeah, him. They're my witnesses. I'm back at the weekend, and you and me are gonna raise some merry hell, yeah?"

He knows as well as I do that I'm really not the hell-raising sort, but I grinned back at him, dismissing him with a wave of my hand, and the grin remained on my face all the way back to Muswell Hill.

Now, back at home, I wish he was still in the house, and I'm sorely tempted to call him and demand he come back immediately. I don't. I make a decision.

It's now or never, I tell myself. I pace back and forth in my room, punctuating my steps with occasional glances at the ceiling. Frank's voice, all casual assurance over the phone earlier this evening, steadied my quaking spirit and I resolve to speak to Tessa, who's home too. My heart rhythmically lashes itself against my ribcage, and my fingers tremble, but I replay his words on a loop in my head.

"You can sort this, Noo. Onwards and upwards, mate."

I inhale deeply, exhale slowly, then repeat. Twice. Then I stride resolutely to the door and fling it open. I pull up sharpish, almost tripping myself in the process. The low growl of men's voices in conversation rises from downstairs, but above me, there's silence, eerie silence. I feel like the lone sheriff in a black and white Western, standing alone on the edge of town, watching moody clumps of tumbleweed sweep across the main drag. She's heading for the saloon where we all know trouble awaits... Resisting the urge to check my trusty Colt 45 and adjust my holster, I launch myself up the next flight of stairs and rap loudly on her door, before I have half a chance to change my mind. An eon passes before I hear her respond, and her advancing footsteps make me flinch and begin to back up. *I could run.* My brain's already in fight or flight mode and would instruct my legs to scarper if I just listened to myself. The door opens abruptly, breaking that chain of thought, and I am left staring vacantly at her scowling face.

"Fin." Her tone is flat, neither questioning nor surprised.

I'm struggling to find my vocal cords and remember that I too am able to speak English. "C-can I come in, Tess?" I allow myself the merest flicker of a glance in her direction, before dutifully examining the carpet pile.

Tessa's eyes narrow slightly, but she opens the door wider before spinning on her heels and striding back to her crumpled bed. I bang out a quick prayer to St Fiacre before I shuffle in and pull the door closed behind me.

"What can I do for you, Fin?"

Again, the monotone voice is an icy finger jabbing me in the chest. *What can you do for me, Tessa? You could smile your beautiful smile, the one that warms me from the inside out, the one that makes me want to smile too. You could take my hand, entwining my cold fingers in yours as you lead me to the edge of your bed. You could draw me into one of your earth-shattering kisses, your fingers softly stroking the back of my head as your tongue invites me to join yours.*

I say none of these things. Instead, I shuffle from foot to foot, both hands still firmly clutching the doorknob behind my back. "I wanted to talk to you, Tess. Can we... Wait! Why are you here?" My brain has suddenly reminded me that it's Tuesday, football practice night, my usual Tessa-free evening at home. Okay, she's spotted my panic diversion, and she is *not* happy.

She fixes me with a look of bored indifference. "Subbed after ten minutes. Head injury. Bloody boot to t'chin. Gotta make sure I've not got concussion if I wanna play tomorrow. That and t'fact that I live here."

My armpits start to prick with a cold sweat. I've never known her to be so emotionless, so detached, and the unexpected chill hits me with a force that literally rocks me back on my heels, leaving me gripping the door frame for support. She opens her mouth to speak then pauses, slowly shaking her head.

My nostrils sting with the heady aroma of her hemp body wash, the sound of my blood is whooshing in my ears, and I am vaguely aware that I am repeatedly rubbing my thumb across the smooth surface of the doorknob in my hand. I steal a glance at her to see her eyebrows knotted in a frown.

"Come in, Fin. Have a seat and stop making t'place look untidy," she says softly.

She gestures with her head at the chair adjacent to the bed and a half smile of relief twitches at the corners of my mouth. I release the doorknob. "Thanks. Th-thank you."

"What's on your mind?"

Tessa sits in the centre of her bed, legs outstretched, and reclines back on her elbows. She's not looking at me, and I know that we're at the now or never point. I suck in a deep breath. "Tess, I want to...need to apologise to you."

Seconds tick by as neither of us speaks. Finally, she scrambles across the bed, props herself against the headboard and looks me directly in the eye. "For what, exactly?" she asks, a slight sneer creeping into her tone. "What is it you're sorry about?"

I shuffle in my seat. I do not want to be here. I want to be anywhere, anywhere else on the planet away from her justifiably unforgiving gaze, but I can't. I need to be here, to do this, and I need to do it right now. "All of it Tess, all of it. I regret allowing myself to get drunk...and all that. I'm sorry that I've been avoiding you ever since, that I'm a spineless little shit, but more than anything I'm so, so sorry that my *stupid*, fucked-up behaviour has caused you this pain." All of that still doesn't feel like enough.

Tessa chews on her bottom lip and stares into space, and I am no longer able to look at her. The air around us becomes thick and oppressive, as if all the oxygen has been sucked out and replaced with some invisible poison which is stinging my throat, pricking the backs of my eyes, making my breath catch. I draw my sweating palms over my thighs, staring at my tingling fingertips, silently willing one of us to speak.

"Yeah," she says, her voice a mere whisper. "It hurt. You hurt me."

I open my mouth to speak, then slap it firmly shut as she continues.

"But, Fin." She repositions herself on the edge of the bed, inches closer to me, our knees almost touching. "What I don't understand is why. Why you come to me and then run away. You start something, build it up, and then you stomp it into t'ground."

Her eyes are searching for an answer I am incapable of giving. She swipes away the tear that has leaked onto her cheek and exhales mournfully, before gripping the edge of the bed with one hand. I remain motionless, cemented in the chair as a scalding tear races down my own cheek before it launches itself onto my jeans with a dramatic splosh.

"Things were going so well. We were going well and then...and then nowt." Her sad eyes reach out to me. "Suddenly Fin's nowhere t' be found, and I have to set up that football trip and t'night at Deborah's to get us back on track. What was all that about? And then again at New Year?"

My mind rewinds to an image of Carl, gleefully grinning as he informs me that Gree will be coming to the New Year party after all. Anticipation and dread. I can't speak. I shake my head. I so want to reassure Tessa, to hold her, to comfort her with some sweet words because I know, I *know* that I am the sole chef of this misery soup, and I'm the only one who can fix it. I don't have the words. "I... Me and Grier...it's complicated." A fiery blaze engulfs my neck, cheeks, and ears. Me and Grier are linked together for life, I think to myself. No, I'm not in love with her anymore, but I do care deeply for her. I still don't know what happened with us, what it was about me that made her leave. New Year? It wasn't love, or lust, or even a desire to find closure that made me fuck her that night. No, it was an altogether different emotion. I wanted to hurt

Novia, to steal from her, to make her feel the same misery that she slapped me with me all those years ago. No matter how I spin it, how I twist the truth to make it less ugly to myself, deep down, I know the real truth. I could've resisted Grier. I could've backed out, but I didn't. I'm so ashamed of myself, so revulsed by my own actions, and I can't tell Tessa or anyone else any of this.

"*What?*" Tessa hisses through her teeth. She leaps from the bed and stands with her mouth gaping in astonishment, her eyes blazing with fury, the knuckles bloodless and white on her clenched fists. "That evil cow. That fucking *cunt.*"

Her words cuff me square on the chin, sending me reeling and recoiling. Gentle Tessa thunders about the room in aimless circles, her sweet face contorted with rage, and I struggle to swallow down the bile in my throat, to catch my breath.

"It's not complicated, you fucking idiot," she screams in my face. "She manipulates you, tweaks your bloody strings, and fucks you over again and again. And you let her. When t'fuck will you grow up, Fin?"

I shrink, slowly shrivelling to nothing in the heat of her fury. I feel like a plastic fork that has accidently found itself on a barbecue grill. Oh, God, please someone scrape me off before it's too late. I need to get out of here, get away from her, but I'm shattered in a million tiny pieces, and she's not done with me.

"Ask anyone, Fin. Ask Frank."

On hearing my brother's name, my pieces snap back together with a jolt. Tessa's face softens a little, and she draws herself back, retreating from my personal space to slump against the edge of the table.

"D'you know what she said to me, Fin, the morning after t'party?"

I shake my head miserably, certain in the knowledge that I do not want to hear whatever it is that she is about to tell me.

"She said, and I'm quoting now, 'Maybe you can take my place in her bed for a while, but Fin will always be mine. Always mine.' That's what she said, and that's what she believes. Is she right? Is that really t'state of play?"

Stop the world from spinning, I want to get off. I pull my knees in and drop my head into my upturned palms. Fucking Grier. Did she? Would she? I already know the answers, and the nausea swells in my stomach. Yeah, I stuck the knife in Tessa's gut, but I did nothing to prevent Grier from twisting it. I just hid myself away so that I didn't have to watch it play out. I can't look at her. I can't bear to see the pain that I know is etched on Tessa's face, knowing that I am the architect of that pain. "Oh, God, Tess. Grier can be so—"

"Yeah."

Tessa returns to the bed and sits on the edge, wrapping her arms around her body. "I don't know what to do about any of this, Fin," she whispers. "I don't know how t'play. You've had loads of relationships, but Emma was...me first."

I nod. When I steal a glance in her direction, I see a worn out, ground down woman staring into space. Her first girlfriend? How did I not know this? She certainly hadn't seemed like a newbie to me. I'd told her about my previous 'arrangement' with Alyssa and the mega-fuck break-up with Grier, but Tessa had said very little about Emma, and my latent jealous streak had nudged me away from probing. "Ah. Your first lesbian relationship?" I try to keep the surprise out of my voice.

Tessa winces as she screws her face into a grimace. She gingerly opens one eye and looks at me. "Me first anything, Fin," she says. She breaks our eye contact, shifting her gaze to the rug before I can comment on that nugget. Then she sighs. "God, we're so different, us. I'm not like you. I've always been a nerd. I read, I study, I take exams. I'm always hurtling on t'next goal. GCSEs, A levels, first degree, Masters, PhD. I'm a history nerd." She shrugs. "I never stopped to think that there might be more to life than study."

Who are you and what have you done with my sex goddess?

"I were twenty-eight years old when she swept me off my feet. Last ditch sliding tackle with me clear on for t'goal. Could've broke me leg, the dirty bastard!" She shakes her head and laughs her delicious laugh, and I bask in the familiar warmth of it. "I got subbed, she got carded. She asked me out after, and I gobsmacked us both by saying yes. The rest, as they say, is history."

She frowns, and I squirm. It's gone. The fleeting balmy flash that her laughter had brought to the room is snuffed out in an instant.

"She didn't want me to take this job. Said I were leaving her behind." She pauses and shrugs again, stealing another glance at me through her watery eyes. "I weren't t'one leaving. She were moving away from me. I felt it every time I went back there, but I never knew what to do because...because I don't know t'rules."

I gingerly slide myself to the edge of the bed, and Tessa doesn't stop me. *I don't know the rules either, Tess. I don't know what's too little or too much, when to charge forward or when to back off. I don't know why the mere mention of Grier's name floods my being with a myriad painful and delicious feelings, even now, even after all these years. It's you that I want, just you.* These are the words I want to say to her, but I say nothing, do nothing. Instead, I stare miserably at the stitching on her pillowcase.

"After New Year," she says softly, "I didn't know what t'rules were with you and me, so I left it."

My eyes slowly slide closed, and my head falls to my chest. *None of this is down to you, Tess. It's me. It's all on me.* The words trip easily through my brain but remain there, my mouth unable to contribute in any way. The dull throb in my head is steadily snowballing, and I have no one: no angels, no devils, no Frank to soothe it. I can't do this. I want out.

"I've left it, thrown myself back into t'job, and left t'ball in your court all these months," she says. "But this." Her hand gestures a circle in the air between us, and her voice rises to a miserable sob. "It can't go on. We need to talk about it, do something about it."

I tentatively move my fingers over the bed toward hers. She glances at me and then away again.

"You know that too, Fin. I mean, I'm a novice here and you're t'queen of avoidance, but you can't be so thick as to think that it's just going to magically sort itself out and—"

And there it is. Sticks and stones. Just words. Just a carelessly tossed out insult, but— *Thick*. A button is pushed. I spring to my feet, cheeks flaming, my jaw clenched with rage. "Fuck you!" I scream into her astonished face before storming out of her room without a backward glance.

I'M COLD. IT'S COLD, it's dark, and my face is awash with a combination of tonight's drizzle and my own hot tears. I run. Pounding the pavements until my heart is fit to burst, I eventually find myself gasping for breath and clutching the wooden arm of a park bench for support. I welcome the seclusion and the pain in my lungs, but I know that she will come.

Casually drawing on a Sobranie Cocktail, my demon girl has found me. She exhales a smoky sneer into my face before she roughly shoves me to the ground. "You disappoint me, Fin."

Her icy stare pins me as I flop onto the bench. My head is spinning, and I'm battling the urge to vomit, but I can't tear my eyes from the leather-clad apparition slowly pacing in front of me.

"What did I tell you? Have you learned nothing from me?"

Her sneering growl lands a stinging blow, and I flinch back to rub the throbbing spot. My heart pounds painfully in my ribcage.

"Oh, don't be so melodramatic."

She positions herself on the bench beside me and whispers into my ear. I do not want to hear her words, to feel her disgust, to relive the memories she is forcing into my mind but I'm powerless to stop her, and she knows it.

"I told you. I told you that she's out of your league, that she's a smarty pants and you're...well..." She looks at me with a flicker of something resembling kindness in her eyes before she huffs and snarls and reverts to type. "You're Fin, and I'm here to help you. My job's to keep them from hurting you, and I'm damned good at it, so stop being such a big baby."

My eyes widen and I make to argue but she drags a thorny

fingernail down my cheek before I can engage my mouth.

"Oh, for Hades' sake! Face the facts. I'm here. I'm here for you." She stretches an arm out and gestures into the night. "Look around you, Fin." She snorts a cruel laugh into the air. "Where's that pathetic angel girl now, eh? Off rescuing abandoned kittens or some such contemptible nonsense. She's got bigger fish to fry than you, kid. And where's that brother of yours? He's off spending time with his favourite sister, leaving you to get on with it. Now Grier..." A thoughtful expression plays over her face as she taps her finger against her chin. "She also disappoints me," she says. "All this recent touchy-feely crap. It's so not like her." Then she smiles, a wide and coolly triumphant smile. "But she'll bounce back. She's focused and determined. She takes what she wants and apologises to no one. I like that!" She runs her tongue over her lips and all but purrs, her eyes gleaming in the darkness.

I'm weak with the exertion of battling the rising nausea in my stomach, the throb behind my eyes, and the stabbing pain in my chest.

"People don't change, Fin. Not her and not you." She sneers. "And I will always be with you, leading you through your mountain of pathetic shit."

She hates me. The realisation hits me like a bolt of lightning. My spinning head hurts. The gurgling contents of my stomach launch themselves upwards as I slide from the bench to my knees. I vomit, retch, and dry heave, snot and tears dripping from my face interspersed with the only word that I can manage to conjure. "No."

"No?"

Her hissed question stabs an icicle into my chest, but I nonetheless haul myself to my feet to face her. I'm hyperventilating, dragging in useless shallow breaths through my tightly clenched teeth, as my knees threaten to give way and send me tumbling. I hear a voice, my own ragged voice, punching out words into the inky darkness. "No. You don't help me... You've never helped me."

She tilts her head to one side, raises her eyebrow, and drags her thin lips into a condescending smile. "Oh, Fin," she whispers lightly, "we both know that you're not the sharpest knife in the drawer, and that I'm all you've got. You're—"

"Done. I'm done." I scream and pinch my eyes tightly shut. "Get away from me. I'm done with you. For good." A tornado of disconnected thoughts howls through my brain, twisting and turning my unanswered questions, demanding answers. Was Sister Mary Agnes right about me never amounting to anything because I once struggled to read? Will getting a degree really make me happy? Why is Grier still in my head? Should I confess to everyone that I love driving, and I really don't want to do anything else with my life? Does Tessa really like me? Could she...*love* someone like me? I have no answers. I have a long, painful shriek rising inside of me that will not be denied. It wants out, and it will rip me apart to find its exit. When I draw a hand across my sweating forehead and will myself to look into demon girl's malevolent eyes, I find myself alone.

When Life Gives You Lemons, Wear Surgical Gloves over Your Papercuts

"Thank you. Thanks. See you on Saturday then."

Therapist Maggie Thorne smiles and nods once before closing the door to her office. Sinking my fists into the pockets of my jeans, I turn and head for my car with a brisk pace. Bloodshot, red-rimmed eyes advertise to the world that I have spent the past ninety minutes ranting and sobbing in the company of Ms Thorne, but I don't care what the residents of this leafy Finchley suburb make of me. My first appointment with Cal's colleague is over, and I'm still standing, just.

I bolted to Cal's house the previous evening a weary, snivelling mess. I don't even remember driving there, but I do remember the look of utter shock on Cal's face when she opened the door to my frantic hammering. Wrung out and empty, I went to the only place I could think of. I don't think I'll ever forget the look on Cal's face when she opened the door and looked at me. God alone knows what she saw.

"I'll get you a cuppa, love," Kevin said, as he made his hasty exit from the snug living room where the two of them had been cosied up together in front of the telly.

Caroline Parker, my dear old friend, held onto me tightly, her body seemingly able to absorb all the shuddering sobs and incoherent ramblings of the unhinged and after a long while, I quietened enough for her to get a word in edgeways.

"Okay?" she whispered softly into my ear, withdrawing her body an inch or two. "You're okay, Fin. You're okay."

"No, Cal." I could only manage a slow and miserable shake of the head. "I'm not okay. I can't cope. I'm going under. I try to hide from it, but it just keeps coming back, and I can't cope. With the questions, with the lack of answers. I can't...deal with myself."

Caroline linked her fingers into mine, brought them to her lips, and gently kissed my knuckles. "Tell me," she said softly as she guided me to the sofa.

I cried. Uncontrollable, shuddering sobs that I was powerless to contain erupted from deep inside of me. I drew my knees up to my chin, wrapped my arms tightly around myself, and caved in while Cal watched and waited. Finally, I stilled, uncurled my body, and looked into her eyes. "What's happened to me, Cal?" I barely recognised the tiny croaking voice that pushed its way from between my lips.

Caroline nodded when she took my hand. "You're having a hard time right now, Fin," she said. "But you will come through it, I promise."

I wanted to tell her. I wanted to scream that I'd hurt Tessa, used Grier, that I'd become this miserable, self-interested person that I didn't recognise. I wanted to tell her that I could feel myself being sucked deeper and deeper into a gloomy place filled with demanding questions to which I had no answers, but I couldn't. How could I tell her, tell anyone, what I had become? I was still shaking, my knee rapidly bouncing up and down, when Kevin tiptoed into the room carrying a tray loaded up with a pot of tea, milk, a packet of mint Clubs, and two mugs. Catching my eye, he cast me a friendly wink before quickly shuffling out again.

"I like Kevin; he's a sweetie," I said, untangling our hands and reaching for a mug.

"I like Kevin," she said, her voice edged with unexpected lecherousness. "He's a sexy beast!" And then, she said, "Now here's what's going to happen."

With all the delicacy of a drill sergeant in a fluffy onesie, Cal told me that she was sending me to meet Maggie, her friend and colleague, who would fit me in for an emergency session. What I did after that would be up to me, but I would be going. Tomorrow.

She would touch base with me at the party, but I could call her any time before if I needed to. She would call me in the morning with the time and the address, and I would go. She told me that she had seen this coming, had detected something in my voice when I had called to cry off our Monday night get together, and had planned to make the appointment there and then. The events of this evening had merely accelerated things. She told me that she was too close to me to hear the things that I needed to say, but she would send me to the person to whom she herself unburdened her soul on a regular basis. I meekly nodded and sipped my near-scalding tea, too exhausted to fight her or anyone's army any longer. We chatted a little then, nonsensical fragments of chit-chat about Penguins versus Clubs and whether PG Tips had the steal on Tetley's, and when she later packed me off home with a quick peck on the cheek, I found my head no longer consumed with thoughts of Tessa, or Grier, or my life of quicksand. No, my focus had veered sharply towards the proposed meeting with Maggie, the anticipation and dread, and the hope of something better to come.

When I got to Maggie Thorne's, I was ready. After a fitful night of tears and broken sleep, I was all too aware that I needed to unburden myself, to let go of the pain, to start to find answers, and forge a way forward. It was strange to sit in this stranger's house, alternating between sobbing and ranting, something I never imagined I'd find myself doing, but Caroline had been right. I needed to do this. Whatever magic wand Maggie has secretly waved over me has worked.

She's helped me erect a set of temporary traffic lights to bring some control to the chaos of my life, a means by which I can manage the bottleneck of intrusive thoughts and emotions that have been threatening to bring me to a standstill. Okay, I'm still living in a multi-car pile-up, but we've called in the emergency services and set up a temporary diversion to allow the bottleneck to disperse. It'll take some time, but I'm actually pretty confident that two sessions a week with Maggie will move me forward to the open road I so desire.

Easing the Beamer into a heaven-sent parking space just outside the house, I shrug off the fluttering butterflies that are assuming battle formation in my belly. In spite of the horrendous encounter with Tessa last night, the harrowing session with Maggie, and Grier's impending arrival, today hasn't been as bad as I might have imagined it would be. The roads have been mercifully clear of HGVs, breakdowns, and kamikaze nobhead drivers, and I have zipped effortlessly between clients, my mind fixed and focused solely on the road ahead. My delight at hearing Frank's ebullient voice through the hands-free speaker was only partially dampened by him informing me that he would be staying at Bernie's on his return on Friday, that he had a bit of a surprise for me, and that my presence was required at the O'Sullivan dinner that night. I guess Saint Dymphna's holding all calls while she focuses on me then. I try to smile as I gently touch my fingers to the rosary beads that are hanging on my rear-view mirror, before bounding out of the car.

Two things occur to me on stepping through my front door and slinging my keys into the bowl on the console table. Tessa's bike isn't propped against the wall, ergo, she is not home. Score one. Secondly, there's a delightful smell wafting up from the kitchen that has Dazza's moniker all over it, and as I don't hear the sound of voices, I can surmise that Grier hasn't arrived yet. Oh, happyish day! I silently mouth the words "Thank you" as I charge down the stairs to investigate and find Carl sitting alone at the table, typing rapidly on his laptop.

"Oh, hey, Carl," I say, opening the oven door to fill my lungs with the delicious aroma of the contents within. "How's yourself?"

Carl continues typing the remainder of his sentence before saving and exiting and flipping down the screen. He raises his eyes to catch me drooling over the shepherd's pie and smiles. "Pretty good, Fin. You?"

This lukewarm greeting typifies our relationship; not exactly abrasive but lacking any real warmth or depth. I note that he's dressed in a grey checked wool suit and brogues, his usual workwear, and that he's finally beginning to show signs of looking his age. Same distinctive high cheek bones and same raze fade haircut, but the boyish dimples on his cheeks are concealed beneath several days' worth of distinctly manly grey stubble.

How exactly am I? I could tell him that my eyes are aching from all the crying, that my brain is struggling to contain the demanding myriad intrusive thoughts and focus on any single one, that my heart is battered and bruised.

"Fair to middling," I say, quick as a flash. Then I scowl, realising I'm speaking like Tessa. Again. I seize the gleaming serving spoon from the counter to distract myself. "I'm bloody starving! Do you think we could just..." I raise my eyebrows and nod in the direction of the pie.

Carl smiles again and shakes his head. "Nah, mate," he says, ruefully eyeing the pie. "I'm off to the Admiral Duncan to have a drink with Alex Durie, then I'll be picking Darren up from work."

Alex Durie? My eyebrows all but launch into orbit at the mention of the name. Alex Durie has only been my very favourite lesbian romcom writer for about a gazillion years, the object of my serious girlie fan crush. A slight blush warms my chest at the thought of her being here in London, which immediately melds with the snarling jab of irritation in my gut at the thought that Carl bloody Johnson of all people should be the one getting to meet her.

"She's brill, isn't she? I know you like her by the number of her books I've found lying around the house." He's clearly clocked my reaction, but he ignores it and ploughs on. "The agents are ironing out the details, but it looks like I'm gonna be directing the film adaptation of *Trying to Think Straight*, so we're getting together tonight before the formals."

My mild irritation rachets up a couple of notches, resentfully fuelled by the glow in his animated eyes. I try to cling to the promise I made to myself only hours earlier, that I wouldn't let anything invade my inner calm, but I find it rapidly evaporating into the air. I push out my lower jaw and avert my eyes as he continues talking.

"Much as I'd love to dive into Darren's pie, I need to go shave and get out of here. Grier'll be here in," he glances at the Longines watch on his wrist, "around half an hour, and she said she wants to talk to you. Has some things to explain. Darren dropped the pie in on his way to work this morning, and we won't be back till late tonight, so you two'll have some time and space to catch up with things."

Carl plants his hands on the table and rises to leave. My simmering petulance overflows, and before I can stop myself, my head jerks up violently. "Oh, yeah? What, things like you and Gree being Mr and Mrs you mean?" I didn't mean to say that. *Why* did I say that? I exhale slowly through my clenched teeth, furiously rubbing my thumb across the knuckles of my other hand,. *I will not explode. I will not lose it. I will breathe. I will recalibrate. I will take care of myself.* Carl sinks back into his chair like a boxer hitting the deck in slow motion, and the colour drains from his face. He stares at me, his eyes rapidly blinking under their furrowed brows. I do nothing to fill the ensuing silence.

"What... How do you... Who told you?" Carl seems genuinely incapable of fashioning a coherent sentence, the splintered words slipping messily from his lips, his pained expression pricking at my conscience.

Cease from anger and forsake wrath.

Do not fret; it leads only to evildoing.

I don't need angel girl to remind me of the psalm that pops up in my head; Mum used to wag her finger and quote it at me so often when I was a kid that I started to think it'd been written especially for me. I'm already struggling to understand just what exactly had possessed me to blurt out the long-held secret.

"It was a very long time ago," Carl says. His eyes squeeze tightly shut before he scrubs his face with both hands. When he raises his eyes to meet mine, I'm caught off guard by the fact that they're filling with tears. "It was before Ellie and—"

His voice falters and breaks, and I am truly ashamed of myself for being the catalyst of his anguish.

"I...I can't." Suddenly, Carl pushes his chair back from the table, screeching the legs against the flagstones as he rises. "Fin, you need to ask Grier about it," he says, all but bolting to the door and away. "Get Grier to tell you."

I hear his retreating footsteps pounding the stairs to the ground floor, along with my own hoarsely whispered, "Holy crap, Batman."

No Good, Some Bad, and Some Downright Ugly

I AM STILL HOLDING the serving spoon, running my thumb and forefinger in soothing circles over the cool metal, when I hear the front door open and then close with a slam. I've been sitting at the kitchen table waiting for her to arrive. Now she's here—they're here—bustling around on the floor above and about to shatter my hard-earned calm into pieces. *Deep breath. Exhale slowly. Feel the smooth metal between your fingers.*

"Fin?"

My body jolts at the sound, her voice now both strangely alien and yet so familiar to me.

"Are you in, Fin?"

The spoon clatters noisily onto the table, my fingers no longer able to contain it in my grasp. I rise from the chair and press my warm palms to the table's cool surface, locking my gaze onto the swirl of the grain. I will not allow my mind to transport me to our New Year encounter, to relive the ferocity of her shuddering orgasm in my bed, to ponder the fact that I had evaded her touch that night, opting instead to hold her body tightly against my own until sleep had overcome her. No, not now.

"Down here, Gree." My voice is an eerie echo in my head, oddly infused with a strength I know I don't possess. Their footsteps clatter down the stairs, and I prepare to greet Grier and Novia. "Into the valley of Death," I mutter to the room. The door swings open, and I dredge up a false smile to greet her. Grier, dressed impeccably in a black shift dress, biker jacket, and DM boots smiles warmly as she crosses the room to embrace me. I'm immediately struck by the curious mass of scarlet curls framing her pretty face and the familiar pale eyes that cause a minor flutter to ripple through my body. She looks a little older, a little stouter, but she is unmistakably Grier. The woman who follows hot on her heels is *not* Novia Delgado, and I am one confused bunny. Grier hugs me tightly, and I neither shrink from nor melt into the embrace. Instead, I recognise and welcome the green shoots of my growth regarding my altogether fucked-up relationship with Grier. I'm going to need to nurture them if I'm to survive this encounter with her, I think.

"Hey, hi." Again with the confident voice that does not belong to me, but I am almighty grateful that St Michael is apparently in my corner right now. Grier smiles up at me, stoking the butterfly tango in my stomach, and stretches a beckoning arm out to the stranger.

"Fin, this is my very good friend, Martha. That's Martha with the H silent."

The stranger dutifully shuffles closer and extends her hand to me. She is a tall, handsome woman, in her early fifties, I'd guess, smartly dressed in dark jeans and a designer hoodie, with long bottle-black hair and a relaxed, smiling face. She is *not* Novia.

"Hello, Fin. I have heard so much about you, I feel as if we have already met," she says, shaking my hand vigorously.

That's Feen as in Spanish Fin, I guess. Martha's voice conveys to me that she too comes from Spain, but she's still not Novia, and I'm still confused. I flash my welcome smile, nodding at her before rounding sharply on Grier, my brows and palms raised. "Novia?" I ask, my voice a little squeakier than I intend.

I have been dreading having to welcome Novia into my home, having to watch her and Grier together, having to suck it up and be civil to the woman who broke my life. Martha raises her eyebrows at Grier's grimace, and a flurried exchange in Spanish ensues. I am none the wiser.

Martha looks at me with a weak smile. "I think that you two need...conversation? To speak together," she says, her tone soft, almost maternal. "I think that I need to take a shower, to unpack." She squeezes Grier's arm and turns to leave. "I will see you later,

Fin."

"First floor, second door," I say, as Grier says the same thing in Spanish, presumably. She nods her head, smiles, and leaves the two of us alone. I feel as if all the warmth in the kitchen leaves with her. I don't look at her. "What's going on, Grier?" The coolness of my tone takes the both of us by surprise, I think, and silent seconds tick by before she answers.

"I'll put the kettle on," she says and lightly grazes my arm with her fingertips as she passes, heading to the counter. "We have some catching up to do. I have a lot of things I need to explain to you, sweetheart."

I feel like I've been dunked in Valium and pegged out to dry. Okay, my heart is thumping against my ribcage, but my brain is weirdly okay with this turn of events. Grier is nervously making the tea, the tremble in her hands clearly visible, as I sit, coolly awaiting the bombshells that are about to pour from her lips. My grumbling stomach struggles to disregard the aroma of Daz's shepherd's pie while my index finger works to break through the small hole I've found inside the pocket of my jeans.

"So. Novia," Grier says, her back to me as she pours the milk into two mugs. "We split up." The teaspoon clatters noisily against the side of the mug. "Eventually."

Good. Great. Hallelujah. May you rot miserably in hell, Delgado, you fucking, fuckwit bastard. I accept the proffered tea with a nod and do not give voice to the explosive thoughts in my head. I'm focused on a mission of self-preservation; meltdown avoidance is the order of the day. I'm blind-sided by an uninvited image of Tessa invading my head. Laughing Tessa, smiling Tessa, twinkle-eyed, kissable Tessa. Teary Tessa, angry, hurt Tessa. No. I shake my head to derail that particular ghost train, trying to focus my attention on Grier.

She has settled herself onto the bench across from me, her ever-beautiful, pale eyes searching my face for signs of reaction. Eight years. Eight years since this woman was mine, and I still feel an urge to reach out and cup her face in my hand, to graze a soft kiss on the side of her cheek. Briefly, I entertain the appearance of my angel girl, who slaps a stinging blow on my own cheek, reminding me to get a grip. I am reluctantly grateful and drop my gaze back to the safety of the wood grain.

Grier sighs and shrugs. "We had... just short of eight years of sizzling intensity," she says in a matter-of-fact tone, curiously devoid of emotion, "punctuated by recurrent bad behaviour, affairs, break-ups, reconciliations, high drama, and more break-ups."

My stomach lurches, and I rub a slow gentle circle across it with my fingertips. I drop my other hand to the table and cover hers with it. "Did she hurt you...physically?" My incredulous whisper quivers in the air between us as the realisation sets in my head; I would kill anyone who hurt Gree, but Novia? Novia, I would torture, crucify, and burn at the stake and enjoy every second.

Grier shakes her head sadly as she tenderly pats my hand. "We both behaved unforgivably," she says firmly.

When our eyes meet, there is a brief moment of pure tenderness between us, before she hurriedly withdraws her hand and all but leaps away from me and stands. I cannot fathom how it is that I'm emotionally still standing, but I am. I'm breathing regularly, but my finger has returned to the task of destroying my pocket, and my body is saturated with a murky grey desolation. I watch Grier as she flicks the switch on the kettle and starts to make another round of tea.

"Fin?" Her voice is so sorrowful, so pained that I start to rise from my seat to go to her and gather her in my arms, but she raises a hand and shakes her head at me. "Don't." She raises her eyes from the floor to mine and inhales deeply. "I have to tell you the truth about me, the truth of all of it, my darling, and I can only hope that you won't hate me at the end. You might, but...but please know that I loved you. I love you now, and I always will. Even if you decide you never want to see me again."

"Oh, fuck, Gree," I say, before I remember how much she

hates to hear me swearing. "Sorry."

Her lips stretch into a smile, but the haunting sorrow in her eyes remains. Grier gathers the tea things and returns to join me at the table. "In all of this, *you* have nothing to be sorry about," she says, her lips still smiling that smile that stops short of her eyes. "But we're going to need more tea, I fear, and I've brought the sugar too."

I sink lower in my seat as I prepare to hear what she's about to tell me, knowing that I will survive. Whatever she has in store for me, the anxiety and dread of it has been worse than the reality could ever be, and I am still standing, still breathing in and out, and I will do, am able to do, whatever I need to do to ensure that it continues.

Kung Fu
Meets the Dragon

"LIVING WITH MARTHA, BEING looked after by Martha and her husband Hugo, has made me realise that I've been a truly awful, selfish excuse for a human being for as long as I can remember. I've caused so much hurt, and I know that it's time that I...that I..."

It's strange to hear Grier describe herself in the way that others had tried, in vain, to have me believe over the years. Neglecting her tea as I sipped mine, she says that she first needs to tell me about Carl. Being no stranger to the confessional myself, I feel compelled to come clean about my conversation with him and the earlier one with Elizabeth.

Grier's eyes widen, and her mouth drops open in amazement as her trembling hand reaches for her cup. "You knew? All this time, you knew, and you never said anything?"

"He said you'd tell me about Ellie," I say, disregarding her incredulous question, unable to look her in the eye.

Grier bolts upright in her seat and clasps a hand across her mouth, as if my words have struck a double-barrelled shot to her heart. In an instant, her eyes fill with tears, a minute exclamation of emotion forcing itself from her lips. In my mind, I see the two of us viewed as if from above, me radiating an aura of calm purple, with Grier swathed in an emotional, red fog. When I reach for her hand, she pulls away from me, shaking her head as the tears race down her cheeks.

"No, Fin. Don't."

I sit, miserably digging another hole in my pocket as she struggles to compose herself with a number of deep breaths before she's able to continue.

"You know that Carl and I met at uni. Ironically, we first met in the Lesbian and Gay group, actually, but what you don't know is that we were together for a time. From the first day we met, we were magnetically drawn to one another, and...and we were good together." Grier momentarily drops her chin to her chest, before ruefully shaking her head as if that might dislodge the memory and send it on its way. "And then ..." Her eyes lock onto mine before she softly whispers, "I got pregnant."

Grier's words cattle-prod me. I always suspected that there had been more to their story than they had let on, but a child? The disclosure welds me to my chair with shock.

"My mum was horrified, and I can never forgive her for her racist attitude to Carl at that time. All she saw was a deadbeat Black guy who had impregnated her blameless little English Rose. But Carl was adamant that he was in it for the long haul, and he convinced me to marry him." She dabs at her eyes, her breath coming out in a shudder. "But I went into premature labour at thirty weeks. Ellie battled for her life, but..." She gulps, her body shaking. "She died in Carl's arms when she was two hours and thirty minutes old."

"Oh, God, Gree," I murmur. "That's truly awful. I can't imagine."

She shakes her head. "You can't. No one can. Something like that either pulls you closer together or drives you apart." Drawing her lips into a tight line, Grier exhales noisily. "It broke us. Carl lost himself in work, refusing to talk about it...about her, and I ...ultimately, I found my way to Ally."

I stare at a cobweb on my ceiling, unable to look at the pain in Grier's face. The visible ache in her brow, the pinched crow's feet at the corners of her eyes. Gathering her into my arms, I ignore her protestations and hold her, folding her into my body, with the quiet of the room broken only by her heaving breaths. Time sluggishly ticks by, with me somehow aging years with every second.

"I'm sorry, Gree. I'm so sorry, babe." A surge of unequivocally unconditional love rockets through my entire body, exiting my mouth as a tender whisper through the kisses I lavish on the top of her head.

"Thank you, thanks. That really means a lot to me." Grier disentangles herself from my embrace and motions for me to return to my seat.

She looks older to me, older and world wearily worn out. I certainly feel both.

Wiping her eyes with the heels of her hands, Grier gives me a sad half smile. "So, now you know, and that's that," she says. "I'm sorry that I've never shared that with you before now. It's not that it was a secret or anything, I just—" She pauses, and a faraway look crosses her face.

When my finger breaks through the hole in my pocket, I remind myself to breathe.

"I should have told you."

She smooths her palms down the sides of her dress, an action that causes me to swallow hard. I know every inch of the body encased in that dress, every curve, every dimple, every sensitive spot. My mouth, my fingertips know how to elicit delicious sighs and moans from this woman. Grier sits back down opposite me, close enough for me to lean across and kiss her if I want to, but I banish such thoughts. This woman isn't mine, hasn't been mine for the longest time, and I have to apply the brakes to my burgeoning inappropriate feelings. My stomach clenches when I hear my voice, cracking and needy, breaking the silence. "Gree? We've never once talked about this, but...why did you leave me?"

Greer blinks once, twice, before lowering her gaze and nodding. "Yes," she says. "You do need to know, I suppose." Wriggling in her seat, she tilts her head, regarding me with a sorrowful gaze. "Do you remember that night at the Hackney Empire?"

We'd spent many nights together at that particular venue but, somehow, I instantly know which one she's referring to, and my heart begins to flutter in my chest. I suck in a deep breath and nod. *Roots and trees, roots and trees.*

Grier launches into her recap of that crushingly boring night at the Hackney Empire all those years ago, the night when she had been commissioned to photograph the so-called performers for a London-wide publication. And there it had begun. Moderately celebrated lesbian artiste Novia Delgado had been the star billing, recounting her dramatic piece entitled *She Who Was Stolen.*

I shiver a touch at the vague memory of a witchy Delgado and her sidekick, the bonkers bongo woman, boring the shit out of me when all I had wanted to do was get the hell out of there and back into the arms and bed of my sweetie. Grier's pale eyes seem paler still, taking on a wounded expression as she stares hard at the wall behind my head. The *she* in question, she explains, refers to the child Novia had given birth to at the age of fifteen, the product of a scandalous liaison with an upstanding clergyman in her congregation at the time.

"Bloody hell!" I clamp my hand over my mouth when her words sink in. I was aware of the Catholic church's shameful scandal of course, but I regarded it as a distant "over there, other people" kind of thing. I fleetingly entertained a sketchy monochrome caricature of anonymous befrocked clergymen with evil leering faces and doleful children dressed in Victorian rags in my head. Now, sitting comfortably in my safe, twenty-first century kitchen, Grier has swept a paintbrush over my ill-defined outline, adding the detail and colour that made it real. Detail that flesh out Novia into a real person.

"Novia was harshly judged and berated, shamed by her own family," Grier says. "Her abuser was barely admonished by the church powers-that-be, before being hastily shipped off elsewhere. The final kicker was her family's insistence that the baby girl be immediately taken for adoption, against her frantic protestations. She was just a girl. Just a desperate little girl who couldn't understand why her baby was being snatched away from her." Grier sighs and closes her eyes. "Novia's dramatisation of having her daughter plucked from her arms an hour after her birth, of her grief, her continual search for something lost that couldn't be reclaimed, spoke to me in a way nothing else had. I couldn't explain that to you, Fin," she says, opening her eyes to look at me. "Not then. I couldn't explain the effect that seeing that, seeing her, had on me without telling you about Ellie and me. And Carl." She pushes her chair back, closes her eyes, and raises her chin to the ceiling. She inhales a deep breath, before puffing her cheeks to release it.

I slowly shake my head, unsettled by the weight of her sombre revelations. Rubbing my forefinger over my thumb in the pocket of my jeans, I remain silent, allowing her to get it all out.

"I was instantly consumed by the need to be close to her," she says, followed by unexpected chuckle. "The fact that she had the reputation of being a serial seducer of all that crossed her path went completely out of the window."

I bristle in my seat, reliving my searing pain at that time. It had taken less than a week for Grier to decide to leave me to go to Barcelona with Novia, and God, that still hurts.

"I was a coward," she says. "I was unable to be resist her magnetism, and I just couldn't face the devastation of your crushed heart. So I ran away."

So now I know. Long lost jigsaw pieces have been retrieved and reunited with their vacant slots, revealing the picture that had long eluded me. I should feel anger, relief, or something forceful, but I don't. I feel empty, desiccated, drained of the ability to feel anything other than the heat of the putrid acid churning round in my stomach. I don't want to be there. I too want to run away, but I sense that Grier isn't done with me, so I tuck my hands under my thighs and order myself to meet her gaze. She pauses, and the waft of a new chill hogs the air between us. Rubbing my forefinger over my thumb in the pocket of my jeans, I remain silent.

"That's not all of it," she says. "I have to tell you this." Her hand moves to cover her mouth, as if she's trying to hold the words in. Then, dropping her hand to her lap, she nods. "When we were together, I cheated on you, Fin. A number of times."

Tick, tick, tick, tick. The clock on the wall punches into the silence in the room, and I forget to breathe.

"I'm sorry," Grier whispers, as she stares at her hands twisting in her lap.

That barbed revelation comes pretty close to toppling me. I draw in a long, slow breath, and remind myself to breathe. Of all the things I've learned this evening, this cuts the deepest. A foot-long paper cut down my chest, awash with a never-ending waterfall of lemon juice, it just hurt and hurt. I'd had no idea.

"And it was my fault that Frank left," she says. "Frank knew. He caught me out one day and demanded that I come clean with you. I was scared shitless. I knew that it'd be the end of us so..." She shakes her head a little. "I called his bluff. Told him that you would believe my denial over his exposé. I told him that you'd always choose me over him, that you loved me more. Two days later, he left for Ayia Napa, and I was...relieved."

She stares at me, as though waiting for an explosion but I don't even flinch. I'm numb. The explosion of anger coils in my belly like a frozen cobra, poised to strike, but hypnotised into submission by her words.

"Carl knew too."

I concentrate on filling my lungs with air and expelling it as the bombs rain down.

"I'm sorry, Fin," she whispers softly. "Sorry that I did that, and I'm sorry that I've never told you. I know I should have. Carl thinks that my keeping you in the dark has prevented you from completing the puzzle and being able to move on, and...I think he's right."

I hurt all over. I feel as if I've been kicked and punched to kingdom come, and I know that the ensuing bruises will bring even more pain when this new information has fully settled in my head. I clench my jaw and pinch the bridge of my nose with my thumb and forefinger. I think of Frank, my grinning, steady rock of a brother, and all the years we had lost. He'd known she was right, that I'd have chosen to believe her, even if he'd told me the truth. With my body weighed down with a leaden weariness, I slowly rise and step away from the table. "I'm going to bed."

I have no idea where that calm, steady voice is coming from, but I need to get out of here, to get away from her. I need to evacuate to the safety of my room, to feel the comfort of cool cotton sheets against my burning cheeks. I leave her sitting there without a backward glance and climb the stairs on autopilot to fall into my bed. I think of Frank, of Tessa, and of everyone I have fucked over because of my misplaced loyalty to Grier Campbell. The woman who surely did not deserve my love.

I'm in serious need of the thumping, crashing dub rhythms of Lee Perry to preserve my sanity. Kung Fu meets The Dragon. No words, no loaded love song lyrics, just me, the jangling crash of the cymbals, and the never-ending reggae bass. Nodding to myself in the safety of my darkened room, I know that Maggie Thorne's survival technique toolkit will see me through—that, and the intervention of the dozen or more Catholic saints whose participation I have been soliciting all evening.

Cymbals crash in my ears, and I momentarily allow myself to drift away with the Dub Master's echo chamber. _Visualise yourself standing still_, Maggie had told me, a lifetime ago it seems, though it was only this morning. _Your feet are your roots, you are anchored deep into the ground. Whatever rains down on you will not topple you. You may bend, sway a little maybe, but you will not break. You will breathe, and your breath will bring nourishment to your roots. You will stand, remain standing through all the storms._

"And reggae music shall be my light and my salvation. Whom shall I fear?" I announce to the room, a tight humourless grin stretching out my lips. I draw a blackout blind down on the thoughts that are bristling in my brain and allow Lee Perry to carry me away.

Waiting to Exhale

"Nearly there. Don't worry, I'll get you there in time."

I smile in my rear-view mirror at the woman who is absently gnawing on her manicured nails in the back as I slowly inch the Beamer forward. We've been stationary for the past twenty minutes or so but are finally, mercifully, crawling forward toward the flashing lights and police cones which announce the accident site: an articulated lorry sprawled on its side, a white Range Rover facing the wrong way, its back wheels on the hard shoulder, two ambulances, three police cars, and a fire engine. My passenger gasps in shock, my grip tightens on the steering wheel, and I resist the urge to cross myself. Not me, and not today. I silently mouth my thanks to God, my eyes locked in focus on the empty lanes ahead.

I had awoken before the alarm this morning with a pain in my left ear and the soulful voice of Nina Simone in my right. When had I changed the music? I scrambled out of my comfortingly warm bed, wincing as I removed the offending bud from my ear, before heading downstairs for my first cuppa of the day. The kitchen was surprisingly warm, exuding tell-tale aromas of the previous night's activities; shepherd's pie, red wine, and cigarettes along with, I fancied, a rather pungent grey cloud of angst. Thanks to Grier's confessions, I'd had no appetite for Daz's pie last night, opting instead to stew in my bed, with my stomach indignantly announcing its protests against my neglect.

Jagged memories bubbled in my brain, noisily squabbling with one another for my attention. Grier and Carl, Grier's infidelities. I frowned when I spied a zip lock bag on the middle shelf of the fridge, my name neatly written on the label in a familiar hand. *Fin, remember to eat lunch.* I audibly snorted back my disdain and shoved the ham and coleslaw sandwich to the back of the fridge as I grabbed the milk carton for my tea. I slammed the door, causing the fridge to wobble on the uneven flag stone.

Grier wasn't getting off that lightly; one sandwich of apology wasn't going to cut it today. Tutting quietly to myself, I apologised to the fridge with a steadying pat, before settling at the table with my brew. How on earth was I going to make sense of the hotchpotch of recently acquired information that was swamping around in my brain? In amongst it all lurked a crocodile or two, smirking, waiting for an opportunity to swallow me whole. The sound of advancing footsteps on the floor above made me groan out loud.

"Hey. I knew it'd be you up at this ungodly hour. Do you have time for a cuppa?" Grier stepped into the kitchen and closed the door, but paused, as if unsure if she should continue.

I stared at her, expecting to feel a rush of emotions, but it never came. I breathed in through my mouth and out through my nose and waited.

Red-haired Grier Campbell, standing in my kitchen, wearing a long, stripey nightshirt and a hesitant look on her face. I shrugged my assent, seemingly incapable of speech, and downed the dregs of tea in my mug. Grier tiptoed across the cold flagstones to the kettle and began busying herself with the tea-making task. I sat uncomfortably on the bench, busying myself with the self-preservation task of keeping my breathing regular, and focused my gaze on her painted green toenails. Part of me wanted to bolt for the door, to escape from whatever situation this proximity would bring, but I remained stiffly motionless in my seat watching her, waiting for her to pop the invisible tension bubble that was keeping us squeezed apart in our respective corners.

"I don't want to leave things as they were last night, Fin." Grier brought the mugs to the table and sat down. "How are you feeling this morning?"

A simple question, but my jaw clenched in response. In an

instant, I became Frankenstein's monster, snapped into life by the jolt of electricity that the question brought to my previously impassive self. "How d'you fucking think I feel, Grier?" I heard my bitter, snarling tone, and I somehow knew that the time for trees, and roots, and steadying breaths had passed. Not even the sight of Grier's flinch could stop me from spewing the venom curdling in my stomach. "Angry, betrayed, confused," I yelled into her face. "Pick one, maybe pick all three, but even that won't come close to cutting it."

Truth be known, I want to break things. To throw my cup against the wall and watch the rivulets of beige chase one another down to the floor. To snarl and upend the table, to take a baseball bat to the crockery on the counter, and to wilfully, mercilessly, destroy everything I saw. Everything but Grier. Grier Campbell, who remained sitting silently opposite me, her head bowed as she held my wrist in her hand, gently rubbing it with her thumb. When had I leapt to my feet? When had I started gulping breaths? Had I really just slammed my fist down on the tabletop? I heard the devil girl's laughter, a gleeful cackle from somewhere far off.

"Bravo! You've grown a spine, Fin, dear!"

I refused to acknowledge her, my lips snarling to dispatch her. I'd screwed my eyes tight, desperately seeking out angel girl's voice.

"Breathe," my angel girl gently whispered against my ear. "Just breathe, and it'll be all right."

The outburst lasted only seconds but felt like minutes, hours even, and all the while, Grier held onto my wrist, releasing her grip only when I lowered my shaking body back into my seat. I stared hard at the tabletop until it went out of focus. "Why, Gree?" Hot tears pooled in the corners of my eyes. Even as I asked the question, I knew that I didn't want to know her answer. Want to know, need to know, can't bear to know. "Why wasn't I ...enough for you?"

Saying the words out loud felt as if someone had reached into my chest and ripped a strip of scar tissue from my heart, exposing the raw, unhealed wound beneath to the elements. Regardless of the pain and the stinging spasm that threatened to annihilate me on the spot, I also felt something akin to relief. How long had I agonised over this question? How many times had it surf-boarded its way to the fore, painfully pricking at my consciousness before receding with the outgoing tide? Want to know, don't want to know. Need to know, can't bear to know. It'd gone on far too long, and I needed an answer.

Grier reeled back in her seat as if she'd been harpooned, a wide-eyed look of incredulity flashing on her face. Shaking her head, she took both of my hands and urgently squeezed them in her own. "No," she said. "Don't ever think that."

I tried to look away, wanting to hide the agony that was surely evident in my eyes, but she wouldn't let me. Finally, I relented and returned her gaze.

"It wasn't you," she said slowly, with an uncharacteristic tremor in her voice. "It was me, always me. I was so fucked up with Ellie and Carl thumping around in my head. I was so confused, and you were—so perfect. I needed to make myself feel guilty." She ran her tongue over her lip. "I was a holy mess," she said and sighed. "I deliberately made myself feel bad, then scuttled back to you. You were—" She visibly winced, as if stung by her own words. "You, your love, was all that was right in the world, and I was selfish. I wanted to keep that."

How many tears does the human body contain? I was pretty sure that I'd expelled every single one in my body and then some the previous night but, sitting in my kitchen this morning with Grier cupping my cheek in her hand, I found my ducts replenished to capacity. The truth, the horrifying reality of the relationship that I had revered above all others had been exposed, laid bare for my consumption and, though I found it distasteful, I gulped it down. Cupping my hand over hers to hold it in place, I allowed the tears to flow for a time. We both did. Then, feeling a little shy, I withdrew from her, wiping my eyes with my palms.

"I've gotta get to work Gree," I said. After all that had been said, all that had passed between us in the preceding half hour, it sounded woefully inadequate, but I'd been too saturated with emotion to come up with anything else.

"Yes, you must." Grier looked down at the table for a beat, before smiling up at me. "Time and the DAC wait for no woman, you know."

I nodded and rose. "We can talk more another time," I said as I crossed the kitchen on shaky legs, pausing only briefly to retrieve the sandwich from the fridge before charging up the stairs, determined to throw myself headfirst into whatever cor-blimey horror show life might fling at me today.

Things I Should've Done Sooner

HOME TO HEATHROW, BASE to Charing Cross station, base to Maida Vale, and White Hart Lane stadium to Peckham Rye. The hours mercifully ticked by without incident, but the persistent drizzle from the battleship grey sky had been irksome, and I was happy to call time on the day's work after the last drop. Being forced to endure the rowdy animated banter of the three elated Spurs fans in the back of the car reminded me that I hadn't spoken to Frank today so I hastily called him after depositing the lads. I should have guessed that I'd find him jubilant and a tad tipsy in his armchair in front of the telly.

"Hey, sis. D'ya see the game?"

When would the man finally come around to the reality of my indifference to his beloved team? "Uh, no. Still working, Frank." I pause to negotiate a right-hand turn, carefully checking for motorbikes, before gliding smoothly into position, with Frank's animated monologue booming through the hands-free. I casually zoned out of his recounting of tackles won, shots tipped onto the bar, and the extra time winning header. I was wrestling with the weight of Grier's words in the kitchen that morning. Her revelations had blown me apart, and I'd struggled all day trying to fix myself back together. Having spent the day grinding out monotonous small talk with passengers I couldn't have cared less about, I was tired, world weary, and I just wanted to sink into the comfort that I knew his voice would bring. Sadly, that comfort was to be short-lived.

"So, how are you doing, Noo? Is Campbell there? Did you talk to Becks?"

A triple whammy for me to negotiate. How am I? Not freaking out and still standing, I suppose. Yes, Grier's here, but I didn't want to get into the details of the conversations we'd had right now. I was going to need time to sift through, to digest and process my thoughts and feelings before I'd be able to share them with him. I'd catch him up on the cor-blimey of that one tomorrow, maybe. And yes, I had spoken to Tessa...sort of. My cheeks ignite into what I imagine is a brilliant shade of red when I relive my abrupt curtailment of that particular episode, and I briefly take my hand off the steering wheel to rub my forehead.

Tessa didn't have had a clue that, in using the word "thick," she had invertedly stomped on my biggest button with both feet. I shake my head and suck my teeth. Poor Tessa had walked right into that one. No way on earth could she have known that seven-year-old Fionnuala, the girl who couldn't yet read, the girl who suffered the daily bullying and torment of her peers and a number of her teachers, would always come out with fists swinging on receiving that particular insult. I sigh, allowing my head to sink onto the steering wheel when I pull up to a red light. I'm no longer seven-year-old Fionnuala and, in the probable words of Sister Ignatius, forty-year-old Fin "must try harder."

"I have to talk to Tessa again, mate," I say, grimacing as I drag my lower lip between my teeth for the umpteenth time. "I sort of fucked it up a bit last time." The understatement of the year jabs me in the chest. Silence. Angel girl rolls her eyes at me. *Give me a break,* I plead.

"Right, right, okay." His uncertainty seems to reach across the miles. "Talk to Becks, Noo. I think she's a good un, as Dad would say." He laughs a little before his voice tenses. "And don't let that Campbell get to you. Don't let her get into your head."

"That ship sailed a long time ago, Frank," I say. "But it's okay. It'll be okay...I think." I pull the Beamer into a tight space outside the house and wish him a good night.

"You've got this, okay?" he says in his big brother voice.

I take a deep lung load of the frosty night air as I climb the front steps of the house, not altogether convinced that I do.

A warm blast of radiator benevolence greets me as I step into hall and fling my keys on the table. I'm relieved to note the absence of Tessa's bike, remembering that she'd told Carl she wouldn't be holding her weekly tutorial meeting in our living room this week. A twinge of sadness accompanies the relief. "Can't live with her, can't shoot her," I whisper. Oh, well, at least I'll only have one ex to deal with tonight. Small mercies, and all that.

My eyes fall on two brown paper packages which are neatly stacked in the centre of the table by the door. I smile when I notice the American postage stamps on the smaller one. After a riotous evening at Deborah's flat spent playing a ludicrous quiz game called, _How butch are you?_ I had ordered its sister, _How femme are you?_ from a San Francisco gift shop, hoping to repeat the revelry with Deborah, Juno, and Tessa. I can't imagine that happening any time soon, so I squeeze that particular memory into a small box in the depths of my brain and rip into the second package. My mouth falls open when I find myself holding a shiny new copy of Alex Durie's latest novel, _Bite Me_, which I know isn't due for release for several months. I fan the pages, drinking in the aroma of the virgin paper and ink, before the annotation catches my eye. Inside the jacket is a handwritten inscription,

To Fin,
Who I will definitely call in the event of a zombie apocalypse.
Keep fighting the good fight, you great sapphic warrior!
Love, Alex.

Wow. Standing in my hallway cradling the book tightly to my chest, the cogs in my brain whir. That Carl Miller of all people set this up, even after I had brought him to tears the other night. That I came so close to being swallowed by the murky quicksand of despair to now find myself standing here in a trance of fan girl ecstasy. That this has been the most bizarre week of my entire life. The sound of the living room door opening interrupts my daydream, and Carl steps through, shuffling awkwardly toward me, his gaze firmly fixed on his shoes.

"Hey. I see you got the book then?"

My stomach tightens as we face one another, neither daring to make eye contact, before the Fin from another dimension grasps his hand and entwines our fingers. When I feel the stiffness in his fingers release, I pull him into a heartfelt embrace, and we stand, silently rocking together for a time. Carl makes to pull back, but I draw him into me again.

After all the years I have spent hating him, I finally face the facts. Carl Miller is not the anti-Christ. He's not my enemy, and he would've been my friend if I'd let him. My mind entertains images of him from our shared past. Carl bringing me a cuppa and flopping himself down on the sofa to watch *Coronation Street* with me, and me inching myself away from him. Carl offering to spot me the five grand I needed for the deposit on the Beamer without so much as a blink, and me barely concealing my resentment when I accepted. Carl interrupting his filming schedule and taking planes, trains, and automobiles to get back to London for Aunt Pearl's funeral, and me all but ignoring him. Without my husband-hating blinkers on, I realise that he's been nothing but good to me, and it's me that's been the arsehole all along. I know that I need to change that. I *want* to change it.

"I'm sorry, Carl," I whisper into his chest. "I'm so sorry, mate."

His arms slide around my shoulders, and we remain locked together in our ungainly hunch as the seconds slip by. I'm acutely aware that I'm unable to recall the last time that we embraced, if indeed we have ever done so throughout the numerous years of our acquaintance. He places a kiss on the top of my scruffy dreadlocked head, before taking a backward step and releasing me. I stare into the chiselled face with the kindly eyes.

"Fin. Thank you," he says, his gravelly voice heavy with emotion.

We fall back into an easy embrace in the hallway of the house that we share, and a long minute passes before he pulls back.

He clears his throat. "We're having pizza," he says, motioning to the living room. "Come and have some."

I decline, telling him that I have a phone call to make. "But tell Gree and Martha hi from me, will you?"

He nods, smiles, and disappears back into the living room, as I haul myself up the stairs to my room. When I open my bedroom door, my eyes fall on a stiff, white envelope that has been pushed under it, and I stoop to retrieve it. I turn it over in my hands, recognising Tessa's scratchy hand in the single written word, *Fionnuala*. I toss it onto the bedside table for later as I focus on the task in hand, my finger trembling when I prod the speed dial number in my phone. A prolonged ring, a second, and then a third. I slump onto my bed with a lump in my throat and tears pricking my eyes when the familiar warm voice comes through the speaker.

"Hello?... Hello?"

It's been too long since I last made this call. Smiling, I release my lower lip from the attentions of my teeth and say, "Hi, Mum."

How Many Lesbian Angels Does It Take To Change a Life Bulb?

Hi Fin,

I wanted to speak to you before the party, but I'm not sure if I'll get a chance, so I've decided to drop you this note. There's so much to say, but I suppose that's been our problem all along, hasn't it? Not saying the things that need to be said.

I'm sorry that our last conversation ended on such a sour note. It seems that we're just not cut out to be together, but I really like you. A lot. I'm absolutely crap at doing the relationship thing, and you've obviously got some unfinished business going on with that woman. I know you. I know that you didn't mean to hurt me, but that happened all the same, and I'm working on dealing with how I feel now, and how I can move forward.

After the New Year thing, I distracted myself by getting involved in the Student Support Service at work. It's been really hard emotionally. I've been supporting a young woman who was assaulted by another student on our campus. She's just a kid, younger than her age really, and steering her through filing a police report, telling her parents, and keeping up with her work has really left me drained. My line manager is insisting that I take some time off to recover and regroup, so I'm planning on getting out to the Cape next week to spend some sun time with Mum and Soph.

I've been thinking that I should probably find somewhere else to live when I get back. It's been great living here with

*you and Carl but, if I'm honest, it's also been pretty hellish
too, being so close to and so far from you. I really want us
to be friends again, and I think we can, given a little time
and space. Perhaps things will fall into place if we're not on
top of one another, so to speak. Haha! You make me smile,
laugh out loud even, and I really miss those things. Bad
timing and a pointy anvil too far have kyboshed us being
together, I fear. Dealing with other people's problems as
a support worker has given me a broader understanding
of the reasons that lead people to doing what you did and
though I can forgive you, it's going to take me some time
to forget it and move on. Right now, I need to draw a line
under that awful chapter and concentrate on getting back
to being myself again, and I think that you need to do the
same.*
*Deborah tells me that you're a wicked dancer so if you ask
me to dance at the party, I just might! Let's try to be friends,
you sweet, crazy woman.*
Love,
Tess

PERCHED ON THE END of the wooden bench at the kitchen table
drinking my morning tea, I stare at the letter. Blue fountain pen ink
on thick writing paper. This is no hastily scrawled Post-it. I've been
turning its contents over and over in my mind since I first dared
to rip into the envelope. Having spent the best part of an hour
bathing in the warmth of Mum's voice, Dad's teasing banter, then
more caressing and cajoling from Mum, I felt sufficiently buoyed
to tackle Tessa's letter. The heat-seeking anvil hit its mark, and its
shock waves are still reverberating through my entire body.

She was still prepared to talk to me. *Good.*

I had been so preoccupied with my angst and navel
contemplations that I failed to detect her need for support through
her challenging work situation. *Crap.*

She wanted us to be friends. *Hopeful.*

She thinks that this can be best achieved by her leaving the house. *No, no, and thrice, no.*

The sound of footsteps descending the stairs jolt me back to the here and now and somehow, I know it's her. Bang on cue, Tessa charges through the kitchen door, stops dead in her tracks, and comically trips herself in the process when she catches sight of me at the table. My stomach performs a minor somersault at the sight of her, dressed and freshly scrubbed for work, sandy strands of damp hair poking out of her bike helmet.

She wrinkles her forehead in apparent confusion as she heads for the fridge. "Oh, hiya," she says over her shoulder.

She appears to be more flustered than I am, and I enjoy that particular role reversal a little too much. "I made you coffee." I nervously shift the letter from left to right with my fingertips across the tabletop. I'm nervous, she's nervous, and all this before breakfast. My stomach announces its displeasure with a loud prolonged growl that makes both of us laugh, momentarily. I gesture to the now lukewarm mug that I have lovingly prepared with an inexperienced hand, and Tessa joins me at the table. We are a couple of feet apart, and I can feel her warm breath hitting my face. A flush of heat creeps up my chest. "How is it?" I mumble.

Her eyebrows furrow a little when she raises the proffered mug to her lips, and she pauses to inspect the contents before she shrugs, obliging me with a nervy first sip. "Brown," she says. "Fin, it's...brown and um...sort of savoury."

There's a silence, a second or two passes and then we both explode with laughter. The dimples in her cheeks put in a rare appearance, making her look like one of Santa's better dressed elves. Those playful twinkling eyes, the laugh that awakens the butterflies in my stomach, that tingling stirring of arousal that makes me want to reach out and touch her... God! Am I some sort of a pervert to be turned on by one of Santa's little helpers, and why the fuck am I imagining Tess wearing a green felt hat with a bell on the end anyway? I purse my lips and exhale. This friendship lark is going to be harder than anticipated, methinks, but I am resolute. I'll do whatever it takes to keep her in my life.

"You know I only do tea." I steal a glance at her, but quickly redirect my gaze when my heart does another somersault. I raise my hands in a gesture of surrender. "This is me wandering into the realms of the unfamiliar and, if I might say so, downright nasty. Me trying to do a matey thing."

She laughs that laugh again, and I gulp a hasty swig of my cold tea in order to swallow down the surprising rush of want that's threatening to launch itself from my mouth in the form of a mournful sob. I miss Tessa, my Tessa, but I'm in no position to make any sort of move on that score. I'm here with her now; we're talking, we're laughing, I'm breathing regularly, and I'm not freaking out in a haze of uncontrollable lights and sounds and smells. I'm still standing.

"Don't go, Tess," I say in a strangled whisper. "Leave the house, I mean. Go to work, of course, but don't move out." When I raise my bowed head to meet her gaze the armies of tiger moths breach the expanse of No Man's Land in my stomach and fully engage. "I'm sorry. I know how much I've hurt you. You deserved so much better from me. I'm so, so sorry." The words shoot awkwardly from my lips as I grip the sides of my chair. I feel like a sad little T-shirt in a tumble dryer, buffeted and billowed by merciless jets of hot air. I have no control over my direction as I am flung; left and right, falling, rising, desperately clawing at the air in a vain attempt to stay sunny side up. The ensuing silence screams into the air between us.

Her eyes are squeezed shut as she rubs at the brow of her nose. "Fin, I'm trying to be t'grown up here. I—"

"Can't we talk about it though?" My hands are encased in woolly mittens as I attempt to clutch the falling straws. "Tonight. Can we get together tonight to talk?"

Tessa smiles as she rises from the table, and I dare myself to look into her eyes.

"No, no, we can't," she says, wagging a finger in my direction.

There's a recovering paper cut on her fingertip, and I wrestle the urge to lean forward and kiss it better.

"You've got your O'Sullivan family dinner thing, remember?"

"Oh, fuckity bastarding hell!" I groan loudly and slap my hand against my forehead in frustration.

"Creative, Fin, very creative."

Tessa's sweet laughter rumbles the air as I pound my fist on the unfortunate table. Indeed I do, though I *was* whipped into it. I scowl a good un and scour my brain, seeking the out clause that will permit me a little more time with her. Fleetingly, I entertain an image of myself in the House of Commons, lumped in with a gaggle of rebellious MPs. The stern-faced Chief Whip is letting them know in no uncertain terms that they *will* be present at the vote, and they *will* vote aye. Turning his attention to me, he states, "Your sister expects you for dinner." His raised eyebrow sends a chill down my spine when he adds, "Need I say more?" Um...*Nah.* I signed on the dotted line, I promised Frank and, chickenshit that I am, I really don't want to incur the wrath of Bernie on the eve of her birthday. The image of Bernie, menacingly armed with a rolling pin and advancing in my direction as she silently mouths the words "Don't even think about it" causes another shiver. Go, I must.

"Wait...how do you know about that?"

Tessa starts shoving her laptop into her rucksack. I didn't tell her and Frank's not here, so how come she knows about my itinerary? She rolls her eyes at me as she fastens the rucksack zip, then flashes me a glimpse of her chipped tooth when she grins.

"Got a pool playing sesh lined up with me best bud tonight," she says.

The lightbulb flickers into life. I stare dejectedly at her rather lovely houndstooth check V-neck, the crisply ironed white shirt beneath, and that kissable star shaped freckle just below her earlobe. Deborah's Tessa's friend, and Juno's her best bud. Frank has eased himself into a back-slapping, arm-thumping matiness with her. Inept bozo that I am, I'm on the verge of careering away from her into a miserable former housemate category. My eyelids blink rapidly as my brain rattles about in my skull, trying to unearth a lifeline.

Anything? Anything? Think, Fin. Don't be a fucking loser all your life.

"I'll drop you over there," I say. *Bloody genius, Fin!* Apparently, St Hildegard has decided to put in an appearance and is whispering a hastily constructed plot in my ear. I'm sure that there are rules about angels employing violence and using profanity, but my angel girl has just headbutted demon girl and is grinning at me with thumbs raised. She's dressed in white Levi's and a white leather biker jacket, but it's her all right. I grin right back.

"I'm picking Deborah up." It's a lie, so I make a mental note to text Deb the plan, and sharpish. "I could drop you off and pick you up on the way back too if you want." It's ingenious. A cunning plan to get Tessa alone, to work on Operation Don't Leave Me This Way. I even manage to crack a smile. Tessa hoists her bag onto her left shoulder, slips an arm around my shoulders, and pulls me in for a brief, somewhat awkward hug. My skin prickles with goose bumps at her touch, and I fill my lungs with the warm, delicious scent of her neck and her freshly showered hair.

"Yeah, okay," she says, releasing me all too soon. "I'll be back by six, but I'm staying over there tonight. Can't say I really trust meself being under t'same roof as madam tonight without sticking one on her." She flashes me a quick smile and an awkward flappy wave as she heads out the door.

"I'll hold your coat," I mutter under my breath.

I resolve to make more of an effort to carve out a place of neutral co-existence with Grier. I'm not sure if she deserves it. I certainly haven't forgiven her, but I rationalise that the most effective way of subduing the angry beast that she has unleashed in me is to deny it nourishment. I'm aware that the bubbling bile in my stomach is meat and drink for the beast, so I'm currently ensconced in the kitchen, frying salt fish fritters for Gree and Martha's breakfast as they sit at the table, drinking coffee and chatting in a mixture of Spanish and English. Later, I'll drive them both to the not-so-surprise party that is being held in my honour at the DAC office. I still don't have a clue what I'll tell them all about my exciting sabbatical plans and how I've decided to remain a DAC driver, but for now I have bigger fish to fry, so to speak. I spear the final fritter and drop it on the pile then carry the plate to the table and sit myself on the edge of the bench.

Grier looks up at me and smiles. "I'd forgotten what a domestic goddess you are, hon."

Her head twitches, and she drops her gaze. I can read her mind. Too soon for such terms of endearment. It seems that, for the first time since we split up, she is genuinely trying to respect the boundaries that separate us, to acknowledge the here and now as opposed to our past relationship, and it's unfamiliar territory for us both.

Grier gently pats Martha's hand. "Of course, Martha here is also not too shabby in the kitchen," she says, a warm smile on her lips. "I don't know what I would have done without her these past months. Starved and withered away, roaming the streets of Las Ramblas taking to myself, I expect."

"Ha, pollita!"

"Mi mejor amiga!"

Martha returns her smile as she rubs Grier's hand with her thumb, the two of them locking eyes tenderly. Sulky, possessive Fin might have been inclined to jealousy at this display of mutual affection, but I'm warmed by the sight. Whatever the future holds for Grier, I'm glad that she has a Martha in her life. I'm grateful that when Novia had thrown a glass of red wine in Grier's face at the dining table, it had been her lifelong friend Martha who had demanded that Novia leave and Grier stay. Tears had spilled down Grier's cheeks when she'd told me of their concluding break-up that night, of the strength she had drawn from the hand of friendship and the roof over her newly homeless head that

Martha had offered. Martha had witnessed the spiralling decline of the relationship in silence, but this single action had proved to be an abuse too far, and she had swept in and scooped Grier up. Blinking away prickling tears of my own, I feel nothing but gratitude as I gaze at the back of Martha's head. When I mutter my excuses and take my leave, I feel a curious sense of satisfaction. My roots are apparently holding strong now, and the earth beneath my feet is solid. Hell, I'm feeling so grounded that I might even attempt a sway in the breeze later.

Onwards and Upwards

"YOU DO KNOW THAT you lose precious butch points for packing like a girlie princess for one overnight, don't you?"

Tessa narrows her eyes and scowls at me as I cautiously inch the car out of the parking space. I chuckle and grin, licking my forefinger and marking an invisible strike in the air with it, before smoothly sweeping the Beamer into the lane.

"My professional drag." Tessa wrinkles her nose in distaste as if the words have released an unpleasant odour into the air. "I hafta to put in an appearance at t'sodding awards ceremony tomorrow night."

I jerk my head to look at her, unable to hide the alarm in my eyes. She has a work do tomorrow? She's going to miss the long-awaited, O'Sullivan shindig? I won't get a chance to fix things, to make them right. A sharp gasp escapes my lips, followed by a deep gulping of air. The thought that Tessa won't be at the party slices me in two, and I fix my gaze on the tarmac and the cars around me ahead in order to remain in one piece. *Breathe. Roots. Squeeze out the screaming thoughts in your head. You can cope with this.*

"Don't worry, I'll be coming to t'party as soon as I can escape."

A muscle in my thigh visibly jumps when Tessa gives my knee a reassuring squeeze. "Good, great. That's good." I resist the urge to sigh and place my head on the steering wheel in relief—never a good idea while doing 40 on the A406—and silently chew on the inside of my cheek as I rattle my brain for something stimulating to add. The fleeting touch of her fingertips turn a small cog of desire somewhere deep in my belly that our proximity in the car is ratcheting higher and higher as the seconds tick by.

"What're ya thinking, Fin?"

Shifting in her seat, Tessa has clearly witnessed my flinch and the creeping flush on my cheeks that accompany it. Reverting to type, I open and shut my mouth without uttering a sound. What am I thinking? I'm thinking *St Fiacre, I'm a taxi driver; get me out of here.* No, wait. I'm a tree… I have roots…yada, yada. I can do this.

I grin. "Just that I can't wait to humiliate you on the dance floor. The dance-off is on, my friend!"

The sound of Tessa's laugh, her grin, and the eyebrow that I know will raise at my comment mercifully fills the space between us with warm and fuzzy. Okay, I have to work diligently at slapping down the *other than matey* sensation in my belly, but my shoulders drop, making normal conversation with her an option.

"You are so full of shit, Fin."

"Aren't you cold, Tess, what with that yellow belly of yours being exposed to the elements?"

The banter between us comes thick, fast, and surprisingly easy as the Beamer hurtles on toward Deborah's, reminding me of all the things I love about being with her, the things I've sorely missed over the preceding months. The gentle teasing, the poking and arm slapping, her hoots of derision at my every selection in a rather illuminating round of "Who'd you rather?"

When we pull up to park in Deborah's street, the revelry vaporises, both of us acutely aware that we have failed to broach the subject of her leaving the house. I think it's fair to say that neither of us actually *want* to talk about it. I kill the engine, and we sit together in silence, her turning her hands in her lap, and me fiddling with my key ring.

"Um, Tess?"

"So, we never–"

We simultaneously begin to splutter nervy, half-finished sentences. Tessa's eyes drop to study her feet, and I shake my head and grin, without a clue as to where the remainder of my question had hidden itself. *You're gorgeous. Your hair seems to have changed colour, more red and less fair, and it's beautiful. I wish it wasn't tucked into your baseball cap. I'd love to see it loose and flowing, to bury my fingers in it, to gently pull your face toward mine, to lean into you and kiss you soundly.* Unfortunately, Fin of old has taken control of my body, and those thoughts remain imprisoned in my head, my lips remain hermetically sealed. Tessa swivels in her seat to face me, locks her eyes onto my own and, for a moment, just one brief moment, we stare at one another, unblinking, eyelids heavy with something akin to desire. I'm convinced that another second would see us melt together into a soft brushing of lips, but my irritating golden sister steals the moment by choosing to announce her presence with a sharp rap on the side window of the car.

"Hell's fucking bells, Deborah!" Tessa's whispered growl punctures the emotional bubble in which we were cosily encased, and we both spring back to our respective corners.

Ding ding, round two.

Old Fin sits motionless and miserable, glued to the seat, staring through the windscreen in a silent sulky strop as Deborah and Juno decant Tessa's bags from my boot to the pavement. New Fin resists the urge to punch Deborah senseless when she clatters into the passenger seat beside me, opting instead to watch helplessly as Tessa steps back from the car, moving a little hesitantly in the direction of the entrance of the block of flats. My mind buzzes as it tries to block out the incessant chatter pouring from my sister's lips. *Look at me, Tess. Please don't go.* My silent pleas go unanswered, and I emit a clipped sigh of resignation when I'm forced to endure the sight of Deborah and Juno mushily snogging their goodbyes through the open passenger window.

"Have a good time." Juno reluctantly steps away from the car, before pounding her fist on its roof to dismiss us.

"You too," I say automatically, without looking at her.

Sister Maria Patricia, Fatty Patty to us girls, chose that

moment to pop into my head, tutting and waving a bony finger of admonishment at my lack of good grace. I conjure a friendly smile when I turn to look at Juno. "And yes, you do get a bonus butch point for coming out in this fuck awful rain in just your shorts and vest."

A laugh from Juno, a throaty gurgle of appreciation from Deborah, and I shove the car into gear and the near moment with Tessa to the back of my mind.

I hate the South Circular almost as much as I love the North Circular. The North Circ takes me where I need to go, whereas the South Circ forces me to endure my annoying sister rabbiting away in my ear, as I sit scowling at the taillights of the car in front. The journey that should have taken an hour has taken a gruelling one hour forty-five and has done little to improve my mood.

I'd promised Frank and Bernie that I'd be there tonight, but why on earth had I volunteered to suffer the torture of transporting my irksome sister Deborah too? I sigh, perhaps a little too loudly, because she shoots me a quizzical look before returning her attention to the text message she had been sending. Yeah, I'd happily pay the annoying sister price for twenty minutes of alone time with Tessa. I'd even resist my escalating urge to shove her out of the door every time the car slowed to a stop. By the time I manoeuvre the Beamer into a fortuitous CPZ slot in the road adjacent to Bernie's, I am bored, hangry, and more than a little miserable. Tessa so close, Deborah so...bloody annoying. I rap the brass knocker on Bernie's front door three times and try to suppress the lump in my throat. The door is opened by a tall woman I don't recognise. She's wearing jeans and a lumberjack shirt and is sporting a broad smile.

She pushes her nerd glasses back up her nose and runs a hand over her steel grey curls. "Fionnuala! You haven't changed one bit," she says, pulling my unwilling frame into a surprise hug. Looking over my shoulder, she extends her other arm and adds, "Oh my God! It's little Deborah, all grown up!"

My stomach flips as realisation seeps into my brain. "Katherine?" When she releases me from the embrace, I slump against the door frame. She extends both arms to Deborah and pulls her into a full body hug. I've never been good with surprises; they make my head throb and my knees wobble, and right now I'm in dire need of the support kindly offered by the door frame. Katherine steps back into the house, smiling broadly as she pulls us both with her. I blink hard and rapidly, struggling to control the buzzing in my stomach and the twinkling stars that have invaded my eyes. Can everyone see them or is it just me?

When I catch sight of Deborah, clearly at a loss for words for a change, I manage to wrestle control of my body and force my eyes to focus on Kath. She's tall, taller than me, and she wears her O'Sullivan corkscrew curls flattened and brushed out into waves around her face. She's as stick thin as I am, but she looks older than her forty-eight years, older than Bernie even. What startles me the most is how much she resembles Mum and not Dad, which is definitely not how I remember her. When she pulls me into another squeeze, I'm surprised to find myself sliding my arms around her and hugging her back.

"It's Katie these days, Fionnuala."

She places a gentle kiss on my cheek, and the contact explodes an unexpected wave of emotion that washes through my body, clear down to my roots.

"Fin, these days." I laugh softly, as Deborah shuffles awkwardly behind us. I revel in that reversal of fortunes until my angel girl pops up to fix me with a scowl. I'm mentally shrugging my protestations of innocence when an unfamiliar male voice booms out of the living room.

"Katie! Where're you at, pet?"

Katie O'Sullivan throws her head back with a snorting laugh and rolls her eyes before grabbing our hands to tug us forward again.

"That'll be Robbie, my other half, and the other half of my

surprise package," she says and grins widely. "Come on, you two. Wait 'til you meet Frankie's surprise!"

Wait, what? There's more? Deborah and I follow our long-lost big sister down the hallway, exchanging shrugs and raised eyebrows as we go. The dualling butterflies in my stomach have somehow found a way into my bloodstream, because I'm tingling from head to foot. I roll my eyes and shake my head when we reach the living room door, pretty sure that this week could not get any more surreal, but I stop abruptly and push Deborah through the door first. Just in case.

Weekends Start with Dinner at Bernie's

HOW MANY DINNER GUESTS can you fit into a three-bedroom semi in Streatham? Without the garden room extension that Bernie and Paul added last summer, probably five or six, but the new open plan living space that I step into sports an enormous, T-shaped dining table arrangement, elegantly dressed for ten.

"Look what I found lurking on the doorstep."

Laughing, Katie ushers us into the room, and I consider the scene. A gaggle of rowdy O'Sullivans standing around the table, laughing and chatting away in animated fashion, all turn to look at us. The raucous cheer that erupts sets my cheeks ablaze.

"Well, about bloody time! Where've you two been? I'm bloody starving!"

Making a show of rubbing his stomach, Frank the Plank picks his way through the crowd to embrace us. He squeaks a kiss on Deborah's forehead, before he hip-bumps me, throwing in a quick poke in my ribs for good measure. We grin at one another before launching into a hand-slapping war. I would've won hands down, so to speak, if I hadn't paused to look at the heavily pregnant woman who appeared at his side.

"You're such a big kid," she says, lightly touching his shoulder, before turning her attention on me. "I take it you're Fin then?"

I'm vaguely aware that my jaw has dropped, leaving me standing in front of them with what is surely a comically gormless expression on my face. "Wha? Um. Yeah. I'm his big sister," I sputter before grabbing her hand and shaking it vigorously.

Frank rolls his eyes at me. "I know you're not great with surprises, Noo, but I wanted to introduce you to these three," he breaks off to slide his arm around the woman's waist, tenderly kissing her cheek, "in person. Ash, this is Fin, Fionnuala. Noo, this is my sweetie, Asha, and our next gen twins."

I feel a little lightheaded. How can my boneheaded brother possibly have landed the attractive redhead with the supermodel smile standing in front of me? More's the point, how can *he* be about to become a father? I mean, this if Frank, for God's sake. Before I can speak, Deborah barges me aside.

"Oh, congratulations you two!"

She throws her arms around them, edging me further out of the loop. Casting a knowing look at me above Deborah's head, Asha accepts Deb's pawing, while Frank takes a step back. I clench and unclench my fists, idly wondering how long I'd get for murdering Deb there and then, and whether doing the time would be such a great hardship. Angel girl gives me the eye, and I give her a shrug. Frank tugs at my sleeve.

"I wanted you to be the first to know," he whispers. "I asked her to marry me, and she only went and said yes!"

Okay. There's cor-blimey bad, and there's cor-blimey good, and this revelation definitely falls into the latter category. When I pull him in for a hug, my delight for him and them is fleetingly interrupted by the wave of trepidation that sweeps through me. I've only just got my brother back, and now he's being ripped away to become a husband and father. He's going to be too busy to be my wingman, my protector, my rock. As if sensing my unease, Frank draws back from the embrace and grasps both my hands.

"Remember what I said…about St Damian and wotsisface?" he says, earnestly holding my gaze.

When the fierce heat in my cheeks spreads to the tips of my ears, I break eye contact and stare at my trainers. I'm being selfish. I'm thrilled that he's apparently banished the ghost of Shar the Terrible to move on to a bigger and better life but…now that he's back in my life, I want to keep him. The devil girl comes creeping into my periphery, toasting fork held aloft, but I banish her with a flare of my nostrils. Hastily adjusting my big girl pants, I remind myself to focus on my roots. Yes, my leaves are fluttering in the wind, but I know that my roots have monster cahoonas. I'm okay. I can cope with this.

"I won't let you go again, Noo," he says. "I got this new job with this firm that specialises in immigration appeals—team leader, if you can believe that! We're gonna relocate back to the Smoke this time next year."

Angel girl is getting overexcited "Woohoo!" She cartwheels and flips, then follows up with a pretty impressive backwards moonwalk. I allow myself a beaming smile. "Aw, mate!"

Cue the back-slapping and noogies, and the goofy, wide-eyed grins that take me back to our childhood. How I've missed this. How have I ever managed without it, this room full of people who fill me with warm and fuzzy? I bang out a swift prayer to Saint Joseph; *May I always make the effort to keep this, keep them in my life. Even bloody Deborah, right royal pain in the arse that she is.* Before I have half a chance to skip down soppy street, I hear my name being called.

"Fionnuala Margaret Mary O'Sullivan! Get your arse in this kitchen. Now!"

Bernie's command slices through the chattering, and the room goes silent, all eyes on me and my rabbit-in-the-headlights demeanour. A cacophony of laughter erupts, before the babbling hum restarts, with everyone resuming their conversations at once.

"Ooh, you in trouble, girl!" Katie wags her finger at me.

I've been avoiding Bernie for no good reason and for far too long. Bernie's my second mum, the one who cuts through the bullshit and sees deep into my soul. I swallow a gulp. I could slide into one of my famous sulks, I could run...

Katie places a soft hand on my back. "Best get it over with, Noo," she says.

The warm smile that spreads across her face takes me back to the girl who would sing "Hill and Gully Rider" as she plaited my hair when we lived above the bakery all those years ago.

"I've had mine, and I'm still standing," she says.

When she mock shudders and crosses herself, I chuckle and shake my head, before making my way to the kitchen. Nervously pushing the door open with one finger, I inhale a deep lungful of the delicious aroma of roast beef and Yorkshire puddings before I step in. I resist the urge to lick my lips at the prospect of Bernie's smooth carrot and swede mash and the ultra-crispy roast potatoes that await. When I cast a contrite look at my sister, cheekily proffering my wrists for her slapping, Bernie barely conceals her smile before holding her arms out in welcome. The feast that she's conjured up in her kitchen is nothing compared to the grilling she's about to subject me to, but I'm ready to accept it. That, and the extended bear hug that she wraps me in, warming me from head to toe. My head relaxes into a comfortable loll on her shoulder and when I close my eyes for a second or two, *home* radiates all around the room. Bernie releases me and takes a backward step.

"I'm sorry," I say, my stupid girlie tear ducts threatening to let loose at any second.

Bernie kisses her teeth, long and slow, before slapping a spoon in my hand and woman-handling me to the cooker. "Stir."

She gesticulates at the bubbling saucepan of thin gravy before she turns to retrieve something from a cupboard. I dutifully apply myself to the task, concentrating on incorporating all of the cornflour before the gravy has a chance to go lumpy on me.

Bernie sloshes a glug of red wine into the pan. "You're too thin, Noo."

She dumps a handful of chopped thyme into my gravy. I stir rapidly, my brow wrinkled in concentration as I inhale the rich, comforting aroma rising from the pan. Yep, good to go. I stoop to reduce the heat under the pan, before turning to face Bernie's music.

"You're a plank, did you know that?" Bernie's tone is less harsh than I imagine she wants it to be right now, and we both slip into smiles and head shakings. "All right," she says, flapping her hand as if to signal her defeat. "Tell me. In thirty words or less, please. I've got hungry mouths to feed. Go!"

I laugh out loud, a genuine laugh that takes me by surprise. I've really missed Bernie's gentle candour, the way she refuses to indulge my adolescent pouting, and the million and one ways in which she reminds me of Mum. I take a deep breath. "Fucked up with Tessa." I take a sorrowful glance at the floor tiles. My heart flinches in my chest and steps up a beat when I say her name out loud. I distract myself by trying to work out the square footage of the kitchen floor and what it would cost to retile it.

Bernie nods and waves her hand at me. "Yeah, yeah. Frank told me about that." She waggles her fingers impatiently at me. "And the rest?"

I puff out a short breath, my eyes now scouring the off-white kitchen ceiling for inspiration, and a hefty dollop of courage maybe. Okay, breathe. I can do this. "I...um, slept with Grier." I wrap my arms tightly around my head in anticipation of the verbal assault to come, but Bernie just stares at me. She just stares. Then she moves to the countertop and busies herself with scooping horseradish into a dish before suddenly rounding on me.

"Why?"

A simple question from big sis, and the "closure" lie is poised, waiting on the tip of my tongue to launch itself, but I hesitate. Jutting my chin out, I bite my lip and say nothing. I've been over this with Maggie. I've wasted far too much precious time agonising and beating myself up for my sins, and I'm done with all that. Standing in my sister's kitchen, I know that there's nothing to gain by rehashing that sorry episode right now—that one's gonna be between me and my therapist—so I stare back into her face, hoping she'll blink first. Thankfully, she does.

"Never mind, never mind." Bernie emits a sigh of resignation and gesticulates with her hand for me to continue. "Twenty-two words, Noo," she says and stabs the carving fork into the joint with a grunt.

She scrapes the knife against the whetstone, and I gulp another breath and force myself to speak. "I got depressed, Bern. Almost lost myself in it." There's a sadness, a choking desolation in my own voice, and an audible spasm of inhalation rakes through my body. *I was close, Bern, so close to sinking and never resurfacing, and I never want to go there again.* Bernie places the sharpened knife on the platter and moves across the kitchen to wrap her arms around me again, and I don't pull away.

"Oh, honey," she says, stretching up to press a series of tight-lipped kisses on my head. "Never, ever go through that alone again. Promise me, Noo? Promise me."

Aunty Ginny arrows into my mind, and I can't help but wonder that if she'd had the love and support that I have to draw on, things would have turned out differently for "poor, sad Ginny." Mentally counting my abundance of blessings, I breathe deeply. "I'm okay. I'm getting back to being okay now."

I draw my arms tighter around her, giving her the assurances she seeks. So many emotions simmer inside me—relief, fear, sadness—bubbling together in a cauldron of unease, but I'm strangely calm, despite that. I'm standing in my sister's kitchen, unloading details of my chaotic, screwed-up life, but I'm actually okay with it. No shallow breathing, no blood pounding in my ears, no overwhelming smells and sounds assaulting my senses. I really am still standing. Wrapped in Bernie's arms, with a roomful of people who care about me just beyond, I'm permeated by an other-worldly beam of sunlight that warms me to my bones, and I know that it's all mine, for keeps. I could bask in this forever but—

"Sorry, sweetie, the mob are about to get their pitchforks out in here. How long?" Paul pops his head around the door.

Bernie and I share a quick eye roll before slowly releasing one another from our embrace, our fingertips trailing to the last second. I busy myself with searching the cupboards for a gravy boat. "It's okay, mate. You can come in." I shoot an enquiring look at Bernie.

"We're done here, right?"

Bernie lets out an imperceptible grunt. She loads Paul up with salvers laden with steaming vegetables and golden Yorkshire puddings the size of cricket balls, before sending him off with a quick peck on the lips. I can't help but smile when I pour the gravy into the boat, the same boat that used to adorn Aunt Pearl's dining table, way back when. Somewhere in my head, an alert chime pings, and I can almost feel the touch of her hand on my shoulder. *"Yuh haf it? Hol' on tight, mek sure yuh na spill me gravy, Noo-la."*

Tilting my head to the side, I cast my eyes to the ceiling, raising my brows in silent salute to my dearly departed role model. I snap out of my reverie when Bernie dumps an enormous dish of roasties in my arms. I start towards the door, but she tugs me back.

"Four words left." She nudges the swing door ajar with her hip. "Then we're done, Noo."

I examine the steaming potatoes, holding the dish a little tighter to my chest, and remind myself to breathe. "I want her back," I say softly. "Tessa." The memory of our nearly moment, our easy banter, and our laughter in the car thrusts a stab of pain into my chest, but Bernie's slow smile swiftly dabs it with her soothing balm.

"Then you'll make it happen. You can, and you will," she says. "Five. That was five, but never mind, never mind. C'mon, kiddo. Dinner is served."

I'm a little unsure as to whether Bernie's making a statement or issuing a command, but I give her a quick nod. This one's on me; it's down to me alone to make it happen. Clearing my mental To Do list, I scratch GET TESSA BACK! in bold red on a new page. I take in a slow, deep breath before releasing it steadily though my nose, and then I smile as I move to take my place at the Clan O'Sullivan gathering.

Woa-wo, Listen to the Music

MAGGIE THORNE USHERS ME into the consulting room in her house with an encouraging smile. She takes her seat on the sapphire blue sofa and silently motions with her hand for me to take the grey velvet snuggle seat opposite.

"So."

"So."

Maggie's tone is calm and unhurried, as opposed to my own, which is breathy with a tinge of antagonism. Maggie's room is a safe place for me to unpack my thoughts and feeling, but I'm not yet entirely comfortable with the fact that I'm here doing it. I do want to, I need to, but... I gulp a breath, allowing the air to swirl deep into my lungs while she waits in silence, her eyebrows fractionally raised as she regards me. We both know why I'm here, the ball squarely hurtled into my court from the minute that I lifted the door knocker, but still, I hesitate. I arrive this morning still bathed in the warmth of a wonderfully pleasant evening at Bernie's, and I'm rather reluctant to step out of that tranquil cocoon. I lace my fingers and begin rapidly tapping my thumbs together. When I realise what I'm doing, I smile ruefully, tuck my hands under my thighs, and look at Maggie, who returns the gesture.

"It's been some week." The understatement of the year falls softly from my lips but seems to bounce off the walls before hovering in the air between us.

"Why don't we start with what happened after you left here on Wednesday evening?"

Yes... no... I suppose so. When I shuffle in my seat and stretch out my long legs, I mouth a silent prayer to St Fiacre: *May my roots hold me tethered to the polished wooden floorboards of Maggie's floor*. Then I projectile vomit the events of the past few days.

I rattle through my list of cor blimeys in an oddly disconnected manner, but when Maggie comments that this is the first time that I have referred to Grier as "my ex, Grier," I'm floored. The tears that prick my eyes rapidly become gushing torrents and heaving sobs. I cry for a full five minutes, with Maggie silently proffering tissues at appropriate intervals. When I quieten and still, I'm drawn in by her gentle gaze.

"It sounds like you've finally let go of Grier. How does that feel to you?"

Devoid of judgement, her utterance is a simple question, but it feels like she has emptied an ice bucket over my head. I pause, scanning the watercolour painting on the wall for inspiration or something, before smiling cheerlessly back at her. "Good, I suppose. Sad," I say, nodding to myself to cement it in my mind, "and long overdue."

Maggie nods, a small smile settling on her lips. To my annoyance, she remains silent, watching me, waiting for me to continue. What's left to say, Maggie? That I've finally severed the red cord that has kept me tethered to Grier all these years? That doing so shoots a physical stab of pain through me that's so acute, I want to cry out? That I'm okay, not okay, maybe okay?

I look down at the floor. "I don't suppose I'll ever let go of her completely," I say, after a time. "I can let go of the shit, of all the angst and heartache, but not of Gree herself." I swallow hard. "She's a part of me and…I love her. I'm always going to love her; I just have to find a way to live without being *her* Fin. We both will."

There, I said it out loud. Maggie Thorne has dragged the admission kicking and screaming from my lips, but she doesn't understand. Frank doesn't understand. Those around me have spent years slagging her off to me, and I've let them. I've endured their scathing condemnations of her in silence, I've resisted the bait. Yes, she hurt me, lacerated my heart so savagely that I'm amazed it kept beating, but...

"Fin, after all you've told me about the pain this relationship has caused you, I'm wondering..."

When her sentence trails away, I force my eyes to move away from the pattern on the cushion I'm tightly clutching to my chest and back to her steady gaze. I already know what she's about to say, and I don't want to hear it. She wants to know why I still love Grier, how I can still love her, and why. There's a cry inside of me, an agonised, tortured wail that I've kept locked in all these years. It's been buried so deep that I know it would shatter my body and soul into wretched, jagged shards if I were to ever release it. How can I tell her, tell anyone? Surely nobody on this earth could possibly understand.

"People don't see the good in her," I say. "People don't notice her giving up her time to help other people...anonymously donating her money to causes she believes in and making sure nobody finds out, but I've always known." I sigh, before I reel off Grier's private list of virtuous and altruistic deeds, struggling to swallow down the feelings of betrayal I feel in doing so. Grier's fierce insistence on my keeping this side of her undisclosed has always filled me with admiration and pride, so I balk a little at Maggie's intrusion, my hands fidgeting, before my mind backpedals. *Maggie's not prying. I chose her to help me, so let her.* Silent seconds or minutes stretch out between us. I blink first.

"Yeah, I know I've made her sound like a right bastard." A sardonic laugh bursts from my lips, and I look up at Maggie, who, irritatingly, says nothing. "She's done some terrible things and some magnificent things." The waver in my voice alerts me to the fact that I'm frowning, staring off into space. The wail readies itself for launch, and I grip my thighs tightly with both hands. If I let go, allow it to see the light of day I know that I'll never stop. "But that's not it...why I still love her."

My heart launches itself forcefully against my ribcage as the memory of that fateful day floods my entire being. "There was this moment..." I realise that my palms are repeatedly smoothing over my jeans, my feeble attempt to still my trembling fingers. I splutter half sentences of explanation at Maggie, who encourages me to continue with her pursed lips and her tiny nods. "It was... otherworldly," I say. "I can't explain it any other way."

I stumble my way through describing the memory to Maggie, fully aware of the inadequacy of the words and my inarticulate command of them.

"So hot... It was a blazing summer day, and we'd snuck off to bed in the afternoon. Unusually quiet too, still and quiet. I don't know why, but we lay on the bed staring at each other. Not talking, just looking. The whole room was yellow. The heat of the sun streamed through the windows, its yellow sunlight illuminating our naked bodies. The buzz of insects seemed to increase in volume, pounding in my ears as we lay together on our sides, looking into and beyond each other's eyes. *I love you.* She'd said it, I'd said it, and we'd been swallowed up by the stifling yellow.

"I couldn't breathe, I was panting, and so was she. I felt like I was being drawn into her. I couldn't stop myself. I couldn't tell where I ended and she began. We were just...one single thing. I shut my eyes, broke the contact, and found myself looking at a hazy image of our fingers entwined. Just for a second. When I opened my eyes, I quickly wiped away the tear rolling slowly down her cheek, and when she touched her thumb to my face, I realised that I was crying too."

I scour Maggie's room for something to focus my watery eyes on, something to rescue me from the swirling yellow that is threatening to overcome me and haul me back to live out the remainder of my days trapped in a nameless, timeless yellow zone. My gaze settles on the line where the off-white cornice meets the sage green wall, and the yellow threat recedes. When I slap my palm against my chest, Maggie gives me a curious look but remains silent, and I don't care. I've dissipated the scream, slapped it back to whence it came, and I've acknowledged the thing that keeps me and Gree tethered. I don't care if Maggie or Frank or the world at large don't get it. *I* get it. I shrug.

"Something happened between us in that moment," I say, my unsteady voice falling to a whisper. "We…I dunno…we connected in a different way." I stop short of telling Maggie about the sex that had followed the connection. Sex with Grier had always been fast and furious but that day, it had begun as a gentle, tentative exploration. Two people, bodies so familiar now unsure, shyly opening up, revealing and discovering one another. Of course, as the afternoon wore on, we'd reverted to type: raw and wild, a feverish marathon session that had left us both bruised and sore when exhaustion had finally overtaken us. The sudden realisation that I have no desire to loiter in the memory causes me to inhale sharply.

Leaning forward on the sofa, I wrap my arms across my chest and exhale a choppy breath. "It was a commitment, I suppose." I slowly nod as the pieces fall into place in my head. "In that moment…" The laugh that bursts from my lips momentarily surprises me. "In that otherworldly moment, on that bat-shit crazy day all those years ago, we committed to loving one another. Forever." I look up at Maggie, clocking the almost imperceptible furrow of her brow. *You don't get it, do you?*

"Me and Gree are over and done, romantically speaking," I say. "We had our chance, but we screwed it up. Well, *she* screwed it up. But we're committed to loving one another. The two things are quite separate." There's an air-punching surge of pride within me at having worked my way to this breakthrough.

"So it was this enduring love that led you to be unfaithful to your girlfriend Tessa and sleep with Grier earlier in the year?"

I'm sucker-punched by the heat that erupts in my chest and powerless to control the searing blush that works its way up my neck to my cheeks, my ears, and my scalp. *Fuck. Fuck. Fuck.* I slump back into the sofa as I fumble in my pocket for something to hold on to. Tracing a finger around the edges of the fifty pence coin, I bow my head, unable to meet Maggie's questioning gaze. *Fuck, fuck, fuck.* Her wall clock replies with a dispassionate tick, tick, tick. When the dualling butterflies in my stomach re-engage, I drop the coin in my pocket, my shoulders slump miserably, and I raise my hand to cover my mouth.

"No." I shove my hands back under my thighs and avoid looking at Maggie, who waits, saying nothing. "It was anything but love. I wasn't thinking of Gree; I was thinking of Novia and how much I wanted to get back at her." I glance up at Maggie, fully prepared to see disgust or outrage in her eyes, but her face remains impassive. She blinks once, before tilting her head to one side.

"I didn't want to reconnect with Gree," I say. "I wanted to hurt Novia. I wanted to punch her fucking lights out." The heat in my cheeks intensifies when I replay the scene in my mind. Grier's head thrown back against the pillows in pleasure, her softly murmured endearments as she writhed under my hand. My lips stretched tight against my clenched teeth, the angry bruise they marked on Grier's shoulder that would leave Novia with little doubt as to what had transpired. And the words, the ugly words that thundered in my head. *Yeah, fuckwit. She's mine. Not yours, mine. Anytime I want, fuckwit. Grier is all mine.* Clearing my throat, I pull myself back to the here and now, to the woman sitting across from me who is silently demanding clarification.

"I was a grade A bastard that night," I say, wearily shaking my head. "I've never, never behaved so badly, so vile... I know that I was vile...and then I justified it by convincing myself that it was because I loved her and needed closure." Swiping away the wetness on my cheeks with my cuff, I steel myself for Maggie's repulsion. Instead, she looks at me with gentle eyes.

"How do you feel about it now?"

Relief floods through me. I take a deep breath. "I'm ashamed," I say. "I'm sad, and I'm ashamed that I used Grier in that way... and mortified that I hurt Tessa for such a pathetic reason. Novia, I couldn't give a flying fuck about though."

This time, Maggie smiles. "We can talk more about that next time we meet," she says, and her smile widens.

When our session concludes, the time having flown away with astonishing rapidity, I feel weary and teary, the grief thrumming in my body like an elongated bow on violin note. When I mumble my agreement to Maggie's suggested appointment times for the coming week, I'm enveloped by an all-over milky sadness but simultaneously sustained by my angel girl's low whisper, *These things shall pass.*

I need to redecorate my bedroom. Lying on my bed, frowning at the thin zig-zag cracks on the faded off-white ceiling, I am gifting myself a quiet, cooldown moment after my session with Maggie this morning. Carl and Darren are engaged in baritone exchanges somewhere downstairs, and I feel a sense of comfort on hearing them. I shuffle my body into a Christ the Redeemer pose and return my attentions to the ceiling. Tessa tiptoes into my head. Tessa, who is not lying on her bed above me. Tessa, who moved in so close to me in the car yesterday that I felt sure we were about to kiss—

"Pah." I spit the word out loud to my empty room. Tessa, who wants to be my friend. I'm wrestling with the quickening pulse between my legs at the thought of said friend when my phone buzzes. I barely have time to take in the picture of Frank on the screen before the phone's ringtone changes to a bellow. "It's your brother... What does he want? What does he waaaant?" Bastard! This is so typical of him; changing my ringtone last night when I wasn't looking. I can't help but smile. "Peanut," I growl, in my best Uncle Gene accent. Frank laughs softly, and I know that his eyes are twinkling with mischief. They're probably ringed red after the number of lagers he put away last night too.

"Just checking in, Noo," he says, before covering the phone with his hand and conversing briefly with Asha.

I catch only brief glimmers of their conversation: "No, I have eaten, and "Sit down, babe, really, I'm good."

"Women!" he says, more to Asha than me, I reckon.

My warm and fuzzy jar fills to overflowing; he reminds me of Mum and Dad all rolled into one.

"Noo," he says, "Bernie's going formal tonight so it's tuxes for you and me, yeah? You still got yours, right?"

I hear muffled giggling and the sounds of a struggle at his end, and my eyes flit to the doors of my wardrobe, mindful of the fact that I have not worn, or had occasion to wear, my smart apparel for more years than I care to remember. "Still got it mate, and it still fits." I hope that's true.

"Don't believe him if he tries to claim the same, Fin. Chubby chops here had to get a new one for his works' do last month."

Katie's laughter shines down the phone as Frank complains to her that our other sister is bullying him. I clutch the phone tightly against my chest while I choke-laugh and when I tell her that I cannot wait to see them all later, my heart swells in my chest and performs a perfectly executed flip.

I hang up and scuttle over to my wardrobe to rifle through the neat row of hangers until I spy the suit bag at the back. How long has it been since I last wore this? I blow a breath over the plastic cover and watch the dust particles dance in the sunlight before unzipping the bag to retrieve the suit. Yeah. So much of me has changed but not my scrawny frame. It'll still fit. Hugging it to my body, I twirl in the sunlight. What will Tessa make of me wearing it? Of me looking like the real grown-up that I'm hopefully on my way to becoming. "Bring it on," I whisper.

Let the Anvils Fall Where They May

"Who are you and what have you done with my moody sister?"

Frank sidles up behind me and squeezes my shoulders, tittering away to himself. When I spin around to face him, a hurriedly constructed scowl on my face, I am powerless to stop the corners of my lips from twitching into a full-blown smile. He's a nob, but he makes a fair point. This evening, I have succeeded in banishing miserable old Fin. I've worked up a sweat on the dance floor, and I've actually been enjoying myself. Okay, yes, I still have a tight little knot festering in my stomach acid at the thought of having to play friends with Tessa when she arrives, but I have bopped and skanked my way through Deborah's set with joyful abandon, and the night is still young.

When Ade and Yemi make their way to us through the crowd, fingers entwined like mushy teenagers, my heart swells. I embrace them both, bestowing heartfelt kisses on each in turn. When I enquire how Yemi is feeling, the memory of her malaise of the other night pricking a knot of worry in my stomach, they glance lovingly into one another's eyes.

"Mother and baby are doing well," she whispers, "though I'll never get used to this damned morning, evening, and anytime sickness malarkey."

She smiles bashfully as she sweeps a hand over her belly, nodding at the incredulous look I give her. Get the fuck out of here! How could I have not known? Tears prick at the corners of my eyes when I hug her tightly, showering first her and then Ade with my delighted kisses. Frank's acute observation, "You ain't happy, Noo," seems like a lifetime ago now, and I grin harder, cast my eyes to the ceiling, and marvel at the events that have rocked my world this week. Am I happy? As near as dammit now, Frank.

I groan half-hearted protestations when the DJ announces the O'Sullivan family "Electric Slide" but surrender without a fight when my bruv tugs gently at my wrist and guides me to the dance floor. Marcia Griffiths, here I come. I acquiesce to the killer sounds of the grande dame of reggae beckoning me onto the dance floor. Step to the right, close, step, close step, close. Our opening moves have us flailing, missing the beat, tripping over one another and our own feet, and roaring with laughter as our friends encircle us on the dance floor, clapping and cheering us on. Deborah holds up her index finger, pointing 5-6-7-8 in the air, and then we're away again, this time, miraculously, in time with the beat. I have to say that I kill it the first time, as my stepping, tapping and rocking comes back to me as effortlessly as breathing. God! How long has it been since we did this, Team O'Sullivan showing off our party trick?

Adding a little head movement to my flawless stepping, I allow my eyes to drift to my siblings, all of whom have eyes on their other halves. Katie, having caught the beat, is gesturing with her hand to Robbie as if to say, "Yep, I'm an O'Sullivan." Bernie has one arm stretched out in front of her, twinkling her fingers at her husband, Paul, who is leaning forward to her, hands clasped over his heart. My brother, the gormless plank, has finally caught up, and he's showing off to Asha, who is smiling sweetly back at him, all the while gently stroking the bump. And Deborah... I catch the tail end of the X-rated tongue gesture that Juno has bestowed on her, and Deborah's scandalous air-humping response, which prompts Juno to throw her head back and roar with laughter. I could die a happy woman right here, right now.

I choose to ignore the niggling reminder that waltzes uninvited into my thoughts. Okay, I don't have that special somebody in my life but, in the here and now, I'm surrounded by the people I love, and that makes me feel good. That and the fact that my *friend* Tessa's once again talking to me. It's more than I had this time last week, so hope springs eternal.

When the music starts to fade, my ears are assaulted by the whooping and cheering in the room, and I take a backward step when the dance floor is overrun by joyful folk, all eager to continue the groove. I puff my cheeks out, undo my expertly knotted bow tie, and hastily run the back of my hand across my damp forehead. To my right, Juno, one tattooed arm slung around Deborah's waist, lets out a piercing wolf whistle and when I follow her gaze, I can see why.

Fresh from her work function, Tessa is standing on the side of the dance floor, eyes searching the mass of bodies and, in all of my forty years on God's green earth, I swear that I have never seen anything more lovely. I've been up close and personal with every inch of her glorious body, but never before have I seen it wrapped up in a dress. A heart-stopping, figure-hugging black dress that shimmers in the sparks of light bouncing off the overhead disco bowl, the side slit revealing a silky-smooth, cycle-toned calf. I'm vaguely aware that my mouth has dropped open as my hungry gaze devours her bare shoulders, the soft wave and the shine of her hair as it falls to those shoulders and her cleavage. I remind myself to breathe. Inhale, exhale. _Stay upright, Fin. Lock your knees in place and ignore that sweet thumping pulse between your legs._

When Tessa spots me looking at her, a shy smile spreads across her lightly lipsticked mouth, and she moves closer. The concept of _friend_ stabs a jagged hole in my heart when she places a finger under my chin and jerks my lips back together. Then she laughs that laugh, and I laugh too, reeling myself back into the here and now with a bump. I see her lips moving but am unable to hear her words over the music and the raucous revelry around us. I raise my eyebrows, shake my head, and point to my ears, so when she tugs gently on my wrist and indicates the fire exit with a nod, I waste no time in complying with her request. _Walk over hot coals with you, Tess? No problem. Stick pins in my eyes just because you ask me to? Abso-fucking-lutely._

Tessa leads me around the dance floor toward the door but drops my wrist, slowing her pace a touch when Grier suddenly appears out of nowhere and approaches us. Without breaking my stride, I hold my palm up at her, stopping her in her tracks when I say, "Not now, Gree," before taking Tessa's elbow and swiftly guiding her through the door. I clock Tessa's small smirk and Grier's minor frown when I do so. The damp spring air shocks my sweating body into a defensive shiver, but I suck in a deep breath and slip my jacket around Tessa's naked shoulders.

"Butch point to you," she says.

My head begins to swim, and I am once again on the verge of hyperventilating. I tug a corner of my lower lip between my teeth. "You're beautiful." I need to lean against the wall for support.

Tessa lets out a quiet sound of disbelief. "You're just a sucker for a girl in a frock, Fin."

My entire body tingles with a pulsating heat, and I need to plunge my hands deep into my pockets to hide the fact that my fingers are curling and uncurling themselves without my permission. She laughs again, the soft sound stroking a warm curl of pleasure which spreads through my chest. I laugh too but despite the heat emanating from my cheeks, I'm shivering.

"Yeah, true," I manage to say, "but you do look... You're so... I've never seen you in a dress before."

She tilts her head to one side and motions with her hands. "Up here, Fin," she says.

Her beautiful soft lips tell me that I'm forgiven for ogling her cleavage. I'm smiling too, despite the fiery blush toasting my cheeks to a frazzle. I'm also floundering. Gawky, tongue-tied, and floundering when I know that I need to be, well, anything other than myself, really. I clear my throat, desperately trying to persuade my saliva to provide the necessary lubrication for speech.

"Frock's for t'work do, but it has been known," she says and rolls her eyes. "Just not that often."

Placing one hand on the waistband of my trousers, she leans

forward, and her head grazes my chest as she steadies herself to remove her shiny black stiletto pumps that look like, if called upon, they could seriously damage someone in a fight. My breath quickens.

"Ah, thank fuck!" She exhales a prolonged groan. "Those bastards were bloody killing me."

We're standing agonisingly close, our bodies separated by an invisible force field that I shouldn't breach. I take a deep steadying breath, and my nostrils are swamped by the intoxicating combination of her fresh citrus and hemp shampoo combined with an altogether Tessa aroma, and I do well not to swoon back on my heels. Can friends get away with sniffing one another? I swallow once, blink twice, and praying that my voice doesn't come out as a squeak, I say, "Welcome back, short arse."

I make a show of standing to my full height so that I can look down at her. She cuts her eyes at me, but her lips part into a grin, and we're back in that comfortable banter zone that I so love. In reality there's probably only a half inch of height difference between us, which I of course claim, but it remains one of our favourite mock-arguments. My mind drifts off to an image of us lying together in her bed, fingers intertwined as we squirm and stretch out our legs, each vying to be the tallest, or the longest. *Friends, not lovers. Friends.* That's uninvited and most certainly unwelcome. Why the fuck do I have to self-anvil right now? I take a step backwards to increase the distance between us and kick out at a stone, for no good reason. My lower lip endures more dental abuse.

"You look good, Fin. I really like this new hair."

Tessa runs her fingers through her own hair as she speaks, then half turns and fiddles with the luscious leaves of the plant behind her. When I catch myself smoothing a hand over my budding dreads, I hastily drop it to my side and focus on running my fingers along the seam of my trousers. Less geeky, I reckon. "Yeah...um... thanks," I say. "I'm trying to... I thought it was time for a change."

When we lapse into silence, I allow my eyes to wander,

composing a pointless mental list of my surroundings. Bench. Tessa. Foliage. Sand bucket. Tessa. Tessa looking straight at me. I smile at her, and she flashes me a most welcome peek at her oddly attractive chipped tooth. Before either of us can speak, the calm is shattered by the sound of someone banging on the window behind me, and I jump out of my skin. Tessa laughs softly and gestures for me to turn around. Inside the building, Frank is performing an elaborate mime, urging us to come back inside and dance. My clench-jawed glare, accompanied by an obscene hand gesture, inform him in no uncertain terms that his interruption is unwelcome. Ever the nonchalant plank, he merely shrugs and throws a wave at Tessa before ambling away.

"He's not wrong though. It's supposed t'be your party. What happened t'dance you promised me?"

Tessa's ramping up of her Yorkshire speak melts the knots in my shoulders, and I capitulate with a grin. "Or you could ask me, Tess. Don't think you can shirk your dance card responsibilities by popping on a dress, woman."

She opens her mouth as if to say something but quickly snaps it shut, before picking her way over the cold paving slabs in her bare feet to stand next to me. Before I can stop myself, my hand lands a light tap square on her backside, and I collapse against the wall in a fit of giggles.

Tessa captures my wrist in her hand, clenches her teeth, and leans in to whisper, "Do that again, and I'll batter t'fucking tar out of you."

I raise my hand to signal my surrender as I try to wrestle my grinning lips into something resembling remorse. I fail, just as she fails to control the twitchy smile which is fighting to spread out across her own lips.

She glances skyward, rolls her eyes, and shakes her head. "Come on, fuckwit. And don't step on me feet."

"Oh, come on, Tess, it was funny, mate."

Tessa is clearly determined to put me through the wringer.

I swear I can see steam coming out of her ears. We've been standing together at the bar for ten minutes solid, me sniggering into my ginger beer, her necking her London Pride and scowling back at me. Even her scowl is bloody sexy. I hold my hand up. "I'm sorry, Tess, really. I didn't mean to wind you up. I just had a bit of a Barney Stinson moment." When her brow wrinkles, my mouth drops open. "Oh, come on! Don't tell me you've never seen *How I Met Your Mother?*"

She points her finger at my face and slowly edges it closer. I go cross-eyed watching it, wondering what she's up to, and if she's finally lost the plot. Her finger hovers in front of my nose for a second before she catches me off guard by flicking a stinging blow on my nostril.

"Tessa! What the fuck? OW!"

She throws her head back and howls with laughter at my feeble attempts to cradle my smarting nose in my hands, then she downs the remainder of her beer in one and slams the glass down on the bar.

"Come on, lass," she says. "Let's dance."

"So, I take it I'm forgiven then?" I yell into Tessa's ear, trying to make myself heard above the music. We've been pumping the beat with the crowd for a while now, our bodies gyrating agonisingly close together. Not close enough though. I scowl when Frank sidles between us, places one hand on her waist and the other in the air, and rotates his hips in front of her. Tessa smiles a wide grin at him, throwing both arms in the air as her body begins to mirror his movements. My feet have stopped moving, my eyes riveted to the sight of my brother artfully maintaining the couple of inch gap between their bodies. Dancing, not dance floor-humping.

Why is it that I can't be that cool, more Shakira and less...well, less Mr Bean? My lower lip pings out in a surly pout when I release the breath I've been holding, and I pick my way through the sweaty bodies back to the bar. If I was a cowboy in an old Western, I'd push my Stetson back with the tip of my finger and growl, "Whiskey, neat…and leave the bottle." I don't do that. "A pint of Pride, pint of Amstel, and a sparkling water when you're ready, mate."

Old Fin is gearing up to take over when Frank and Tessa come crashing off the dance floor, laughing at some comment or other that I haven't heard. New Fin rolls her eyes at her, prodding her sharply in the chest, reminding her that "It's a party, for fuck's sake," and that she needs to "bloomin' well lighten up." I opt to roll with New Fin.

Curling an arm around my shoulders, Frank pulls me close, plants a kiss on my head, and exclaims, "Mate!" before lifting the glass to his lips.

Forgoing the formalities, Tessa stands on my other side and ravenously guzzles her pint. When she thumps the half empty glass back on the bar, I feel a surge of warmth sweep through my body. She's gorgeous. I resist the urge to run my thumb across her lips to remove the trace of beer beard from the corner of her mouth and elect instead to study the stitching on my shiny brogues. *Breathe, Fin, breathe.* By the time the thumping dance track fades and the next one begins, I've managed to squash my nerves back to a manageable level, and I'm back in the game. I allow my eyes to wander back to Tessa's lips, ignoring the quick catch in my breath when the tip of her tongue slips out to moisten them.

"Mm, Van Morrison," she says, softly grazing my clenched fist with the tips of her fingers. "Come on, Fionnuala, you're up!"

Why does my heart do a flip whenever she says my name? When I reach for her proffered hand, she links her fingers into mine and gives them a gentle squeeze as she leads me to the dance floor. *Sweet Thing.* The memory of her calling me that when she reminded me that I was allowed to be happy sizzles in my brain. The light fluttering of her fingers on my back as our bodies dovetail and sway into the song leaves me feeling like butter on a crumpet. For three and a half minutes, we remain silently locked together, and I'm transported to another dimension where nothing exists other than the warm press of her body against mine and the soft croon of Van's voice. For the second time in as many days, I realise that my heart is so achingly full that I could die of contentment, right here and now.

When the song begins to fade and my eyes reluctantly open, I realise that we're clinched tightly together, our foreheads touching. I force myself to release her and step back. Our fingers remain linked as we lock eyes and I open my mouth to say something, anything, to prolong the moment. There's a tiny frown on her eyebrows, but her eyes tell me that she doesn't want this moment, this searing chemical moment between us, to end either.

Saved by the DJ! When the first strains of Al Green's "How Can You Mend a Broken Heart?" waft from the speakers, Tessa casts her eyes to the ceiling and emits a throaty groan.

"Ar, 'eck. I fucking love this song," she says.

The cosmic magnet sucks our bodies back into sync, and she cups the back of my neck as our bodies sway ever so slightly to Al's deliciously pleading voice. I last for a total of two verses and a chorus before I tilt my head to graze her earlobe with my lips. Vaguely aware that we have stopped moving, I ghost a slow trail of tiny kisses along her jaw line before our mouths meet in the softest of kisses. She tastes glorious, of salt mingled with that unique body scent that drives me nuts and makes me thirst for more. Her lips part slightly, and my heart and other vital organs perform a rhumba when I feel the tip of her tongue meeting my own, but she pulls up abruptly and places a hand on my chest.

"I can't do this, Fin," she gasps, withdrawing her body and stepping away. "I can't."

Shaking her head rapidly, she turns and heads for the fire exit, leaving me on the dance floor, eyes wide in astonishment and breathing heavily through my gaping mouth.

"Go after her," Katie's voice is gentle, but her shove in my back is anything but.

"Tess, wait up. Please!"

Katie throws my jacket to me, and I give her a grateful nod. I waste no time in charging after Tessa and manage to grasp her elbow before she gets to the door. When she lifts her head to look at me, I see panic and confusion etched in her expression. I open my mouth to say something, but I don't have the words. I struggle to ignore the electric tingle in my fingertips as they rest on her warm skin and the manic pounding of my heart in my chest.

"Not now, Gree." She smirks, her voice oddly cool and measured.

I had barely registered Grier approaching, but when Tessa directs a death ray glare at her, Grier stops dead in her tracks and turns her face to me, her eyebrows raised.

"Fin, I wanted to ask—"

"Really? Really, Gree?" The tightness in my chests erupts, and the words explode with unexpected fury from my mouth before I can stop them. I can count on one hand the number of times my temper has gotten the better of me over the years, yet here I am, teetering on the brink because Grier has the audacity to act like she's at the top of my priorities list. She's not. I'm no longer *her* Fin, no longer the woman-child that she would coddle and manipulate in equal measure. I'm Fionnuala Margaret Mary O'Sullivan the grown up, and I'll do whatever is needed to rescue my real, grown-up relationship. I'm no longer a woman-child incapable of making good decisions. I take a deep breath and when I lead Tessa toward the exit, she doesn't resist.

"I'll catch up with you tomorrow," I yell in Grier's general direction before stepping outside with Tessa. Yes, we still have things to talk about but right now, all I want, what I *need* is to be with Tessa, and Grier needs to back the fuck off. The sharp night air bites at my sweating body and slaps me back to reality with a jolt. I hand my jacket to Tessa, my stomach knotted so tightly that my hand snakes up to rub comforting circles over it. I scrape my other hand along the rough wall, fingertips mapping the level brick and coarse cement, as the acid in my stomach threatens to appear.

"I can't do this, Fin. I can't do this again." Her voice is soft, small, and restrained.

I take a step towards her, but she holds up a hand to stop me, her head slowly shaking from side to side.

"No," she says. "Just stop."

The soundless air holds her words aloft between us, and I stare miserably at the ground.

"This," she gesticulates into the space between us, "this has never been a problem. Yeah, we fit together so sweetly." Her eyes half close, but she shakes her head and exhales.

I feel her eyes on me and have no choice but to meet her gaze. Green eyes, flecked with brown. My breath hitches, the duelling tiger moths in my stomach holding their rapiers aloft. "Tess. I want to..." My stuttering words crash and burn. My hands fly to the sides of my head, and I tug at my hair. Why, God, why? Why must I be this inarticulate, lumbering idiot? My thoughts, my words are an inexperienced ice skater, flailing, hands hopelessly clutching at thin air before crashing spectacularly to the frozen ground.

Tessa wraps her arms across her chest and runs her teeth over her lower lip. "When you let go, it's fucking glorious! You're glorious. I like you, really, really like you. I like us." She swallows hard and sucks in a deep breath. "You leap in and fill your boots, but then run for t'hills. It's just you, Fin. It's what you do, but..." Her lips purse tightly. "I'm drowning with this misery, and I have to get away from it. From you."

A low strangled sound gurgles in my throat when my mouth flies open in response to her words. *Breathe. Don't gulp, it doesn't help. Breathe, focus, speak. Speak now!*

"I know, Tess, I know." I squeeze my eyes shut and slap my forehead. "I've been such a woman-child," I manage to blurt out. "I let the misery swallow me up. I just let it happen. And then I let it pull me down and keep me down. Like I didn't matter. Like you and me didn't matter, like I didn't have any control over what was going on around me." I scrub my face and see her nostrils flare ever so slightly as she listens. "I let it go on far, far too long but...I've got a grip though."

My entire body is a mass of contradictory sensations and emotions. My hands tingle with cold, my head sears with white hot needles, and my heart's skipping beats and furiously launching itself against my ribcage. When a warm swirl of fresh citrus and earthy hemp punches my nostrils, I force myself to visualise the ground beneath my feet and the roots that tether me to it. I am unable to meet her gaze though; my eyes are unwilling to risk what they might find in it. *Breathe, Fin, breathe.*

"I took people's advice. Well, insistence really." My lips stretch out in a wry humourless grin, but I shake my head and plough on, determined to force my mouth and brain to collaborate. "Seems I need some chemical help right now to stop the blackness from swallowing me up." I risk a quick glance at Tessa, but her expression is indecipherable. I want to be anywhere else in the world right now, doing anything but this, but I owe her this explanation, and I need to do this here and now. I clear my throat and continue, the softness of my tone taking me by surprise. If I'd ever thought about this conversation, the one about me owning the uncomfortable, embarrassing shambles that lies beneath my fabricated cool, I would surely have imagined my jaw being clenched and my hands squeezed into fists. Now, standing face to face with an uncharacteristically dejected Tessa, I'm filled with a need to explain, to have her know me, the real me.

"I needed to talk about myself with someone, so I did. I am, and it helps. I still get spooked and feel like I want to run away, but I don't want to be that person anymore. There's too much at stake, too much to lose." My chin falls to my chest, and I close my eyes. "I'm working on it." I throw my arms out to the sides and allow them to slap back against my thighs. I dredge up a silly smile when I look at her. "So, anti-depressants and therapy. I'm a fucking catch, Tess!" The chuckle that escapes my lips holds no mirth.

Silent seconds pass as Tessa considers this information, her head slowly nodding. My head tilts to the side when it dawns on me that she's the first person I've shared this information with, and it feels okay to have done so. *Fionnuala needs help.* My eyebrows twitch upward when I realise that the statement in my head doesn't sit as uncomfortably as I had imagined it would. I'm okay. *Fin gets by with a little help from her family, her therapist, and a shit load of little white pills.* I've barely had time to register her movement before Tessa has moved tantalisingly close.

"You must be freezing," I murmur, my eyes scooting nervously over her bare feet as I try to recall whether her toenails were bright red the last time that I saw them. I am, of course, avoiding her gaze, still fearful of what her eyes might tell me, but when she dips her head and raises mine with a gentle finger, I have nowhere left to run.

"Nah," she says, giving me a lop-sided grin, "I'm from Ilkley, mate. Feels like August to me." She balls a lump of my shirt in her hand. "Ya great southern softie!"

I grin along with her. Then the grin slides from her face, her pale eyebrows furrow, and I realise that the fleeting moment of levity has ended.

Tessa takes a backward step and tractor beams my eyes. "I'm glad you told me, and I'm here for you, Fin."

She tries to maintain eye contact, but I look away, fearful of the menacing *but* that lurks in the air between us.

"Really, Fin, believe me. Whatever happens with us," she scowls and sucks her lip briefly, "I will be there for you, on t'second floor, whenever you need me."

The tiger moths throw down their weapons and shift into an at ease stance, gently humming into my stomach acid. The *but* stomps its way to the fore.

"But I do need to get away right now," she says gently. "I need some serious R&R before I really screw up at work and—"

"Don't go to Cape Town, Tess. Come to Jamaica with me."

The plea shoots from my mouth before my brain has time to settle on the same page. I have no idea what I'm saying, or why I'm saying it, but I do know that I can't bear the thought of weeks away from her. Not after all the time I have stupidly wasted. I blink twice and silently plead for the assistance of St Jude, St Monica, Saint Anthony, and any passing goddess who might be listening.

"What? Why?" Tessa's eyebrows go into orbit.

"Don't go to Cape Town. I want to take you to Jamaica. I want my parents to meet you—they'll love you, by the way! I want to climb Dunn's River Falls with you and go scuba diving in Port Royal. I want to stuff you with saltfish and ackee and curry goat and rice and peas. Don't make that face, you'll love it! I want us to sit in Mum and Dad's garden sipping ice-cold jelly coconuts and snacking on mangoes straight from the tree. I want us to swim with the dolphins in Ocho Rios and wallow in the Luminous Lagoon— God! We've got to do that! Maybe we can even go night fishing with Dad and Uncle Devan. I want to do it all, and I want to do it with you, Tess."

I break off from what is almost certainly the longest monologue of real sentences that I have ever uttered, wondering just how I have managed to get my brain and mouth to work in sync. Tess continues to stare at me, bemused, and I swallow. "There's so many things I'd do differently if I could go back in time"

That's it. That's all I've got. I still don't know where it all came from, but I know that I want this, want her. *Breathe, Fin, breathe. Trees and roots. The ridges on that pound coin in your pocket against the rub of your thumb.*

Tessa says nothing at first, but she lifts her hand to the collar of my shirt, my ludicrously ruffled baby blue tuxedo shirt, and smooths it between her finger and thumb before she whispers, "Like iron yer bloody shirt properly, eh?"

My eyes fly open, confused. Tessa slips her other hand around the back of my head, gently pulling my head to her. Her lips brush a feathery kiss on the corner of my mouth, and I remember to breathe before she leans in fully and snogs the face off me.

~ THE END ~

Thanks for reading my debut novel. It'd be great if you could stick a review on Amazon for me!
And if you want to find out what I'm writing next, maybe you can sign up to the Butterworth Books newsletter? (bit.ly/ButterBookers).

Cheers,
JP

Other Great Butterworth Books

Escape in Time by RJ Nyx
Working in the past is hell on your future.
Available on Amazon (ASIN B0DSJFDZ7R)

Ship of Dreams by Brey Willows
Two rival captains, one deadly mission, and secrets that could set the skies ablaze.
Available on Amazon (ASIN B0DRW1X75N)

Unwritten by Helena Harte
No strings is fun 'til it unravels.
Available from Amazon (ASIN B0DGQFFHYB)

Chucking Putty at the Queen by Simon Smalley
A heartbreaking, humorous, and courageous exploration of what it takes to be ones authentic self.
Available from Amazon (ASIN B0DGGBV22W)

The Promise by Addison M Conley
When the world keeps pulling you under, who do you reach for?
Available on Amazon (ASIN B0DDY9FH6Z)

Back to Back by Jo Fletcher
."When Fred and Ruby's worlds collide, can love rise from the rubble?"
Available on Amazon (ASIN B0D6M499K2)

Heart of the Storm by Ally McGuire
Sometimes a storm is just what you need to clear the skies ahead.
Available on Amazon (ASIN B0CYTSQXWW)

Sanctuary by Helena Harte
Passions ignite and possibilities unfold. Welcome to the Windy City Romance series.
Available from Amazon (ASIN B0D4B42RRW)

Brave Enough to Love by Valden Bush
In a dance between truth and sacrifice, can they rewrite the rules of love?
Available on Amazon (ASIN B0CQP8PMVB)

Dead Ringer by Robyn Nyx
Three bodies. One killer. No motive?
Available on Amazon (ASIN B0CPQ8HFK7)

Medea by JJ Taylor
Who will Medea become in her battle for freedom?
Available from Amazon (ASIN B0CK2FB7GW)

Virgin Flight by E.V. Bancroft
In the battle between duty and desire, can love win?
Available from Amazon (ASIN B0CKJWQZ45)

Fragments of the Heart by Ally McGuire
Love can be the greatest expedition of all.
Available on Amazon (ASIN B0CHBPHR6M)

Here You Are by Jo Fletcher
.Can they unlock their hearts to find the true happiness they both deserve?
Available on Amazon (ASIN B0CBN935ZB)

Stunted Heart by Helena Harte
A stunt rider who lives in the fast lane. An ER doctor who can't take chances. A passion that could turn their worlds upside down.
Available on Amazon (ASIN B0C78GSWBV)

Dark Haven by Brey Willows
Even vampires get tired of playing with their food...
Available on Amazon (ASIN B0C5P1HJXC)

Green for Love by E.V. Bancroft
All's fair in love and eco-war.
Available from Amazon (ASIN B0C28F7PX5)

Call of Love by Lee Haven
Separated by fear. Reunited by fate. Will they get a second chance at life and love?
Available from Amazon (ASIN B0BYC83HZD)

What's Your Story?

Global Wordsmiths, CIC, provides an all-encompassing service for all writers, ranging from basic proofreading and cover design to development editing, typesetting, and eBook services. A major part of our work is charity and community focused, delivering writing projects to under-served and under-represented groups across Nottinghamshire, giving voice to the voiceless and visibility to the unseen.

To learn more about what we offer, visit: www.globalwords.co.uk

A selection of books by Global Words Press:
Desire, Love, Identity: with the National Justice Museum
Aventuras en México: Farmilo Primary School
Times Past: with The Workhouse, National Trust
Young at Heart with AGE UK
In Different Shoes: Stories of Trans Lives

Self-published authors working with Global Wordsmiths:

Max Beeken
Maggie McIntyre
John Parsons
Dani Lovelady Ryan
Kit Stone